Susan Ferrier

Destiny

Or, the chief's daughter. Vol. 1

Susan Ferrier

Destiny
Or, the chief's daughter. Vol. 1

ISBN/EAN: 9783337422912

Printed in Europe, USA, Canada, Australia, Japan

Cover: Foto ©Andreas Hilbeck / pixelio.de

More available books at **www.hansebooks.com**

DESTINY

OR

THE CHIEF'S DAUGHTER

BY THE AUTHOR OF

'MARRIAGE' AND 'THE INHERITANCE'

'What's in a name?'—SHAKSPEARE

Edinburgh Edition

IN TWO VOLUMES

VOLUME I.

LONDON

RICHARD BENTLEY & SON

Publishers in Ordinary to Her Majesty the Queen

1882

Printed by R. & R. CLARK, *Edinburgh*.

TO

Sir Walter Scott, Baronet

THESE VOLUMES

ARE RESPECTFULLY DEDICATED

BY AN OBLIGED FRIEND

THOUGH ANONYMOUS

AUTHOR

EDINBURGH, *March 15, 1831.*

DESTINY.

CHAPTER I.

ALL the world knows that there is nothing on earth to be compared to a Highland Chief. He has his loch and his islands, his mountains and his castle, his piper and his tartan, his forests and his deer, his thousands of acres of untrodden heath, and his tens of thousands of black-faced sheep, and his bands of bonneted clansmen, with claymores and Gaelic, and hot blood and dirks.

All these, and more, had the Chief of Glenroy; for he had a family tree upon which all the birds of the air might have roosted. Doctor Johnson, to be sure, has said that there are no such things as family trees in the Highlands; but the Doctor's calumnies against trees of every description, or rather of no description, throughout Scotland, are too well known to require refutation.

Glenroy, therefore, *had* a tree; and as for his rent-roll, it was like a journey in a fairy tale, "longer, and longer, and longer than I can tell." However, as the Chief himself was not particular in ascertaining the precise amount of his income, but lived as if the whole Highlands and Islands, with their kelp and black cattle, had been at his disposal, it would ill become his biographer to pry into the state of his affairs for the gratification of the curious. Suffice it therefore to say that the Chief of Glenroy lived in a style which was deemed suitable to his rank and fortune by all—and they were neither few nor far between— who partook of his hospitality. In person, as in fortune, Glenroy had been equally gifted. He was a tall handsome man, with fine regular features, a florid complexion, an open but haughty countenance, and a lofty though somewhat indolent air. The inward man was much what the outward man denoted. He was proud, prejudiced, and profuse; he piqued himself upon the antiquity of his family, the heroic deeds of his ancestors, the extent of his estates, the number of his followers, their physical strength, their devoted attachment. On the other hand, he was of an open temper, of a social disposition, liberal to his tenantry, generous to his dependants, and hospitable to all. His manners, though somewhat coarse, were by no means vulgar; and, when a little under control, he could be both pleasing and gentlemanly in his deportment.

His supremacy being universally acknowledged throughout the extensive district where his possessions lay, he bore his faculties with that sort of indolent pomp which betokens undisturbed power. He

felt himself a great man; and though he did not say,
even to himself, that he was the greatest man in the
world, he certainly would have been puzzled to say
who was greater.

Such was Glenroy; and with all these advantages,
it was naturally expected that he would form an
alliance worthy of himself and his clan, all of whom
identified themselves with their Chief, and consequently looked upon his marriage as an event in
which they had an undoubted interest. As it was
impossible, however, that any one so great in himself
could make a great marriage, his friends and followers,
being reasonable people, merely expected that he
would make the best marriage possible.

Greater speculation could scarcely have been excited at the court of King Ahasuerus as to a successor
to the rebellious Vashti, than that which prevailed
amongst the clan on the subject of forming a suitable
alliance for their Chief. Each had his favourite and
exalted fair, in one or other of the most illustrious
Scottish families, on whom he conceived that Glenroy
should place his affections. But vain are the schemes
of man! Instead of these glorious results, Glenroy
did what many wiser men have done before him; he
fell in love, and made what was called a "most unaccountable marriage;" for he married a merely pretty
girl, of neither family nor fortune, the orphan daughter
of a poor hundredth cousin of his own. The fact was,
Glenroy was too proud to consider it a matter of much
importance whom he married: he could derive no

consequence from his wife; his wife must owe all her dignity to him. This was a blow to the clan, which all the youth, beauty, and sweetness of the lady could not reconcile them too; and it was not till the birth of an heir that they recovered their spirits. But then bonfires blazed, bagpipes played, tartans waved, whisky flowed—all, in short, was done to welcome to this vain world an heir to its vanities. Alas! how short-sighted are sometimes even second-sighted mortals!

At the end of two years a daughter was born, but far otherwise was her birth commemorated. A lifeless mother, a widowed father, a funeral procession, tears, regrets, lamentations, and woe—these were the symbols that marked her entrance into life, and cast a gloom upon her infant days. The child was christened Edith after its mother. And so ended Glenroy's first attempt at connubial happiness.

CHAPTER II.

GLENROY mourned the loss of his wife as much as it was in his nature to do; but he was not the man either to live with a breaking heart, or to die of a broken one. In due time, therefore, it occurred to him that, great as his loss appeared to be, it was nevertheless one which might be repaired. But, too proud and indolent to take any measures for the accomplishment of his design, he left it entirely to time, chance, or circumstances, to carry it into effect; and these did seem to conspire to bring it to pass. During an occasional visit to London, he more than once happened to find himself in parties, where he was so much in the background, that but for the notice of the Lady Elizabeth Waldegrave, he would have passed almost unobserved. Great as Glenroy was, he therefore found he was capable of being still greater: yet greatness by means of a wife—a woman—and that wife an Englishwoman! this was a startling thought to the proud Chief. But his stay in town was protracted: he continued to meet the Lady Elizabeth, who was so very affable and agreeable—such an enthusiastic admirer of tartan and Highland bonnets and Highland scenery—that Glenroy was captivated; and he even came to the conclusion that he would not be the worse for being connected with some of the highest families in the kingdom. Then, although Lady Elizabeth was somewhat *passée*, she was still a showy-looking woman, quite suitable to him in point of years, and more likely to make a good staid step-mother than a younger wife would have been. To be sure, she was not very bright; but Glenroy hated clever women, they were all so managing and man-œuvring: in short, from an admirer the Chief became a suitor, and thought himself a lucky man when he was the accepted lover. Had Glenroy been better acquainted with the character and circumstances of the lady, he would not have been quite so much elated with his good fortune.

Lady Elizabeth Waldegrave was sister to the Marquis of Heywood, and widow of the Honourable Edward Waldegrave, a fashionable spendthrift, who had closed a brief career of folly, leaving his widow and infant daughter to the charity of relations. It may be supposed, then, that Lady Elizabeth's circumstances were anything but affluent. She was, in fact, struggling to keep her place in society upon a small annuity from her father-in-law, Lord Waldegrave, who, having had to pay largely for the extravagance of his son, was little inclined to be liberal to his widow and child. Glenroy's proposals, therefore, came in good time; and the union being of course warmly approved of by the lady's family and connec-

tions, no obstacle stood in the way; so that, as soon
as the lawyers and milliners had done their parts,
the marriage was celebrated with the utmost *éclat*.
On the one side, there was a special license, the
presence of a prince of the blood, the benediction of
an archbishop, with peers and peeresses, lace and
pearls, a magnificent saloon, an elegant *déjeûner*, a
line of splendid equipages, etc. Such was the scene
in St. James' Square; while at the Glenroy Arms
the event was celebrated by a numerous meeting of
the tenantry and vassals of the Chief with "barbaric
pomp;" a roasted ox, and half a score sheep, barrels
of ale and bowls of whisky, long speeches, loud shout-
ing, toasting, cheering, bonfires, bagpipes, and the
Highland fling.

Much as Glenroy loved pomp and retinue, he was
somewhat startled at the magnitude of his lady's
bridal train. In addition to his own travelling carriage and servants, there followed Miss Waldegrave's
equipage, containing that young lady, about five years
of age, her French governess and English sub-gover-
ness, and attended by her own maid and the Lady
Elizabeth's footmen. Glenroy thought less might
have served her; but it was too soon, or rather too
late, to say so; and Lady Elizabeth expatiated largely
upon the goodness of old Lord Waldegrave in allowing her to take his favourite son's only child to Scotland with her. The Chief tried to feel sufficiently
grateful for the favour conferred upon him in this
addition to his family; but in spite of himself he

felt something like shame at this importation to Glenroy. The arrival of the new-married pair was celebrated with great rejoicings. Lady Elizabeth was dressed in the clan-tartan, wore a Highland bonnet, looked well, made a speech, and was at once pronounced to be a most charming woman.

But scarcely were the rejoicings over before Glenroy began to suspect that he had not drawn the capital prize in the marriage-lottery; and these his first faint misgivings began to assume a less questionable shape as the features of the lady's post-nuptial character became to be more fully developed. At length they boldly resolved themselves into tastes, habits, and pursuits of the most decided dissimilarity from her husband's.

How it happened that this discovery had not been made before marriage instead of after was one of those mysteries which, though of common occurrence, have never yet been fully cleared up to the satisfaction of single-minded people. Whence it is that two persons who seem to have been born only to hate each other, should, under any circumstances, ever fancy that they actually love each other, is a phenomenon which even philosophers may have encountered, but which they certainly have not yet explained.

No two human beings born and bred in a civilised country could be more different than the Chief and his lady; and as both were independent, and both had arrived at years of discretion, it seemed but natural that they should remain as fate seemed to place them—perfect antipodes. The lady had been accustomed to a gay London life, and she had also lived abroad. She had seen much of the world, and the world had seen much of her. She had been admired for her talents, her manners, her music, her taste, her dress; and although the admiration had long been on the wane, the craving still continued. She was, in fact, when without her adventitious aids, a mere showy, superficial, weak woman, with a fretful temper, irritable nerves, and a constitution tending to rheumatism, which she imputed entirely to the climate of Scotland.

In direct opposition to all this, Glenroy detested London; depised every part of the globe save Scotland; hated all music except that of the bagpipe; had little enjoyment in any society but that of his friends and followers; and when he spoke of the world, meant only his own county and clan. He had also become subject to attacks of the gout, which he ascribed to his visits to London, and therefore vowed he never would set foot in it again.

Although Glenroy saw much good company at his hospitable mansion, yet it was only during a short period of the year; for the Highlands may be said to open for the season as the King's Theatre shuts; and, thanks to grouse and deer, the one has become almost as fashionable a place of amusement as the other. During this season, therefore, Lady Elizabeth lived pretty much in her own element; but when that was over, a long and dreary interval ensued: not that the

house ever emptied of visitors, be the season or
weather what they might, but the company was not
suited to her taste, for it must be owned Glenroy was
not nice in the choice of his associates. Although his
vanity was gratified with occasionally entertaining
the best in the land, still the same principle, together
with his love of case, made him prefer in general
being what is called the king of his company.

Amongst sundry of his adherents whose persons
and manners were particularly obnoxious to the Lady
Elizabeth, the most offensive was the Laird of Benbowie, a friend and clansman of the Chief's, who,
from having been all his life in the habit of paying
long and frequent visits at the Castle, had gradually
become domesticated there, to the infinite annoyance
of its mistress. The Laird of Benbowie was an
elderly man, of the most ordinary exterior, possessing
no very distinguishing traits, except a pair of voluminous eyebrows, very round shoulders, a wig that
looked as if it had been made of spun yarn, an
unvarying snuff-coloured coat, and a series of the
most frightful waistcoats that ever were seen. Benbowie's mental characteristics were much upon a par
with his personal peculiarities. He was made up of
stupidities. He was sleepy-headed and absent. He
chewed tobacco, snored in presence, slobbered when
he ate, walked up and down with a pair of creaking
shoes, and drummed upon the table with a snuffy hand.
Nay, more; with that same obnoxious snuffy hand
he actually dared to pat the head or shoulder of the

elegant, refined Miss Waldegrave, as often as she came within his reach. But all these things were mere leather and prunella to his Chief, whose feelings and perceptions were by no means so refined as his lady's. Benbowie was the very apple of his eye, for he was devoted to *him.* He never contradicted him, or rather he invariably coincided with him. He rode with him, or walked with him, or sailed with him, or sat still with him. He played at backgammon with him, and when there was no one else, did well enough to be beaten at billiards. Yet no one could call Benbowie a hanger-on ; for he had a good estate and a pretty place of his own, both of which he neglected for the sake of living with his friend ; and although he was not profuse of his own money, yet, to do him justice, he was equally sparing of his Chief's.

What pleasure or profit Glenroy could find in Benbowie's company no one could discover. But so it was, and Glenroy could have better spared a better man ; although, if pressed for a reason of his preference, he could only have resolved it into that unanswerable argument, " Je l'aime parceque c'est lui," etc. Lady Elizabeth had at once attempted to expel Benbowie from the house ; but she might as well have attempted to move one of his own brown mountains. Benbowie was invulnerable in his stupidity and obtuseness, and nothing less than the united efforts of the fairy and the genie who lifted up Prince Camaralzaman, and carried him a thousand leagues without waking him, could have made Benbowie dream of leaving a house where habit had completely domesticated him, and where his instinct made him feel comfortable and happy.

Some one has well said, "Lorsqu'on ne peut éteindre une lumière, on s'en laissé éclairer;" but Lady Elizabeth did not adopt this wise maxim. She could not extinguish Benbowie's light, faint and dark as it was, neither would she permit it to shine even in its native dim eclipse. The consequence was that poor Benbowie, who seemed to have been born without a single spark of fire in his composition, became a sort of smouldering brand in the family of his friend. As neither the Chief nor his lady were young enough to be moulded anew, or wise enough to make the most of what each mutually thought a bad bargain, it may be supposed their lives did not glide away like that of Parnell's Hermit, in one clear, unruffled stream, but rather resembled the course of their own mountain torrents, which chafe, foam, murmur, and take their own way.

CHAPTER III.

Time rolled on, but did nothing to smooth the asperities of Glenroy and his lady. Pride was the ruling passion of both; and unhappily there was no mutual object on which they might concentrate this predominant principle. The Lady Elizabeth added no branches to the family tree; and thus the unjust and overweening partiality of each parent for their own separate offspring continued to grow with *their* growth, and strengthen with their strength.

Such was the state of the Chief's family when he received a visit from his brother-in-law, Sir Angus Malcolm, with his only son, a spoiled handsome boy about the same age as his cousin Norman. Sir Angus was a widower, and had been recently appointed to a high command in India, whither he was to proceed when he should have found a situation for his son, suited to the anxieties of a fond parent. But that was a matter of difficulty, as indeed it must be to any one to part with his choicest treasure, and commit it to untried love and alien tenderness. Why did he leave it? For wealth—that which tempts so many to "leave each thing beloved most dearly." Sir

Angus had a fine estate, but it was loaded with debt.
Time, self-denial, and management might have re-
trieved it; but to wait on the one and submit to the
other was not in the nature of an impetuous, open-
hearted, open-handed Highlander; and he preferred
the easier task of retrieving his fortune by methods
more congenial to him in a foreign land. His only
care was to secure a safe and happy asylum for his
child; and as, besides being allied to Glenroy by
marriage, he was also his nearest kinsman by blood,
he flattered himself the Chief would take charge of
his son, and educate him with his own. His only
doubt was with regard to Lady Elizabeth, of whom
he had not heard the most favourable reports; but
he was a sanguine, good-natured, undiscerning man,
and his little misgivings were quickly dispelled by
the affectionate and gracious reception he met with.
Glenroy was more than hospitably kind; and his lady,
won by the admiration expressed for her darling, and
the beautiful presents bestowed upon her, acted a most
amiable and delightful part. Glenroy at once anticipated the subject uppermost in the breast of the
parent by inviting him to leave his boy with him
during his absence; and in a few minutes all was
settled to the mutual satisfaction of both parties.
Lady Elizabeth was flattered by seeing that it was
to her the father looked for care and protection to
his son; and her vanity was gratified at becoming
the patroness of the young heir to an ancient title
and noble fortune. But above all, her favour was

secured by the predilection evinced by the young Reginald towards Florinda. Upon being asked by his father which of his two cousins he would choose for his wife, he declared instantly in favour of Florinda, as being by far the prettiest; he then followed up the avowal of his admiration with an offer to marry her, which was no less promptly agreed to on the lady's part, especially when she heard of the gold and diamonds and pearls that were awaiting her.

The little Florinda was indeed an uncommonly pretty child, with a skin of dazzling whiteness, a profusion of golden ringlets, large blue eyes, a sylph-like figure, and an air of distinction which, although not always the accompaniment of high birth, is rarely to be seen except among the true patrician orders. She was also of a gay, sportive disposition, and winning manners; thus her natural endowments and early acquirements rendered her a perfect epitome of feminine grace and beauty. Edith, on the contrary, possessed no uncommon attractions for the superficial observer. Her features were soft and delicate, her countenance mild and thoughtful, and her manners more grave than is usual at her age; for no fond mother's heart had ever pillowed her infant head, no tender mother's hand had wiped away her childish tears, and even a father's arms were seldom open to her, for Norman's place was there. Disregarded or checked in the natural expression of her feelings, she gradually learnt to repress them within her own breast; and while to careless observers the feelings themselves seemed wanting, the roots had only struck the deeper into the heart, while the shoots were thus carelessly trodden down.

Edith was too much accustomed to see Florinda preferred to her to feel any of the envy and heart-burnings of an offended rival, but meekly yielded up the prize. Lady Elizabeth was silly enough to feel gratified at this childish fancy, and continued so kind and caressing to her little son-in-law (as she styled him) during the week his father remained, that he departed with a mind relieved from all doubts and fears as to the situation in which he had left his son and heir.

CHAPTER IV.

FOR a little time all went on smoothly in the youthful circle of Glenroy; but, unhappily, inconstancy is known in childhood as well as in manhood, and Reginald began to discover that even the beautiful Florinda had her faults. She was very greedy, and was too much petted, and wanted everything her own way; and as he had been accustomed to be no less despotic, many a childish squabble ensued. At length, not having the fear of damages for breach of promise of marriage before his eyes, he in a transport of indignation one day declared that he had quite changed his mind; that she was not to be called his wife any more, for that he was going to take Edith; she was much better tempered, would part with any of her playthings to him, and never cried when she was contradicted; and, at any rate, brown hair and pale cheeks were much prettier than yellow hair and pink ones; in short, "for any other reason why," his affections were transferred. Lady Elizabeth was weak enough to resent this affront, and to enter into all the childish feuds that followed, aggravated as they often were by nurserymaids, to whom a spoiled unruly boy is always a subject of torment, and, of course, of blame.

The consequence was, her fondness for Reginald, which had always been of a very precarious nature, now turned into downright aversion; while he, unused to control at home, and encouraged by Glenroy in all his freaks, set her authority completely at defiance. Even Benbowie, his tobacco, his snore, his shoes, and his waistcoats, almost all ceased to be objects of animosity compared with this new annoyance. At length matters came to a climax, and threatened to add one more to the many proofs that great events do often spring from trivial causes.

One day, when the two boys and Edith were engaged in some play in which Florinda was deemed incompetent to join, to get rid of her importunities Reginald lent her his watch, the parting gift of his father; receiving many assurances in return that she would take the greatest care of it. These promises, however, were soon forgotten; the watch was opened, examined, wound up, and broken. Summary revenge is always the first impulse of the childish heart; and Reginald, in his rage, shook Florinda with all his might, slapped her on the cheek, and even left the print of his nails on her arm. Her shrieks soon brought Lady Elizabeth to the spot, when she found her darling almost convulsed with terror and indignation at this rude assault. The extreme fairness and delicacy of her skin rendered the slightest touch at all times perceptible, and on the present occasion

showed the offence in glowing colours, and told a tale
of outrage that raised all the mother in Lady Elizabeth's breast. In vain did Norman and Edith attempt
to palliate the offence by detailing the provocation,
and declaring that Reginald had not meant to hurt
her. They were sure he had only just given her a
slap for breaking his watch. Lady Elizabeth would
listen to nothing but the sobs and exclamations of her
darling; till at length she worked herself up to assert,
and of course to believe, that her child had been
seriously hurt, and would have been killed, had not
she come to her rescue; the whole was wound up
with the soothing assurance to her angel that the
savage should be sent from the house that very day.

"But this house is not yours," retorted Reginald
with equal warmth; "it is *my* uncle's house, and I
am to stay here till my papa comes home, and then I
shall make him send that wicked monkey to prison
for breaking my watch. The little wretch! I hate
and despise her for telling lies,—yes, you shall go to
prison and be fed on bread and water, you little
lying, yellow-haired wasp!" And he shook his hand
at her with renewed vehemence.

"This is past all endurance," cried Lady Elizabeth,
with violence; "begone, all of you!" And in the
recklessness of her anger she pushed Edith, who had
been upon her knees caressing and soothing Florinda,
as she lay in her mamma's lap. Edith fell, and struck
her temple against the corner of the chair, but she
uttered no cry.

"There!" cried Reginald, as he flew to help her up; "see what you have done to Edith, and how good *she* is! But Betty M'Ivor says you are very bad to Edith, and don't love her, because she is not your child; but *I* love her, and she is to be *my* wife, and she shall be all covered with gold and diamonds that my papa is to bring me. Yes, that you shall, Edith! But *she* shall have nothing but dirty old rags to wear, and good enough, too; for Betty M'Ivor says her skin is just like cream cheese, and her hair like a lint-tap."

A fresh burst of screams and tears from the fair Florinda made Lady Elizabeth hastily withdraw with her from the scene of action. In the tumult of exasperated and exaggerated feeling, she hastened to Glenroy; and, denouncing Reginald as the destroyer of her child, demanded that both he and Betty M'Ivor should be sent from the house. A scornful and peremptory negative was of course returned. The lady persisted, as she commonly did; and rising in her passion at the contemptuous indifference her complaints met with, she at last declared her determination of leaving the house and taking her child along with her, unless her demand was complied with. This threat being treated with anger and derision, led to a scene of altercation and mutual recrimination. When people are ready primed for quarrelling, a very little matter will serve the purpose, just as a single spark applied to a train of gunpowder will do the business of an earthquake. So it was with Glenroy and his lady. It had been touch-and-go with them

for many a day; and now, from less to more, from
bad to worse, it ended in a threatened separation.
The lady declared she *would* go, and the Chief would
not ask her to stay. Glenroy would have been the
last man to have turned his wife and her child from
his house, however obnoxious they might have been,
and he felt rather annoyed at the thoughts of such a
thing being said; but he was too proud to betray his
feelings or to make any concession; he merely contented himself with remarking to Benbowie that if
her Ladyship chose to go she might go; she was
welcome to go or stay for him.

"Very right, Glenroy; on my conscience, that's
very right," responded Benbowie; "but if she goes,
I wish you may not have to aliment her."

The acrimonious feelings of the parents could not
fail to keep alive the resentment of the children. A
spirit of absolute hatred towards each other seemed
to burn in the young hearts of Reginald and Florinda;
and they never met without mutual provocation
being given and taken in full measure. In vain the
gentle Edith strove to reconcile them; no sooner was
an old offence patched up than a new one broke out;
and the only thing they both agreed in was in liking
her.

It was at this crisis that an afflicting dispensation
in the Waldegrave family accelerated the separation
between the Chief and his lady. At the time of their
marriage Lord Waldegrave had two sons, then in the
prime of life; but nearly about the time that the

oldest was killed by a fall from his horse, the youngest
died of the yellow fever in the West Indies.   Thus
the young Florinda became at once presumptive heir
to her grandfather, who, broken-hearted and paralytic,
was not likely to stand long in the way of the succession; and as the title and estates descended in the
female line, she might now be considered as future
Baroness of Waldegrave.   With such prospects before
her, Lady Elizabeth felt as if there were degradation
in her remaining longer under the roof of a coarse-
mannered, overbearing Highlander; and she therefore
signified her intention of immediately removing her
daughter to England, in order to be near her aged
grandfather.   She yielded so far, indeed, as to say,
that, provided Glenroy would send the boys to school,
and engage to spend eight or nine months of the year
in or near London, she would have no objections to
pass the other three or four in the Highlands.   But
an indignant refusal being returned, arrangements
were immediately made for a final separation.   The
approaching departure of the mother and daughter
caused universal satisfaction throughout the house,
which had long been divided into two parties as
fierce as the Montagues and Capulets.   Glenroy's
adherents did not of course like his lady, and his
servants had long looked with fiery indignation on
the importance attached to Miss Waldegrave, and the
airs of superiority assumed by that young lady's *suite;*
while the governesses and ladies' maids hailed with
transport their emancipation from a long dull winter

at Glenroy, as the contrasted gaieties of London rose
to their mind's eye. Glenroy's own sensations were
of a mixed nature; he felt that his lady's absence
would be an inexpressible relief; but there was something of wounded pride which alloyed the pleasure of
the parting. Edith shed many tears at the thoughts
of losing Florinda, to whom she was really attached;
for her warm and affectionate heart was ready to love
everything that did not repel her by harshness or
indifference; and Florinda loved Edith as much as a
spoiled child can ever love anything beyond self.

"Do not cry, Edith," said the little future baroness,
with a patronising air; "for when I have a house of
my own in London, I shall make a point of having
you to stay with me; indeed I shall; but I will not
invite *you*, nor *you*," to the boys.

"If you did, we should not go," retorted Reginald;
"we are too glad to get rid of ugly lint-tops to follow
them to dirty, smoky London."

"How happy I am to leave this ugly dull place,"
exclaimed the indignant Florinda; "and Jenkins says
it is quite inconceivable how we have been able to
exist here so long; only, dear Edith, I am very sorry
to leave you; but I hope I shall never see Glenroy
Castle again!"

"And we hope we shall never see you here again,"
retorted Reginald, as Florinda skipped past him to
the carriage, from which, with an air of insolent
triumph, she smiled and waved her little white hands.

Edith was the only one of the family who grieved

at the separation which had taken place. Her warm,
tender heart had fondly attached itself to Florinda;
and her only consolation at parting had been Florinda's
promise of writing her a letter whenever she got to
London. Poor Edith had watched from day to day
for this letter—her *first* letter; and all may remember
the anticipations of their first letter—anticipations
fully realised by the actual receipt of it. What a
new world broke upon us with the breaking of the
first seal! What glorious visions unfolded themselves
as we for the first time unfolded a letter to ourselves,
containing perhaps some few words of *full text!*
Who ever received a first letter that did not spell and
con it fifty times over; who did not lay it under their
pillow at night, and fall asleep, longing for morning
that was to give the treasure again to their eyes?
But these were joys only pictured to Edith's imagination, as each day she rose in fresh hopes that that
was the day her letter would arrive. Thus "dupe of
to-morrow," days passed away, till at length poor
Edith's expectations died the natural death of "hope
deferred."

CHAPTER V.

THE lady's departure was the signal for a gathering of the clan, who, as upon all occasions either of condolence or congratulation, failed not to rally round their Chief in full force. Even Benbowie, although in general obtuse as a hedgehog, seemed to feel this as an epoch to be commemorated; and he therefore ordered a new waistcoat ten times more hideous than any of its predecessors. His characteristics also began to expand more freely, and as if they owned some genial influence. He slept more and snored louder than ever; he inhaled his soup with an inspiration that might have sucked in a fleet; his wig grew more small and wiry; and when his feet were not creaking up and down the room, they were to be found reposing on the bars of his neighbour's chair. Halcyon days ensued; Glenroy was himself again; and a never-ending, still-beginning, course of revelry was kept up, till the Castle more resembled a petty court than a private dwelling.

A tutor had been provided for the boys by Sir Angus before leaving Britain, and to his care they had been committed. He was an Englishman, a first-rate scholar, a man of elegant, refined manners, fond of study, yet skilled in lighter accomplishments, somewhat epicurean in his taste and habits, and altogether such a one as was calculated to form the perfect gentleman, and nothing more.

At first Glenroy grumbled a good deal to Benbowie at what he called the insufferable airs of the fine English dominie; but as they did not interfere much with his own ways, he was too indolent to resent them; and at last he became gradually accustomed to bear with Mr. Ellis as the most consummate puppy he had ever known.

A governess was talked of for Edith; but that was such a secondary consideration that Glenroy could not be troubled to make any exertion to procure one. So, in the meantime, she received lessons from Mr. Ellis in the solid branches of education along with the boys; while the more feminine accomplishments were supposed to be communicated through the medium of a sort of half-and-half gentlewoman, the widow of one of Glenroy's factors, and herself the fag-end of his clan, being a cousin not many degrees removed from the Chief himself. Mrs. Macauley was now an elderly woman in years, but in nothing else. She was plain, but pleasing in her looks: she had a little thick active figure; a broad, clear, brown face; and two of the happiest, merriest, little black eyes that ever lighted up a head. She had an agreeable voice; but her accent and pronunciation were provincial, and some of her phrases were altogether peculiar to herself, which rather gave a zest to her conversation.

But Mrs. Macauley's great charms with old and

young were her unconquerable good-humour and her unceasing good spirits. She was one of those happily-constituted beings who look as if they could "extract sunbeams from cucumbers," and who seem to have been born *sans* nerves, *sans* spleen, *sans* bile, *sans* everything of an irritable or acrimonious nature. But with all these wants, there was no want of a heart—a good, stout, sound, warm heart, which would cheerfully have given itself and its last drop for the honour and glory of the race of Glenroy. She had also just as much religion as an irreligious man could tolerate; for her religion was a compound of the simplest articles of belief, and certain superstitious notions of second-sight, visions, dreams, and so forth, which sometimes afforded amusement, or, at any rate, always served for ridicule. As for her accomplishments, they were many and various; and being mostly self-acquired, they possessed a sort of originality, which in some degree compensated for other deficiencies. She was a perfect adept in the now much-despised art of needlework; and, besides the more vulgar arts of hemming, running, stitching, splaying, basting, etc., she had a hand for

" Tent-work, raised-work, laid-work, frost-work, net-work,
Most curious pearls, and rare Italian cut-work,
Fine fern-stitch, finny-stitch, new-stitch, and chain-stitch,
Brave bred-stitch, fisher-stitch, Irish-stitch, and queen-stitch,
The Spanish-stitch, rosemary-stitch, herring-bone, and maw-stitch,
The smarting whip-stitch, back-stitch, and cross-stitch."[1]

---

[1] " The Needle."

Not satisfied with these her supreme excellences, Mrs. Macauley also aspired to the knowledge of music and painting. She had a good ear, a tolerable voice, and a great collection of old Scottish songs, which she sang to herself in very blitheness of heart.

Her performances in drawing were no less limited, as all the efforts of her genius had been concentrated in one single view of Glenroy Castle, which, after much toil and trouble, she had accomplished to her own satisfaction, and to which she had faithfully adhered for upwards of forty years. From this parent view had descended an innumerable progeny of various shapes and sizes, but not of aspect; as all, to a leaf, were impressed with the self-same features. These, mounted in the several forms of letter-cases, pocketbooks, watch-papers, etc., were most liberally dispensed by her to the friends of the family, including every one who had ever set foot in the castle.

Mrs. Macauley's vanity was so inoffensive, and she contributed so largely to the amusement of every one, that her company was in great request, and by none more than by the Chief himself. In proof of this, besides many other acts of liberality towards her, he had not only fitted up for her a cottage in the vicinity of the Castle, but had likewise assigned her an apartment there; from which, however, in Lady Elizabeth's time she had been wholly banished, but in which she was now become a fixture. This chamber was the favourite rendezvous of the children, who delighted in beating upon her old spinnet, and in being allowed to daub paper, dirty their fingers, and look at cloth-dogs, calico-peacocks, tinsel-grottoes, fili- gree figures, birds made of *real* dyed feathers, and all the rest of Mrs. Macauley's monstrosities; while she, her good-humoured face beaming with pleasure, was no less happy in the belief that she was rendering the most essential benefit to her benefactor in thus im- parting her accomplishments to his children.

Glenroy, to be sure, scouted the idea of her teach- ing them anything but her own brogue, and took great delight in ridiculing her accomplishments even to herself; but then, as he said to Benbowie, Mary Macauley, although a great idiot, was a kind-hearted, well-meaning body, and was fond and careful of the children; and if they learned little good from her, they would learn as little evil, for she was a simple, honest creature as ever breathed: to which the usual affirmative, or rather *confirmative*, was returned.

"That's very true, Glenroy; on my conscience there's a great deal of good sense in that. Molly Macauley is a *very* decent girl, and costs nothing."

Such was the preceptress of the Chief's daughter, and in the genial warmth of her social love and sym- pathy Edith's young heart expanded as a flower to the sun.

It is a trite remark that the most important part of our education is given by ourselves. If Edith was not so regularly and well instructed as she might have been, she escaped the still more dangerous error of having her mind overworked and overloaded with premature knowledge: and how many a mind has been worked perhaps to the weakening of those very powers which it was the aim of the teacher to strengthen and expand! In the moral, as in the physical constitution, Nature is the best guide; and Nature spoke wisely even by the lips of Mrs. Macauley when she said, "Childer will be childer, let us do as we will; we cannot put gray heads upon green shoulders!"

CHAPTER VI.

SCARCELY had Glenroy begun to enjoy his emancipation from one species of domestic tyranny, when he found himself groaning under another of a very different description—that of the minister of the parish; and if the Chief and his lady could have agreed even in their antipathies, Mr. M'Dow might have had the merit of reconciling them. But Glenroy had not even the luxury of openly complaining of this torment; for, like his former one, it was one of his own providing, placed there not merely with his consent, but by his own free will. Mr. M'Dow was the man of his own choice; the chosen of many candidates. The church having become vacant by the death of the former minister, much canvassing and competition had of course ensued; and at least twenty "licensed graduates" had presented themselves, each with testimonials and credentials enough to have entitled them to a bishopric.

But of the two whose recommendations carried most weight, the one was the present pastor, the Reverend Duncan M'Dow, and the other was of the Evangelical side—a party whom Glenroy, although professing Christianity, held in the utmost abhorrence. Not that he knew very well what it was they *did* profess; he only guessed it was something he did *not* practise. He had a vague, confused apprehension that an Evangelical pastor was a sort of compound of a Popish priest, a stiff-necked Presbyterian, a sour-faced Covenanter, a lank-haired Seceder, a meddling Jesuit, a foul-tongued John Knox, a what-not, that had evil in its composition.

No reasonable person surely can doubt that there have been, and still are, many bright ornaments of the Church amongst both parties of Christians; and it is much to be lamented when prejudice runs high on either side, and a man is applauded or defamed, not according to his practice, but his profession. As little may it be questioned that in their respective congregations the wheat and the tares grow promiscuously even to this day. But this was not the view Glenroy took of the subject; and he was loud against all high-fliers, new-lights, gospellers, bigots, zealots, enthusiasts, saints, and so forth.

Being a moderate man, he, like all moderate people, was most violently opposed to the admission of any person of that description within the precincts of the parish. As the other heritors were few in number, the patronage in this instance was conceded to him; and his choice fell upon the present minister, who had been twenty years tutor in the family of the Laird of Kindullie, and who never had been branded with any of these appellations, but bore the character of being an easy, good-humoured, sensible, moderate man, who troubled nobody, but minded his own affairs. This last qualification he certainly possessed, as Glenroy soon found to his cost.

The Reverend Duncan M'Dow was a large, loud-spoken, splay-footed man, whose chief characteristics were his bad preaching, his love of eating, his rapacity for augmentations (or, as he termed it, *owg*mentations), and a want of tact in all the *bienséances* of life, which would have driven Lord Chesterfield frantic. His hands and feet were in everybody's way: the former, indeed, like huge grappling-irons, seized upon every-thing they could possibly lay hold of; while the latter were commonly to be seen sprawling at an immeasur-able distance from his body, and projecting into the very middle of the room, like two prodigious moles, or bastions. He dealt much in stale jokes and bad puns; he had an immense horse-laugh, which no-thing ever restrained, and an enormous appetite, which nothing seemed to damp, and which he took care always to supply with the best things at table. He used a great quantity of snuff, and was for ever hand-ing about his mull, an ugly cow's-horn, with a foul dingy cairngorm set in silver on the top. To sum up his personal enormities, when he spoke he had a prac-tice of always advancing his face as close as possible to the person he was addressing. Although a strong-bodied, sturdy man, he was extremely careful of his health; and even in a fine summer's day was to be seen in a huge woolly greatcoat that reached to his heels, trotting along on a stout dun pony, just high enough to keep its master's feet off the ground.

Such were the outward man and beast: the inward man was very much of the same stamp. Mr. M'Dow's principal object in this world was self, and his constant and habitual thoughts had naturally operated on his outward manners to such a degree as to blunt all the nicer perceptions of human nature, and render him in very truth his own microcosm. He was no dissembler; for a selfish dissembler is aware that in order to please one must appear to think of others and forget self. This fictitious politeness he had neither the tact to acquire nor the cunning to feign; consequently he was devoid of all the means of pleasing. Not that we mean to recommend dissimulation, or to insinuate that Mr. M'Dow would in reality have been a better man had he been able and willing to form himself on the model of the Chesterfield school. He would merely have been less offensive in the ordinary intercourse of life, and would have sinned less against the common observances of society. But had he been earnest in his calling, had he sought to have his mind enlightened by the knowledge of those divine truths which he professed to teach, their unction would have softened and refined even the ruggedness of his nature, and have rendered him an object of respect instead of a subject of ridicule.

From the moment he was "ordained" minister of the gospel, Mr. M'Dow had done nothing but make demands for augmentation of stipend, enlargement of

glcbc, additions to the manse, new offices, and so on.
Now there was no way in which his money could go
that was so unsatisfactory to Glenroy as when it was
claimed as a matter of right, more especially by the
clergy, whom he looked upon as the worst species of
land-tax. Besides, like all idle, indolent people, he
had an utter abhorrence of everything that occasioned
trouble, or was a *bore*, and Mr. Duncan M'Dow was a
bore that beset him on all sides. He was a stum-
bling-block in his path, a thorn in his side, a weed
that had taken root in the very heart of his estate,
and which it was impossible for him to extirpate.
True, he was not molested with spiritual admonitions,
plans for building churches, subscriptions for establish-
ing schools, or schemes for employing the industrious,
or relieving the indigent, or reclaiming the wicked;
but then he was haunted with estimates for enlarging
the manse, and repairing the barn, or hints for re-
building both house and offices; or he was beset with
a copy of the new locality, or an extract of the last
decreet, or a notice of a second summons for augmentation, or an interlocutor of the Teind Court in
favour of some other minister; one or other, if not
all, of which missiles Mr. M'Dow bore as constantly
about his person as a highwayman does his pistols.
But what provoked Glenroy even more than all this,
was the utter impossibility of overawing the minister,
or keeping him at a proper distance; for Mr. M'Dow
possessed that sort of callous good-nature which
rendered him quite invulnerable to all rebuffs: as

well might a needle have been applied to the skin of a rhinoceros as a gibe or a taunt to the feelings of the minister; they were all received as good jokes, which only called forth roars of laughter in return. Besides, the impression was so completely implanted in his brain of Glenroy's extreme predilection for him, from having appointed him his pastor in spite of all opposition, that anything he now said or did could not possibly remove it. In a word, Henry the Second and Thomas à Becket were a joke to Glenroy and Mr. Duncan M'Dow.

CHAPTER VII

GLENROY'S property was too princely in extent to admit of any very near neighbours who could vie with him in state and consequence. Yet two of his nearest kinsmen had dwellings within a short distance of him; or rather the distance was reckoned short in a country where stormy firths and pathless mountains oppose no such obstacles to social intercourse as are enjoined by the flimsy forms of fashion and etiquette.

All that Glenroy's eye looked upon of hill and glen, lake and forest, were his own, with the exception of one single feature in the landscape, and that the fairest in all the goodly scene. This was a beautiful richly-wooded promontory, which stretched far into the bosom of the estuary that almost surrounded it, and gave it the appearance of a sylvan isle. It had once formed part of the Glenroy estate, and had even been the original seat of the family, as was indicated by some gray, ivy-grown walls which crowned the summit of one of its green knolls. But by one of the many mutations land is subject to, it had been severed from the greater part of the property, and had passed to a younger branch of the family, by whom it had

for generations been possessed. This younger branch
had now dwindled away to one "sear and yellow leaf,"
a rich and childless old man, who had lately succeeded
by the death of a nephew, whose first act, upon coming of age, had been to repair and furnish such part
of the old castle as could be rendered habitable for
the shooting season. His successor was not personally
known in the country, as he had left it at an early age
to push his fortune in a remote provincial town in
England, and had only visited it once since. Glenroy
had long looked with a wistful eye towards this property, which, indeed, was the very crown jewel of
the family, and for which he would gladly have exchanged many thousand acres of muir and mountain;
but hitherto he had coveted in vain. All his overtures had been rejected; for, to tell the truth, Glenroy had everything but money to offer for it; and
money, unfortunately, is the only thing that ever
induces people to part with their lands. But now he
seemed in a fair way to gain possession of it, not by
conquest, as the law terms purchase, but by gift, or
inheritance, as he *said* he was the nearest heir to the
childless old man who was now the proprietor. Even
if it had been otherwise, it was of little consequence,
as the property was not entailed, and it was but
natural to suppose he would leave it to him as the
rightful owner and the head of the family; especially
as he could have nobody else to leave it to, having
quarrelled with all of the clan with whom he had
ever come into contact.

At a more respectful distance from the proud tur-
rets of Glenroy stood the humble dwelling of his
cousin, Captain Malcolm, a half-pay officer in delicate
health, the possessor of a paternal farm, and the father
of eight children. In early life he had made a love-
marriage with a lady of good family and great beauty,
but no fortune. This step had of course displeased
the friends (so called) on both sides, and the young
pair had been left to struggle through life as they
best could—and a hard struggle it had been. But,
as has been truly said, "unfitness of *minds*, more than
of *circumstances*, is what in general mars the marriage
union; where these are suited, means of contentment
and happiness are within reach." And in this instance so it had proved. Mrs. Malcolm, though highly
born and delicately bred, had followed her husband
through all the changes of a soldier's life, had shared
his hardships and privations with cheerfulness, and
had now retired with him to a bleak Highland farm,
with that contentment which was ready to find good
in everything. If their claims had been strictly in-
vestigated, it would probably have been found that
Captain Malcolm was still more nearly related to the
Inch Orran branch of the family than the Chief himself; but his chance of the succession was such a
hopeless one that he never had allowed himself to
indulge the slightest expectation. In his first outset
in life he had disobliged Mungo Malcolm, the present
proprietor, by refusing to be received into his office
and bred to his profession—that of a scrivener. One

offence was quite sufficient to make an enemy for life
of Mungo Malcolm ; but when this act of disobedience
was followed up by a rash and imprudent marriage,
assurance was made doubly sure : the door was completely closed and barred against him, and it seemed
as if little less than a miracle could ever open it again.

When this family first came to the neighbourhood,
Glenroy had shown them considerable kindness and
attention, in an ostentatious, patronising way; and
they had received his favours as people willing to be
obliged, because they felt that in similar circumstances they would have been happy in obliging
others.   But, at the same time, the Chief's pompous
civilities were met with a simple courtesy, which,
while it showed they were not insensible to them,
yet denoted minds of too elevated a cast to be over-
whelmed by condescension, or oppressed by trivial
favours.   This, however, was what Glenroy could not
understand, and did not like.   He was more lavish
than generous; he gave freely, but he loved to
brandish his favours, and always looked for an immediate return in gratitude or adulation.

The calm manner and moderate expressions of
Captain Malcolm were therefore ill calculated to
feed the cravings of his vanity.   Boast as he might,
his boastings never called forth any bursts of admiration or applause from his poor kinsman ; nor did all
the display of his wealth and state appear to excite
the slightest envy, or even astonishment, in his breast.
Yet there was nothing sour or cynical in this plain-

ness; nothing that betrayed a contempt for what he could not attain. On the contrary, his manners were mild and pleasing to all who could value simplicity and sincerity; and he was ever ready to commend and admire when he could do so consistently with truth.

There is, perhaps, nothing more baffling to pride than when it meets with contentment in a humble station; it is then like the wind wasting its strength where there is nothing to oppose it, or the waves spending their foam upon the smooth, printless sand. In like manner, the lofty bearing and arrogant pretensions of the Chieftain met neither with encouragement nor opposition in the quiet but independent satisfaction of his poor cousins.

Pride is easily instilled even into generous natures; and the Glenroy children were not slow in learning how greatly they were thought superior to the young Donald Begs, as the Chief contemptuously nicknamed his kinsman's family. This knowledge, however, availed them little in practice; for the young Malcolms, though gay, good-humoured, and obliging, were free from that servile spirit which denotes the mercenary dependant, and in their childish intercourse preserved an ease and equality as remote from false shame as from vulgar forwardness. Educated by pious and enlightened parents, their young minds were imbued with that most elevating of all principles, the genuine spirit of Christianity; and by it they were early taught to distinguish between those

things which the world despises, and those things
which are in themselves despicable. Though poor,
they therefore attached no degrading ideas to poverty,
nor affixed undue importance to wealth. Their minds
were kept free from sordid passions and vulgar prejudices, while all the nobler qualities of their nature
were strengthened and improved by the constant
exercise of the mind's best attributes. Love, charity,
contentment, fortitude, temperance, and self-denial—
these were the treasures the parents sought to lay up
in the hearts of their children; and if they did not
always succeed in raising these plants of heavenly
growth in that strange and wayward soil, the human
heart, the very attempt produced a wholesome influence in displacing pride, prejudice, and selfishness—
those bitter roots of envy, hatred, and malice.

There was something so sweet and attractive in
Mrs. Malcolm, and so pleasing in the whole family,
that Edith was never so happy as when allowed to
spend some days at Lochdhu; but she would have
been ashamed to acknowledge how much she loved
them all, for she was accustomed to hear them spoken
of in a slighting and somewhat contemptuous manner.
Thus is many a pure and generous feeling stifled in
the young heart by the withering breath of ridicule.

CHAPTER VIII.

It was at this time that the new Laird of Inch Orran was expected to take possession of his inheritance, and nothing else was talked of throughout the district, while many and various were the rumours afloat concerning him. The only point they all agreed in was, that he was a very particular man—which is the next thing to being called a Hydra. But particular men, and particular women too, well deserve a chapter to themselves, which they shall perhaps have at another time; but this one must be devoted to the particularities of Inch Orran. Of that "particular man," then, it was generally reported, that he was of a very capricious bad temper; or, according to the nursery phrase, that he was very apt to have the black dog on his back. When that happened, it was said he was in the practice of sitting in profound silence all the time the fit lasted, with a red nightcap on his head; which red nightcap he would not have lifted for the king himself till the black dog had taken his departure, and then it was hung up on its own particular peg till the return of the said black dog. Another edition was, that he always allowed his beard to grow with

the growth, and strengthen with the strength, of the
fit; till at length, in a melting mood, he had again
recourse to the razor, and came forth with a new-
mown chin ready to salute all the world. Others
said that Inch Orran hung out no dead-lights on the
approach of a storm, nor hoisted any signals by which
the enemy could be warned of their danger. His
black dog, it was said, was seldom off his back, and
went and came just as it happened, without saying
by your leave. That he *had* a black dog, nobody
doubted; and that he was most thoroughly disagreeable was never disputed. Whether he had a wife
was not so certain: some said they had seen her;
others had never even heard of her; a third reported
her dead; and a fourth in confinement. There was
also much speculation as to how he would come,
when he would arrive, where he would reside, whether
he would entertain the county, etc. Glenroy had
written a pressing invitation to his kinsman to take
up his abode for the present with him; but a very
brief dry refusal had been returned, which had fired
the Chieftain's blood, till he recollected that he was a
particular man: and even a great man must give way
to a particular man, inasmuch as the one is sometimes
a poor man, and the other is always a rich man.
Glenroy's next step was to have scouts stationed to
give him the very earliest intelligence of Inch Orran's
arrival; and no sooner was that announced than he
ordered his barge to be manned, and, accompanied by
Benbowie, he embarked on the smooth surface of a

summer's sea to welcome the old Laird to the seat of
his forefathers. It is sometimes difficult to believe
that all things are in their right places in this round
world. Certainly Glenroy and Benbowie did not
seem in character with the scenery, as they were
borne along on the bosom of the blue waters, which
reflected, as in a mirror, the varied beauties that
skirted their shores; the gray rocks, the graceful
pendent birch, the grassy knolls, the gushing stream-
let, the fern-clad glens, the lofty mountains glowing
with heather, save here and there where patches of
tender green relieved the rich monotony of colour;
while, above all,

———" the gorgeous sphere
Lit up the vales, flowers, mountains, leaves, and streams,
With a diviner day—the spirit of bright beams."

To the eye of taste and the feeling heart there
would have been rapture in every beam of light and
breath of heaven on such a day and amid such scenes.
But Glenroy and Benbowie cared for none of these
things; though the woods and waters, hills and dales,
suggested ideas to them, such as they were, as they
sailed along, and they were pleased holding parley in
their own way. And "as imagination bodies forth
the form of things," so the two friends "turned them
to shapes," and gave to "airy nothings a local habitation and a name." Glenroy and Benbowie, then,
although they could not be said to find "sermons in
stones, tongues in the trees, or books in the running
brooks," yet found much profitable matter of discourse

in the various objects of nature that presented themselves. The crystal depths of the limpid waters over
which the sun was shedding his noonday effulgence
suggested to their minds images of herrings, fat, fresh,
or salted, with their accompaniments of casks, nets,
and busses; the mountains in their stern glory, with
their lights and shadows and lonely recesses, to them
showed forth heath-burning, sheep-walks, black-faced
wedders, and wool. The copsewood, tender and
harmonious in its colouring, free and graceful in its
growth, was, in their language, "hags and stools" of
price and promise; and as they touched the shore of
Inch Orran, they broke into no idle raptures about
the water-plants, the fern, the wild flowers, the tall
foxglove, the gray rocks and bright mossy stones, half
hid beneath the broad-leaved coltsfoot, that formed
the rich and variegated foreground; for they were
casting searching looks for "black tang" and "yellow
tang," and "bell wrack" and "jagged wrack," and
such other ingredients as enter into the composition
of that valuable commodity called kelp. Such were
the speculations which came most home to the business and bosoms of the friends; so grovelling and
sordid are the results of human pride and selfishness.

Although the ruins of Inch Orran Castle had an
imposing effect when viewed from a distance, the
respect they excited was considerably diminished on
a nearer survey. They stood on the summit, and
close to the edge, of a romantic eminence which rose
abruptly from the water, and gave them an air of

grandeur to which they could not have otherwise
aspired. The building had been originally in the
form of a square, with a court in the centre; but two
sides of it were now mere shapeless, weather-stained
masses of stone, which time was every day crumbling
into more picturesque forms, and mantling with ivy
and wall-flowers, thus "making beautiful what else
were bleak and bare;" while such parts of the building as had fallen down were overgrown with creeping
plants and briers, that gave it an appearance of intri-
cacy, and thus heightened the interest which the
mouldering and dilapidated remains of a human
dwelling never fail to excite. One side of the square,
that next the water, had been repaired, and now
formed the dwelling-house; but it was so sombre,
and so perfectly in harmony with the rest of the
building, that it gave no offence, for it conveyed no
impression of any modern usurper having invaded
the precincts of the departed; it rather seemed as if
some of its former inmates still lingered there amid
the wreck of former ages. Glenroy knocked at the
door; but it was some time ere his summons was
answered. At length a very corpulent, red-faced,
sour-looking serving-man appeared, and after a little
seeming hesitation in his own mind, acknowledged
that he *believed* his master was at home; then with a
slow, toddling, reluctant gait, he led the way to the
apartment where sat the Lord of the Castle.

CHAPTER IX.

IT was a spacious room, panelled with oak, and handsomely furnished in the modern-antique style. Three windows looked upon the loch, and one at the end of the apartment confronted an ivy-mantled tower, which admitted few of day's garish beams at any time, much less at present, when there stood stationed there the huge person of Mr. Duncan M'Dow.

On the entrance of the Chief he instantly hastened towards him with his grappling-irons extended; and before Glenroy knew where he was, Benbowie and he were actually led forward in a triumphant manner, and presented by the minister to the master of the house.

"I am amazingly proud," said he, in his loudest and most emphatic manner, "that it has fallen to my lot to introduce my respected friend and pawtron, Glenroy, to you, Inch Orran, and likewise my very worthy friend, Benbowie; this is really a treat!"

Glenroy certainly had been struck dumb, else he never could have borne this in silence; but he began to rally his forces, although he refrained from breaking out before his kinsman. He therefore merely bit his lip and cast a look at Mr. Duncan, which, if looks could have killed, would certainly have laid the pastor senseless at his feet. He then turned to Inch Orran, who had risen to receive him from before a table, on which lay some law books, ledgers, bundles of papers, and parchments.

Inch Orran was a little, meagre, sickly-looking man, with a sharp, bitter face, a pair of fiery, vindictive eyes, and a mouth all puckered up as if to keep in the many cutting things which otherwise would have got out. And indeed it must be owned that but few escaped in comparison of the multitude that lodged within; for he was one of those gifted individuals who have "un grand talent pour le silence." Neither red cap nor black dog was visible; but, on the contrary, the marks of the razor were still visible on his chin, and he welcomed his visitors with something that approached to bare civility. However, people may be thankful when they meet with even bare civility from a particular man, and Glenroy was not one to be daunted even by bare civility; so he shook his kinsman heartily by the hand, and expressed his pleasure at seeing him in a very cordial manner.

"You are welcome to the Highlands, Inch Orran," said he warmly; "and I hope you will like us well enough to remain amongst us."

"Sir, I thank you," was the reply, with a full stop.

"When did you arrive, Inch Orran?"

"On Tuesday evening, at a quarter past six, sir," in a loud, sharp, cracked voice.

"I wish I could have prevailed upon you to take up your quarters at Glenroy," said the Chief; "I think I may venture to say you would have found yourself comfortable there."

"There, sir, you must allow me to judge for myself," was the reply.

Here, Mr. M'Dow thought, was a fit opportunity for him to strike in.

"I assure you, Inch Orran," said he, "however little Glenroy may think of this house in comparison of his own, yet I can only say I would be very well pleased if I had a room half the size of this in the manse."

'You are very moderate, sir," returned Inch Orran, with a bitter sneer, which was quite thrown away upon Mr. M'Dow, who went on—

"This house has been wonderfully well repaired and improved; it's really a most commodious, comfortable dwelling, and most handsomely furnished: but in general it's my opinion a man should not think of adding to or repairing an old house. A man will never make his plack a bawbee by repairing: for instance, there's the estimate of the addition and repairs for the manse and offices that I was mentioning to you when my worthy and respected pawtrons came in. My house is really a poor affair; my byre's in a most dreadful state, and my stable's not a great deal better; and by-the-bye," as if recollecting himself, "I'm not sure but I slipped the estimate into my pocket before I came away." Diving into an enor-

mous pouch, like a sack, he drew forth a large bundle
of papers, which he turned over, as if to ascertain
their identity, although every letter was as familiar
to him as his own fingers.

"Ay, here it is—estimate of the necessary repairs
for the manse, offices, etc., of Auchterbruckle. You
can take a glance at it any time you are at leisure,
Inch Orran;" upon which he laid it on the table, and
making another dive, fished up his snuff-mull, which,
shaking and patting, he offered to Inch Orran, who
in the same dry, caustic manner, said—

"Sir, snuffing is a practice which I despise and
abominate."

"Hoot toot, Inch Orran, you must not say that,"
cried the undaunted Mr. M'Dow, with a great roar of
laughter; "here's my excellent friend, Benbowie, has
no objections to a snuff any more than myself." Here
Benbowie and he exchanged boxes. "And, by-the-
bye, that puts me in mind of a *bong mote* I read in the
Edinburgh Caledonian Mercury of the 29th ultimo
that I was very much taken with—I thought it really
very good—I really had a good laugh at it—hach,
hach, hach, ho. Two snuffers happened to meet one
day, at the Cross I think it was. Says the one to the
other, as they exchanged their mulls, just as we have
been doing,—says the one to the other,

"'A friend's a good thing at a pinch.'

"'Yes,' says the other, 'but is it not still better
for friends to be laying out their money this way, at
scent per scent?'"

Here a tremendous volley of laughter broke forth, peal upon peal, roar upon roar, while he rubbed his hands, rocked upon his chair, and threw his body about in all directions, in perfect ecstasy. "Cent per cent, Benbowie, would soon build the manse and mend my byre!" And this witticism was followed by another roar, in which no one joined except Benbowie, who did not know at any time what he laughed at. But Mr. M'Dow and his mull were not done yet. "Though you are no snuffer, Inch Orran, you may perhaps admire the setting of my mull; it's a topeuss on the top, a Highland cairngoreum, an uncommon large fine stone. It was given to me in a present by my excellent friend, Kindullie, on the occasion of my leaving his family. It was a very gratifying token of his regard for me, and of the manner in which he was satisfied I had performed my duty in educating of his seven sons. Our Highland mulls and cairngoreums are all the fashion now, Inch Orran."

"I am no lapidary, sir," said Inch Orran, without deigning even to cast his eyes upon it.

"That's just my own case, Inch Orran!" quoth the undaunted minister. "I know very little about these things myself; I have always had other things to mind, and I have never given much attention to your fashionable gimcracks."

"It's a pity, sir!" said Inch Orran, in that significant tone which would have conveyed the most cutting sarcasm to every ear but that of Duncan M'Dow.

Glenroy all this time was fuming to himself at the

laconic dryness of his host on the one hand, and the facetious familiarity of his minister on the other; and indeed a more discordant party scarcely ever met together in friendly semblance; and it seemed in vain to expect anything pleasant from such a compound. However, Glenroy thought of the family seat and the fifty thousand pounds, and he made another attempt to be agreeable.

"You have been a great stranger in Scotland, Inch Orran; it must be a long while since you have visited your own country?"

"Forty years, sir, and upwards."

"Forty years! That is a long time; what wonderful changes you must see!"

"I do see a change, sir; but that is not wonderful."

"The impertinent old cur!" thought Glenroy; "what does he mean by snarling at my words?" And he sat in sullen silence, while the old man kept his scrutinising eyes fastened upon him with that terrific expression which eyes sometimes have, of being not only eyes, but ears.

"Forty years is a long time," said Benbowie; "on my conscience, it is a very long time."

"If there were any ladies present, Benbowie, you and I, who are bachelors, would not be very keen, maybe, of kenning anything about forty years," said Mr. M'Dow, with a sly wink and a loud laugh. Then paused, in hopes of being rallied on the subject of his celibacy, but in vain; so he went on—"Many's the

gibe I get from my excellent friend Kindullie, about
not having provided a dow for my nest yet—ho, hoch,
ho! But I tell him I must first get my dookit before
I think of providing a dow for it. Don't you think
I'm right there, Inch Orran?" with a thundering
peal of laughter.

"Sir?——"

"Oh, it's entirely a joke, on both sides—you understand it, Glenroy? I must get my addition, if not
an entire new manse and offices, before I can ask a
lady to come and preside there. I can give you no
Mrs. M'Dow till you give me my drawing-room and
my byre, at all events. Don't you think that's but
reasonable, Inch Orran?"

"Really, Mr. M'Dow, this is not a time to introduce your private affairs," said the Chief haughtily.

"I beg your pardon, Glenroy; but I really must
differ from you there. Only consider, here's a meeting of my three principal heritors! Who knows when
I may have such another opportunity; though, I am
sure, I trust we may have many pleasant meetings for
all that. But, however, since I have the pleasure of
seeing my principal heritors convened, I think there
can be no harm in just taking a slight glance at my
Summons of Augmentation, which, with the interim
locality, I happen to have by mere chance about me."
And, plunging his arm into the other bottomless gulf
of a pocket, out came a huge bunch of papers, from
which even Benbowie instinctively drew away his
chair. "You see it is no great bulk; you'll soon

glance over it. There's first the Summons—that's it, No. I. Summons, at the instance of the Rev. Duncan M'Dow, minister of Auchterbruckle, for an augmentation of stipend, etc. Then there's the interlocutor of the Court, with the interim locality and decreet; for you see, although my allocation is upon the teinds of——"

"I hope you have brought Mrs. Malcolm with you, Inch Orran?" said Glenroy, making a desperate attempt to get the better of the teinds.

"Certainly, sir," was the laconic reply.

"I trust I shall have the pleasure of paying my respects to her, then, if convenient?"

"Do you wish to see my wife, sir?" demanded Inch Orran in no very sweet accent.

"If quite convenient and agreeable, I should be happy to welcome your lady to the Highlands."

Inch Orran rang the bell, which was answered by the fat serving-man. "Be so good, Simon," said he, in a voice like a lamb, "as desire Mrs. Malcolm to come here."

"She is dressing, I believe," said Simon.

"Send her here when she is ready, Simon." And Simon, with a bang of the door, withdrew.

CHAPTER X

In a few minutes the door opened and the lady entered. She was arrayed in a bright amber silk gown, a full-dress cap, decorated with scarlet ribbons, and even more than the usual number of bows that tied nothing, and ends that evidently had no ends to answer, save that of swelling the milliner's bill. She had a mean, vacant countenance, and a pair of most unhandy-looking hands crossed before her, clothed in bright purple gloves, with long empty finger-ends dangling in all directions. All artists admit that there is as much character displayed in hands as in heads, and Mrs. Malcolm's hands were perfectly characteristic; they proclaimed at once that they could do nothing—that they were utterly helpless, and morally, not physically, imbecile.

Inch Orran seemed instinctively aware of her approach, for without looking the way she was, he merely said, "Mrs. Malcolm, gentlemen;" and Mrs. Malcolm, advancing in an awkward, trailing manner, made sundry low curtseys to her guests, and extending her empty finger-ends (which were eagerly caught at by Mr. M'Dow), she, in a peaking, monotonous voice, expressed her pleasure at sight of them.

Why. Mr. Malcolm had married Mrs. Malcolm
was one of those mysteries which had baffled all
conjecture, for she had neither beauty, money, connections, talents, accomplishments, nor common sense.
Not that she was ugly, for she would have looked
very well in a toy-shop window. She had pink
cheeks, blue eyes, and a set of neat yellow curls
ranged round her brow. She was much younger than
her husband, and looked still more juvenile than she
really was, for not all the contempt and obloquy that
had been poured upon her for upwards of twenty
years had ever made her change either countenance
or colour; in fact, she had neither passions, feelings,
nerves—scarcely sensations. She seemed precisely
one of those whom Nature had destined to "suckle
fools and chronicle small beer;" but fate had denied
her the fools, and Inch Orran had debarred her from
all interference even with the small beer; for such
was his contempt for the sex in general, and for his
own portion of it in particular, that he deemed a
woman quite incompetent to regulate a household.
His domestic concerns were therefore conducted
ostensibly by himself, but virtually by his fat serving-
man, who was his foster-brother, and had been his
factotum long before he married. Even his dress, to
the most minute article, was all of Simon's providing.
Simon alone knew to a hair the cut and colour of
his wig, the pattern of his pocket-handkerchiefs, the
texture of his shirts and neckcloths, the precise latitude
and longitude of his flannel waistcoats, with various

other particulars incident to a particular man.　Now, the chief occupation of Mrs. Malcolm's life was trailing from shop to shop, in search of anything or nothing, and she would have liked to have the dressing of Mr. Malcolm for the pleasure of buying bargains for him.　She had therefore attempted to wrest this privilege out of Simon's hands, but in vain; she had picked up a pennyworth of a wig, which she said "looked remarkably neat on the head," but which Simon turned up his nose at, and his master threw into the fire.　She had haggled till she was hoarse about a dozen of cotton pocket-handkerchiefs, which after all Simon pronounced to be perfectly useless, as they were of the diamond pattern, and his master would not blow his nose with anything but a spot.　Her improvements upon flannel jackets had very nearly caused a formal separation, and from that time her active energies, not being permitted to exercise themselves either upon her household affairs or her husband's wardrobe, had centred entirely in her own person.　She lived in a perpetual, weak, impotent bustle about nothing, spent her money in buying hoards of useless clothes, and her time in looking at them, folding and unfolding them, airing them, locking them up, protecting them from the moths in summer and mildew in winter, and so on.　To crown the whole, she set up for being a sensible woman, and talked maudlin nonsense by the yard; for she was one of those who would ask if the sea produced corn, rather than hold her tongue.　Here it may be remarked that it requires a great deal of mind to be silent at the right time and place. True, there are some few gifted individuals whose conversation flows like a continued stream, fertilising all around, enriching others without impoverishing themselves; but how different from the idle chatter of empty heads, whose only sounds are caused by their own hollowness. "Two things there are, indicative of a weak mind," says Saadi, the Persian sage, "to be silent when it is proper to speak, and to speak when it is proper to be silent." Such was the helpmate of Inch Orran.

"I am happy to see you, gentlemen," said she, in her little tiresome croaking voice; "indeed I'm thankful to see anybody, for this is such a lonely out-of-the-way place. I was just saying this morning what an improvement a town would be on the water-side; it would be a great ornament, and of great use in making a stir and giving employment to poor people, and very convenient too. I'm surprised it has never struck anybody to set such a thing a-going, when there's such a want of employment for the poor."

"Rome was not built in a day, you know, ma'am," said the facetious Mr. M'Dow, with one of his loud laughs; "but if you will use your influence with Inch Orran, and prevail upon him to begin, there's no saying where it may end"—another peal—"and I hope the kirk and the manse will not be forgot, Inch Orran."

"Still less the stipend, sir," said Inch Orran, with one of his vicious sneers,

"I'll answer for it the stipend will no get leave to

be forgot," returned the incorrigible Mr. M'Dow, with one of his loudest roars; "you may trust the minister for keeping you in mind of that."

"I believe I may, sir."

"And let it be a good one at the first, Inch Orran, that he may not have such a battle to fight for his augmentation as I have had. I really think the Teind Court has taken an entire wrong view of the subject there, or they would have given me the decreet at once. You'll no go along with me there, Glenroy?"

But Glenroy disdained to reply, so the little old man said, "It was the saying, sir, of one of the wisest judges who ever sat upon the Scottish bench, that a *poor* clergy made a *pure* clergy; a maxim which deserves to be engraven in letters of gold on every manse in Scotland."

"'Deed, then, I can tell you, Inch Orran, the gold would be very soon piket off," returned Mr. M'Dow, with redoubled bursts of laughter. "Na, na, you must keep the gold for your fine English Episcopalian palaces, where it's no so scarce as it's among us;" and Mr. M'Dow perfectly revelled in the delight of this *jeu d'esprit.* Mrs. Malcolm now struck in. "I'm quite tormented with these midges. I don't think they'll leave the skin upon me. I wish they would bite you, Mr. Malcolm."

"Perhaps, sir, you would wish some refreshment," said Inch Orran, addressing Glenroy, in a voice louder and shriller than that with which Punch denounces Polly. The Chief, who was still under the influence of a late and luxurious breakfast, declined; but upon the same offer (if offer it could be called) being put to Benbowie, he was so little in the habit of refusing anything, except to give money, and besides had such a willing appetite, that he at once greedily assented. Mr. M'Dow rubbed his hands, drew out his pocket-handkerchief, placed his hands upon his knees, and began snuffing the air, as though he already caught the scent of some savoury mess.

The bell was faintly rung by Inch Orran, but some minutes elapsed, and no one answered.

"That's always the way with that Simon," said Mrs. Malcolm; "I'm sure I wish we had a well-behaved, clever, active boy, for——"

But a bitter look, and a sh——sh from her lord, stopped her tongue, while a fierce tingle of the bell brought forth Simon.

"Refreshments, if you please, Simon," said his master, in a softer tone and manner than he had yet evinced.

"Refreshments, sir?" repeated Simon, putting his hand to his forehead, with an air of great perplexity.

"I think some warm broth would be the best thing in such a warm day," said Mrs. Malcolm; "for when people are warm they should never take anything cold, it's very dangerous; I had an aunt once——"

"Something cold, Simon," said his master decidedly.

"Cold, sir?" repeated Simon; then, seeming to recollect himself, he withdrew.

Then ensued a great deal of heavy tramping to and fro, and a mighty clattering of plates, knives and forks, which was music to the ears of Benbowie and Mr. M'Dow.

At length entered Simon, and, with much seeming exertion, began to rub down a table (although there was neither speck nor spot upon it) in the most ostentatious manner, puffing and blowing all the while, as though he had been in the tread-mill.

"Take care of the carpet, Simon," said his mistress; but Simon seemed as though he heard her not. He then unfolded and carefully laid a table-cloth with mathematical precision, retiring a few paces to judge of its general effect, and then returning to adjust what his eye pronounced to be amiss.

"I think the cloth should be rather more this way, Simon," said his mistress, drawing it towards her, with an air of great importance.

"Tut," muttered Simon, as he jerked it in the contrary direction.

Once more he withdrew, and another pause ensued, during which Glenroy made another attempt to draw his host into conversation.

"This is a beautiful situation of yours, Inch Orran," said he,—"I really know nothing finer."

"It is a very *desirable* property, sir," returned the old man, with marked emphasis.

"You have one of the noblest views in Scotland from these windows," said the Chief proudly, as he looked on his own princely domain.

"It may be, sir; but I have other things to look to than fine views on this neglected property," replied Inch Orran.

"That's precisely my own case, Inch Orran," said Mr. M'Dow. "One person has been saying, when they came to the manse, 'Oh, what a beautiful situation, Mr. M'Dow!' Another says, 'Oh, such a grand view, Mr. M'Dow!' Another cries, 'I really think you beat Glenroy himself in your prospects, Mr. M'Dow.' 'That may all be,' says I; 'but the best prospects I have in view are a comfortable manse, an addition to the glebe, and the decreet for my augmentation.' Ho, hoch, hoch, ho."

Neither Glenroy nor Inch Orran took the smallest notice of this sally; and the former continued to address the latter.

"I have the advantage of you in one respect, Inch Orran; for this place of yours forms one of the finest features in the view from my drawing-room windows; though, without vanity, I may say Glenroy is also a very fine object from yours."

"Probably, sir, *you* may have more pleasure in the view of *my* property than I have in contemplating yours."

Glenroy felt his cheek flush at this palpable hit; but just then the door was thrown wide open, and Simon appeared with his arms at full stretch, bearing a tray, which he deposited on a side-table, and then proceeded to arrange its contents with the same bustling importance.

At the top of the table was placed the wizened nib of a tongue, and *vis-à-vis* the almost bare blade-bone of a shoulder of mutton; on one side a thin slice of bread was confronted with a few potatoes; at the corners were a jug of whey and another of water; a decanter containing a few glasses of port, and a bottle of currant wine, stale and sour, and tasting, as currant wine sometimes does, of brown sugar, blue paper, yellow soap, cork, candle, twine, and vinegar.

The two expectants had felt their appetites considerably damped at sight of the cheer provided for them; they, however, seated themselves, though with rueful faces. To do them justice, neither of them was nice, but they both loved a savoury mess, something to make a slop with; something to eat with their knives—what they ought to eat with their forks. But, alas! here was no room for such a display; for, though Mr. M'Dow, as the younger and stronger man, contrived both to cut and chew the inflexible remains of the tongue, poor Benbowie was completely baffled in the attempt; and all he could do was to crumble down a bit of bread, and spill half a glass of wine on the table-cloth, after which he declared he had had enough—quite enough, on his conscience. While the master of the revels drank to the health of his guests very graciously in a glass of green whey.

"I shall let the old miser see what good living is!" thought Glenroy, as he began a pompous and pressing invitation to his kinsman to spend a few days with him, accompanied by ostentatious offers of barge, pinnace, carriages, horses, servants, etc. "It is *my* intention to spend a couple of days with you, sir, before I leave the country," replied Inch Orran; "and, if agreeable to you, when I can make it convenient to myself, I shall not fail to apprise you."

This was more than Glenroy had expected, or perhaps wished for, now that he had experienced the nature of the man; but of course he was all pleasure, gratification, and so forth. A hope was then expressed that Mrs. Malcolm would join the party.

"Most certainly, sir," replied Inch Orran. "*I* keep no separate establishment for my wife."

"I'm sure I shall be very happy to go," said she; "for I'll be thankful to go anywhere—this is such a dull place. Only, if the ladies here dress much to go out to dinner, I'm sure I don't know what I shall do, Mr. Malcolm, for a cap for——" But a "sh—sh," and a wave of his hand from her husband, stopped her mouth, and the visitors took leave.

As they traversed the long passage, they descried Simon at the other extremity, waddling along with a foaming tankard in one hand, and a long-necked bottle in the other; and, at the same time, the nostrils of Benbowie and Mr. M'Dow were assailed with the smell of some very gusty viands, towards which Mr. Simon seemed to have been steering his course.

The half-open door of a housekeeper's room, from whence issued the fragrance, induced them both to thrust in their heads; and there stood disclosed a table neatly laid for two, with a smoking tureen of

hodge-podge, and a magnificent jowl of salmon. At
this sight the two stood as if entranced, with open
mouths and outstretched necks; but it was of short
duration; for directly a quick foot, an invisible hand,
and the door was shut with an angry slap.

"On my conscience! but I would rather be the
man than the master," said Benbowie, with a grunt
of dissatisfaction, as he followed his friend to the
barge.

"At least, I would rather take pot-luck with him,"
said Mr. M'Dow, with a faint attempt at a laugh, as,
with a discomfited air, he betook himself to his
Amailye (as he had christened his pony, in honour
of the Lady Kindullie), and trotted away in quest of
better cheer.

CHAPTER XI.

GLENROY returned home much dissatisfied with his visit. He had been provoked at the dry impertinence of the old man, disgusted with the tiresome weakness of his wife, and incensed beyond measure at the innumerable offences of Mr. M'Dow. Neither was his ill-humour appeased when, at the end of a week, he received the following despatch, written in the plainest and squarest and most inflexible of hands :—

"Mr. Mungo Malcolm presents his compliments to Mr. Norman Malcolm of Glenroy, and if still convenient for him to receive a visit, Mr. Mungo Malcolm will, in pursuance of his original intention, wait upon him on Wednesday next, the 20th inst., in the course of the afternoon, and purposes to be his guest till the following Saturday forenoon, when he positively takes leave. Mr. M. Malcolm will be accompanied by his wife and male servant."

Glenroy chafed like a boar at being thus addressed as Mr. Norman Malcolm, and scouted the whole style of the billet; but it is much to be wished that the world in general, and many very worthy people in

particular, would follow the example of Mr. Mungo
Malcolm, in thus precisely marking the limits of their
intended stay.

All householders, whatever they may pretend,
must at some period or other have groaned under
the indefinable misery of an undefined length of visit,
and every family must have felt the want of a chro-
nometer for ascertaining the respective ideas of both
parties as to the reasonable latitude and longitude of
a visit. In good old times Scotland had its regular
standard measure for visiting, as it had for its oatmeal
and potatoes. A rest day, a dress day, and a press
day, were the appointed measure of a visitor's days.
The first was consecrated to repose, after the fatigues
of the journey, whether there had been a journey or
not; the second was allotted to showing off the full-
dress suit, prepared perhaps for the occasion; and
the third was delicately appropriated to the pressing
solicitations of the host, and always conferred as an
act of bounty over and above. Thus both parties
were pleased, the presser and the pressed; the presser
at having conquered, the pressed at having conceded;
and thus they parted, happy to part, happy to meet,
and happy to part again.

But since this barrier has been broken down by
modern innovation, visiting has no longer any limits,
except such as exist in the minds of the respective
parties; and accordingly "there's the respect" that
makes cautious people pause before bringing upon
themselves a visit. A visit! How vague, how unde-

fined, how dark, how immeasurable, how obscure, how unfathomable, how mysterious, is a visit! A visit may be meant for a day, or a week, or a month; and it may be taken for a winter, or a summer, or a year! A visit may be the cement of friendship, or it may be the bane of domestic happiness! A visit may be like an angel's coming, brief and rare, or it may be like a wounded crocodile, drawing its slow length along.

But none of these evils could befall the host of Mr. Mungo Malcolm, for the day and hour and minute of his departure were always settled, as upon this occasion, long before his arrival. Glenroy anticipated anything but pleasure from this visit, but he comforted himself by considering it as a compliment, and the next thing to being declared heir to Inch Orran. He therefore resolved to pay all honour to his guest, and to win his heart by the good cheer and gaiety he would provide for him.

The appointed day arrived, a raw, bleak, chill, unhappy-looking day; not stormy enough to be grand, but just rough enough to be disagreeable. The hills were covered with mist, the sky with clouds, the sea with foam, and doubts were entertained whether the old man would venture forth in such a day, when, in the midst of mist and clouds and rain and foam, a little black dripping boat was descried rowing along, which being run ashore, out stepped Inch Orran, his aspect completely harmonising with that of nature. Next was dragged forth Mrs. Malcolm, a mass of cloaks and shawls. Next followed Simon, with a small bundle under his arm, his person snugly ensconced beneath a large umbrella, which he affected to hold carefully over his lady, but of which she got only the droppings.

The Laird and his lady were welcomed by Glenroy with every demonstration of courtesy and good-will. They were received by him in his great hall, decorated with banners and broadswords, and dirks and claymores, and targets and deers' heads, and warlike trophies of every description, amidst which a consequential, full-plumed piper paced to and fro. Altogether, the effect was grand and imposing, but it was quite lost upon the guests. Inch Orran, if he noticed at all, noticed only to hate such trumpery, and his lady did not know a dirk from a deer's horn. Glenroy's attempts at striking them with awe on their first entrance were therefore all in vain; it was to no purpose that he pointed out the stately banner of one chief, and the singular dirk of another, and related anecdotes pertaining to each.

Inch Orran's horrid listening eyes were bent straight upon him, but he never opened his lips unless to utter a monosyllable. But still more enraging was his lady's commotion upon discovering that she had lost one of her gloves; it was a new glove, a pink glove, a French glove, a habit glove; it was the fellow of the glove she had on; she must have left it in the boat, or it must have fallen into the sea, or she must have dropped it on the road, or Simon *must* have seen it, or it *must* be in

Mr. Malcolm's pocket, for it could not be lost, and it was not about her; and she shook herself round and round in testimony thereof.   These her surmises and lamentations were uttered in a low, slow, monotonous tone to Benbowie and Mrs. Macauley, as with a *dementit* air she looked all round about, and not seeing her pink glove, she saw nothing else.   Mrs. Macauley and Benbowie bestirred themselves with all their might in search of the stray glove, for it was a case that came home to both their bosoms; they had each lost gloves at different periods of their lives; they therefore knew what it was to lose a glove.   They entered into the nature of the loss; they did not idly sympathise in it, they exerted themselves to seek for it, they wondered for it, they lamented for it, they poked about for it in all improbable as well as impossible places; in short, all the energies of their heads, hearts, and hands were put in motion for the recovery of the glove, but in vain.

Simon was next summoned, and he ended the matter at once by boldly declaring that he had seen the glove drop into the water as his lady was coming out of the boat, and that just as he was trying to recover it, a monstrous wave had swept it away, and he could see no more of it.

"I'm sure I never know whether to believe Simon or not," said the lady to Mrs. Macauley; "for I think he'll say anything just to save himself trouble."[1]

[1] It will doubtless be a relief to the compassionate reader to learn that the glove was all this while in Mrs. Malcolm's own pocket.

A rich repast, under the head of luncheon, was now served up; but this Inch Orran refused point-blank even to approach, and upon being pressed by his host to partake in a manner that savoured more of hospitality than of free will left to his guest, he said in his most peremptory manner, "Sir, I make it a rule to dine but once a day." This was uttered in a tone not to be disputed; but he added in a some-what softer key, "But I request, sir, I may be no re-straint on your usual practices;" and motioning his host towards the table, he betook himself to a far-off corner of the room, the most remote and inaccessible, where he began to read a newspaper; and Glenroy, already boiling at his dogged impertinence, left him to chew the cud of his own reflections, while he did the honours of the banquet.

CHAPTER XII

THE party were scarcely seated when young Norman came bounding into the apartment in all the exuberance of unchecked animal spirits, just let loose from the restraints of the schoolroom, and evidently master of his own actions everywhere else. He was a handsome sprightly boy, with a haughty, careless air, that showed he was already aware of his own importance. He eyed Inch Orran for a moment, with a look that seemed to say, "Who are you?" as he brushed past him to the table, followed by a large greyhound.

"Go and shake hands with that gentleman, Norman," said his father; "that is Inch Orran." But Norman heard as though he heard him not.

"I am *so* hungry, papa," said he, casting a wandering glance from dish to dish all over the table; "I hope you have got something good for me. Oh, do make haste, pray. No, no, I won't have a mutton-chop," drawing away his plate quickly as Mrs. Macauley was preparing to help him; then, as suddenly retracting, "Yes, you may give me one for Fingal. Here Fin, Fin, my pretty fellow, here is a mutton-chop for you; now eat it like a gentleman, and don't grease the carpet."

"Norman, did you hear me desire you to go and shake hands with our friend Inch Orran?" said Glenroy, in a more authoritative tone.

"Yes, papa, I will presently, but——"

"Go, then, sir, when I desire you," cried the Chief, in rising displeasure.

"Yes, papa—ah! ham-pie, that is so good!" and he jumped and shook his hands in ecstasy. "Now, do give me some, papa; there is nothing I love so much."

"Unless you do as I desire you, sir, deuce a bit of anything you shall taste to-day," cried Glenroy angrily; his authority over his son always requiring to be backed by a threat, or a bribe, or an oath—sometimes by all three.

"Well, then, remember you promised me some ham-pie, papa;" and slowly approaching Inch Orran, with his head riveted to the table and his eye upon the dish, he extended his hand to him; but it met with no corresponding movement on the part of Inch Orran, whose hands remained firmly closed before him. Nowise disconcerted, however, his young kinsman made a sort of snatch at his hand; and then, satisfied he had done his part, skipped away back to enjoy the reward of his obedience. Glenroy took a glance at the old man in the corner, but he did not like his look. His lips were drawn in till they were invisible; his cheeks were distended like Æolus's bags, and his eyes glared like a cat's in the dark. His lady was all this while seated between Benbowie and Mrs. Macauley, and enjoying herself to her heart's content in conversing with them.

"What's become of Reginald and Edith to-day?" inquired Glenroy, and at that moment the sound of young voices in the hall seemed to answer the question. Fingal pricked up his ears and wagged his tail, while his master sprang up and bounded away, followed by his favourite, who almost jumped over Inch Orran, in his eagerness to gain the door.

"What are these children about?" demanded Glenroy angrily, as the uproar increased.

"You *must* come in—you *shall* come in—don't let him go—hold him fast," resounded through the hall, and presently entered a youthful group, consisting of the three children of the house, all hanging round a fine, manly-looking boy, dripping wet, and evidently of a different stock from his more dainty-looking companions.

"There is Ronald, papa," whispered Edith, as she ran up to her father.

"Well, and what of that?" answered he in a dissatisfied tone. "Do you see no greater strangers than him here, that you should be making all this noise?"

Edith blushed, and turned to Mrs. Malcolm; then, but with still more timidity, went to Inch Orran, who, relaxing from his sternness, took the little hand that was held out to him, and even bestowed a pat on the head, as if to make up for the rebuff she had met with from her father. Meanwhile the two boys had com-

pelled their guest to approach to the table, quite
unconscious of the haughty looks with which Glenroy
regarded him.

"Now you are our prisoner," cried Norman; "so
sit down, and you shall have something to eat, though
you deserve to be fed on bread and water for attempting to escape. Here, Fin, at him, if he offers to stir
without my leave."

"How your dirty shoes have stained my trousers,"
said Reginald pettishly, as he rubbed some spots of
mud from his white trousers; "I wish I hadn't gone
near you; and I am so hot," putting his fingers
through his hair; and throwing himself at full length
upon two chairs, he began to fan himself with a
napkin.

"So, Master Ronald, what has brought you here
this bad day?" inquired the Chieftain, in no very
encouraging accent.

The boy coloured, as if he felt the rudeness of the
inquiry; then answered, "I came to return Norman's
fishing-rod."

"Phoo; there could be no hurry in that," said the
Chief, still more coldly.

"I had *promised* to bring it to-day," said Ronald.

"Pshaw, what signified that?" said Norman carelessly; "you needn't have got yourself wet for a
promise, if that was all."

"I would rather have to swim for my life than
break my word," said Ronald warmly.

The two boys burst into a fit of laughing.

"On my conscience, but there's a great difference," said Benbowie, with a look of alarm.

"Come, come, let us have no more nonsense," said Glenroy impatiently; "and if you're for anything to eat, boys, make haste, for everybody's done."

Ronald declined the ungracious invitation, and was retiring, when he was again seized by his two friends.

"Oh, you know, you are our prisoner; so you needn't attempt to get away. You *must* stay, and you *shall* eat. So sit down."

"*Must* and *shall?*" repeated Ronald, with a smile; while his open countenance and fine intrepid air showed that he yielded more from good-humour than from false shame or fear; for he wore

> ——"upon his forehead clear
> The freedom of a mountaineer;
> A face with gladness overspread,
> And looks by human kindness bred."

Altogether there was an air of noble, artless simplicity about the boy extremely prepossessing, and rendered still more striking when contrasted with the more artificial elegance of his companions, and the saucy capricious airs of superiority which marked the children of consequence.

"Now, although you are a prisoner," said Norman, I shall allow you to choose for yourself. What will you have? Here is a ham-pie which I can recommend. Papa, I told Barclay that I thought he had put rather too many truffles and morels in the last, and not enough of eggs; and, by-the-bye, plover's eggs are much the best. If you like venison, Ronald, here is a hash, which is by far the best way of eating venison, at least in my opinion."

"I'll take a mutton-chop," said Ronald, helping himself to what was next him.

"A mutton-chop! horrible!—that's Fingal's dish; but he wouldn't eat them now, for they are almost cold."

"It is very good," said Ronald, eating with a hearty appetite.

"Perhaps you choose a cold potato too," said Reginald contemptuously, holding one up.

"Warm ones are better," said Ronald, taking a potato; "but I don't care—it doesn't signify."

"No; to be sure, if people have no taste, it does *not* signify," said Norman, piqued at the indifference of his guest, and bent upon showing his power and consequence, especially before such queer-looking people as Inch Orran and his lady.

"You are quite wet, Ronald," said Edith softly, as she put her hand on his arm. Then whispered to her father, "Pray, papa, give Ronald a glass of wine."

"Here's a glass of wine for you," said Glenroy, pouring it out ungraciously, and as if he wished to end the scene; but Ronald declined taking it.

"Do take it, dear Ronald," said Edith.

"We shall *make* him take it," said the young heir, whose hospitality was of the most peremptory nature.

"If I were to take it for anybody, it would be for

Edith," said Ronald; "but I don't choose any wine, thank you."

"Come, drink it off, and go away and amuse your-selves somewhere else," cried Glenroy, in a very bad humour.

Ronald instantly rose, but was again seized by his two tormentors.

"Oh you shall not stir till you have drunk it to the last drop."

And Norman, taking the glass of wine, would have forced it to his lips; but he shook him off.

"Nothing will make me drink wine," said he firmly.

"Oh, you are a Turk, a Mussulman!—a Turk, a Turk!" shouted the two boys in derision.

"He is an obstinate dog," said Glenroy; "let him alone." Ronald's colour rose, but he said nothing.

"What is the reason you refuse to drink, my boy?" demanded Inch Orran, emerging from his corner, where he had been an attentive spectator of all that had passed. Ronald met his sharp inquisitive glance with the clear ingenuous expression of his full blue eye; but he was silent for a moment, then said—

"Because my father wishes me not to drink wine."

"And why?"

Ronald cast down his eyes.

"Oh, I know the reason now," whispered the two boys, nodding to each other with half-suppressed smiles, then whispering, "it's because they're so poor."

Ronald instantly shook off his embarrassment, and

looking up, said, "He can't afford to give us wine at home."

"On my conscience, and that's the very reason you should get leave to take it when you can get it elsewhere," said Benbowie.

"Well, well, we have had enough of this," cried Glenroy impatiently; "go away, and divert yourselves elsewhere, children.—Good morning, Mr. Ronald."

And Ronald, in spite of the forcible attempts of his friends to detain him, shook them off with ease, and darted away in the midst of a heavy rain.

"That's the son of Jack Malcolm of Lochdhu?" said Inch Orran, fixing his inquisitorial eyes full upon Glenroy, who felt that an apology was due for this ill-timed meeting with the son of the man he detested, and he replied, "Yes. I'm sorry this should have happened, Inch Orran; but the father is a tacksman of mine; I couldn't be off letting him have a farm that joined to his own bit of property, and that boy has got a sort of footing here through the children; they're glad of companions near their own age."

"How many children has Jack Malcolm?" asked the old man abruptly.

"About a dozen, I believe," said Glenroy contemptuously.

"And that is his eldest son?"

"Yes; and if he had been mine, and I had been in his father's situation, he shouldn't have been idling away his time at home. I gave them my advice,

which was to send that boy to some cheap public
school in England, where he would learn something
of the world, which is the thing for a boy that has
his way to make in it. But they wouldn't hear of
it; said they would rather live upon bread and water
than send any child of theirs to a great school. However, they are not just at that, for they can at least
give them kail and porridge;" with a laugh of derision.

A spark shot from the corner of Inch Orran's eye
as he turned abruptly away, muttering something
between his teeth. The rain fell without intermis-
sion for the rest of the day, which seemed of endless
duration to both parties, and Glenroy was at last
obliged to have recourse to Mrs. Macauley's much-
despised musical powers to wile away the time.

CHAPTER XIII.

THE following day cleared up, and there was a bright sun and a sweet blowing wind, and everything looked gay and everybody pleased except Inch Orran, who minded neither sun nor wind, and was alike insensible to the charms of nature and the influence of weather.

Glenroy had invited a large party—that is, he had summoned all who were within call to do honour to his kinsman's visit—and the house (which indeed was seldom empty) had continued to fill during the whole morning with invited guests, as also with chance droppers-in of various descriptions. The Chief felt as if there was safety from his kinsman's ill-humour in the multitude that surrounded him; his courage rose, his spirits revived, and he was himself again. But it was a transitory calm. The dinner-hour was drawing near, the guests were all assembled, when suddenly, borne on the breeze, came the distant neighing of a steed. Glenroy started and turned red; another and another loud and long and shrill and joyful burst; it was the well-known happy neigh of Amailye, announcing the approach of Mr. Duncan M'Dow! Had the Castle possessed a drawbridge it certainly would have been raised on the instant, but as there were neither javelin-men nor moat to oppose him, the minister rode boldly on, arrayed as usual in his large woolly greatcoat and red worsted comforter.

Mrs. Malcolm caught the *sough* of his name, and thereupon thought proper to address Glenroy.

"Is that the Mr. M'Dow that was so good as to call one day at Inch Orran? What an uncommon pleasant, sensible, well-informed man he is! I was really very much pleased with him; he's so polite and well-bred, and has so much to say; he seems a very superior man; it must be a great advantage to have such a man for a clergyman, and I'm sure you have great credit in your choice, for there's really something so very—ahem—a—so uncommonly—a—a—so much of the gentleman about him."

Glenroy disdained to reply.

Here the announcement of Mr. M'Dow put a stop to the remarks, and presently his heavy foot announced itself. Although there was a large assemblage of ladies and gentlemen present, Mr. M'Dow as usual made a point of grappling with each individually, right and left, here and there, cross hands and down backs, in the most indefatigable manner. Then fastening upon his host, he burst out with one of his *avant courier* roars of laughter.

"Well, Glenroy, there's one thing, I'm sure, you'll not say of me, as was said of a poor friend of mine, who was thought rather neglectful of his parish in the visiting way, and something too metaphœsical in his discoorses from his pulpit; it was really very neatly said—ho, hoch, how—that he was a most wonderful man, for he was invisible six days in the week, and incomprehensible on the seventh; very clever, rather severe, to be sure, but it was really just the truth—how, how, ho, hoch."

Glenroy was not like Hamlet. He could have used daggers, but he could not speak them. He did not excel in *repartée* at any time, for, when provoked, he was instantly in a passion; and not daring to give scope to it in the present instance, all he could do was to dart a furious glance at the intruder, and turn on his heel. But heel or toe, it was all one to the minister, who was quite insensible to all rebuffs, especially as he met with a warm reception from such of the party as, being more remote and inaccessible in their dwellings, and having nothing to say as to the augmentation, were not favoured with so much of his company in their own houses.

And as one person of easy manners—no matter how vulgar—is always acceptable to the guests, whatever he may be to the host, Mr. M'Dow's bad jokes and hearty laugh were very palatable to some of the party, who found them much more relishing than the overbearing pomp of Glenroy, or the morose silence of Inch Orran. Mr. M'Dow, therefore, was very soon riding on the rigging of his own good spirits; and peal upon peal, roar upon roar, followed in quick succession, and raised many an echo from the lower

orders of the company. His staying to dinner was a
matter of course. In the first flush of his gratified
feelings, at having got the man of his choice—a moderate man, an honest fellow, and also pleased with the
convivial habits and jolly manners, which he saw
would be no restraint on his own, Glenroy had in a
rash moment given him a general invitation to his
house, which the minister had not been slack in avail-
ing himself of, particularly if there was anything
going on that promised better cheer or more amusement than common. As surely, therefore, as Glenroy
had any new arrivals of consequence, or a larger or
more ceremonious party than usual, or an extraordinary influx of company, or any strangers of great distinction, he might depend upon Mr. M'Dow's dropping
in. It was quite wonderful how and where he acquired
such speedy and certain intelligence; for in a remote
and thinly-peopled country, where dwellings were few
and far between, it could neither be by seeing nor
hearing nor smelling. But so it was; no wild Indian
could have tracked his prey with greater certainty
and finesse than Mr. M'Dow did a good dinner;
indeed, nothing could surpass the accuracy and success with which he followed the trail of a jolly party,
or what he termed "an innocent recreation."

Glenroy having surmounted the first shock of his
appearance, though still boiling with wrath against
him, resolved to make it plain that his company was
not expected at dinner, and therefore said, in his
stateliest manner, "You are too late for luncheon,

Mr. M'Dow; but if you wish for any refreshment, I shall order some to the eating-room for you."

"You are really extremely kind and considerate, Glenroy," replied his guest, with much hearty warmth of manner; "but it is quite unnecessary in you to put yourself to that trouble, as I had a snack at your friend Captain Malcolm's; and indeed I was pressed to stay still there, which I would have done, if I had not previously intended myself the honour of taking my pot-luck with you, as you were so very polite as to assure me of being always welcome; a piece of kindness and hospitality which I am sure I shall never forget."

"That's just as it should be," remarked a laird who had three ferries between him and Mr. M'Dow. "There ought always to be an open door to the minister."

"It's a pleasant thing to see the heritors and ministers on a friendly footing," said another, whose teinds were valued and exhausted.

"In that respect, I have really reason to be proud," said Mr. M'Dow, rapping his mull with an air of modest importance; "for ever since my induction, I have met with uncommon attention and hospitality, not only from my respected pawtron here, but likewise from the very gentlemen who thought proper to oppose the presentation. There's Captain Malcolm, for instance, he was very keen against me; more so, indeed, than what many men in my situation would have overlooked. But he's a little of the high-flier:

the very—hem—the unco gude—hoch, hoch, how!
one o' your gospellers, in short; what one of my
worthy brethren calls your saunts—hoch, hoch, ho! ·
but I believe he is a well-meaning man for all that,
so I made a point of showing him that I bore no ill-
will against him, and that I had no objections whatever to be on a friendly footing with him," with
another long, self-sufficient pinch of snuff.

"He's a very honest man, Captain Malcolm," said
a good-natured bluff laird; "and has as fine a family
as I ever saw, and as well brought up, too. There's
not a prettier girl in all the shire than Lucy Malcolm; and he'll be a lucky man that gets her for his
wife."

Mr. M'Dow now addressed Inch Orran. "I was
just saying, sir, that I had the pleeshure this forenoon
of paying my respects to a very worthy gentleman, a
clansman, and, I believe, a relation of yours—Captain
John Malcolm." A slight, stiff bend from Inch Orran
was the only reply; but Mr. M'Dow went on. "My
principal object in calling on him to-day was, that I
wished particularly to see a set of farm offices which
I heard he had lately built, and also some improvements which he had made upon his house; and I
thought I might pick up some useful hints from them,
to lay before my excellent pawtron here, especially
in respect of a byre. There's nothing in my remembrance that there's been greater improvements in than
in byres. However, I must say I was disappointed;
he has made no addition of any signification to the

house; and the offices are really upon a very moderate scale—very much so ; extremely moderate, indeed."

"I understood, sir, moderation had been a favourite virtue of yours," said Inch Orran drily.

"Ay—yes—to be sure, in some things—indeed in most things, I may say; moderation is the safest coorse. Moderation will never lead a man far wrong, Inch Orran."

"Yes, sir, it leads a man far wrong, if it keeps him from doing his duty," returned Inch Orran.

"There I quite agree with you, Inch Orran—there can be no doubt of that. But, in respect of the offices —it's really my unprejudiced opinion, that when a man has his hand in the mortar tub, a little money, more or less, is ill saved, when the question is between a good, handsome, complete building, and a poor, paltry, insignificant thing. I used the freedom to say something of that sort to the Captain himself, but he only laughed and shook his head, and said he had eight strong reasons against extravagance—pointing to his children. 'Ay, to be sure, there's no arguing against such facts as these, Captain,' says I ; 'they're the next thing to the Ten Commandments'—hoch, hoch, hoch !—how, ho !" Here, strong in conscious freedom, Mr. M'Dow roared and laughed, rapped upon his mull, drew in about a quarter of a pound of snuff, and displayed all the extent of a Pulicat handkerchief.

At dinner things were, if possible, still worse. The manse and the byre, to be sure, were forgot, while he revelled amidst a profusion of fish, flesh,

fowl, and game of every description, with the ardour
of a man who, with all the inclination, had not the
means of faring sumptuously every day. The rest
of the party ate, drank, talked, and disputed in the
usual manner, all save Inch Orran, who ate little,
drank none, and preserved a profound silence, except
when now and then provoked to utter some sharp
and biting sarcasm.

CHAPTER XIV.

THERE is something very appalling in the silence that precedes a storm. At such a time the imagination and the conscience are left to the full and undisturbed exercise of their powers; and, however vague and undefined may be their operations, they nevertheless continue to oppress us with that deadliest of all fears —"the fear of something yet to come."

It was probably this instinctive dread which had made Glenroy hitherto shun every approach to a *tête-à-tête* with his silent guest; but as the hour of his departure drew near, he began to muster his courage, and to consider that it was due to himself to come to some sort of understanding with the old man, as to the strange bearing he had held ever since his arrival. It was impossible he could have met with any real ground of offence, for everything had been done to grace his visit and gain his good-will; but something might have occurred which he was not aware of, or there might have been some imaginary failure that had given umbrage, and a few words of explanation might set all to rights. For this purpose, therefore, Glenroy sought a private interview with his guest, the morning of his departure, and began in the usual terms, by expressing his regret at the prospect of losing him so soon, mingled with gentle upbraidings at the shortness of his stay, hopes of his speedy return, and of being favoured with a longer visit. Then Inch Orran spoke, and he said very deliberately,

"Sir, this is my first visit, and it will be my last."

This was coming to the point with a vengeance. Glenroy was startled, but drawing himself up he said, "I flatter myself, Inch Orran, you have found nothing wanting on my part to make your stay here pleasant?"

"Have I made any complaint, sir?" was the true Scottish answer.

"I should be sorry if you, or any man, had anything to complain of in my house," replied the Chieftain proudly.

Inch Orran smiled—that is, he uncurled his little purse-mouth for the first time since his arrival; but it was a scornful, ill-omened smile.

"I—I'm at a loss to understand you, Inch Orran— 'pon my soul I am. I am used to speak my mind to every man, and I expect every man to do the same to me," said Glenroy, waxing warm.

"I have no objection to speak my mind to you, sir," said Inch Orran, with a horrid gleam of his little vindictive eye; "but are you quite sure you have none to hear it?"

"I don't know why I should," returned the Chief, affecting great coolness, to conceal the abhorrence which all men, women, and children, feel at that awful and portentous threat, whether from friend or foe, of speaking their mind. It is then "conscience makes cowards of us all," as it did of Glenroy, who, in spite of the high opinion he had of himself, felt an instinctive dread at the idea of Inch Orran speaking his mind, either *to* him or *of* him. And, indeed, speaking the mind is generally understood to mean neither more nor less than that the speaker means to be most thoroughly disagreeable and abusive.

There was, however, no escaping Inch Orran's mind, or rather matter, as he looked exactly like a tiger cat who had got his claw stuck hard and fast in his prey, and was in no hurry to despatch it.

"Then, sir, on what particular point is it that you wish me to speak my mind?" demanded he, with the firmness of a rock. This was much too precise for Glenroy, who would rather have kept in vague generals than have been brought to particular points, and who, moreover, had expected the questions to be all on his side, the answers on the other.

"I—don't think—in—a—I, in short, I—don't think you seem to have been pleased with something or another, Inch Orran?" said Glenroy, with some awkward hesitation.

"I don't say that I have, sir."

"Then, sir, I wish you would have the goodness to say what it is you complain of ; have you met with anything to offend you in me or any of my family?" demanded the Chief, strong in conscious importance.

Inch Orran was silent for a moment, then answered in the most decided manner, "I have, sir."

"I'm sorry to hear it, Inch Orran; very sorry indeed that you or anybody else should have met with anything unpleasant in my house, or should consider yourself as having been ill-used by me or any of my family."

"Sir, you mistake me; I never said I had been ill-used."

"I beg pardon; but I certainly understood you to say so, Inch Orran."

"Then, sir, you *mis*understood me."

"I'm happy to hear it, Inch Orran; for I assure you I should have been very sorry if any misunderstanding had taken place between us; for there are few men for whom I entertain a higher respect than I do for you."

"Excuse me, sir, there *is* a misunderstanding."

"Sir," said the Chief, "I am really at a loss to understand you. If I have failed in any attentions——"

"No want of attention, sir," in a tone as much as to say, "Rather too much of it."

"Has there been anything in any of the company to offend you, Inch Orran?"

"Much!" pronounced in a most emphatic manner; then, after a little pause, "Everything, and in all of them, sir."

"Indeed! upon my soul, sir, you are ill to please! You have met with some of the first gentlemen in the county, I can tell you, whatever you may think."

Again his mouth was contemptuously curled, while the Chief took a turn up and down the room to cool himself; he then stopped, and having gulped down his anger, said, "Come, come, Inch Orran, I see how it is; you are a sober man yourself, and you have been a little scandalised at seeing some of my friends take their glass so freely; but every country has its own customs, you know, and I didn't suppose you expected to find a company of hermits in the Highlands of Scotland."

"Sir, if by hermits you mean anchorites or holy hypocrites, I despise them as much as you do; but I was not prepared to witness such excesses in eating and drinking."

"Excesses! that's a very strong expression! I have always been used to keep a full table, and to make my friends welcome to it; people must live according to their station; my style of living is perhaps different from what you have been accustomed to."

"Very different, sir," quickly interrupted the old man; "*my* life, sir, has been a life of labour, of frugality, of abstinence. *Your* life, sir, is one continued idle, extravagant, intemperate soss."

"Anything else, sir?" demanded Glenroy, boiling with indignation.

"There *is* something else, sir."

"Then you had better go on, sir; much better say all you have to say; you have already found fault with the company I keep, and the style I live in."

"Sir, you mistake; I find no fault, I only speak my mind."

"Call it what you please, sir; you object to my friends and my table."

"Excuse me again, sir. I object to neither. I have sat at the one, and associated with the other, though they were both highly offensive to me."

"And I can tell you, sir, your behaviour has been no less offensive to me and my friends. By heaven, there is not another man on the face of the earth I would have suffered to stay in my house, and sit at my table for three days without opening his lips. Sir, let me tell you such behaviour is more like that of a spy than anything else." And Glenroy's passion was now at its height.

"Exactly, sir," said his antagonist, pursing up his mouth with an air of sovereign contempt. "I came to your house not as a babbler and winebibber; but as a noter and observer, and I have accomplished my purpose."

By a violent effort Glenroy regained his temper, and, seeing all was at hazard, he resolved to humour the old man, and let him go his way in peace; he therefore said with a laugh, "Well, well, Inch Orran, you've hardly dealt fairly by us, considering that we were met to celebrate your arrival, and drink to the Laird of Inch Orran. Perhaps we did exceed a little last night; but, since that's all, we shall part good friends, I hope."

"No, sir; it is not all."

"What else offended you, sir? The boys have been rather noisy, perhaps; but you know boys will be boys."

"Noisy and disagreeable all boys are," replied Inch Orran; "but epicures and puppies all boys are *not*. Sir, your son is an epicure, and I look upon an epicure as little better than a drunkard. I have known drunkards, sir—that is, men who what you call liked their glass (degraded as they were to a level with the brutes)—who still retained some manly feelings; but I never knew an epicure who cared for any one thing on the face of the earth but his own inside."

Glenroy had stood the attack upon himself, his friends, and his table, with wonderful equanimity; but this invective against his son and heir, the very apple of his eye, was too much for him; and, uttering an oath, he stalked away to the window. But there lay full disclosed the seat of Inch Orran—the family seat!—its venerable towers, its green uplands, its noble woods, all reflected on the bosom of the clear waters.

"There's the respect" that made him pause; and after a severe struggle, he recovered himself and said, "I'm sorry, Inch Orran, you should have taken up such a prejudice against Norman; for, although I say it, there is not a finer or more manly boy in the country than he is. And as for his eating, if he is a little nice, it's all owing to that English dominie, who, by Jove, beats all for gormandising that ever I met with. I've a good mind to give him his dismissal this very day."

"As to that, sir, you may take your own time, for it is now too late. Epicurism is a vice that never cures. Your son, sir, is an epicure, and an epicure he will remain, in spite of your teeth."

Here Glenroy could scarcely refrain from seizing the old man by the nape of the neck, and whirling him out at the window, which stood most invitingly open. While he stood irresolute how to testify his fury and contempt, Inch Orran proceeded:

"Now, sir, I have spoken my mind to you, and I have done it with deliberation. I have spent nearly three days, sir, under your roof, in the midst, I may say, of a human hog-sty, for the purpose of studying your son, and the result of my observations is, that he is an epicure. Allow me, sir," as Glenroy was about to interrupt him; "I am aware, sir, that you look forward to your son succeeding to my estate—sir, I beg I may not be interrupted—the expectation is perfectly natural, and in your situation I should probably have done the same. The wish to regain the inheritance of your forefathers is also unblamable; I find no fault with it."

Glenroy brightened up a little, and began to breathe more easily.

"But, sir, I think it right and proper to undeceive you. Your son will never inherit a foot of my land, or a farthing of my money."

Glenroy was absolutely dumb with rage and astonishment; the old man therefore proceeded: "But, sir, you have another child, who, although of the wrong

sex, promises fair. She is a quiet, inoffensive, tem-
perate creature, which is all that can be expected of
a female. My intention, therefore, is to settle the
property upon her and her heirs-male."

"This is a most extraordinary proceeding," cried
Glenroy, interrupting him, as he suddenly recovered
from the shock he had sustained; "upon my soul, I
don't know what I am about. It is a proposal so
wholly unexpected, so very unnatural and improper,
to pass by the boy for no reason whatever. I, sir—I
can't possibly agree to such a thing."

And he walked hastily up and down in great agitation, while the old man sat looking as demure as a
cat. "Sir," continued he, "I don't deprive you of
your son, or your son of anything he has any right
to; so neither you nor he has any business to say
buff or sty in the matter. My intention, sir, is to
mend the breed, which has degenerated, and is still
degenerating."

Bursting with half-restrained rage, Glenroy uttered
some unintelligible ejaculations, and allowed his kinsman to go on.

"Sir, the one to mend a degenerate breed is he
who speaks the truth, who keeps his word, who
honours his parents, who is no gormandiser, who
minds neither wind nor weather, and who has been
born and bred in wholesome poverty. Such a one is
the lad I saw scorned and browbeat at your table;
and provided he, Ronald Malcolm, will, at a proper
age, consent to take your daughter to wife, and she

has sense enough to accede to the proposal, the property shall be settled upon their heirs-male; on the other hand, should he refuse——"

But here an oath burst from Glenroy's lips like a thunderbolt, and the flood-gates of his long-repressed fury were opened—loud and fierce was the torrent that broke loose; but the old man sat and bore it all with the most perfect composure, and even seemed as if he enjoyed the storm he had raised.

At that moment a servant entered to say that the boat was ready, and the tide answered. Inch Orran rose.

"Time and tide will no man bide, Glenroy. I have now spoken my mind to you, and I shall leave you to deliberate on my proposal."

"I would rather see any daughter of mine in her coffin than the wife of any beggarly tacksman's son," cried Glenroy, in a perfect foam. "I have other views for my daughter, and I will dispose of her as I think proper."

"Quite right, sir, if you can."

"Sir, I both *can* and *will*."

"You are a lucky man, sir, it seems. I have no more to say."

"Sir, I have something to say to you. This behaviour of yours is not to be borne!"

"That is unfortunate, sir, for I am no duellist. I wish you good morning," was the cool reply; so, disregarding all remonstrances, Inch Orran walked off, and was joined by his lady and Simon.

CHAPTER XV.

OPPOSITION was a thing Glenroy was little accustomed to at any time; but to be thus bearded and got the better of in his own house, in the very heart of his friends, guests, and countrymen, was an indignity he could not away with: for a time he gave full play to his passions, and like a very dragon of old, breathed fire and fury all around. But as what is violent is never lasting, he soon cooled down to his usual temperature, and being of a sanguine disposition, he even began to look upon what had passed as a sort of bad joke, or ill-natured whim of the old man's, which would go no farther, and would not be followed by any bad consequences. The calm, however, was of short duration. The first intelligence he heard was that Ronald Malcolm had been invited to Inch Orran, and was actually living there in high favour with his kinsman.

This went so far beyond Glenroy's worst anticipations that he disdained to be in a passion about it. He was perfectly cool and composed, as everybody might see, only his colour was considerably higher than usual; and though he hummed a song, it was much out of tune, and when he laughed very heartily

nobody knew very well what it was at. In short, he
had all the gaiety and indifference which people commonly have when very much agitated and discom-
posed. It was only by fits and starts that anything
like ill-temper showed itself; but upon his son, as
usual, choosing the richest dishes at table, he was for
the first time in his life checked with an angry exclamation and an oath, followed with, "And I'll be
hanged if I'll suffer any epicures in my house. I
hate an epicure, and you shall not be an epicure, sir.
You shall live upon porridge and mutton as I did, or,
by Jove! you shall starve."

This threat was, of course, null and void the very
next day, when the young Chief was to be seen, as usual,
picking his way amongst the intricacies of the luxurious
board; but that day had brought new matter to light
which made it unnecessary for Glenroy either to sing
out of tune, or laugh out of time, or contradict his son,
or do anything out of the common course of nature. It
was reported that Ronald Malcolm, so far from having
been invited to Inch Orran, had been sent there by
his father to try to bring about a reconciliation; that
instead of that, he had met with a very bad reception, and been even turned from the house late one
stormy night, when he had lost himself amongst the
hills, and had been glad to take refuge in the shieling
of Duncan Macrae, the hind on Benvalloch, from
whom the deponent had his information.

Glenroy was not a malignant man, but different
passions often lead to the same result. He was a

proud and a selfish man; but his pride was called
family pride, and his selfishness natural affection;
and both these much-admired qualities operated precisely as envy and malice would have done.

His pride had been galled and his self-love wounded
at the thoughts of his poor despised kinsman's son
being preferred to his; and now his heart unconsciously exulted in the downfall of his hopes, and he
felt ready to patronise and befriend him in any way,
except that of becoming Laird of Inch Orran. Flushed
with his own generous feelings, he resolved to pay a
visit to the family at Lochdhu, and offer him his advice
and assistance in the disposal of Ronald. Perhaps a
little curiosity to hear a true account of Ronald's visit
to Inch Orran mingled with the motives, for he had
heard so many various statements as to what had
passed between the old man and his young kinsman,
that he was at a loss what to believe. In one particular, however, they all agreed, and that was the
main point, that a violent quarrel had taken place;
but whether Ronald had left the house in dudgeon,
or been turned from it in disgrace, had not been
clearly ascertained. Whichever it was, it mattered
little to Glenroy; the result would be the same, and
the restoration of his son would follow, as a matter
of course; he therefore flattered himself that it was
simply the desire to arrive at the truth which lay at
the bottom of his curiosity. Accordingly, one fine
summer's day he set forth on his ride.

Lochdhu was as ugly as any Highland place *can*

be; but there was a wild grandeur in its dark mountains and roaring streams and trackless heaths, and
a varying interest in the lights and shadows of its
stormy firth, which atoned for the want of more
florid beauties. There was perfect neatness, and
even some embellishment, around the house; but the
shrubs were yet in their infancy, and the flowers
were not so luxuriant as in brighter climes, and beneath more costly culture.

As the Chief drew near, he descried Captain and
Mrs. Malcolm, with their children, on the little lawn
before the house, which was strewn with coils of new-
mown hay. Mrs. Malcolm, though no longer young,
still bore a fair and youthful aspect, and seemed like
the elder sister of the sweet, Madonna-looking girl,
the senior of the family, who sat by her side. Captain Malcolm had been a very handsome man, but
the hardships of war and varieties of climate had
impaired his looks as well as health. What he had
been was now pictured in young Ronald—

> " By his ingenuous beauty, by the gleam
> Of his fair eyes, by his capacious brow,
> By all the graces with which nature's hand
> Had bounteously array'd him."

The younger children looked healthful and bright
as opening buds and blossoms.

Mrs. Malcolm and her daughters were seated with
a book and their work. Captain Malcolm and the
bigger boys were turning over the hay, and the little
ones were frolicking about.

But Glenroy saw no beauty in this family picture on which his eye could long dwell; for he despised women, and never was amused with any children but his own. The first brief salutations over, he therefore walked apart with his host, expatiating upon hay-mowing, making, stacking, etc., and describing the magnificent manner in which these operations were performed on his model of a farm. He then entered upon the subject uppermost in his mind, by inquiring of Captain Malcolm if he had seen Inch Orran since his arrival in the country. A simple negative was all the reply.

"Your son would tell you he had met him at my house," said Glenroy, with some hesitation.

"Ronald was then ignorant who he was; but I suspect he was indebted to your good offices upon that occasion."

Glenroy coloured, and stammered out something in the way of denial.

"I am very sensible of your kind intentions," said Captain Malcolm, "although——"

"Not at all, not at all," interrupted Glenroy hurriedly. "I did not—that is to say, I—I—"

"You did all you could, I believe, Glenroy," said his kinsman; "but all would not do."

"I assure you—you give me more credit—than I am at all—entitled to," said the Chieftain, in increasing confusion.

"No, no," cried Captain Malcolm. "The fact speaks for itself; it could only have been to your friendly offices Ronald owed his invitation, for no sooner had Inch Orran returned from his visit to you, than he sent for him to his house."

"And he went, of course?" inquired Glenroy, eager to pass over any more undue compliments.

"Yes, he did; his mother and I saw no reason against it; on the contrary, we were both in hopes it might lead the way to a reconciliation, and I trust we were actuated by something better than mere worldly motives in wishing it, though, no doubt, these had their influence too; but whether as Christians or as mere self-interested parents, we certainly did most earnestly desire it; it has, however, been otherwise appointed, and we are satisfied."

"It was reported," said Glenroy, "that your son had been taken into high favour; was there then no foundation for that?"

"He was well received and kindly treated," said Captain Malcolm; "but——"

"But it didn't last?" cried Glenroy, with something of triumph in his tone; "I could have told him that, for, between ourselves, the man's as mad as a March hare. But how came Ronald to quarrel with him, for at one time he seemed to have got into his good graces?"

"Thanks to you for that, Glenroy," said Captain Malcolm; "and he might perhaps have been there still if he had not preferred his parents to a fortune. It was such a strange, unnatural proposal the old man made him, that I can only account for it on the plea

of insanity : he kept Ronald for three days, showed
him all his property, told him of all his wealth, and
then offered to adopt him, to make him his heir, and
settle his whole fortune upon him, on condition of
his renouncing all intercourse with his own family !"

"Ay, that's just of a piece with his threatening to
disinherit Norman for asking for the back of a moorfowl one day at dinner; the man's certainly mad!
And what did your son say to that?"

"Few boys, I believe, would have been base and
sordid enough to have yielded to the temptation, but
some of them might have listened to it more calmly;
instead of which, Ronald, whose temper and feelings
are warm, was so indignant that he instantly left the
house, and set out to walk twenty miles in a dark
stormy night."

"He should have come to me," cried Glenroy
warmly ; "my house was all in the way, and I would
have made him welcome at any hour of the night;
for, I assure you, I approve highly of his behaviour;
he did just what he ought to have done ; it gives me
a very good opinion of your son, it does, indeed—*very*
good !"

This was uttered with great emphasis, and as if his
encomium would be the making of Ronald's fortune.

"We have indeed reason to thank God that he is
deserving of our affection," said Captain Malcolm,
with emotion.

"Yes, he seems really a promising boy, and he
acted in that matter just as he ought to have done ;

to be sure, it would have been very bad if he had
done otherwise. And, by-the-bye, what are you going
to make of him? Is it not full time you were thinking of that?"

"I have had many an anxious thought on that
subject," said Captain Malcolm, with a sigh.

"Ay, to be sure, it's no joke setting out a lad in
the world, now every profession is so overstocked;
but it's time Ronald should learn something."

"I trust he has learnt something, and is every day
learning more," said his father.

"Oh, I have no doubt you have done all you could
for him," said the Chief slightingly; "but we all
know there are few gentlemen fit to educate their
sons."

"Yet I believe it is from their parents that children
receive by far the most important part of their education,"[1] replied Captain Malcolm.

"The deuce you do! then I for one can assure you,
I take no sort of charge of my son's education. I pay
four hundred a'year, which I think a pretty fair allow-
ance for a dominie, and I should think it rather hard
after that if I was expected to educate him myself!"

Captain Malcolm smiled, perhaps at the ostentation
with which this was uttered, then replied, "Yet his
habits and opinions will be much more influenced by
you than by his tutor, and these are what I consider
as the most important parts of education."

"Do you so? then education must be a very easy

[1] See Mrs. Barbauld's admirable Essay on Education.

matter with you, it seems; if that were all, I might
have saved my four hundred a year. Habits and
opinions! I really never happened to hear of boys'
habits and opinions. I should like to know what
sort of things *their* habits and opinions are!"

Captain Malcolm was quite accustomed to hear his
Chief talk "high nonsense," loud, arrogant, overbearing nonsense, the most insufferable of all the varieties
of nonsense, and he had the merit of always answering him as calmly as though he had been conversing
with Plato himself.

"The actions of each day and hour are what form
the habits," he replied, "and the taste and affections
are what influence the opinions; both combined, are
what insensibly form the character. Ronald is deficient in many things, but I trust he has imbibed good
principles. I am sure he possesses kindly affections;
he is not wanting in solid learning, and his habits are
those of a hardy Highland boy, who minds neither
wind nor weather, hunger nor thirst, and who can
climb the rock, swim the water, and sleep among the
heather."

"My good sir, any herd's son in the country can
do all that," said Glenroy contemptuously. "But
that's nothing to the purpose; we were talking of
your son's education, which is quite a different thing.
There's my own boy! although I say it, I don't believe
there's a boy in the kingdom farther advanced in his
education than he is."

"Those who can afford to purchase instruction for

their children are in the right to do it," said Captain Malcolm mildly; "for a liberal education is a great advantage; but those who cannot, ought to be satisfied with giving their children a virtuous and a useful one. You and I, Glenroy, are differently circumstanced; wealth educates your son, but poverty must train mine, and the best education a poor man can give his son is to make him know and feel betimes that he *is* the son of a poor man."

"That's all very true," said Glenroy; "but what are you to make of him? What would you think of making a preacher of him? I could be of some use to you there; I have a good deal of patronage of my own, as well as something to say in other quarters."

"I thank you, but Ronald's bent does not lie that way, and no motive of worldly interest will ever prompt me to urge any son of mine to enter on so sacred a vocation. Ronald has decided for the sea."

"A very good, sensible choice," cried the Chief, "just the very thing for him, and the sooner he goes the better; 'learn young learn fair,' is, you know, a good old saying."

"He will go, I expect, next year," said Captain Malcolm. "A cousin of his mother's, Captain Stanley, a worthy man, and gallant officer, has offered Ronald a berth in his ship."

"Ah! that's very well, but you ought to send him in the meantime to a public school; it's a great advantage for a boy who has his way to push in the world to have had some training before he begins, and he'll learn more of the world in one year at a great public school than he will do all his life at home."

"I am no friend to a premature knowledge of the world; it comes soon enough to most of us. I greatly prefer the safety which results from good principles and virtuous habits, to that purchased by an early knowledge of vice."

"Most of our great men, however, have been educated at public schools," continued Glenroy.

"That is an opinion which has been completely refuted,"[1] said Captain Malcolm; "and even were it otherwise, I should prefer having my son a good man, rather than a great one."

"Oh ay, that's fine romantic talking," said Glenroy contemptuously, "but it's a great deal too fine for me; I have no notion of your romantic schemes."

"Then we are agreed," said Captain Malcolm, with a smile; "for I too think the plainer and simpler the system of education, especially for the children of a poor man, so much the better; however, I thank you from my heart for the interest you take in Ronald; if you knew him better, I flatter myself you would not find him so deficient as you suppose. He has his faults, but he has many a hard lesson yet to learn before the system of moral discipline will be completed. I trust God will order all for the best, and when the time comes, to His care I will with confidence commit his future destiny."

"Well, I hope it may answer, for Ronald's a good

[1] See *Edinburgh Review*.

boy, and I shall always be ready to assist him ;" and with a shake of the hand to his kinsman, and a hurried adieu to the rest of the family, Glenroy returned home, satisfied that he had nothing to fear from Ronald's rivalship.

CHAPTER XVI

THE good-natured laird's recommendation of Lucy Malcolm had not been thrown away upon Mr. M'Dow, and from that time he had been very frequent in his visits at Lochdhu, much more so, indeed, than was at all agreeable to any member of the family, for between his mind and theirs there was a gulf which seemed impassable. But, never dreaming that he could presume to cast his eyes upon their fair sweet Lucy, the parents ascribed his frequent visitations to better motives, and flattered themselves that, faintly as their own light shone, it might yet prove the means of enlightening the still more darkened steps of Mr. M'Dow. He seemed to them to be kind-hearted and well-meaning in his own coarse way; at least so Captain and Mrs. Malcolm construed the many attentions he was now in the habit of paying them, together with the softened tone of his conversation at times, and the anxiety he evinced to make himself useful and agreeable to the young people. At one time he would amble over on the back of Amailye, his huge pockets filled to the brim with nuts from his own premises, "most uncommonly sweet and delee-chuz," which he would take out in large handfuls, and deposit on the ladies' work-table; another time he would arrive laden on each side with apples from his garden, "uncommonly high-flavoured and jisey;" on another occasion he appeared with a basketful of small fresh-water trouts, which he had caught himself, and which he said would be "most uncommon delicate picking," but he hoped Miss Lucy would take care of the bones. But the consummation of all was, when he entered with his shooting-bag over his shoulder, containing a brace of "most beautiful young termagants,"[1] trophies of his prowess on the moors. It often fell to Lucy's lot to receive these testimonies of the minister's good-will, which she did with her usual sweetness of manner; and though few things could be more offensive to her than the company of Mr. M'Dow, she yet behaved towards him with that polite endurance which, to one of his gross ken, was equal to the most flattering encouragement.

"There are some uncommon fine prospects about the manse, Miss Lucy," said he, as he found her one day sketching the view from the parlour window; "I think you would make a fine hand of them."

"The views in your neighbourhood are indeed very beautiful," said Lucy; "and I have long wished to take a few sketches there, if it were not too presumptuous in me to attempt it."

"Oh, Miss Lucy!" exclaimed Mr. M'Dow, "how can you say that? But I'm really happy that you admire the situation of the manse."

[1] Ptarmigans.

"Everybody must admire it," said Lucy; "it is quite charming."

"I'm delighted to hear you think so," cried Mr. M'Dow; "for it's rather a remote, secluded situation, though, to be sure, the prospect's much more animated than it was, now that the steamboat comes our way regularly twice a week, and touches at the village, which is not above a gunshot from the manse. She's an amazing convenience, besides making a most interesting object in the view; for instance, I get my tea and sugar brought to my very door by her for a mere trifle. I can even get a loaf of bread from Glasgow, within four-and-twenty hours after it's out of the oven, for a penny or so additional, which is no consideration to *me*, in comparison of the comfort of the thing; it's uncommon fine bread, too."

A pause ensued, for the minister's communications called for no reply; and Lucy busied herself with her drawing. Mr. M'Dow resumed:

"Eh, Miss Lucy, if I might but hope for the honour of seeing you at the manse some day, you would really make me very proud."

"I should be sorry if a visit from me were to have that effect," said Lucy, smiling; "but certainly I shall be very happy, some day when papa and I are taking a ride, to bring my sketch-book to Auchterbruckle, and carry off, if I can, some of its beauties."

Before the minister had time to utter his raptures, Captain Malcolm entered the room; and, after the usual preliminaries, Mr. M'Dow began: " I have just been admiring Miss Lucy's painting," pointing to her pencil-sketch; " I'm no great *connyshure*, indeed ; but it strikes me as being uncommonly well executed ! "

"And, in return, I have been praising Mr. M'Dow's fine views, papa," said she ; "and have even been bold enough to talk of attempting to sketch some of them."

" I assure you, sir, I am very much flattered with Miss Lucy's approbation of my prospects ; and I was just requesting, as a most particular favour, that she would do me the honour some day to come over with you, and take a look of my premises. There's not much to be seen, to be sure, just now about the manse ; but the prospects all round are much admired ; and when I get my decreet, things will be made more decent about the doors than they are at present."

"You little know what you are about, when you invite such a noted sketcher as Lucy to visit you," said Captain Malcolm, with a smile ; "she is such an enthusiast, and you have so great a variety of fine views in your neighbourhood, that, I warn you, you will find it difficult to get rid of her again."

" I'll take my chance of that, Captain," with a prodigious roar of delight; " I'll take my chance of that; and now, Captain, will you not just do me the favour to fix a day when Miss Lucy and you will ride over, and take a look of my premises ?"

" We had better take our chance of a fine day," said Lucy, who privately thought the minister's absence was not the worst that could befall them.

"I beg your pardon, Miss Lucy; but really the disappointment would be dreadful, if I was to miss the honour of a visit from the Captain and you— perfectly dreadful! And it *might* happen, for I have occasion to be a good deal from home; in fact, I consider it as a principal part of my duty to visit a good deal, and to be on the best footing with the heritors of my parish. It's a discreditable thing when the minister and the gentry are no just at one; and wherever I have been, I have always made a point of keeping the very best company."

"A clergyman who faithfully discharges his duty must see great varieties of company," said Captain Malcolm; "and ought neither to consider himself as elevated by the notice of the higher orders, nor debased by mingling occasionally with the lowest and poorest of his flock."

"There I perfectly agree with you, Captain," replied Mr. M'Dow, with much hearty warmth; "these are precisely my own sentiments on the subject. From the honourable nature of my office, I have always looked upon myself as upon a footing—if not rather *shoopayreor* to gentlemen of larger fortune, and who may, perhaps, make a greater dash in the world than I do; and, on the other hand, I never refuse, when properly called upon, to attend to the poorest man or woman in the parish."

This was uttered with a modest air of self-approbation, and concluded with a long, self-complacent pinch of snuff.

"There is, indeed, a reverence due to the clergy as a body," said Captain Malcolm; "and in a Christian country they are always sure of meeting with it; but that is a feeling which operates very slightly upon the minds of the community; and, unless ministers can claim *individually* the respect due to superior piety and excellence, I fear collectively it is of little avail."

"You're perfectly right, Captain. I agree with you entirely. Every clergyman is called upon to keep up the dignity of his station, and to cut a respectable figure in the world. It doesn't do for a man to let himself down too much."

"In my opinion, a clergyman who is in the way of his duty never can let himself down," said Captain Malcolm; "for he must be endeavouring to raise the minds of those around him to the highest standard of moral excellence."

"That's really not an easy matter, Captain," said Mr. M'Dow; "for the common people are a bad set. But here comes Mrs. Malcolm; I hope I'll get her on my side to fix a day for the visit to the manse."

And herewith Mrs. Malcolm was assailed with entreaties to use her influence for that purpose, or, as the minister elegantly expressed it, "just to nail the business at once." Mrs. Malcolm was pleased at the thought of a little excursion for Lucy; so she seconded the minister's proposal, and, to his great delight, a day was fixed when Captain Malcolm and his daughter were to pay a morning visit at the manse of Auchterbruckle.

CHAPTER XVII

GLENROY'S anger against Inch Orran had much abated since he had ascertained what he called "the defeat of the Donald Begs."

"After all, Inch Orran is not a bad body," he would say to Benbowie ; "he knows what he's about, and will not be easily taken in, or I'm much mistaken. I begin to think I was rather short with him when he was here, though the wretch was most confoundedly provoking too ! But he's an old man, and a particular man, and he has such an idiot of a wife ! I really believe, after all, he meant nothing."

"On my conscience, I believe so," responded Benbowie. "Nothing—nothing—nothing at all."

Still this nothing had left an awkwardness, which Glenroy did not know very well how to get over. Something ought to be done to prove there was nothing ; but what that something was he could not tell. After what had passed, he could not possibly renew the overtures in person ; still less could he send Benbowie as his ambassador. Had Inch Orran been like anybody else, he might have felt his pulse with a haunch of venison ; but that most likely would only lead to fresh hostilities; so difficult is it to manage people who have no weak side, or rather no favourite sense to gratify.

Inch Orran had a weak side, indeed, but that was rather his strong point; for the love of money was his prevailing passion; and, of all besetting sins, that is perhaps the most difficult to gratify. Harpagon, to be sure, had his Frosine; but in general the difficulty of administering to the pure love of gold must be greater than that of pampering any other evil propensity.

Glenroy was, however, relieved from his embarrassment, by receiving the following despatch from his kinsman :—

"Mr. Mungo Malcolm of Inch Orran presents compliments to Mr. Norman Malcolm of Glenroy, and requests the favour of his company, and that of his friend, Mr. Lachlan Malcolm of Benbowie, at his house, on the afternoon of Wednesday the 24th instant, to remain till the forenoon of Saturday the 27th instant. Mr. M. Malcolm begs to intimate that he can also accommodate Mr. N. Malcolm's body servant."

An invitation to Inch Orran was what Glenroy had not looked for; and though the manner in which it was couched was highly offensive, yet that was passed over with a slight oath or two. The visit itself, indeed, would be an act of the severest penance, both to mind and body. Ill-humour, impertinence, and starvation, to be endured for three days—even Glenroy's stout heart quailed to think of! But to refuse would be at once to renounce all hopes and expectations. It was a golden opportunity for bringing matters to the point. It was evident Inch Orran was making up in his own way. It would be madness to refuse to meet him—go he must, even in the face of the blade-bone of mutton! Benbowie at first made a faint resistance, as even his dull fancy pictured to itself the "flesh-pots" of Glenroy, in mournful contrast with the bare bones of Inch Orran; but he was so little in the habit of opposing his Chief, that he soon succumbed. So, after much consideration, the following answer was despatched :—

"Glenroy returns kind compliments to Inch Orran, and assures him he will allow no engagements to stand in the way of his accepting his friendly invitation for Wednesday the 24th; and will, if possible, make such arrangements as may enable him to remain till the 27th with his worthy kinsman. Benbowie begs his best respects, and will do himself the honour of waiting upon Inch Orran at the same time."

"Well, for my part," said Mrs. Macauley, when she heard the invitation discussed, "I cannot say I like it. Three people invited, and for three days. There's something—I cannot tell what—in such an invitation!"

"You are a complete goose, Molly Macauley, and if you had just as much sense as would stick on the point of one of your own needles, you never would open your mouth," was the Chief's courteous reply.

"Well, Glenroy, you know it is not so much sense

that I set up for having, as just a sort of a something else—I cannot tell what it is—that makes me see things that people a great deal wiser and sensibler than I am do not see."

"You pretend to the second-sight, do you?"

"Oh no, 'deed I am not so favoured as that; but if you would be guided by me, Glenroy, you would not go to that cankered body's house."

"I suppose you think there will be a boar's head served up, as a signal to despatch Benbowie and me, with knives, and perhaps forks?"

"No, Glenroy, I have more sense than to think that Inch Orran would behave in such a way as that; but I don't like people being so perjink in paying back their entertainments. You see there was himself and his wife, and Simon his servant, all came here on a Wednesday afternoon, and stayed till the Saturday forenoon; and then he asks you and Benbowie, and your servant, just to do the same thing; and is not that saying, I'll give you neither less nor more than what you gave me"?

"Oh, you're a soothsayer—a diviner, are you? You can tell what's passing in people's minds? But I would advise you, Mrs. Mary Macauley, to stick to your needles and thread; for you know no more of mankind than one of your own worsted monsters."

"Well, well, Glenroy, I·know you're a great deal wiser than me; but we'll see who's right for all that."

Wednesday the 24th arrived, and looked most auspicious. The Chief and his friend having made a

hearty luncheon, and sighed to think it was the last
plentiful meal they should behold for three days,
embarked with a favourable gale, and were in due
time safely landed at Inch Orran.

If Glenroy had any misgivings in his own mind
as to the sincerity of the reconciliation, they were
soon dispelled by the courteous reception he met
with. No symptom of displeasure appeared either
in the looks or manners of his host; on the contrary,
he was studiously polite, and even accosted him with
a smile, or something intended for such, though of so
suspicious a character that it would have made any
one else instinctively bethink him of the canny old
Scottish motto — "Touch not the cat but a glove."
However, Glenroy was not the man to be daunted
by a smile, so he returned it in full measure, and a
most cordial greeting took place. Inch Orran even
inquired, in a mild and courteous manner, after the
health of young Norman, which Glenroy considered
as the next thing to declaring him his heir.

"I have had three gentlemen residing with me for
some days," said Inch Orran, addressing the Chief,
"whom it was my wish that you should see here.
One is my law-agent, or man of business, Mr. Mel-
drum; another is my factor, Mr. M'Farlane; and the
third is Mr. Crowfoot, an eminent land-surveyor.
Their business with me has been of an important
nature, and has proved highly satisfactory in its results. It was concluded this morning; but the
gentlemen remain with me till to-morrow, in order to

celebrate the termination of our labours, and also to afford you, sir, an opportunity of acquiring any information you think proper on the subject."

This went far beyond Glenroy's most sanguine anticipations. In fact, what did all this amount to, but that, having had his estates valued, his rent-roll proved, and his settlement made, he now took this method of declaring him his heir? In common delicacy, therefore, he could do no less than waive all appearance of curiosity or interference on the subject, which he did, but in a manner that plainly showed what was passing in his mind. At this Inch Orran's mouth was curled up in a most suspicious manner; and one better acquainted with the character of the man would have felt rather distrustful of this supernatural sweetness and openness after what had passed; and to those who knew him, this "faire seemlie pleasaunce" would have been anything but an "augur of good purpose." It was one of Inch Orran's peculiarities that whenever his mind had settled into a fixed hatred or contempt for an individual, from that time his manner towards him was marked by the most scrupulous attention to the ordinary rules of politeness; not with any design to deceive, for he despised all duplicity and double-dealing, but from a certain malignant delight, akin to that with which a cat gently strokes the victim she is preparing to immolate.

But Glenroy was too superficial himself to be at all aware of the depths profound of others. He

could not see beneath the surface, and when that was
smooth, he judged all was sound; he therefore drew
the most flattering conclusions from his kinsman's
behaviour, and without pretending to the second-sight,
he already beheld, by anticipation, the long-coveted
property in his possession, the family honours again
fixed in the family seat, and a clear five thousand
per annum added to his rent-roll. They were now
joined by the men of business, who were each introduced with marked emphasis to Glenroy. Next
followed Mrs. Malcolm, "in outward show elaborate,"
and as sensible and edifying as usual. The dinner
hour arrived, and, to the agreeable surprise of Glenroy and his friends, they sat down to a most plentiful and excellent repast, such as would not have
disgraced even the Chief's own board, while wines of
the best quality were liberally dispensed. The most
perfect good-humour prevailed. Glenroy's gascon-
ades passed without comment; and even Mrs. Malcolm's *sottises* escaped with impunity.

The agent and factor were silent, ironbound-look-
ing persons; but Mr. Crowfoot, the surveyor, whose
more active habits had probably given a greater freedom to his tongue, discoursed largely upon the survey
he had made of Inch Orran, its pertinents and pen-
dicles, the prodigious rise in the rent when the leases
should fall, which would happen in a year or two; then,
if there should prove to be a seam of coal, of which
Mr. Crowfoot was very sanguine, there was no saying
what might be the value of the property; and so on.

"Whatever the value may prove," said Inch Orran mildly, "one thing is certain, sir, that it will prove of more benefit to my heir than ever it can to me."

Glenroy's face flushed with the consciousness that he was the man; and he expected the next thing would be the proclaiming of him; but though he could have decreed, and even assisted at the apotheosis of Inch Orran, he was not prepared to make a speech upon the occasion; for, fond as he was of talking, he was not gifted with eloquence. He, however, showed by his manner that he took the hint to himself: his spirits rose; Inch Orran's smiles redoubled; and, strange to say, the day passed pleasantly, and the evening closed peacefully!

CHAPTER XVIII.

ACCORDING to Mrs. Macauley's theory, things looked still worse the following day, when there arrived in rapid succession the self-same party who had been convened by Glenroy, when he did the honours of his house to Inch Orran. There were lairds of every description — good-natured and ill-natured, fat and lean, tall and short, red and blue, rich and poor, some with wives, and some without. Nor was Mr. M'Dow wanting, though he protested that nothing but respect for his worthy heritors would have brought him there that day, as he had just received the melancholy accounts of the death of his sister Mrs. Dr. M'Fee's youngest child, a most uncommon stout infant, named after himself, M'Dow M'Fee. It had died of the cutting of a back tooth very suddenly; a severe stroke upon his poor sister and the worthy doctor. Under these circumstances, Mr. M'Dow thought proper to be rather in a pensive mood, though, as he owned to a touch of the rheumatism "up one side" of his head, and testified an immense swelled jaw, it was at least doubtful whether his spirits were most affected by his own cheek, or the catastrophe of little M'Dow M'Fee.

So it was, he was less obnoxious than usual, and uttered no *bong motes* worthy of being recorded. If Glenroy had been surprised with the dinner the preceding day, he was confounded at the banquet round which the company were assembled. It had evidently been got up by an artist of the first eminence. The *sough* went round the table that Inch Orran had brought a cook all the way from Glasgow—Edinburgh —London—Paris, to dress the dinner. Be that as it may, the dinner was evidently dressed by no mean hand, and all testified the work of man, and not of woman. Certainly not Mrs. Malcolm's, who, between her own finery and that of the dinner, seemed quite bewildered, and, like Mr. M'Dow, was more silent than usual. Such of the party as could not be accommodated within the walls of Inch Orran, found lodgings, some at the factor's, some at the Clachan, and some in the hay-loft; but all returned to the charge the following day, like giants refreshed. Even Mr. M'Dow's cheek had fallen, and Mrs. Malcolm's tongue was unloosed.

Everybody who has made one of a party in a large house in the country must have observed how great a portion of time is consumed in what is politely called the pleasures of the table ; and upon this occasion the prevailing practice was duly observed. The host, indeed, continued his own abstemious mode as usual ; but he begged his rules might be no restraint upon the company, and that they would, in all things pertaining to good cheer, take their Chief as their example.

The intervals between the meals were filled up in the usual manner, by sauntering out of doors, walking up and down the rooms, playing at billiards, reading newspapers, discussing politics, canvassing county meetings, etc.

"Here's a most entertaining game," said Mrs. Malcolm, drawing forth a large sheet of pasteboard, on which was displayed the royal game of the goose; "it's a thing I brought with me in my trunk; for I thought it would be a fine amusement for Mr. Malcolm and me in the country, when we had nothing to do; but I can't get him to play at it, if I would do ever so."

"Most men find it enough to have played the fool with a wife, without having to play the goose with her next," said Inch Orran, with one of his bitter smiles.

A burst of laughter from the unmarried part of the company testified their approbation of this sentiment.

"That's really very severe, Inch Orran," said Mr. M'Dow, coming forward as the champion of the ladies; "very severe, indeed, upon the fair sex, and I'm sure most extremely misapplied in your own case, with such a lady as yours," bowing to Mrs. Malcolm, who sat quite unmoved with her goose spread out before her.

"A man may learn a useful lesson even from a goose, sir, if he can take a hint in time," said Inch Orran sarcastically.

"A well and a prison are pretty broad hints, to be sure,"· said Mr. M'Dow, surveying the detail of the goose ; "but I hope there's nobody here that will ever have occasion to take such hints ; for my own part, I don't think I'm in any danger either of the one or the other, even if my decreet should go against me—hoch, hoch, hoch, ho !"

"These, sir, are emblematic, I presume, of Truth and Reflection," said Inch Orran ; "the one is said to lie in the bottom of a well, and the other, I believe, is often found at last within the bars of a prison. I know few men who may not profit by such hints ;" and a small fiery spark shot from the corner of his eye at Glenroy, on whom it fell harmless, so intrenched was he in the firm belief that all was doing and saying in honour of himself. Not Haman, when he seemed to be at the pinnacle of his wishes, felt more secure than Glenroy.

The third day arrived, which was to wind up the Inch Orran festivities, and nothing remained but that the guests should now take their departure. The usual stir had begun amongst them, as their several conveyances were successively announced.

"I assure you, Inch Orran," wheezed a fat laird, who was the first to move, "I am sorry to be the first to break up this party ; for I can with truth declare I never, in the whole course of my life, spent two plea-santer days ; and I am sure I speak the sentiments of the whole party when I say so."

"I believe you, sir," replied Inch Orran, with one

of his little horrible smiles; "but the credit of these revellings is due to our Chief. Had it not been for him I should have entertained you in a different style; but he has given me a lesson which I hope I shall not soon forget; and I have only been discharging the debt I had incurred to him by his splendid hospitalities towards me."

Glenroy was not prepared for this eulogium, and his face glowed and his whole person distended with the proud triumph of having the meed of praise thus publicly awarded to him; but while he was preparing a suitable reply, Mr. M'Dow, as usual, broke forth with a tremendous hach, hach, ho!

"Well, Inch Orran, for my part, I can only say that I hope from my heart this innocent rivalship between my two worthy pawtrons may long continue to subsist; and I daresay I may answer for all present, as I do for myself, that, like the Swiss troops, we shall always be ready to lend our assistance to either side, and serve both to the best of our power for the time being—hoch, hoch, hoch, hoch, ho!"

A clamour of mirth succeeded, which drowned Inch Orran's reply, as, with one of his bitterest looks, he said, "Sir, your services are not likely to be required by me in a hurry." Then, as the roar still continued, he muttered, "I would at any time rather sit down to table with two devils than with twenty angels."

The guests had severally departed, all save Glenroy, who still lingered in hopes that Inch Orran would now come to the point, and disclose the deeds that had been done; but Inch Orran's lips seemed now as if hermetically sealed, and he heard all Glenroy's hints and innuendoes in profound silence. At length the Chief saw it was time to take leave; and as he did so he expressed a hope of soon seeing his kind host at his house.

"Never, sir!" was the reply, with a look and an emphasis that made even Benbowie start.

The Chief was confounded; but he was now outside the door, which was already closed upon him.

"He is a very particular man," said Glenroy.

"On my conscience, it would not do for everybody to be so particular," said Benbowie.

"It's just his manner," said Glenroy; "I'm convinced he means nothing."

And his echo answered, "Nothing."

CHAPTER XIX

THE day arrived for the long-promised visit to the Manse, and a most propitious one it was, worthy of the lovely scenes on which it smiled. The father and daughter set out early on their excursion, and after a ride of about five miles found themselves in the environs of the Manse. These were of the grandest and most romantic description; there were lofty heath-covered mountains, softened by gently-swelling green hills, diversified and enriched by patches of natural copsewood, which completely supplied the place of trees; here and there were openings to the bold rocky shore, with its gray cliffs and broken fragments mingling in peaceful amity with the dark-blue waters that curled around them. Far as the eye could reach, the sea was studded with isles and islets, some gleaming through misty showers, some glancing in the full blaze of sunshine. In short, nothing could be more varied, animated, and picturesque, yet beautifully tranquil and secluded, than the scenes which presented themselves, at every step seen under different aspects. Lucy was enchanted, but the enchantment fled on approaching the Manse. It was a thin tenement, built

of rough gray stone of the usual pattern, a window
on each side of the door and three above. At one
side was the garden, with cabbages and marigolds
growing pell-mell, and in the rear was the set of condemned offices, partly thatched and partly slated.
There were no attempts at neatness in the approach
to the house, which was merely a rough jog-trot road,
flanked on each side by a dyke. Presently Mr. M'Dow
was seen hurrying to the door to meet his guests, and
there, as they alighted, he was ready to receive them
with open hands.

Great was the joy expressed at this honour, as Mr.
M'Dow led the way to the interior of his mansion,
which was just such as might have been expected from
its outward aspect. There was a narrow stone passage,
with a door on each side, and there was a perpendi-
cular wooden stair, and that was all that was to be
seen at the first *coup-d'œil*. But if little was revealed
to the eye, the secrets of the house were yielded with
less coy reserve to the other senses; for there was to
be heard the sound of a jack, now beginning with
that low, slow, mournful whine, which jacks of sensibility are sure to have; then gradually rising to a
louder and more grating pitch, till at length one
mighty crash, succeeded, as all mighty crashes are,
by a momentary silence. Then comes the winding-
up, which, contrary to all the rules of the drama, is,
in fact, only a new beginning, and so on, *ad infinitum*,
till the deed is done. With all these progressive
sounds were mingled the sharp, shrill, loud voice and

Gaelic accents of the *chef de cuisine*, with an occasional clash or clang, at least equal to the fall of the armour in the Castle of Otranto.

Then there issued forth with resistless might a smell which defied all human control, and to which doors and windows were but feeble barriers or outlets; till, like the smoke in the Arabian Nights, which resolved itself into a genie, it seemed as if about to quit its aerial form, and assume a living and tangible substance.

Lucy would fain have drawn back as she crossed the threshold, and, quitting the pure precincts of sunshine and fresh air, found herself in the power of this unseen monster—this compound of fish, fat, peats, burnt grease, kail, leeks, and onions, revelling, too, amid such scenes, and beneath such a sky!

"You see I have brought my sketch-book, Mr. M'Dow," said she; "so I must make the most of my time, and be busy out of doors."

"You'll have plenty of time for that, Miss Lucy; it's early in the day yet; you've had a long ride, and you'll be the better of a little refreshment; pray sit down, and do me the favour to take a mouthful of something;" and he handed a plateful of shortbread, which, with a bottle of wine, stood ready stationed on a side-table. "You'll find it uncommonly good, Miss Lucy; it comes all the way from Glasgow; it's made by my mother, now in the seventy-eighth year of her age; she sends me always a bun and half-a-peck of shortbread for my *hogmanay*, and it's surprising how it keeps. This is the last farl of it, but it's just as good as the first was!" helping himself to a piece which would have qualified anybody else for six weeks of Cheltenham. "And, by-the-bye, that's a picture of my mother, taken when she was a younger woman than she is now," pointing to an abominable daub of a large, vulgar, flushed-looking, elderly woman, sitting on a garden-chair, with a willow at her back, her hands crossed before her, and a large hair ring on her forefinger. "That's reckoned a strong likeness of my mother; she was an uncommon fine woman when in her prime; she measured five feet ten and three-quarters on her stocking soles, which is a remarkable height for a woman, and she carried the breadth along with it; yet she was the smallest of six daughters. It's told of her fawther, Mr. M'Tavish (who was a man of great humour), that he used to say he had six-and-thirty foot of daughters—hoch, hoch, ho!—it was very good! very good!" Here Mr. M'Dow indulged in another fit of laughter, while his guests turned their eyes to another picture, but it was no less obnoxious to the sight. "That, again, is my fawther, and a most capital picture! there's a great deal of dignity there! for though extremely affable, he could assume a great deal of dignity when it was necessary."

This dignitary was a mean, consequential-looking body, with lowering brows and a bob-wig, seated in an arm-chair, with a flaming Virgil, portrayed in red morocco and gold, in his hand.

"I am no *connyshure* myself, but they strike me as

being very good pictures; and I can vouch for their being most capital likenesses." Neither Captain Malcolm nor Lucy could violate sincerity so far as to bestow a single commendation on the pictures; so Mr. M'Dow went on—"That book which you see in my fawther's hand was a present made to him by his scholars when he was master of the Myreside School. I confess I look at it with great pride, as a most flattering testimony of the honourable and——" Here a prodigious crash from the kitchen, followed by very loud and angry vociferations, arrested Mr. M'Dow's harangue; and opening the door he called in a very high, authoritative tone, "What's the meaning of this noise?" upon which the tumult ceased. "Make less noise there, and keep the kitchen door shut!" A violent slam of the door was the only answer returned. "I understand it's all the fashion now in great houses to have the kitchen as near the dining-room as possible," said Mr. M'Dow, wishing to throw an air of gentility over his *ménage*. "But for my own part I must confess I would prefer it at a little distance, for it's impossible, do what you will, to get servants to be quiet; and it's really not pleasant, when I have a friend or two with me, and we are just wishing to enjoy ourselves, to be disturbed as we were just now. What I want in my addition is this: I would turn my present kitchen into my drawing-room or study, just as it shuted, for there's an exceeding good light scullery off it, which I could make my own closet, and keep my books and papers in. The kitchen I would throw to the back, with a washing-house and small place for the lasses. Then upstairs I would have a pretty good family bed-chamber, and a good light closet for keeping my groceries within it, besides a press fitted up for my napery (of which I have a pretty good stock), and——"

"You would have a very comfortable house, I have no doubt," said Captain Malcolm, who, although rarely guilty of the ill-breeding of interrupting any one, yet could not refrain from cutting short these ministerial arrangements. "Even as it is," added he, "you don't seem to be ill off—this is a very good room, and such a view from your window! Will you dare to attempt it, Lucy?"

"Not before witnesses," replied Lucy. "So I shall look about me elsewhere, and perhaps I may find something better adapted to my pencil." And she was leaving the room, when Mr. M'Dow stepped forward, and interposed his huge person between her and the door.

"Oh, Miss Lucy, you're not going to run away from us, I hope? You'll find it uncommonly warm out by, just now; the sun's extremely powerful on the rocks."

"A noted sketcher, as papa calls me, minds neither heat nor cold," answered Lncy; "and I shall easily find either a shady spot or a cool breeze."

"Well, then, since you will go out, trust yourself to me, and I'll take you where you'll find both, and the most beautiful prospect into the bargain."

At that moment the door opened, and a thick yellow

man, with no particular features, dressed in a short
coat, tartan trews, and a very large ill-coloured neck-
cloth, entered the room, and was introduced by the
minister as his cousin and brother-in-law, Mr. Dugald
M'Dow, from Glasgow, then on a visit at the Manse.

"We're just going to take a turn in the garden,
Mr. Dugald," said his host; "will you get your hat
and join us?"

"With the greatest pleasure," replied Mr. Dugald,
with a strong accent and a stiff, conceited bow; then
popping down a seal-skin cap from a peg in the passage, he was instantly accoutred, and the party set
forth.

"I wish it had been earlier in the season, Miss
Lucy," said Mr. M'Dow, as he ushered her into his
kailyard by a narrow, slimy path, overrun with long
sprawling bushes; "a month ago I could have treated
you to as fine berries as perhaps you ever tasted.
They were uncommonly large and jisey, and at the
same time extremely high-flavoured. I have a little
red hairy berry that's very deleeshus; and there's the
honey-blobs, an uncommon fine berry—a great deal
of jise in it. I was rather unlucky in my rasps this
season; they were small and wormy, and a very poor
crop; but my currins were amazingly prolific and
uncommonly jisey. In fact, I couldn't use the half
of them, and it was really vexatious to see them absolutely rotting on the bushes. The want of a lady at
the berry season is a great want, and one that's sorely
felt; for though my lass is an exceeding good plain cook,

yet she's not mistress of the higher branches of cook-
ery, such as the making of jams and jeellies, and these
things ; but I would fain flatter myself, by the time
the berry season comes round again, I may have a
fair lady to manage them for me. Do you think I
may venture to hope so, Miss Lucy ?"

Lucy was not aware of the nature of the minister's
hopes, nor even conscious of his faltering accent and
tender look ; for she was considering whether she
might not make a sketch from the spot where she was
standing ; and at the same moment Captain Malcolm
turned round and directed his daughter's attention to
some particular beauty in the landscape, that had
attracted his own.   And again Lucy's book was
opened, and her pencil in her hand, ready to begin,
when again Mr. M'Dow struck in.

"Now, before you begin, Miss Lucy, I would beg
as a most particular favour, that you would just take
a look of my offices ; they are in a shameful state, to
be sure, for a lady to visit, but the instant I get my
decreet, they shall be all clean demolished ; and what
I'm very desirous of, is to have your opinion as to the
most proper situation for the new ones."

"I don't think Lucy's opinion will be at all a
sound one," said Captain Malcolm ; "she is too fond
of the picturesque ever to consider the useful, so you
had better leave her to her sketch."

" I'll not take your word for that, Captain ; I have
a great respect for a lady's opinion, and there's no
lady whose opinion I set a higher value on than Miss

Lucy's. Ah! Miss Lucy, you'll really oblige me if you'll give me the benefit of your fine taste;" then, in a lower tone, and with great (intended) softness, "I'm really extremely anxious to please you!"

And Lucy, good-humouredly laughing at the idea of Mr. M'Dow's desiring to please her in a matter so perfectly indifferent to her, again put up her sketch-book, and suffered herself to be conducted over the localities of the glebe.

CHAPTER XX

HAVING given her assent to all the projected improvements, Lucy flattered herself she should now be free
from further molestation.   Again she attempted to
rid herself of the assiduities of Mr. M'Dow, and was
gliding away, as she hoped unperceived, when, strid-
ing after her like a seven-league ogre, he called,
"Miss Lucy—Miss Lucy! you're not running away
from us, I hope? this is just about the time I ordered
a slight refreshment to be ready," pulling out his
watch; "you'll do me the honour to partake of it, I
hope?"

Lucy declined, on the plea of having already had
ample refreshment, and being much more inclined to
sketch than to eat; but Lucy must have been made of
stone and lime to have been able to withstand the
importunities of Mr. M'Dow: he was as urgent as
though his very existence had depended upon her
partaking of his "slight refreshment," and she was at
length compelled, much against her inclination, to
return to the *salle à manger*.   During their absence a
table had been covered, but the arrangements were
not finally concluded, for a stout, ruddy, yellow-haired
damsel was rattling away amongst knives and forks

as though she had been turning over so many down feathers.

"I expected to have found everything ready by this time," said Mr. M'Dow; "what have you been about, Jess?" But Jess continued to stamp and clatter away without making any reply.

"I'll just show you the way to my study, till the refreshment's put upon the table," said Mr. M'Dow; and finding all remonstrance in vain, his guests submitted with a good grace, and were conducted to a very tolerable room upstairs, where were a few shelves of books, a backgammon board, a fowling-piece, and a fishing-rod, with shot, lines, and flies scattered about. There was also a sofa, with a dirty crumpled cover, where Mr. Dugald seemed to have been lounging with a flute and a music book. In one corner stood a table with a pile of books, some of them in bindings very unlike the rest of the furniture.

"That's a parcel of books," said Mr. M'Dow, "that I bought at the Auchnagoil rouping. I just bought the lot as you see them. I believe there's a good deal of trash amongst them, but I've had no time to examine them yet."

Lucy began to examine the books, and opening a little volume of Gambold, she exclaimed to her father, "What a charming picture of a clergyman, is it not, papa?" And Captain Malcolm, taking the book, read the passage aloud—

" He was a man so pure in private life,
    So all devoted to the things above;

So mere a servant both of Christ and men,
You'd say he acted without spark of nature,
Save that each motion flow'd with ease and beauty."

"Oh, as to that," said Mr. M'Dow, throwing one of his huge arms over the back of his chair, and swinging himself to and fro, "I can truly say, for my own part, I should think it due to myself to feel at my case in all companies;" and a long, self-complacent pinch of snuff followed.

"Don't you think, papa, that is exactly the description of our good Mr. Stuart?" said Lucy, as she again looked over the volume.

"Mr. Stuart certainly does bear a strong resemblance to this picture," said Captain Malcolm; "and it is always pleasing when we can recognise in a living character the lineaments of such a portrait—we are so apt to look upon it as the *beau ideal*. You are, of course, acquainted with Mr. Stuart," added he, addressing Mr. M'Dow, "and can also bear testimony to the likeness?"

"I *am* acquainted with Mr. Stuart," replied Mr. M'Dow coldly; "but I don't know how it is, we don't often meet; he's not a very social man. But I wonder if that woman's going to give us our refreshments to-day?" Then going to the door, he bawled down, "Jess, woman, for any sake, what are you about? I've no bell in this room, which is a great inconvenience; and I don't think it worth my while to be at any expense till I get my decreet."

"Ah, here is my favourite Goldsmith!" exclaimed

Lucy, trembling for a dissertation upon teinds, localities, and decreets; "familiar as his *Deserted Village* is, I never can refrain from reading it whenever I meet with it."

"*Apropos* of clerical pictures," said Captain Malcolm, no less sick of his host's vulgar egotism, "I don't know a more delightful one than that of his parish priest."

"I'm really amazed what that woman can be doing with our refreshments," said Mr. M'Dow, pulling out his watch, with visible marks of impatience.

"In the meantime, we may refresh our memories with an old acquaintance, the Village Clergyman," said Captain Malcolm, reading the following lines:—

> " His house was known to all the vagrant train,
> He chid their wanderings, but relieved their pain ;
> The long-remember'd beggar was his guest,
> Whose beard descending swept his aged breast ;
> The ruin'd spendthrift, now no longer proud,
> Claim'd kindred there, and had his claim allow'd ;
> The broken soldier, kindly bade to stay,
> Sat by his fire—— "

Here Mr. M'Dow burst forth with, "Well, Captain, I'm really amazed how, with your excellent abilities and good principles, you can think that man a pattern for a dignified clergyman ! His house must have been a perfect receptacle for blackguards. I would think it highly improper in me to allow one of those vagrants to set their foot within my door ; if they want to hear me, let them come to my church."

"But they would rather wish you to hear them," said Mr. Dugald.

"I've no doubt of that," said Mr. M'Dow emphatically; "but I would have little to do if I was to sit up listening to all the worthless vagabonds that come in my way."

"Perhaps," said Lucy timidly, "their vices are often the effect of their ignorance, and a word spoken in season might go far to enlighten and reclaim them."

"Oh, Miss Lucy," said Mr. M'Dow, with an air of gallantry, "there's nothing I admire more in your sex than your gentleness and softness; but I'm sorry to say, it exposes you very much to be imposed upon, and most shamefully taken in; and I'll just appeal to you yourself, now, how it would answer in a house, I'll suppose you're the mistress of, to have your kitchen filled with all the clamjamphray of the country—drunken soldiers, randy beggars, ill-tongued tinklers, and so on—how it would do, I say, for a young lady of your delicacy and refinement going down to order your dinner, to find the very scum of the earth sitting, perhaps, on your kitchen-dresser?"

"That is, indeed, a climax to be avoided," said Captain Malcolm, laughing; "and I'm afraid, Lucy, you must admit that, charming as your favourite picture is, it is one which in these days it would not do to copy too closely. We may please ourselves by such representations of primitive manners; but I fear they no longer exist, except in the poet's page, or your imagination. Steamboats and stage-coaches have now brought each village and hamlet in close contact with some great town, even with London itself; and the evils the poet so beautifully predicted are, I fear, coming on apace. I doubt we should now in vain seek from the Land's End to John-o'-Groat's House for a 'sweet Auburn,' whose 'best riches' are 'ignorance of wealth.' But I see Lucy won't give up her love for beggars, for all we can say."

Lucy smiled as she replied, "Mr. M'Dow's representation of Christian charity is certainly very different from the poet's; but I am still inclined to side with him, and to think that much may be made of human nature, even in its worst state, by kindness, as Mrs. Fry has testified; and so I believe good Mr. Stuart has often found it. The lines that follow are still more descriptive of him. Pray, papa, read them;" and Captain Malcolm went on—

> " Thus to relieve the wretched was his pride,
> And even his failings lean'd to virtue's side ;
> But in his duty prompt at every call,
> He watch'd, and wept, and felt, and pray'd for all ;
> And as a bird each fond endearment tries,
> To tempt its new-fledged offspring to the skies,
> He tried each art, reproved each dull delay,
> Allured to brighter worlds, and led the way."

"Allow me, in the meantime, to lead the way to something more substantial, Miss Lucy," cried Mr. M'Dow, seizing her hand, as Jess put her head in at the door; and having given a glare with her eyes, and wide opened her mouth, emitting a sort of guttural sound, importing that "aw's ready," galloped downstairs again as hard and fast as she could.

"Give me leave, Miss Lucy; but the stair's rather narrow for two; you know the way; turn to the left hand of my trance.[1] It's very easy for these poets to preach; but it's not so easy always for us preachers to practise—hoch, ho!"

This sentiment uttered, a grace was hurried over; and the company seated themselves at table, which was literally covered with dishes, all close huddled together. In the middle was a tureen of leek soup, *alias* cocky-leeky, with prunes; at one end, a large dish of innumerable small, clammy, fresh-water trouts; at the other, two enormous fat ducks, stuffed to the throat with onions, and decorated with onion rings round their legs and pinions. At the corners were minced collops and tripe, confronted with a dish of large old pease, drowned (for they could not swim) in butter; next, a mess of mashed potatoes, scored and rescored with the marks of the kitchen knife—a weapon which is to be found in all kitchens, varying in length from one to three feet; and in uncivilised hands used indiscriminately to cut meat, fish, fowl, onions, bread, and butter. Saucers full of ill-coloured pickles filled up the interstices.

"I ordered merely a slight refreshment," said Mr. M'Dow, surveying his banquet with great complacency; "I think it preferable to a more solid *mail*

---

[1] Trance—in England, a deep swoon; in Scotland, a narrow passage.

in this weather. Of all good Scotch dishes, in my
opinion, there's none equal to cocky-leeky; as a friend
of mine said, it's both nectar and ambrosia. You'll
find that uncommonly good, Miss Lucy, if you'll just
try it; for it's made by a receipt of my mother's, and
she was always famous for cocky-leeky; the prunes
are a great improvement; they give a great delicacy
to the flavour; my leeks are not come to their full
strength yet, but they are extremely sweet; you
may help me to a few more of the broth, Captain,
and don't spare the leeks. I never see cocky-leeky
without thinking of the honest man who found a
snail in his: 'Tak ye that snack, my man,' says he,
'for looking sae like a plum-damy;' hach, hach, ho!
There's a roasted hare coming to remove the fish, and
I believe you see your refreshment; there's merely a
few trifles coming."

Lucy had accepted one of Mr. Dugald's little
muddy trouts, as the least objectionable article of the
repast; and while Mr. M'Dow's mouth was stuffed
with prunes and leeks, silence ensued. But having
despatched a second plateful, and taken a bumper of
wine, he began again: "I can answer for the ducks,
Miss Lucy, if you'll do me the favour to try them.
A clean knife and fork, Jess, to Mr. Dugald to cut
them; I prefer ducks to a goose; a goose is an incon-
venient sort of bird, for it's rather large for one person,
and it's not big enough for two. But my stars, Jess?
what *is* the meaning of this? The ducks are perfectly
raw!" in an accent of utter despair. "What *is* the

meaning of it? You must take it to the brander, and
get it done as fast as you can. How came Eppy to
go so far wrong, I wonder!"

Jess here emitted some of her guttural sounds,
which, being translated, amounted to this, that the
jack had run down and Eppy couldn't get it set
agoing again.

"That's most ridiculous!", exclaimed Mr. M'Dow
indignantly; "when I was at the pains to show her
myself how to manage her. She's the Auchnagoil
jack, which I bought, and a most famous goer. But
you see how it is, Miss Lucy; you must make allow-
ance for a bachelor's house; there's a roasted hàre
coming. Jess, take away the fish, and bring the hare
to me." The hare was herewith introduced, and
flung, rather than placed, before her master. "Oh,
this is quite intolerable! There's really no bearing
this! The hare's burnt to a perfect stick! The
whole jise is out of its body!"

"Your cook's not a good hare-dresser, that's all
that can be said," quoth Mr. Dugald.

"Very well said—extremely good," said Mr.
M'Dow, trying to laugh off his indignation; "and,
after all, I believe, it's only a little scowthered.[1] Do
me the favour to try a morsel of it, Miss Lucy, with a
little jeelly. Jess, put down the jeelly. Oh, have
you nothing but a pig[2] to put it in?" demanded he,

---

[1] Scorched.

[2] Pig—in England, an animal; in Scotland a piece of
crockery.

in a most wrathful accent, as Jess clapped down a
large native jelly-pot upon the table. "Where's the
handsome cut crystal jeelly-dish I bought at the
Auchnagoil roup?"

Jess's face turned very red, and a downcast look of
conscious guilt told that the "handsome cut crystal
jelly-dish" was no more.

"This is really most provoking! But if you'll not
taste the hare, Miss Lucy, will you do me the kindness to try the minced collops? or a morsel of tripe?
It's a sweet, simple dish—a great favourite of my
mother's; both you and the Captain are really poor
eaters, so you and I, Mr. Dugald, must just keep each
other in countenance."

And another pause ensued, till at last an order was
given to take everything away, "And bring the few
trifles—but *will* you make less noise? there's no hearing ourselves speak for you;" but Jess rattled away,
nevertheless, till she vanished, leaving the door wide
open. A few minutes elapsed before she reappeared,
with the greasy apparition of Eppy at her back, standing on the threshold with her hands full.

"Now, take the pigeon-pie to Mr. Dugald; bring
the puddin' to me; put the puffs and cheesecakes at
the sides, and the cream in the middle. I'm sorry
I've no jeellies and *blaw mangiys* for Miss Lucy. If
you won't taste the pie, do me the favour to take a
bit of this puddin'; it's quite a simple puddin', made
from a recipe of my mother's."

Lucy accepted a bit of the "simple puddin'," which,

as its name implied, was a sort of mawkish squash, flavoured with peat-reek whisky.

"I'm afraid the puddin's not to your taste, Miss Lucy; you're making no hand of it; will you try a jam puff? I'm sure you'll find them good, they come from Glasgow, sent by my good mother; I must really taste them, if it were only out of respect to her. Oh! Miss Lucy, will you not halve a puff with me?"

The minister and his friend having now ate and drank copiously of all that was upon the table, Captain Malcolm said, "My daughter has not yet accomplished the object of her visit here, and we must soon be returning home, so you have no time to lose, my dear," to Lucy, who started up from table like a bird from its cage, "if indeed it is not lost already," he added, as Lucy and he walked to the window. The bright blue sky had now changed to one of misty whiteness, showers were seen drifting along over the scattered isles, and even while they spoke, a sudden gust of wind and rain came sweeping along, and all the beauteous scenery was in an instant blotted from the sight.

Captain Malcolm was not a person to be disconcerted by trifles; but on the present occasion he could not refrain from expressing his regret, as he every moment felt an increasing repugnance to the company of Mr. M'Dow and his friend, and still more on Lucy's account than his own; it seemed like contamination for so fair and pure a creature to be seated between two such coarse barbarians. Mr.

M'Dow affected to sympathise in the disappointment; but it was evident he was exulting in the delay.

Shower after shower followed in such quick succession that Lucy found the object of her visit completely defeated. At length the clouds rolled away, but the day was too far advanced to admit of .further tarriance ; and besides, both the father and daughter were impatient to extricate themselves from the overpowering hospitalities of Mr. M'Dow.

"I hope you will have many opportunities of taking drawings here," said he, with a significant tenderness of look and manner, as he assisted Lucy to mount her pony; "and when the manse is harled, and I get my new offices, the view will be much improved."

Lucy bowed as she hastily took the bridle into her own hands, and gladly turned her back on *the manse* and the minister.

CHAPTER XXI

THE showers had passed away; the rainbow was "smiling on the faded storm;" the fragrant air was mild; the herds and flocks were cropping the dewy grass; the declining sun shot "a slant and mellow radiance;" and all things seemed imbued with new life and beauty. Captain Malcolm and his daughter proceeded for some time in silence; each felt the beauty and the harmony of nature, and as they slowly paced, side by side, amongst the windings of the green hills, they needed not words to utter the feelings of their hearts. Captain Malcolm was the first to speak.

"You are unusually meditative, Lucy," said her father. "What is engaging your thoughts so much?"

"I have been thinking, papa," said Lucy, rousing herself from her reverie, "what a sweet thing silence is."

"That is to say, you admire silence as La Bruyère did solitude?"

"Oh, certainly, silence is sweeter when shared with another who can understand its beauty. But after such a day, such a coarse unpleasant day as we have spent, even solitary silence would be sweet and grateful. Had Mr. M'Dow given us some nice clean well-boiled potatoes and milk, and have allowed us to walk about and enjoy the beautiful scenery, how much more pleasantly and profitably the day would have been spent!"

"Mr. M'Dow is, indeed, a coarse specimen of a coarse propensity," said Captain Malcolm, "and has fallen into a common error, that of seeking to raise himself by appearances; as if these could exalt the character, especially of a minister of the gospel—of one who is 'as poor, yet making many rich; as having nothing, and yet possessing all things.'"

"One is always pleased with the humble fare of a cottage," said Lucy; "and I am sure most people would feel additional respect for the simplicity of a clergyman's, or indeed any one's style of living, when proportioned to their means."

"Certainly," said Captain Malcolm; "poverty in itself is never despicable or ridiculous except to vulgar or thoughtless minds. It is only when it carries pretension along with it that we feel privileged to laugh at so preposterous a union. We are also apt to be more disgusted with a coarse gourmand than with a refined epicure, though there certainly is not more moral or intellectual superiority evinced in the love of turtle and venison, or even *fricandeau* and *blanquette*, than in cocky-leeky and ducks."

"Oh, how much I lament having lost this day!" sighed Lucy, as she stopped her pony to admire a lovely peep between the hills.

"I fear your lost day is not to be understood in the same sense as the Emperor's was," said her father. "I suspect it is only your lost sketches you lament."

Lucy smiled as she acknowledged the fact. "But surely, papa," she added, "you must allow it was rather hard, instead of roaming amongst rocks and glens, and filling my *portefeuille* with sketches, to be shut up all day with Mr. M'Dow! Indeed, papa, his company is anything but agreeable."

"I am aware of that, my dear, but as a clergyman, I wish to show him all the respect in my power. His sacred office I consider the most important in which a human being can be engaged, and the most difficult, when one considers what various states of mind a faithful pastor must be called upon to minister to."

"But you surely cannot call him a faithful pastor, papa? I cannot possibly conceive any one consulting him about spiritual matters, or even asking him for a prayer; I am sure I could not."

"I never heard you so severe upon any one, Lucy. When you have lived longer in the world, you will find there are worse characters in the church than Mr. M'Dow, though, happily, there are also others whose genius, learning, and piety shed a lustre over the age in which they live. Mr. M'Dow is not an immoral man, otherwise I would not have gone to visit him."

"The most offensive part of his character, I think," said Lucy, "next to his love of eating, is his constant jocularity; not that I should like a morose, austere pastor, who would look upon all gaiety as sin, but I should like to see one, as Cowper says, 'serious in a serious cause.'"

"I agree with you," said her father, "that when a clergyman views in its true light the importance and the responsibility of the office he has undertaken; an office which, as an old writer says, is 'a weight under which angels' shoulders might shrink,' his great object will be to get men to think seriously, not to laugh lightly; though wit being a natural talent, like every other, it may be turned to good account."

"Ah! there is old Sandy!" exclaimed Lucy, as a sudden turn of the road gave to view an old gray-haired shepherd on the hillside, basking in the rays of the evening sun, with his book and his dog. "How finely he is in keeping with the landscape! I wish we were nearer, to have a little conversation with him, for I find both pleasure and improvement in conversing with him; he is simple and artless, but not vulgar, for he knows his Bible, and that truly 'maketh wise the simple.'"

"He is indeed a very favourable specimen of humble life," said Captain Malcolm; "for I have always found that where common education is built on solid religious principles it never fails to elevate the mind, and give that contented and independent spirit which is a nation's truest strength and safety."

"How perfectly he realises Grahame's picture of a Sabbath evening shepherd," said Lucy, still gazing on the picturesque figure of her old favourite :—

———" Behold the man!
The grandsire and the saint ; his silvery locks
Beam in the parting ray ; before him lies,
Upon the smooth-cropt sward, the open book,
His comfort, stay, and ever new delight."

"And there is a setting sun," said Captain Malcolm,
as they emerged from the glen, and the blazing lumi-
nary burst upon their sight, "that would defy all
painting, for, as Wordsworth says,

———" Such beauty varying in the light
Of living nature, cannot be portray'd
By words, nor by the pencil's silent skill ;
But is the property of him alone
Who hath beheld it, noted it with care,
And in his mind recorded it with love !"

"Oh, papa, do let us alight here for a few minutes
to feast our eyes with this lovely sunset," cried Lucy,
when they had gained the summit of a hill which
gave to view all the glories of the scene—the sun,
with all his retinue of flaming clouds, sinking to rest
in the bosom of the waters.

Captain Malcolm loved to encourage in his children
a taste for the beauties of nature ; a pleasure so cheap,
so pure, and so elevating, and he readily assented to
his daughter's request. Seating themselves on a
grassy spot by the side of a wild mountain brook,
they gazed "with eyes intent on the refulgent spectacle." At length Lucy said, "How perfectly Barton
has realised such an evening as this, with all its accom-
panying feelings, in that sweet poem of his, 'Morning
and Evening ;' every verse seems to me a perfect pic-

ture in itself, and a picture, too, that excites such pure
and holy thoughts!"   And her soft blue eyes shone
with an expression of love and adoration as she contemplated the glories of the heavens, and recalled the
beautiful imagery of the poet.

"It is a comparison he draws between the rising
and the setting sun, is it not?" said Captain Malcolm;
"my memory for these things is not so good as it
was, Lucy; but I daresay you can repeat it to me
word for word, and this is just the time and place for
hearing it."   Lucy, in a sweetly-modulated voice and
simple manner, then recited the last stanzas of Bernard
Barton's "Morning and Evening":—

            " 'Tis when day's parting light,
               Dazzling no more the sight,
            Its chastening glory to the eye is granting,
               That 'thoughts too deep for tears,'
               Unearthly hopes and fears,
            And voiceless feelings, in the heart are panting.

            " While thus the western sky
               Delights the gazing eye,
            With thrilling beauty, touching and endearing!
               What still of earth is fair,
               Borrows its beauty there,
            Though every borrow'd charm is disappearing.

            " Ere yet those charms grow dim,
               Creation's vesper hymn,
            Grateful and lovely, is from earth ascending;
               Till, with that song of praise,
               The hearts of those who gaze
            With solemn feelings of delight are blending.

            " Then from those portals bright
               A farewell gleam of light

Breaks with unearthly glory on the vision ;
   And through the folding doors
   The eye of thought explores
Seraphic forms and fantasies elysian.

  " These pass like thought away !
   Yet may their hallow'd sway
Rest on the heart—as dewdrops round adorning
   The drooping silent flowers,
   Feed them through night's dark hours,
And keep them fresh and living till the morning.

  " Thus should the sunset hour,
   With soul-absorbing power,
Nurse by its glories the immortal spirit ;
   And plume its wings of flight
   To realms of cloudless light,
Regions its God hath form'd it to inherit.

  " Fair, bright, and sweet is MORN !
   When daylight, newly born,
In all its beauty is to sense appealing ;
   Yet Eve to me is franght
   With more *unearthly thought*,
And purer touches of *immortal feeling !*"

The shades of evening began to gather around,
but the gloom was still enlivened by streaks of sunshine on the mountain tops ; the silence and solitude
that reigned, and the stupendous objects that surrounded them, filled the hearts of the father and
daughter with solemn thoughts, and as they journeyed
slowly home they felt this was indeed the time for
"unearthly thought" and "immortal feeling."

CHAPTER XXII.

LITTLE more was heard of Inch Orran for some weeks. He had gone upon a voyage of discovery to two of the Isles where the principal part of his property was situated, and was actively employed in detecting abuses, redressing grievances, making surveys, getting estimates, quarrelling with his neighbours, discarding his factor, threatening his vassals, and so forth, and all in the face of the worst and stormiest weather that ever was seen, even on a western island. At the end of some weeks, he returned to Inch Orran, and Glenroy and he soon after met at a county meeting. The Chief, as well as every one present, was immediately struck with the change that had taken place in the old man's appearance since his first arrival in the country; in fact, he more resembled a livid skeleton than a living man.

"I am glad to see you safely returned to us, Inch Orran," said Glenroy, accosting him with much cordiality. "I'm afraid you have had but a fatiguing expedition?"

"Sir," returned his kinsman, "I desire to be excused from being either congratulated or interrogated."

And with a slight wave of his hand he turned away.

Glenroy could scarcely keep from strangling him for his insolence; but he saw death in the old man's face already, and he refrained. So, swallowing the indignity, even although put in open court, he consoled his wounded pride by anticipating the rich reward that soon awaited his forbearance. Indeed, to all human appearance, the time was not far distant when the possessor of the long-coveted lands would be called on to relinquish them. It was evident he was then labouring under severe indisposition, though, when some one remarked to him that he appeared to have caught cold, he denied the fact with much asperity. Then, as if to give the lie to the offensive insinuation, he mounted his horse, and rode home ten miles in a pour of rain, without greatcoat or umbrella. The following day he was still worse; but, nevertheless, being in one of his invincible fits of ill-humour and obstinacy, he chose to stand out for six hours in wind and rain, seeing his potatoes lifted, carted, and measured, that he might take *his* measures accordingly.

The cold, bad as it was, might perhaps have ended like other colds, had it been treated in a gentlemanly way; but it was not Inch Orran's mode to treat anything gently, or give place to any of the beggarly elements of human nature. He had likewise an utter contempt for doctors, without having a well-grounded faith in anything else, unless it were in that phantom called Nature, which was the only thing (Simon excepted) that had any control over him. To Nature then he, in the first place, committed himself; but the cold grew worse and worse, in the most natural way possible. He then submitted himself to Simon, who boldly undertook the cure; but Simon had only two recipes in the world, the one was *ale saps*,[1] the other was *Atholl brose*.[2]

In spite of nature and Simon, and saps and brose, Inch Orran's case became desperate, and then a doctor was called, but came in vain. Another was summoned, but with no better success. Glenroy was most attentive, but to no purpose. The patient grew gradually worse and worse, till at the end of a few weeks, all solicitude was vain, for Inch Orran ceased to breathe.

Mrs. Malcolm behaved "as well as could be expected" on this trying occasion. She said it was just to be expected, for Mr. Malcolm was an old man, and a very particular man, and it was no wonder he died, for he never minded a word she said; and with Mrs. Macauley to sit by and assent to all her propositions, and listen to her complaints of Simon, and concert with her about her mourning, and talk over the ceremonials of the funeral, Mrs. Malcolm was soon "wonderfully well."

It is a tormenting law which exists in Scotland of keeping the will of the deceased a dead secret until after the interment, especially as wills are things so

---

[1] Porridge made with ale.
[2] A composition of honey and whisky.

capricious in their nature as to defy the speculation of the living, and baffle all their attempts at anticipation. During that dread interval, how are the hearts of the nearest of kin of a childless miser, or a wealthy old bachelor, or a saving elderly spinster, agitated with the emotions of hope and fear! Doubts resolving themselves into certainties, and certainty fading away into doubt, as their omissions of duty and commissions of offence rise successively to view. In the present instance, the only parties who seemed privileged to entertain either hopes or fears, doubts or certainties, were Glenroy and Captain Malcolm, as the nearest relatives of the deceased, and both standing much in the same degree of propinquity. But the latter waived his pretensions in favour of the Chief, who therefore took upon himself the arrangement of the funeral, and also bore the whole burden of the fortnight's suspense which intervened between the death and burial. Having seen the last remains of Inch Orran safely deposited in the family vault, Glenroy returned to the mansion of the departed to unseal the repositories, and cause them to render up their secrets. The search was soon ended. The first thing that presented itself was Inch Orran's settlement, or general disposition, new and neat, formally drawn up, and regularly signed and attested in the most business-like manner possible. But as the reading of a settlement is a tax too heavy to impose upon any save those who are to profit by it, it will be sufficient to extract the kernel from the voluminous husk in

which, for wise purposes, the law has thought proper
to encase it, but which it is not every one's jaws that
can penetrate. Suffice it therefore to say that the
settlement set forth, in the usual strain, for good
causes and considerations, giving, granting, assigning,
and disponing all houses, lands, heritages, debts, move-
ables, goods and chattels, writs and evidents, etc. etc.
etc., to Christopher Blancow, Isaac Knipes, and Mark
Lipptrot, attorneys and scriveners, in trust, for behoof
of Ronald Malcolm, eldest son of Captain John Malcolm of Lochdhu, and his heirs and assignees, the
proceeds during the life of the said Ronald Malcolm,
until he shall have attained the age of twenty-six
years, to be invested in the three per cent consols,
there to accumulate. Not a farthing of the money
was to be touched under any pretence; and the said
Ronald Malcolm was not to be alimented or subsisted
therefrom, but to be considered as having no right
whatever in the premises, until he should have attained
the aforesaid age. Failing the said Ronald Malcolm,
his heirs, etc., the whole was to go to his father,
without restriction of any kind. A small jointure
to Mrs. Malcolm, five hundred pounds to each of
the trustees, a legacy of a thousand pounds, and an
annuity of thirty, to Simon Small, for his faithful services, were the sole bequests contained in this incon-
sistent and capricious "disposition."

Glenroy was too much confounded at first to be
able to be in a passion; it was only when he had col-
lected his senses that his energies were roused, and

he was able to articulate, with his face in a flame, and his eyes flashing fire and fury, "Ronald Malcolm! Oh, certainly, a very proper person—*very*—I—hem— I wish you joy, sir," to Captain Malcolm, stamping his foot as he spoke. "Your son is very welcome!" in a voice of thunder—"perfectly welcome for me!" and with a muttered oath the Chief took an abrupt leave of the party of mourners; and, tearing off his crape and weepers, threw them into the loch, and returned home.

CHAPTER XXIII.

ALTHOUGH everybody declared they had expected a most extraordinary settlement from Inch Orran, still this far surpassed the anticipations even of the most experienced, and afforded an ample field for animadversion to all. Yet perverse, unjust, and capricious wills are things of such common occurrence, the only surprise is that people should still continue to be surprised at them. Surprised, however, every one was, and none more so than the family at Lochdhu, who were perhaps the only people of the name who had not dreamt of either lairdship or legacy. Neither Captain nor Mrs. Malcolm were people to be much elated with any portion of mere worldly prosperity, and this succession of their son's was not such as to call forth any very exuberant demonstrations of joy. It could be of no immediate advantage to themselves or their children; for, situated as they were, with a narrow income and a large family, necessarily enduring many privations, a single year's rent of the estate would have been more beneficial to them now than the accumulated treasures of a long minority might prove hereafter. But, above all, they dreaded the effect this seducing prospect might have upon the mind of their son, with wealth and consequence thus placed before him, as the goal at which he must ultimately arrive, without any exertions of his own. Convinced as they were that the moral part of our nature is best developed amidst struggles and difficulties in the outset of life, they dreaded the various temptations to ease and pleasure which would beset his path. Yet, in spite of these sobering reflections, they hailed with gratitude the prospect that was still afar off, even though it neither gilded the present nor cast any delusive glare on the future.

As for the young heir, he felt much as any other generous, warm-hearted boy would have done upon such an occasion, and many were the romantic schemes which passed through his mind and burst from his lips in the first ardour of youthful emotion. Great was his disappointment at finding he could not, till the appointed time, dispossess himself of a farthing of his nominal wealth, and his heart revolted at the injustice that had been committed against his parents. He loved his mother with that deep and earnest love which a mother's virtues only can excite in the hearts of her children; and, contrasting the poverty and privations she endured with the comforts and luxuries he witnessed elsewhere, he was indignant at the barriers that were opposed to the gratification of his wishes.

Bent upon discovering some means by which his future wealth might be turned to the immediate benefit of his family, Ronald's mind became restless and dissatisfied; and his thoughts, occupied with vain wishes and impracticable projects, wandered far from the daily occupations he was wont to pursue with ardour and alacrity. Yet his was the restlessness of a noble mind, aiming at good which he could not realise.

He was beginning, as usual, one day with, "Oh, how I wish!" when his father gently stopped him.

"My dear Ronald," said he, "I was in hopes your good sense would, before now, have suggested to you what a dangerous habit you are acquiring of constantly wishing."

"Dangerous, papa!" repeated Ronald; "how can that possibly be?"

"I consider it very dangerous," replied his father mildly; "and so will you, I am very sure, when you come to reflect upon it. It is positive waste of time and thought and contentment. Wishing has been called the hectic of a fool. If it is not the proof of a dissatisfied mind (which, in your case, I trust it is not), it inevitably leads to it; for wishing is not very far from murmuring. It is not to inculcate an improvident habit, but a contented mind, that we are charged to take no thought of to-morrow."

"But in my situation it is scarcely possible to avoid wishing," said Ronald.

"You surely do not mean to say it is scarcely possible for you to avoid indulging in an idle and foolish habit?" said his father mildly. "We have indeed little control over circumstances—these are regulated by a higher power; but as rational and reflecting beings, we are accountable for the exercise of our faculties."

"But my wishes are not so much for myself as for others," said Ronald, reddening a little at the reproof.

"I am aware of that, my boy, for yours is not the sordid spirit that would merely seek its own gratification; but, nevertheless, you can do us no good by indulging those vain wishes of yours; perhaps, eventually, you could do us none had you the power of gratifying them, as it is very certain we know not the things that are best for us, and were our wishes granted, it might often be to our ruin. One thing you may be assured of, your mother and I would rather see you poor, if possessed of a grateful heart and contented mind, than master of millions with a restless and dissatisfied spirit. I forget what philosopher it is who says, 'It is better to be born with a cheerful temper than heir to ten thousand a year.' For my part, I think its value is incalculable, when it springs from the right source—faith and love. Such, I am sure, I have found it in your mother. You know but little of the privations she suffered in marrying me; but never have I even heard her utter a wish for any mere temporal benefit. *Her* wishes, Ronald, have been prayers; and we flattered ourselves we should, by the blessing of God, be enabled to make our children rich in contentment, if in nothing else. You will not, then, disappoint us, Ronald?"

Ronald could not answer, but his feelings were depicted on his open countenance, as he wrung his father's hand in silent emotion. From henceforth he sought to stifle his murmurs amid the sober realities of practical duties, kept in wholesome exercise throughout the daily walks of life.

But Ronald seemed destined only to feel the disquiet of riches without partaking of their enjoyments. The news of his succession had spread far and wide throughout the district; but the particulars were (as all particulars are) very variously and imperfectly stated, and of course much error and exaggeration prevailed, particularly amongst the lower orders of the more remote vassals and tenants. The consequence was, the young heir was assailed from all quarters with petitions for, and remonstrances against, this, that, and the other evil, while a hoard of grievances, that had lain slumbering for many a year, were now brought to light, and laid before him, in the sure and certain expectation of being all speedily redressed. Wives came from afar to speak for the renewing of their husbands' leases; and mothers walked many a weary mile to get a word of the young laird about the enlarging of their sons' crofts; and widows crossed many a rough ferry, and climbed many a long hill, to petition for a cow's grass, or to claim favour, in right of their husbands or their fathers having lost an arm or a leg, serving under a Captain Angus Malcolm (some tenth cousin of the last laird) in the American war. In vain did Ronald protest to these poor people that he possessed no more power than they did themselves. He was heard with sorrowful incredulity, or renewed entreaties that, if he could not help them himself, he would speak a word for them to those who could. But Ronald had already found of what stuff Messrs. Blancow, Knipes, and Lipptrot were made, and that it was in vain to attempt to seek favour at their hands. Faithful to the trust confided in them, that of turning everything to money, they had already commenced their operations in the most systematic manner, and were deaf as adders to all appeals that came merely recommended by mercy or liberality. But it was in vain Ronald sought to convince the malcontents. It is at all times difficult to convince the poor that those they deem rich and powerful *cannot* relieve them, if they choose; but with the lower class of the Highlanders, it is next to an impossibility to make them comprehend how their superiors should not have the power to redress every grievance and supply every want, as promptly as it is made known.

Many was the slow reluctant step Ronald saw at length turn away from him, as if still lingering in the expectation of being recalled; and many was the groan, and the sigh, and the shake of the head, and the shrug of the shoulder, and the discontented "weel-a-weel!" he received in answer to his protestations. Such was the young heir's initiation to his inheritance.

CHAPTER XXIV.

But Ronald's cares, had they been weighed in a balance, would have been found light as feathers compared to Glenroy's wrath. Not even the pains of the gout, which ensued, could drive the disappointment from his mind. There are people—alas for those who know them!—who have never done with a subject, especially if it is of a disagreeable nature. "They feed upon disquiet" themselves, and force others to partake of the same sorry fare.

Such was Glenroy's practice; and upon this occasion his colloquial powers had received an *impetus* which seemed likely to keep them going to the last. It was a still-beginning, never-ending theme;—morning, noon, and night, he spoke of the injury he had sustained, as though he had been robbed, and his son murdered; till, by dint of hearing the same thing so constantly repeated, he at length talked himself and all around him into the firm belief that he had been cheated and circumvented in the most shameful manner by the Lochdhu family; and as his head was none of the clearest, or his reasoning powers of the strongest, the proofs, for or against, were all mixed up in one solid mass of invective.

"It is not the value of the property that I care about," he would repeat, at least ten times a day, to his all-enduring friends, Benbowie and Mrs. Macauley, as they sat by his gouty chair, the one with his tobacco-box, the other with her work-basket, shaping-scissors, and spectacles. "But I hate the dirty, under-hand way these people have gone about the business; I was completely thrown off my guard by them; but I never knew one of these canting dogs that wasn't a complete hypocrite."

"On my conscience, that's very true, Glenroy," said Benbowie.

"I'm as sure as I am of my own existence," con-tinued the Chief, "that there was a regular laid down plan, from the moment of the old man's arrival in the country. You may remember he had hardly entered this house when that Ronald—that young saint—was at his heels; sent to play the spy, and show off before him. The father knew better than to face the old dragon himself, and so he set his son to dodge him and fawn upon him; he had his lesson, and knew what he was about the day he came here. I saw through them even then."

"On my conscience, I really believe so," said Ben-bowie.

"I have no doubt it was these incendiaries that were at the bottom of that insane proposal the old scrivener made me about Edith; but I would rather a thousand times have seen her in her grave than the wife of any beggarly tacksman's son—and to cut out her brother, too!"

"Well, now, is not that very curious!" said Mrs. Macauley; "are not these just the very words that I heard Mr. Reginald using the t'other day? 'Edith,' says he, 'I would rather see you killed a thousand times than that you should have disgraced yourself by marrying the tacksman's son.'—'Oh, Reginald,' said she, 'you know that could not be, for I am engaged to be married to you, and so I would not marry Ronald even if he were a king.'"

"You'll really make these children as great fools as you are yourself," cried Glenroy impatiently. "How can you put such nonsense into their heads!"

"Me, Glenroy! 'deed I never put anything into their heads. I would be very sorry; so far from that, when the boys said that you hated Ronald, for he was a bad boy, I said to them, 'Well, childer, your papa may say what he pleases, and you ought to mind everything he says, when it is good and fit to be remembered; and when he happens to say what is maybe not just so right, then you must be sure to forget it.'"

"I really don't believe there is such another fool as yourself in existence," cried Glenroy; "and I only wish you had this gout of mine in your tongue, to silence it."

"Well, I'm sure I wish I had, if it would take it out of your toe, Glenroy; but wait till you hear.

'Oh,' says Norman, 'I shall take care never to forget that he cheated me out of an estate.'—'Nor I,' says Reginald, 'that he had the impudence to want to marry Edith; a pretty husband indeed for Edith, a poor tacksman's son!'—'Childer,' says I, 'I fear you read your Bible to little purpose, or you would not speak evil of your neighbour, or be so scornful of anybody for being more humbly born than yourselves; for we are such curious creatures, we cannot tell what may happen to us. You ought to remember how Joseph, that was sold for a slave, came to be a ruler over his proud brethren; and was not there King David, the greatest of all the kings of the earth,—what was he but a poor shepherd boy? But it pleased God to make him a great king, and if it please Providence to appoint that Ronald should live to become a great man, who knows but he may be married to Miss Edith——' "

"Providence!—appoint! What is it you mean, Mrs. Macauley? do you know what it is you are saying?" cried Glenroy furiously.

"'Deed I do, Glenroy, and I'm sure so do you, that it is Providence that appoints our lot——"

"Providence!—appoint!—lot! Do you mean to make my children predestinarians?" cried Glenroy passionately. "I thought you had been merely a simpleton, but I see you're a most mischievous creature, and I cannot suffer you in my family, if you sport such doctrines as these."

"Well, Glenroy, if you think so, I cannot help it;" and poor Mrs. Macauley's heart rose at the thoughts of having to choose between her Chief and her conscience.

"But I don't believe you know yourself what it is you mean," cried he, somewhat mollified at sight of her distress.

"'Deed, then, but I know very well, Glenroy."

"Then I say you are a very dangerous and mischievous woman," cried Glenroy, enraged that she would not take advantage of the loophole he had opened for her escape.

"Well, maybe I am, Glenroy," was the humble reply; "but I'm very sure I do not mean it."

"You are really not fit to associate with either men or children," cried the Chief, striking his crutch on the floor as he spoke.

"Well; maybe not," was said in a very dejected tone; "but you may say what you please of me, Glenroy, for there's no harm in that; but I do not like to hear you casting out with Providence."

"Who's casting out, as you call it, with Providence, you old goose?"

"Well, I really thought you was affronted at my saying that we did not get everything our own way in this world, but that Providence appoints our lot for us."

"Then I tell you again, Mrs. Macauley, that I will not suffer such doctrines in my family; I'm for none of your predestinarian notions here. I suppose you'll have my servants cutting my throat, and saying it was appointed. I—I—it's really a most infamous doctrine."

"Oh! Glenroy, that is not the Christian notion of the thing at all; it's only poor ignorant heathen craaters, or them who do not take pains to read their Bible, who can misuse it that way; for how can we think we are appointed to do mischief to one another, when does not He tell us that we are to love our neighbour as ourselves? 'Deed, if an angel were to tell me the contrary, I would not believe it."

"You really—you know nothing about the matter, and I desire I may hear no more such doctrines; there's no knowing where it would end."

"'Deed, then, I think it would just end in our being of contented minds, and learning to walk humbly with God, casting all our care upon Him who careth for us."

"Oh, you are setting up for a saint too! but I'm for no saints in this house, remember."

"Well, you know, if you wish me to go my way I cannot help it; it is my duty to go." Here tears streamed down Mrs. Macauley's cheeks.

"Yes, yes, you're ready to go, and leave me at the very time when you might be of some use; you might at least have the discretion to stay till I have got somebody to take your place; but do as you please."

"Oh, Glenroy, how can you think it would please me to leave you and your children!" cried poor Mrs. Macauley, quite overcome.

"Well, stay where you are," cried Glenroy, somewhat softened; "only don't go and fill the children's heads with these pernicious doctrines of yours." Mrs. Macauley's face fell at the conclusion of this sentence.

"I must speak the truth to them, Glenroy," said she, with a sigh, "whatever may come of it; and I think we are such curious craaters, and know so little, that we cannot tell what may happen to us. It may be God's will to raise us up, or to cast us down."

"Are you at it again," interrupted Glenroy furiously; "when I tell you, Mrs. Macauley, I will not suffer these doctrines in my family?"

"Well, Glenroy, I am sorry it should be my lot to displease you, for I owe you a great deal of kindness, and I would lay down the hair of my head for you and your childer, but I cannot give up my principles."

"Who's meddling with your principles?" demanded Glenroy, again softened at sight of her distress.

"Well, I thought it was not like you to do it; you who have such good principles of your own."

"It's my opinion," said Glenroy, "you know nothing about principles, I don't believe you know what they are; are they flesh and blood, or are they skin and bone?"

"Oh! Glenroy, I wonder to hear you, who have so much good sense, speak that way, when you know what respectable things principles are, and what poor craaters we would be without them. No, Glenroy, when I die, I will leave those things behind me; but I expect to carry my principles along with me, for no doubt they will be of use to me in the next world."

"That's very true," said Benbowie, waking out of

a doze; "on my conscience, we should keep all we can."

"I don't believe there's a man on earth but myself that could put up with two such idiots," muttered Glenroy.

"Oh! 'deed, we have all our appointed trials, Glenroy," said Mrs. Macauley, looking in his face with the most perfect good-nature and sympathy; "but we have all a great deal to be thankful for, too, and myself most of all, for 'man proposes but God disposes,' and so He has disposed you to be a good and kind friend to me, Glenroy."

"You speak a great deal of nonsense," said the Chief, whose wrath, having had its full swing, now evaporated; "but I don't believe you know what you say, and I daresay you mean well; and there's the children calling you." And he graciously extended his hand, which received a kindly pressure from the placable Mrs. Macauley.

"Oh, Glenroy!" cried she, while tears of joy twinkled in her eyes; "is it not a great blessing that you have not cast out with me, and that from no power in me to hinder you?—Well, my dears, I'm coming," as another call from the children made her hasten to join them in a little excursion.

CHAPTER XXV.

If it is difficult to impress truth upon the minds of children, it must be owned there is nothing so easy as to instil prejudice. The effect produced by these and similar invectives, which the young Glenroys were in the daily habit of hearing, may therefore be easily imagined. The Lochdhu family became gradually associated in their minds with everything that was base and treacherous; while Ronald in particular was the object of a sort of undefined ill-will to the two boys, who had already learnt to ape the Chieftain's tone and adopt his sentiments. Even the gentle, timid, loving Edith was insensibly borne along in the stream. She was still too young to comprehend the nature of the case, or to conceive how pride, prejudice, and envy, may distort the fairest and simplest statement. Neither could so monstrous a supposition ever enter into her young imagination as that her papa could be in the wrong. She could therefore only grieve in silence that her once dear friends should have been so wicked as to have told lies and cheated, and that Ronald, dear Ronald !—who had given her a white owl, and was training a starling for her—

should have been such a bad boy as to rob Norman, and to want to have her for his wife, when he was only a poor tacksman's son and she was the daughter of the Chief.

Such was the taint already communicated by pride and prejudice to the young and simple heart, by nature "rich in love and sweet humanity."

With all Glenroy's violence and gasconading, he nevertheless did not proceed to open hostilities with the Lochdhu family. When they met, which was but seldom, he even felt his spirit so rebuked beneath the mild and unassuming, yet open and fearless aspect of Captain Malcolm, that his blustering subsided into a dead calm, or merely showed itself in a still haughtier deportment. His kinsman was at no loss to guess that this accession of dignity in his manner was occasioned by anger and disappointment, and he was aware how unavailing argument or expostulation would be against prejudice so unreasonable and inveterate. He also knew that offended pride is only to be propitiated by the humiliation of the object of offence. To attempt, therefore, to conciliate the Chief, on the footing of equality, he perceived would only exasperate him the more; and as there was nothing on his part which called for concession, he deemed it the wisest plan to allow matters to take their course, without either seeking or avoiding an explanation.

Although Captain and Mrs. Malcolm were not so Utopian as to attempt to bring up their children in utter ignorance of the wickedness of the world in

general, still less were they given to point out particular living instances of it, as they found quite
enough on record to serve their purpose, without
applying the scalpel to the characters of all their
acquaintances. Glenroy's behaviour, therefore, called
forth no animadversions from them in presence of
their family. They knew that reason, and the improvement of the understanding, nay, religion itself,
are often insufficient to destroy prejudices imbibed in
early life, and that children cannot possibly discrimi-
nate or comprehend the vast variety of shades which
are to be found in the same character. With them
everything and everybody is either good or bad, and
of course either loved or hated with all the ardour
of unregulated minds. They were therefore unwilling to impress their young hearts with feelings of
enmity and aversion against one, who, with all his
pride, vanity, and littleness of mind, nevertheless
possessed claims upon their forbearance and good-will.

Some childish disorder which showed itself in the
family soon afforded a plausible excuse for the continued estrangement, and Captain Malcolm trusted
that by the time that was over, the Chieftain's disappointment would be somewhat mollified. And so
it gradually was in some degree, although, for want
of something better or worse to say, he had got into
the habit of regularly abusing the whole family at
least five times a day, unless otherwise engaged.

Such was the state of affairs when Captain Malcolm
received a letter from Captain Stanley, offering to

take Ronald on board his own vessel, the *Brilliant*, then under orders for North America. The commander and the voyage were both unexceptionable; but Captain and Mrs. Malcolm, who had never been very desirous of their son's entering on a seafaring life—a life of such hardship and danger—were now decidedly averse to it, when, by the change of circumstances, a profession had become a very secondary consideration. But in vain they endeavoured to combat this inclination. Ronald had conceived that strange and unaccountable predilection for the sea which, like all extraordinary propensities, when once it has taken possession of the mind, is not to be expelled by anything short of dear-bought experience. He said, indeed, that he would give it up rather than distress his father and mother; but he said it with sorrow, and the disappointment hung so heavily on his spirits that his parents thought it wrong to oppose so decided a predilection, and the point was yielded. They gave their consent, not without hope that a single voyage would do more to cure him of his naval ardour than all that could be urged against it. Preparations were therefore immediately made for his departure; but he said, before he went away, he must go to Glenroy to give Edith her starling, and to take leave of them all. They had been very shy of late. He did not know what was the matter, but he would go and see them, and make it up whatever it was. And full of kind feelings, Ronald set forth.

At a little distance from the house he met the

two boys and Edith at play upon the lawn, and his
heart bounded at sight of them. He accosted them
with all his wonted gladness and frankness of manner,
but the boys reddened and looked at each other,
while Edith cast down her eyes and looked sorry. If
children are sometimes slow to speak the truth, they
are commonly quick to show it in their behaviour.
The tongue seems in childhood the only member
which can yield a ready assent to falsehood. The
kindling or downcast eye, the blushing cheek, the
constrained air—all speak the feelings of the heart,
and 'tis long ere the ingenuous mind is tutored to
regulate and control them.

The young party met Ronald's salutation with cold
averted looks, unlike the familiarity of their usual
manners.

"You look as if you did not know me," said Ronald,
with some surprise, as his friendly greeting met with
no return; "although it is a long while since we
have met, surely you cannot have forgotten me?"

"Oh, no!—we have not forgot you," said Master
Norman scornfully.

"Then why don't you speak to me, and shake
hands with me?"

No answer was returned.

"And why do none of you come to Lochdhu?
You need have no fears of the measles now, for the
little ones have been quite well for more than a
month; and——"

"It isn't for that," said Reginald haughtily; "but

it's of no use to ask any questions; we don't choose to answer them, and that's enough. So, good morning to you."

"No!" cried Ronald in some agitation. "I won't go till you have told me why you are not friends with me. I'm sure I never did any of you any ill!"

"You have, though!" reiterated Norman passionately; "and papa says we are never to speak——"

"Hush, Norman!" said Edith, putting her hand on his lips, and whispering softly. "You know papa told us we were not to repeat anything he said; and I'm sure he would not be angry if we were to bid Ronald good-bye."

"I wish you would tell me what it is I have done that has made you quarrel with me; for I'm sure I don't know," said Ronald, in vain trying to recall any offence he had committed.

"We shall perhaps *make* you know some day," said Norman.

"The sooner the better," said Ronald boldly; "for I am going away."

"Where are you going?"

"To sea."

"And what have you got in your hand?"

"It is Edith's starling," said Ronald, displaying his captive.

Curiosity got the better of pride. Edith uttered an exclamation of pleasure, and the boys drew near, with looks of eager expectation.

"Can it speak, Ronald?" cried she, in a flutter of

delight, and quite forgetting her reserve. Ronald answered by opening the little cage he held in his hand, when the bird flew out and perched upon his wrist, jabbering something, which he said was, "Forget me not !" but which rather puzzled the uninitiated, and certainly was not so plain as the "Can't get out" of Sterne's sentimental starling.

Such as it was, it was a novelty, and consequently hailed with eagerness by the young group, who, one and all, for the moment forgot their animosity.

"Give it to me—make it come to me—let me have it," cried all three at once, eagerly extending their hands to it.

"You are frightening it," cried Ronald, raising his arm to save the starling from its assailants.

"Well, but I won't frighten it," cried the two boys, again attempting to get hold of it. "Give it to me—give it to me !"

"No, no, I won't give it to either of you. It is Edith's bird, and I will give it to nobody but her."

"If it is Edith's bird, why don't you give it to her ?" cried Reginald.

"Well, stand away both of you," said Ronald, "for it is frightened. It is rather wild yet to strangers; but see how it stays with Edith !"

"Now, Edith, give it to me !" cried Reginald, darting forward to seize it; but Ronald hastily stretching out his arm to ward him off, the shock threw him back, and his head striking against the branch of a tree, he fell, and the blood sprang from his nostrils.

Edith screamed, while Norman sought to stanch the blood with his handkerchief, and Ronald flew away for some water, which he brought in his cap.

"I am very sorry for this, Reginald," said he, as he returned breathless with haste. "Here is some water—drink a little of it; it will do you good."

But Reginald pushed away his hand with indignation.

"I'm sure I didn't intend to hurt you, Reginald," said he earnestly; "I was only trying to save the starling from you."

"You had no business to keep it from me," said Reginald passionately. "You had given it to Edith, and she had promised it to me, and you ought to have been very proud of our touching your bird, or anything belonging to you."

"Proud!" repeated Ronald.

"Yes, *very* proud," added Norman; "but we shall not demean ourselves any more, so you may take away your ugly stupid starling; Edith is not to take it."

"Edith is not to be dictated to," said Ronald warmly; "she is to do as she likes, and I know very well that she would like to have the starling. Would you not, Edith?"

"Edith, I shall never speak to you if you take his bird," cried Reginald; "so take your choice."

Edith, with tears in her eyes, looked imploringly at her tyrants, and then at the starling.

" You are not to take his bird, I tell you, Edith,"
cried Norman, in a passion. "It will tell lies and
cheat."

"What do you mean?" cried Ronald, kindling.
"Do you mean to say I tell lies and cheat? Who-
ever says so is a liar, and if either of you were as
strong as I am, you durst not say so; but you know
I won't fight with a less boy than myself."

"If you hadn't given me this cowardly blow," said
Reginald, "I should have fought you on the spot, and
so I will yet some day."

"I did not intend to strike you," said Ronald.
"I told you I was sorry for it. I didn't come here
to fight you : I came to be friends with you all, and
to shake hands with you before I go away; but if you
are determined not to do it, I can't help it."

The boys looked a little ashamed, and walked
sullenly on, while Edith lingered, and cast many a
loving look to her starling.

"I shall carry home the bird for you, Edith," said
Ronald, "and give it to you there, and Mrs. Macauley
will take care of it for you ; at least, *you* will part
friends with me, won't you?" and Edith, with downcast eyes, uttered a faint affirmative. The party
walked on in silence till they reached the Castle, when
Ronald said, " Here is your starling, Edith ; take it,
and let us be friends before I go."

Edith looked with soft earnest eyes, as if she longed
to be reconciled, and her hand was extended, when
Reginald interposed.

"You must choose, then, between him and me," said he passionately. "I shall never speak to you if you are friends with him."

If Edith had followed the dictates of her heart, she would most probably have chosen the unvarying, kind, generous, protecting friendship of Ronald to the somewhat capricious and often tyrannical preference of Reginald; but, too timid and gentle to dare to have a will of her own, she trembled at the thoughts of even betraying her good-will towards him, for fear of the displeasure it would draw down upon her. Thus early is " the fear of man a snare " for the young heart.

"I cannot take it, Ronald," said she, bursting into tears ; and all three walked into the house, and shut the door in Ronald's face. Ronald felt both anger and sorrow at such unkind behaviour, and, deeply mortified at Edith's joining against him, in a paroxysm of disappointment he tossed up the starling in the air. "There," cried he, "you may go ; since Edith won't have you, no one else shall;" and in bitterness of heart he retraced his way to his own kindly home.

It may be supposed what a sight and a story this was for Glenroy ; his children all dabbled over with blood—the noble blood of his nephew shed by the plebeian hand of the tacksman's son—his own blood boiled to think of it! Dire were the anathemas uttered against the perpetrator of this outrage ; and though not naturally a sanguinary man, yet, had the power of former days been in his own hands, there is

no saying in what manner he might have thought
proper to avenge this indignity. Most likely in the
Rob Roy strain—

> " And to his sword he would have said,
> 　Do thou my sovereign will enact;
>
> .　　.　　.　　.
>
> Judge thou of law and fact."

But after Reginald's face had been washed with
vinegar, and his dress changed, there appeared no
injury to redress. The traces of it did not, however,
pass so easily from Glenroy's mind; he was never
weary of detailing and denouncing the exaggerated
statement of Ronald's enormities, till his name became
a byword and reproach throughout the family.

CHAPTER XXVI.

BUT Ronald was soon to be beyond the reach of Glenroy's contumely, for the day and hour of his departure had arrived. The parting hour! that hour which, even in all its bitterness, we would yet fondly prolong, and when past, would many times gladly—oh! how gladly—recall! There is something peculiarly affecting in the first separation that takes place in a family, which, amidst many difficulties and privations, has ever preserved in its own bosom the elements of happiness—of sweet domestic happiness; those precious elements which, once scattered, are so seldom, if ever, united again!

> " My home of youth! oh, if indeed to part
>   With the soul's loved one be a mournful thing,
> When we go forth in buoyancy of heart,
>   And bearing all the glories of the spring
> For life to breathe on—is it less to meet
> When these are faded? who shall call it sweet?
>   Even though love's mingling tears may haply bring
> Balm as they fall, too well their heavy showers
> Teach us how much is lost of all that once was ours."[1]

Yes; search as we will, let us ransack east and west, earth and sea, for their peculiar treasures; it is

[1] Felicia Hemans.

not these, even in their fullest attainment, that bring
joy to the heart, which can only find its happiness in
the exercise of its best affections; and which, when it
survives these, lives but to sigh over its withered
hopes, its buried love. Alas! if in the long and
dreary interval of separation, it were foreseen what
griefs were to be borne, what ties were to be severed,
what hearts were to be seared or broken; who of
woman born could bear the sight and live? But 'tis
in mercy these things are hidden from our eyes!

No foreboding of evil greater than the present
filled the hearts of the sorrowing family who were
now assembled to part with him who was the loved
one of all; for his parents' hearts were strong in faith
in that Almighty Power, in the shadow of whose
wings there is safety for all who put their trust in
Him. They knew that it was not in an arm of flesh
to save when the decree had gone forth to smite; for
they had seen—as who has not?—the child of a thousand cares, the hope of some noble house, the heir of
some mighty name—the only, the all, the idolised one
—whose pillow had been a mother's heart, whose
safeguard a father's arms, smitten even when pressed
to their hearts, and torn from their unavailing grasp
by the stern hand of Death; while the wet sea-boy,
whose cradle had been the waves, who had been
buffeted by the stormy winds, and tossed on the
raging billows, with none to watch over him, none to
care for him, had been upheld and preserved by Him
whose "way is in the sea," and whose "path is in the

great waters," and in whose "hands are the issues of life and of death."

It was this heavenly confidence which gave fortitude to the father and resignation to the mother as they blessed again and again the object of their love and their prayers, and gazed upon the treasured features, dimmed as they were by their parting tears. Years might pass away before they should behold them again, but the remembrance of them, they felt, would never pass away till the last hours of life.

But different from the calm and holy sorrow of the parents are the feelings of the young and imaginative upon these solemn occasions. Amidst *their* grief there is still a spirit of joy within them, and their hearts beat high with fond anticipations of a world their fancy has pictured so fair, and which is fraught to them with all, with more than all, the world ever gave, or has to give.

And what though there be error and exaggeration in their romantic dreams? And what though dangers and disappointments are sure to quell their towering hopes of youthful enthusiasm? The delusion springs from a lofty source, from which all that is great in thought and noble in action has its rise; from those aspirations after a higher destiny than that of mere everyday existence, which seem inherent in minds of noble stamp, and

"Speak their high descent and glorious end."

Such were the feelings of young Ronald as the pic-

tured joys of a sailor's life dwelt upon his imagination,
and braced his heart to leave all those beloved most
dearly. The stately ship, the swelling sails, the dashing waves, the freshening breeze, the unknown lands,
the excitement, the perils, the renown, over all these
his ardent spirit had cast a charm which he longed to
realise. Yet when the time came, still he lingered
amidst the encircling arms and the linked hands, and
the fond tones, and the tears, and the kisses, and
mutual promises *not to forget.* But last and longest
did he remain locked in his mother's arms—that
mother so loved, so adored ; must he then leave her ?

It was a mighty effort to break away from all he
had ever known and loved ; the tender parents, the
happy playmates, the dear familiar faces, and scenes
which had stamped the first impressions on his heart.
His very dog, his faithful Bran, how his long, mournful
howl rang in his ear as the boat put off from land,
and he was left ! For the moment Ronald's bright
prospects all melted away beneath the warm gush of
tender affection, as he thought, "Why have I left
them ? I might have stayed; and now, perhaps, I may
never see them more !" But the day was one to chase
all sadness from the heart ; the blue waters glittered
in sunshine ; a summer breeze filled the sails of the
little boat, which skimmed along like a thing of life ;
and other and fairer scenes soon met Ronald's eye
than those of his mountain home and native shores.

CHAPTER XXVII

By the succession of his son, and his own eventual inheritance, Captain Malcolm was now in a different situation from what he had hitherto been, as the proprietor of a small farm, and the tenant of his proud Chief. But although he met with all that deference and attention which ever waits upon worldly prosperity, there was no alteration in his simple habits and demeanour, to the surprise of those selfish, sordid spirits, who look upon wealth as the *summum bonum* of human felicity. Whether Mr. M'Dow was of the number we do not pretend to say; but at this time the following letter arrived from him :—

"My dear Sir—The preparations for the departure of your son, and the consequent bustle and confusion which such an event unavoidably creates in a family, prevented my having the honour of communicating with you sooner upon a subject of an extremely delicate and most interesting nature. From the various small attentions I have for some time past been in the practice of paying to your eldest daughter, Miss Lucy, I have no doubt you will be pretty fully prepared for the communication I am about to make

to you, looking upon this mode of proceeding as by
far the most honourable and manly on such an occasion. From the first period of my entering on the
ministry it was my firm determination to embrace
the earliest opportunity of entering into the married
state, not only as being most conducive to my own
comfort and respectability, but as what the world
would naturally expect from me when placed in independent circumstances and in an elevated station in
society. I was very soon captivated with the modesty,
good temper, beauty, and accomplishments of your
daughter; but the difficulties which I found myself
involved in, in consequence of having to raise a
summons for augmentation, together with the uncer-
tainty as to the final result of my reclaiming petition,
made me at once resolve to act as became a man of
honour and integrity, by refraining from paying my
addresses until such time as I should have obtained a
final decreet. I have now the pleasure of informing
you that by last night's post I received the agreeable
intelligence that the Court has found me entitled to
my augmentation, and also decern for a small addition to the manse and thorough repairs to my offices,
which, although not what I by any means think myself entitled to, yet, upon the whole, will make things
pretty decent. That being the case, there no longer
remains any necessity for my concealing the attachment I have for a considerable time entertained for
your daughter, and for soliciting her hand in marriage.
From what I have observed, I think I have every

reason to flatter myself with a favourable response from her, although, in justice to myself, I must again assure you that I have made no direct appeal to her affections but such as you have been privy to. With regard to my family connections and private fortune, I beg leave to subjoin the following statement for the satisfaction of yourself and Mrs. Malcolm.

"My father, as is well known, was for upwards of forty years schoolmaster on the mortification of Myreside, and although the emoluments were not at that time what they are now, still they were such as enabled him to live like a gentleman, and to cut a good figure in the world. I need scarcely add that he was a man of a most highly respectable character, and of uncommon learning and abilities—in fact, quite a superior man; he was nearly related to the great M'Dow of M'Dow. At the same time he set no great value upon these things himself, and for my own part, I am no genealogist either, and have never given myself any trouble to prove the antiquity of my family. With respect to my fortune, I have not been much in the way of amassing wealth, but what I have is vested in the three per cent consols, and amounts to something upwards of £200. I have likewise two substantial top flats in the Gallowgate, Glasgow, one of which my mother liferents; the other I let off for £16 per annum. I am far from expecting, my dear sir, that, with your numerous family, you should be able to afford splendid fortunes to your children; at the same time, as your prospects,

my dear sir, are very materially improved, I have no
doubt you will at once see the propriety of doing all
that lies in your power to enable your daughter to
cut a good figure in the world as my wife.   But as it
is well known that money has never been the principal object with me, I think I may safely trust to
your own good sense and liberality, and gentlemanly
conduct, for a suitable and genteel portion with your
daughter.   On my part, I am willing to make such
settlements as may be deemed just and reasonable on
my wife, who in addition will, in the event of surviv-
ing me, be entitled to £30 per annum from the
Widows' Scheme.[1]   I beg the favour of an acknowledgment of this per bearer, and I hope I may be
permitted the honour of waiting on the ladies in the
course of to-morrow forenoon; in the meantime I
request you will do me the favour to deliver my
respectful compliments to them, with my most special
devoirs to Miss Lucy, and with the utmost regard,

" I am, my dear Sir,
" Your most faithful humble Servant,
" DUN. M'DOW.

" P.S.—For your further satisfaction, I think it
proper to hand you over a sight of the testimonials of
my character, which, in justice to myself, I thought
it necessary to procure at the time when I was applying for the presentation.   D. M'D."

---

[1] In English, a matrimonial design ; in Scotch, a pecuniary
compensation.

The "Testimonials" were, as usual, such as might have entitled the *testified* to the honours of an apotheosis, and the eulogy uttered by Mark Antony over the dead body of Julius Cæsar would have sounded tame and cold in comparison of the panegyrics lavished on Mr. M'Dow to his own face. From a voluminous mass of evidence, the following may serve as a slight specimen :—

"MY DEAR SIR—It is with the most unfeigned satisfaction I take up my pen to bear my public testimony to worth such as yours, enriched and adorned as it is with abilities of the first order—polished and refined by all that learning can bestow. From the early period at which our friendship commenced, few, I flatter myself, can boast of a more intimate acquaintance with you than myself; but such is the retiring modesty of your nature, that I fear, were I to express the high sense I entertain of your merit, I might wound that delicacy which is so prominent a feature in your character. I shall therefore merely affirm, that your talents I consider as of the very highest order ; your learning and erudition are deep, various, and profound ; while your scholastic researches have ever been conducted on the broad basis of Christian moderation and gentlemanly liberality. Your doctrines I look upon as of the most sound, practical description, calculated to superinduce the clearest and most comprehensive system of Christian morals, to which your own character and conduct afford an apt illustration. As a preacher, your language is nervous, copious, and highly rhetorical; your action in the pulpit free, easy, and graceful. As a companion, your colloquial powers are of no ordinary description, while the dignity of your manners, combined with the suavity of your address, render your company universally sought after in the very first society. In short, to sum up the whole, I know no man more likely than yourself to adorn the gospel, both by your precept and example. With the utmost esteem and respect,

"I am, dear Sir,

"Most faithfully and sincerely yours,

"RODERICK M'CRAW,
Professor of Belles Lettres."

But Lucy was not dazzled either by the Testimonials, or the Decreet, or the Augmentation, or the flats in the Gallowgate, or the Widows' Scheme; and, to Mr. M'Dow's astonishment and indignation, a polite though peremptory refusal was returned to his modest proposals.

CHAPTER XXVIII

LIFE seemed to be now holding its most even tenor both at the Castle and the farm, for both showed so little variety beyond the most common casualties that for some time not a single occurrence in either family would have served to adorn a tale, scarcely even to point a moral. The Chief, although his rancour was gradually abating, still preserved a stately distance towards his kinsman; and as their habits and pursuits were quite opposite, they seldom came in contact with each other. Glenroy, in spite of the downfall of his hopes, still pursued his course of revelry and reckless profusion, while Captain Malcolm, undazzled by the glare of future wealth and consequence, continued his former simple, frugal mode of life; his chief aim being to render his children happy, virtuous, and independent.

But the blank Ronald had left in the domestic circle remained a dreary chasm for many a dull day and long night; for Ronald had been the beloved of all, and all missed him, from the eldest to the youngest. The accounts that had hitherto been received, both of and from him, had been highly satis-

factory. His captain and he were mutually pleased
with each other, and the young sailor's naval ardour
had suffered no diminution during the time the ship
had remained at the Nore, after he had joined. But
soon after that its destination had been changed, and
instead of being despatched, as was originally intended,
on a six weeks' voyage to a healthy climate, it had
been ordered to cruise in distant seas, and in another
hemisphere. This was a disappointment to Captain
and Mrs. Malcolm, and an aggravation to the anxiety
they naturally experienced on their boy's account—an
anxiety which, even under the influence of pious trust,
could not fail to be felt by fond parents for a son of
such promise. Their hearts were indeed occasionally
cheered by letters from both Ronald and his captain,
when they happened to hail a ship in their progress,
and the contents were always of a gratifying nature.
Captain Stanley was delighted with Ronald, and
Ronald was delighted with the sea, and said he would
not exchange his hammock for all Inch Orran. All
he wanted was to witness a battle and a storm, and
when he had seen these, he should be satisfied.
"Heaven forbid his wishes should be soon gratified!"
said his mother, as she read the young enthusiast's
letter; but it seemed as if Heaven, in its mysterious
decrees, had otherwise ordained.

Many months passed after this, without either
letters or tidings, and the anxiety of the parents
became gradually more intense. Winter days and
stormy nights and summer suns rolled on, and still

all was silence. To the watchfulness of expectation
now succeeded the feverishness of apprehension, and
then came that awful stillness, the oppressive weight
of time which we have loaded with our own dread
presentiments—when all nature seems to be wrapped
in silence and in gloom, when every object appears to
proclaim the downfall of our hopes, when the gayest
scenes only move us to tears, when the gladdest tones
only sound as the death-knell of our happiness. Oh!
many were the midnight prayers breathed from a
sleepless pillow wet with a mother's tears, and duly
wore the streaming eyes and supplicating hands raised
to Heaven, while "Thy will be done!" yet trembled
on the lip. In vain the anguished parents strove
to hide from each other the dismal forebodings which
filled their souls. The averted look, the stifled sigh,
the listless step, the sudden start, the vacant yet
searching eye, all betrayed the secret of those hearts
which for the first time were closed against each other.
At length the bolt fell, and by one stroke these hearts
were laid bare. The ship had foundered, and every
soul on board had perished! A plank, on which were
a few letters of her name, and a shattered boat, had
been picked up, and all was told. In the ocean depths
all had gone down, and many a wave since then had
dashed over the trackless spot where lay the young,
the brave, the loved—their tale a secret till that day
when the seas shall give up their dead.

> " Oh, were her tale of sorrow known
> 'Twere something to the breaking heart,

The pang of doubt would then be gone,
  And Fancy's endless dreams depart.
It may not be !—there is no ray
  By which her doom we may explore ;
We only know she sail'd away,
  And ne'er was seen, nor heard of more !"

Ah ! who can tell the anguish of a parent's heart sorrowing for the loss of their child? He only to whom all hearts are open, and who, remembering we are clay, forbids not those fond and mournful recollections with which we invest the perished form of the object of our love. Alas ! how does our startled fancy recoil from the first dread thought, and seek to cheat itself, by conjuring up, and enthroning anew, that image in our hearts which our reason sternly tells us is no more. No more ! the being all life and motion, and strength and beauty, whom we have so lately held to our breasts—whose voice even now sounds as sweetest music in our ear—in whose eyes we were wont to read as in a book—whose vacant seat still stands before us—whose thousand mementoes lie scattered around us—is that being indeed gone from the face of this bright earth for ever? Still, still would we seek the living among the dead ! In vain does human sympathy seek to pour its oil on the dark and troubled waters of affliction. 'Tis a hand divine can alone stem the torrent which overflows our soul ; 'tis a voice from heaven alone that can speak peace to our stricken hearts, when it tells us the dust we so loved on earth, whether it be scattered o'er the trackless desert, or be buried in the dark and fathomless abysses of the ocean, He will again build up in immortal beauty, and restore to that divine inheritance, where there is no more sorrow or death. Oh, blessed are they who, even in the anguish of their spirits, can bring their fainting hearts to His footstool, and there, with meek submission, say, "Not my will, but Thine be done." With such, "weeping may endure for a night, but joy cometh in the morning."

CHAPTER XXIX

In the affliction of the bereaved family it would have been no small comfort to them to have been visited occasionally by a faithful and spiritual-minded pastor, one who could have soothed their downcast spirits, and have strengthened their religious faith, and have recalled to their startled minds those cheering promises which in the first moments of anguish are so apt, even by the best, to be forgotten or but faintly remembered. But it was not in the house of mourning that Mr. M'Dow's presence was wont to shine. He called, indeed, but he saw only Captain Malcolm. "Sorrow is a sacred thing," not to be subjected to the common eye, and Mrs. Malcolm and Lucy felt as though the presence of Mr. M'Dow would only have profaned the memory of the departed, and harrowed up the feelings of the living. Sorrow had indeed sunk deep into the soul of the bereft mother. Ronald had been unconsciously the idol of her affections, and in the anguish of losing him she felt that he had been the dearest to her of all her children. She bowed, indeed, with meek submission to the will of Heaven, but the elasticity of her mind seemed gone.

All was calm and resigned, but it was the calm of
deep suffering, the resignation of a silenced heart.
Often in the dead of night there seemed to break
upon her startled ear the sound of the raging sea, and
the tempestuous winds, and the cry—the piercing cry,
of her drowning boy; and then to wake to silence
and sad conviction that all was not a dream! But
prayer would again bring down its holy calm to the
troubled mind, and the pious mourner would meekly
confess that it was good for her to be thus brought,
even by the hand of sorrow, to the throne of grace.
It was at this time that a visit from the good Mr.
Stuart came to cheer and invigorate her drooping
spirit.

He was a man whose whole appearance and deportment were so emblematic of the sanctity of his character, that even a child would have felt that there
was a holy man. He was of a pale, thoughtful cast of
countenance, but his thoughts were evidently such as
savoured more of heavenly things than low-born
cares, for its expression was at once elevated and
benign. He

" Bore his great commission in his look,"

and the sense of that sacred trust gave a certain
dignified humility to the apostolic simplicity of his
demeanour.

It is difficult to describe a piety so consistent in
all its parts, and so unvarying in its practice, which
sheds a living unction over the whole character,

whose influence is deeply felt in the daily intercourse
of life, but whose results do not dazzle by any sudden or powerful impression. Human life, indeed, is
composed of such an unceasing succession of minute
occurrences and humble duties and undignified occupations, that it would seem tedious and trivial to
narrate the course of even a good man's one well-
spent day; but, as some one has well observed, it is
fidelity in the aggregate of these little things that
forms the true solidity and greatness of the Christian
character. Even so it was with the venerable pastor
of Auchnagoil. Grandeur, worldly grandeur, would
have heard with a disdainful smile the simple annals
of his obscure life; but how much of moral grandeur
was there in the self-immolation of his Christian
course—a course at once humble and sublime! He
was indeed a "living sermon" of the truths he taught,
and to inculcate these truths by precept and example
was the sole aim of his consecrated office. To succour
the distressed, to minister to the sick, to help the
poor, to comfort the mourner, to cheer the penitent,
to reclaim the wanderer—for this he laboured in the
far-extended district which his parish contained; for
this he visited the distant village and the lonely hut,
seeking out each individual of his widely-scattered
flock; for this he braved the winter's flood and summer's heat; for this he crossed many a rough and
tempestuous ferry, and climbed many a rugged and
dreary mountain, and traversed many an unfrequented
glen.

" Yet would not grace one spark of pride allow,
   Or cry, ' Stand off, I'm holier far than thou !'"

For he was no wild enthusiast, nor narrow-minded
sectarian, nor hot-headed zealot ; but he was a man,
plain, artless, and simple in deed and word : his highest gifts meekness, temperance, patience, faith, and
love, and the highest words wherein he taught them
were words from the Book of God.

But though Mr. Stuart's character was thus fair
and consistent in the eyes of others, in his own estimation how differently did he view it ! "Unworthy
and unprofitable servant that I am," he would exclaim
to himself, " how mixed are all my motives ! How
selfish are my best intentions ! How polluted my
purest affections ! How deficient are my best works !
But Thou hast told the weary troubled soul to come
unto Thee, and Thou wilt give it peace :" peace, how
different and how superior to the outward satisfaction
of the vain, self-satisfied, worldly mind !

Such are the feelings of the true Christian. His
warfare is within, and in proportion as he is enabled
by the eye of faith to discern the holiness and purity
of God, so shall he also perceive the guilt and frailty
of his own imperfect nature.

He spoke, and his words came like balm to the
wounded hearts of the sorrowing parents, for they
came fraught with cheering promises, and glorious
hopes, of eternal life. He bade them turn their
thoughts from the contemplation of that on which,
at such a time, our thoughts, alas ! are too prone to

dwell, even the material part of that immortal being once so precious in our sight.

He had known Ronald, and he knew the good seed that had been sown in his young heart, and felt convinced that in the hour of peril that would not have failed him.

"I am far from saying that you ought not to weep for him you have lost," said the good pastor, while his own eyes were moistened with sorrow. "Such a state, even if attainable, would be far from desirable; it would defeat the purpose for which God hath been pleased to bestow upon us warm and kindly affections. We know that afflictions are sent not as punishments, but as messengers of love to lead us unto Him."

"I feel it is so," said Mrs. Malcolm meekly; "but still, my rebellious heart——" She stopped, but struggling to overcome her emotion, added, "Alas! I often think, had my boy but died in my arms, I could have yielded him up with less reluctance to the will of God. I feel as if I could then have said with greater sincerity than I fear I do now, 'The Lord gave, and the Lord hath taken away; blessed be the name of the Lord.'"

"That is a natural feeling," said Mr. Stuart; "the horrors of death always come aggravated to our minds when accompanied, as in this case, with anything of suddenness or mystery; we are then apt to imagine it more dreadful than any reality, forgetting that 'the Lord is mightier than the noise of many waters, yea, than the waves of the sea.' True, 'the silver cord is loosened, and the golden bowl is broken,' and the dust has returned to the dust, but the spirit has also returned to God who gave it. What matters it, then, *how* we enter on the valley of the shadow of death, when we know we are to pass through it by the light of those Divine footsteps which have trod it before us? They still remain, and will remain till time shall be no more, to guide us to our heavenly home, where this 'corruptible shall put on incorruption, and this mortal shall be clothed with immortality;' where we shall enter on 'glory such as eye hath not seen, nor ear heard, and which it hath not entered into the heart of man to conceive.'"

"With such glorious prospects of perfect and endless felicity at the end of the Christian course," said Captain Malcolm, "it indeed matters little whether we enter upon them by lingering decay, or by a stroke of the sword, or the shock of a wave; whichever it is, we must believe that it is the means our Heavenly Father deemed the best; and in that belief let us humbly acquiesce."

"And in that simple act of acquiescence we shall feel a sure and certain rest for our souls," said Mr. Stuart. "Time, it has been truly said, indeed obliterates sorrow from the worldly heart, and leaves it no better than it found it; but religion beautifies and sanctifies affliction in the heart of the Christian, and causes it even to bring forth new and more abundant graces; the fountain of bitter water may yet become the well of living water springing up to everlasting life."

"Feeling and acknowledging as I do the truth of these things," said Mrs. Malcolm, "how weak, how sinful, it seems to allow my soul to be thus cast down! I know the conditions on which every blessing is bestowed—that we must one day part with it; and I believe that God knows best when that parting should be; and yet," she added, while the tears flowed silently down her cheek, "my son! my son!"

"Do not judge yourself thus strictly," said the good pastor; "you do not mourn as those who have no hope; the spirit is willing to believe all things, though the flesh is weak to endure them. You believe that God *gives* in love, believe that He also *takes* in love, and your heart will not be troubled beyond measure; for 'light is sown for the righteous, and gladness for the upright in heart;' be of good courage, then, for God's promise is not made in vain: 'They who sow in tears shall reap in joy.'"

Such, though imperfectly detailed, was the tenor of the faithful minister's conversation with the afflicted parents; and he left them soothed by his visit, and cheered by the promise of repeating it as often as his wanderings brought him near their dwelling.

Perhaps the first pleasurable emotions of an outward kind to which the bereaved heart is awakened are to be found in the deep and simple enjoyment of the beauties of nature. And where to the reflective mind and cultivated taste are not these beauties to be found? Even on the barren mountain and the dreary moor, on the ever-flowing waters and the ever-changing clouds,

> " No plot so narrow, be but Nature there,
> No waste so vacant, but may well employ
> Each faculty of sense, and keep the heart
> Awake to love and beauty ! "

To those whose eyes and hearts have long been closed, whether by sickness or sorrow, but are again opened to the soothing influence and gentle harmony of nature,

> " The meanest floweret of the vale,
> The simplest note that swells the gale,
> The common earth, the air, the skies, "

are indeed to them " as opening paradise," and insensibly they " feel that they are happier than they know."

CHAPTER XXX

WHILE the mansion of Lochdhu was thus darkened by the shadow of death, we may turn to the habitation of Glenroy, which was basking in the full blaze of prosperity. Ronald's mournful fate, however, had not failed to excite its due share of sorrow and of sympathy. Even the Chief's animosity had been greatly softened, and the two boys remembered with shame and compunction their unkind treatment of him at their last meeting; while Edith shed many a tear of remorse and regret over the memory of the loved companion of her childhood. She was again permitted to renew her intimacy with the family at Inch Orran, and her affectionate heart felt as though its only reparation could be in devoting herself to the consolation of the mourners.

Years rolled on, and the young people either gradually outgrow their childish faults, or exchanged them —as is often the case—for others less obvious to common perception; but so it was, the spoiled, forward, petulant boys were now transformed into handsome, spirited, pleasing youths, the pride and delight of the Chieftain—the admired and applauded of all his friends and followers. Not that Norman possessed any distinguishing traits of excellence in himself, for he inherited much of his father's character, along with his features. He was proud, overbearing, and selfish, but he was handsome, light-hearted, active, and brave, which, with his figure and fortune, were requisites sufficient to ensure his popularity as a future Chief. Had it been possible for him to have been eclipsed in his father's eyes or house, he certainly would have been so by his cousin Reginald, who was a perfect model of manly beauty, and seemed in his person to have realised all that Grecian sculpture had imagined of faultless form and feature. The materials of his mind and character seemed also of a richer and nobler stamp than Norman's. He had good feelings, great sensibility, an ardent, romantic imagination, and a high-spirited scorn of everything mean and base ; and although he was at the same time headstrong, self-willed, and impetuous, the slave of impulse and the sport of passion, yet, as his impulse often led him to what was good, and his passion was a mere gust, these in early life showed scarcely as defects, but seemed merely the natural exuberance of youthful blood and unchecked spirits. The seeds of many good qualities had been sown in him by nature, but not much had been done by education to bring them to maturity ; the tares had been suffered to grow up with the wheat, and both were now so completely blended together that it would have required no common skill and pains to have distinguished and

separated them.   The attempt, however, had not
been made, and which should predominate, would
depend upon the circumstances in which he might be
placed, and the temptations to which he might be
exposed.   Hitherto, nothing had occurred to call forth
any of the latent feelings of the heart, or proclaim the
master-passion of the soul, for his life had merely
been that of an indulged and pampered boy, who had
never known a trial, or had a wish ungratified.   So
bright and sunny an existence, then, could scarcely fail
to produce a pleasing influence on the naturally good
temper and high spirits, as the soil will be richest in gay
flowers where the harrow has never entered.   But,

> ———" not only by the warmth
> And soothing sunshine of delightful things
> Do minds grow up and flourish."

Alas! who has ever beheld the endowments of
nature and the advantages of fortune realise in the
happiness of their possessor the splendid visions they
seemed destined to fulfil?

Mr. Ellis had frequently urged on Glenroy the propriety of sending the young men to finish their studies
at an English university : but his remonstrances were
always answered by a quotation from Dr. Johnson,
the only one the Chief had ever burdened his memory
with, that "an English education could only tame a
Highland Chieftain into insignificance."—"And, sir,
my son shall not be tamed into insignificance at any
of your English universities."

Mr. Ellis was therefore obliged to give up the

point; and having written on the subject to Sir Angus, he only waited to receive his instructions as to the future plans to be adopted for the completing of Reginald's education before he took leave of his pupils, and relinquished what was now a mere nominal office—that of their preceptor.

Glenroy liked his daughter as well as he could like anything incapable of holding or transmitting the chieftainship, yet still she was rather an insignificant person in his estimation. He was, however, pleased to hear on all hands that Edith was reckoned the prettiest girl in the county, and that Reginald and she had already formed an attachment to each other; as that was at once securing a good establishment for her, and saving himself all trouble as to her future disposal. Although it has been said, the love which grows by degrees is more nearly allied to friendship than to passion, nevertheless the attachment of the cousins seemed to form an exception to this general rule, for *their* love had continued to grow with their growth, and strengthen with their strength.

As the attachment was sanctioned by both sides of the house, the course of their love, contrary to that of all other loves, seemed destined to run in a very smooth channel, and it was already settled that the marriage should take place upon Reginald's attaining the age of twenty-one. No envious cloud, therefore, marred the brightness of their horizon; they stood on "the threshold of life," and all life's fairest prospects lay spread out before them.

A too strict similarity of character is perhaps not favourable either to love or friendship, and the difference of dispositions in the young lovers seemed only such as would give greater charm to their attachment. Reginald was all fire and impetuosity, while Edith was all gentleness and timidity. With her father and brother she found little congeniality of mind, or interchange of sentiment, for their characters were cast in a different mould from hers; but there was much of a kindred nature in the more romantic and imaginative mind of her cousin, and she loved him with her whole heart, as the only being with whom she could hold unreserved communion. Possessed of deep sensibility, and dwelling with the object of her earliest affection amid scenes of grandeur and beauty, calculated to call forth and nourish all that was romantic and tender in her nature, it was not surprising that Edith should yield to the dominion of an artless affection, unsullied by the tarnish of the world, and live in a creation of her own. Outwardly calm and serene, all the powers of her mind were concentrated in those feelings, which, hidden from the common eye, had entwined themselves with every fibre of her heart, and choked each plant of humble, wholesome influence.

Her mind, though sensitive and feminine, was naturally strong, but it was relaxed and enfeebled from the constant habit of looking to Reginald as the ruler and arbiter of her very thoughts. The materials of excellence and happiness had been largely bestowed upon her, but she was ignorant of their value, and confided them wholly to the keeping of another. It was to Reginald she looked for her daily portion of happiness; it was in his heart she anchored her trust, and there sought her abiding place of rest and refuge.

ONE of the many gifts Mrs. Macauley had received from nature was her faculty of dreaming, which she piqued herself upon in no small degree; and although it never had been productive of any good either to herself or others, yet she nevertheless entertained the utmost respect and veneration for this endowment, and placed the most perfect reliance on her own oracles.

Glenroy, of course, affected to treat her dreams and visions as he did herself, with great contempt, but secretly he had rather a relish for them, especially as Mrs. Macauley was not a public dreamer; her dreams always related to his house and family, and there was therefore a sort of importance annexed to the idea of having his own peculiar dreamer in his household. It was a piece of state almost equal to that of keeping a dwarf, or a fool, or a henchman, or a piper, or any other of those prerogatives of grandeur.

The natural contempt, however, which is felt in this enlightened age for old wives' dreams, and even for young women's fables, together with the profound respect we entertain for the understanding of our

readers, withholds us from relating upon this occasion
the cabalistic narrative with which Mrs. Macauley
one morning regaled the breakfast table; suffice it to
say, it was all a dream should or could be. It was
grand, confused, dark, incoherent, contradictory, senseless, and sublime; and in spite of the ludicrous tones
and gestures of the narrator, it produced more or less
an impression upon the minds of her audience. From
the cloud of her misty imagination various distinct
images emerged. There was a large raven with a
wedding-ring in its mouth; there was a troubled
sea, and a dove with a bleeding breast; there was a
shroud, two coffins, and a grave; and there was the
minister, Mr. M'Dow, all dressed in white, standing
in the kirk with Miss Edith, who was all dressed in
black, and somebody else, with such a mist upon
them she could not make out who it was, etc. etc. etc.

A few days after this memorable dream there
arrived accounts of the death of Sir Angus Malcolm.
He had died of the fever of the country, just as he
was on the point of embarking for Britain. He had
had sufficient warning of his danger, however, to
admit of his making arrangements as to the management of his affairs, and the disposal of his son. Sir
Angus seemed to have felt that Reginald had been
left too long to Glenroy's superintendence, for he
directed that he should as soon as possible be entered
at one of the English universities, under the superintendence of Mr. Ellis. After spending two years at
college, he was to set out on a tour to the Continent,

accompanied by Mr. Ellis, to remain abroad until he came of age. He was then to return home and celebrate the event among his own people, in a manner befitting the heir of an ancient house and noble property. A sanction was given to his marriage with Edith, and a hope expressed that he would then settle for life in his own country.

"Oh, what a mercy it is I had the good sense to tell my dream before this came to pass!" whispered Mrs. Macauley to Benbowie; "for if I had not told it, nobody would have believed me now. Oh! what wonderful creatures we are! the great black raven! I cannot forget it! Little did I think that was Sir Angus, poor man! and the wedding ring that he had in his mouth too! was just to show like, that he was coming over to marry his son to Miss Edith."

"On my conscience, he was a very lucky man, to have cleared his estate before he died!" responded Benbowie.

Reginald showed much warmth of feeling on the occasion of his loss; but from the length of the separation that had taken place between the father and son, it was not to be expected that his sorrow should be lasting; and in due time he was comforted.

Glenroy had now arrived at the period of life when any change in the domestic arrangement is dreaded as the severest of evils, and the more so, as the gout had now become so frequent in its attacks as to render him more than ever dependent on domestic society. It may therefore be supposed Sir Angus's injunction did not accord with his inclinations, and he as usual vented his displeasure in apostrophising Benbowie.

"Finish his studies! finish his fiddlesticks! *I* never finished my studies—*I* never was at any of their English universities. I should be glad to know what my son could learn at an English university! Reginald may go if he chooses, but I'll be hanged if I'll allow Norman to accompany him. He shall not be tamed into insignificance if I can help it. It is a fine preparation for a Highland Chief to be cooped up in one of their musty colleges with a pack of priests and dominies, and sailing about their plainstones in a black gown and a trencher skull-cap!"

"Very true," responded Benbowie, "on my conscience, it's all very true—a philabeg would set him better."

"A fine thing, to be sure, for a Highland Chief to have B.A. tacked to his name!"

"On my conscience, a man need not go so far to learn to cry BA!" said Benbowie.

"And then the scheme of sending him to the Continent is, if possible, still worse," continued Glenroy. "What can he learn there but to dance and speak gibberish, or to be running after old bridges and broken statues, when he ought to be building new bridges and entertaining the gentlemen of the county? Statues! a pack of rubbish. I would not let one of them within my door."

"On my conscience, I think you're quite right,

Glenroy. I would not give a three-year-old stot for
any stuccy babbies that ever were made."

Such was the style of colloquy held by these two
worthy gentlemen; and had Reginald been inclined
to disregard his father's dying injunctions, plausible
pretexts would not have been wanting for him to
have at least postponed the fulfilling of them. But
Reginald was eager to enter upon the course pointed
out to him, and Mr. Ellis lost no time in taking the
necessary steps for getting him entered at Oxford,
whither he was to accompany him. Nothing could
induce Glenroy to part with Norman; and as Norman
attached no great ideas of pleasure to a student's life,
he was easily prevailed upon to relinquish it, and to
remain at home his own master, so called, though
still more the master of all around him.

Edith beheld with meek and silent sorrow the
time approach for the departure of Reginald: to be
separated from him for more than a few days was an
evil she had never contemplated; and now weeks
and months were to drag their slow course along,
while Reginald and she were to dwell apart. Oh!
what a solitude would hers be! the dreariest, the
saddest of all solitudes—the solitude of the heart.

Reginald's sorrow at parting with Edith, it might
be supposed, was pretty much swallowed up in the
anticipated novelty and variety that awaited him;
and he strove to comfort and reassure her, as he
talked cheerfully of the shortness of the time of his
probation. Three years were nothing; besides, he

should certainly make a point of seeing her often again before he left England; and, at any rate, he should write to her constantly, every day, that she might never for a single day forget him. He would then reiterate his own vows of eternal love and constancy, and call upon Edith to repeat the same, while each favourite haunt was visited and hallowed in their imaginations by the pensive thought that it would be long ere they should again revisit them together. Thus the intervening days glided away with the rapidity of a stream, and thus feeling stamped the value of ages upon the duration of moments. Then swiftly came the parting hour—

——" that hour,
When love first feels its own o'erwhelming power."

"This, Edith, is a ring of betrothment," said Reginald, as he placed one upon her finger. "Remember, there it must remain till I exchange it for a bridal one. Edith, do you promise?" and he held her hand locked in his, while Edith tried to smile an affirmative through her parting tears.

Again and again the farewell was spoken: again and again Edith was pressed to his heart, and now he was gone, and she was left alone.

CHAPTER XXXII

By degrees the loss of Reginald's society was almost atoned for to Edith by the new enjoyment of corresponding with him. It was a different, a more abstracted and concentrated feeling, but scarcely a less delightful one than that which she used to enjoy in his presence. True, he was no longer with her; but then, what though the image itself was gone? The impression remained almost as vivid as the reality, and she had his ring, his picture, his letters—those mute but eloquent pledges of his faith; the almost daily assurances of his love, the oft-repeated vows, the fond anticipations of their future happiness. Deep and earnest in her love, but timid and reserved in her manners, her heart expatiated more freely upon paper than ever it had done in the daily intercourse of her whole life, so that she was ready to exclaim—

> " O Fortune, ...
> . . . . . . thou canst not divide
> Our bodies so, but that our hearts are tied,
> And we can love by letters still, and gifts,
> And thoughts, and dreams."

Thus was her mind kept in a state of constant excitement, more inimical to its repose than the presence even of the object of her affection. Imagination left to itself had awakened in her that extreme sensibility so destructive to happiness, which, in seeming to give us " a sweet existence in another's being," is only fixing more firmly its barbed arrow in the heart.

So passed days, weeks, and months; and when the college vacations permitted, Reginald revisited with delight his early home. Absence, so far from abating the attachment of the youthful lovers, seemed if possible to have augmented it, and the lapse of time had only added new attractions to each, in the eyes of the other.

But now a longer period of absence was to intervene, and seas were to divide them. The time for Reginald's visit to the Continent had arrived, and painful was the parting of the lovers. Yet the sanguine spirit of Reginald imparted comfort to Edith, as he fondly reminded her that two out of the three years of their probation were over, and that this parting should be the last.

Many was the fond and impassioned letter she received from Reginald, and many were the tender and confiding ones she wrote in reply. At length his letters became less frequent, but that was not surprising, considering that he was constantly moving from one place to another; and then when they did come, they were as affectionate as ever. He still reminded Edith of their engagement; he still assured her that time and absence only rendered her dearer to him, and that he longed impatiently for the time when he was to return to her to part no more. But after receiving one of those letters, breathing all that a fond lover could say to the idol of his heart, a long pause ensued; and then, when the next came, Edith thought, but it must be fancy, that the style was changed. It was short, too; but he pleaded a head-ache—perhaps he was ill and concealed it from her; and many an anxious day and sleepless night she passed, till another arrived; it was still shorter, but he was just setting out upon an excursion, and had not time to write more than a mere line, to assure dear Edith he was well. Other long and dreary chasms ensued, and were but faintly attempted to be filled up by meagre letters, full of little else than apologies for their rarity, and promises of writing oftener and longer ones. But the same excuses continued; one time the heat was so excessive he could scarcely hold the pen, then he was interrupted by a friend, or he was just returned from a fatiguing excursion, or he was setting out upon a pleasure tour, or the time was now drawing near when he should be returning to Scotland, and therefore it was unnecessary to say much more at present.

So absorbed was Edith in anxiety about Reginald, that she was quite unconscious of the attentions, or rather intentions, of another lover, in the person of the young Lord Allonby, who, from partaking occasionally of Glenroy's hospitalities, had now become a more frequent visitor, and, having no small opinion of

himself, he concluded he had only to pay his addresses
to have them instantly accepted. Edith's ideas of
love were much too romantic to enable her to construe
the flimsy gallantry of a modern fine gentleman into
anything like a serious passion, and her surprise at
his lordship's hasty and self-assured proposals could
only be surpassed by his amazement at the rejection
of his suit. It was one that, in other circumstances,
Glenroy would have been gratified with, but as Edith
was engaged to Reginald, he could only have the
satisfaction of chuckling over it in private, or throwing out innuendoes in public.

Thus wore away time; but still Reginald came not,
and his birthday, the day of his coming of age, which
his father had recommended him to celebrate at home
among his own people—that day which he himself had
so fondly anticipated, and which Edith had looked forward to with no common interest—that day passed
unnoticed, unheeded on his part, and on hers only
recorded as a day of disappointment and gloom.

Glenroy chafed and fumed at this disrespectful
delay. Norman, still more sanguine and impatient
in the self-assumed anticipations of his cousin's return,
had scarcely been restrained more than once from setting out to meet him. Mrs. Macauley dreamed and
wondered in vain. Neither dreams nor wondering
could solve the mystery. Edith sighed and feared,
she knew not what, for her heart was too simple and
guileless to harbour suspicion. She had heard and
read of such a thing as inconstancy, but to associate

it with the idea of Reginald never entered her imagination, or if it did, it was instantly dismissed.   She
had only to recall the remembrance of past days, to
look at his picture, to meet the gaze of those fond
eyes, to read his letters fraught with vows of everlasting love, and all her doubts fled as by the touch
of a talisman.   Thus imagination still held sway over
her, while time, as it moved slowly along,

> " Deposited upon the silent shore
> Of memory, images and precious thoughts,"

which it was the delight of her solitary hours to
treasure up in the inmost recesses of her heart.   She
knew not—who in early life does know?—that such
treasurings up of the frail records of human love
prove but as landmarks to note where the tide of
passion and of sorrow hath been.

CHAPTER XXXIII.

YEARS had passed away since Ronald Malcolm had left his native home, when, one bright summer's day, a tall and sunburnt youth, coarsely and scantily clad, but with something wild and noble in his air and aspect, stood on the shores of Lochdhu, and for a moment surveyed its dark mountains and roaring waters, with the look of one to whom they bore no common interest.

That youth was Ronald, and many a sad sight his young eyes had looked upon since last he left the spot where he now stood, and many "a strange and moving accident" burned within him, to relate to the dear ones he had left. He had to tell of the wonders of the raging sea and the angry heavens, which had shivered the stately ship, and sunk so many "high hearts and brave" beneath the devouring billows. He had to tell of his own escape, with others of the gallant crew, and of the hunger, the thirst, the cold, the heat, the hardships, and privations they had endured, and under which many of those brave spirits had sunk. He had to tell of the survivors reaching the coast of Africa, only to become captives to the

wild and lawless natives, by whom they were driven
as slaves to the interior of those wild, desert, and
unexplored regions, where his companions, one by
one, fell victims to the severity of their lot. But his
youth and dauntless spirit, his habits of endurance
and activity, the flexibility and sweetness of his
temper, had, under the blessing of a superintending
Providence, enabled him to bear the heavy load
assigned him, and had even gained him favour in the
eyes of his barbarous captors. How many a summer's
day and winter's night would it take to tell of all
that he had seen and thought, and felt and suffered
and done, during his dreary captivity! and how, even
in the depths of his desolation, he had ever cherished
that trust divine which a mother's lips had early
breathed into his infant soul! Then came his escape,
with all its dangers and privations, his wanderings by
land, his perils by sea; all these, and much more, had
Ronald to tell; but all was forgotten in the tumult
of his feelings as he stood once more on his native
shore, and looked on his father's house, and recalled
the dear familiar scenes of his childhood.

Memory flew over the intervening years, and all
faded from his mind save the loved ones, whose looks
and tones had sometimes haunted his very heart to
agony, as fancy pictured the joys of home to the far-
distant captive. And now in a few minutes he should
behold them again; already he seemed to feel their
kisses on his lip, their tears of gladness on his cheek,
their arms enfolding him; once more he was pressed

to a mother's beating heart! All these thoughts
rushed through the young adventurer's mind, as he
gazed for a moment on the well-remembered features
of his mountain home. These were unchanged, for
their stern and massive outline was unchangeable;
but something of a still wilder, a more desolate and
mournful cast, seemed to dwell upon them, for all was
silent and voiceless. Ronald stayed not to conjecture
or to fear, but in an instant he was at the house—his
father's house! He had crossed the threshold of his
once-happy home, but still there was none to meet
him, none to welcome him. Everything was dis-
placed and in disorder, and he sought in several of the
rooms before he discovered an old purblind woman,
who seemed the sole inhabitant of the house he had
left so full of life and joy, and youth and beauty.

In this ancient crone he recognised an old pensioner
of his mother's, more famed for her fidelity and attachment to the family than for the sweetness of her
temper or the urbanity of her manners. In a voice
choking with agitation, he inquired for Captain Malcolm, for the family; but he had to repeat the question three times before he could obtain an answer; for,
though not positively deaf, her ear was slow to catch
a strange accent, and Ronald's voice and accent were
both so totally changed that his own mother could
scarcely have recognised them. At length, in a sharp
Highland tone, he received the satisfactory reply of—

"Captain Malcolm?—ay! whar should he be but
in his ain hoose?"

"But this was his house," said Ronald, reviving at this information, scanty as it was.

"Ay, and wha says it's no his hoose, noo? but it's no his dwelling-hoose, if you mean that; he's ower great a man to dwell here noo—ay, that he is!"

The truth now flashed upon Ronald, and, with a pang he said, "What!—he now lives at Inch Orran, I suppose?"

"To be sure—whar else should he live? But sit down, sit down. You maun be a stranger here, it seems, frae the Low Country? Maybe, a friend o' the faamily?"

"Thank you; but first tell me, is Captain Malcolm well, and my——, and all of them, are they all well?" And Ronald's lips quivered as he put the question.

"Oo, surely, surely—they're all well. What should ail them?"

"Nothing, nothing. And my——" Ronald's heart fluttered as he thought of his mother; and he could not find voice to name the name dearest to his heart.

The old woman went on. "No, no, there's nothing ails them noo; they've gotten a'thing they can want. Och ay, God be praised! they are very prosperous noo, an' very happy."

"They have met with some good fortune, then, it seems?" said Ronald, trying to speak with composure.

"Och ay! 'deed an' they have done that, and well they deserve it. Not but what they paid for it, too, poor craaters! ay, that they did. God knows, their fine fortune cost them sore hearts at the time;

but that's past—an' noo, what should they be but pleased an' happy?"

Ronald's heart heaved, and he was silent a few moments, then said, "But they have been afflicted—they have suffered?"

"Och! 'deed they were that; they were sore distrest, poor people! at the droonin' o' their boy—a fine boy—a pretty boy he was—och ay!" Here old Nanny groaned, and wiped her eyes with the corner of her apron.

"But you say they are happy now—they have forgotten him?" said Ronald, with emotion.

"Oh! surely, surely—God be thank't, he's forgotten noo, an' it's time—'deed is it—och ay! And we little know what's for our good in this world; for it was God's merciful providence, after all, that the boy was ta'en, or they tell me they would ha'e been but a puir needfu' faamily the day—'deed would they!"

A strange pang shot through Ronald's heart. "What a vile unfeeling creature," thought he, "to talk in such a manner!" and he was about to leave the house, when old Nanny resumed—

"Och ay! Providence was really kind in that particular, for the droonin' o' the boy, poor thing, (that ever I should say't!) has been the savin' o' that whole faamily, 'deed has it! And weel they deserve it, for they're a worthy well-doin' faamily; and Inch Orran himself is a good man, and does a deal o' good, that he does; and he is a reall blessin' to the country —that he is!"

"But he might have been a blessing to the country although his son had not been drowned," said Ronald.

"No, no—they tell me not. That if the boy had lived, he would have keepit his father a poor man a' his days; and wou'dna that have been a sin and a shame! No that it wad hae been the poor boy's fault, poor thing, but the fault o' them that would have made him keep his father's head below the water. Och! it was God's providence to tak' the boy out of his worthy father's way; and noo a'thing's as it should be, and he has gotten his ain, honest man; and long, long may he enjoy it!"

"And you say they are all quite well,—and—— happy?" said Ronald, his heart swelling, in spite of the contempt he tried to feel for the unfeeling narrator.

"Ay, ay! they are that. Happy they are, and happy may they be; and shouldna they be happy when there's gawn to be a grand marriage amang them? Miss Lucy, that's her that's the eldest o' the faamily, isna she gawn to get a husband, and a braw one, too—no less than the young Laird of Dunross? No but what Miss Lucy is well worthy of him and the best in the land—ay, by my troth she is; but she wadna ha'e gotten him wantin' the tocher; for the auld Laird's ower fond o' the siller to let his son tak' a tocherless lass. Och ay, shame till him! Wasna poor Miss Lucy maist broken-hearted because he wouldna let his son get her when she was the poor man's daughter? And the Captain wouldna let him tak' her wantin' his father's will; and the poor young craaters were just beside themselves like; and so the young man went into the army, and has been in the Indies, but noo he's come back; and they're so happy. And the Captain—that's Inch Orran—is to give her five thousand gold guineas on her weddin'-day, they tell me, forbye this hoose that they're comin' to dwell in; and him paintin' it all from top to bottom, and makin' everything so genteel for them; and all comes o' the droonin' o' the bonny laddie! Och ay!"

Many little circumstances that had taken place before he left home here darted into Ronald's mind, in confirmation of old Nanny's words. Young Dunross and Lucy had been lovers even then, and want of fortune on her part had been the only obstacle to their union; and now that was removed, and he had returned only to blast their happiness!

"But what if he has not been drowned—what if he should yet return?" said he, with agitation.

"Och, sorrow bit he'll ever return noo, poor bairn; and it would na do for him to come back in the body noo—'deed, an' he wad be but a black sight; no, no, that it would not—he's been owre lang dead to come back noo—'deed has he, och ay! he's dead and gone, an' it would na do to bring him back again—no, no; wae I was when I heard o' the poor thing's droonin', but I was ignorant then. I did not know that it was God's providence to set up the faamily like by that same means, and make them all so comfortable and genteel and happy, och ay!"

"And my mother?" said Ronald faintly, as he covered his eyes with his hand, while his whole frame thrilled with emotion.

"The mother?" said Nanny, catching the sound imperfectly. "Ay, his mother—that's the leddy hersell, you'll mean? och, God only knows the mother's sorrow, och ay! But she's a quiet craater, and she knew whose hand it was that was upon her—ay, that she did—and so she demeaned hersell like a good Christian as she is; but they tell me she has never had her ain colour since."

Tears forced their way through Ronald's fingers; he started up, and was hurrying away, when Nanny interposed, rather unwilling to part so soon with a visitor from whom she had as yet extracted no information in return, and visitors to Nanny were few and far between.

"And what's taking you away, my lad, in such a hurry? canna you sit doon a wee and rest you, and tak' a drap this warm day?"

"The day is far spent, and I have a long walk before me," said Ronald.

"Ay? maybe ye'll be going to Inch Orran? I'm thinking you'll be a friend o' our young laird's?—that's Mr. Angus—for I guess by your tongue you're a gentle."

"Is he at home?" asked Ronald, waiving the question and the compliment.

"I'm thinkin' so that he's at home the noo; but he goes away for months and months at a time to one

o' their places in the Low Country, where young gentlemen go to learn everything—they're no schools—
they're universals, or something like that; you'll
ken what I mean; for he's very bookish, and they
tell me he will be a great man yet, since his father
can give him such a grand education; but he's no such
a fine, roving, spirity craater as the 'tother poor boy
was—what a craater that was! Nothing feared him,
and he was so good-natured and so kind to everybody,
och ay! he would 'have run a mile to flit a sow,' as
they say. But, no doubt, he has got his reward noo,
though we cannot see it; for if he can but see what
a great blessin' his death has been to his faamily, I'm
sure he'll no begrudge it, wherever he be."

"Surely his family would be happier to have him
back again?" said Ronald, after a pause.

"Troth then, and to tell the truth, I'm no sure o'
that—no but what they were very fond of him, and
thought much of him when they had him; but now
you know, like good Christians, their minds are made
up to want him, and maybe they could na want other
things so well—och no. No, it would never do for
him to come back in the body, for they tell me if he
was to come alive again, the money would be all ta'en
from Inch Orran; and would not that be very hard
noo, when he's doing so much good with it? forbye
keepin' such a genteel hoose, is na he ga'en to build a
grand new one, and does na the leddy ride in her
own coach noo, and is na he setting out his childer so
well in the world, and himself upon a footin' wi' the

best in the land? ay, and the good that he's doin' is no to be told. No but what he's ower keen o' what they ca' improvements.—Och, sorrow tak' some o' thae improvements! They'll no leave a bunch o' heather in the country; but nae doot, he's doin' good, for a' that. Och! hunders and hunders are blessin' the day that made Inch Orran a rich man—'deed are they; but for that, mony's the poor craater that would ha'e been trailin' owre the saut sea wi' their wives and their childer, awa' frae a' their kith and kin, and toilin' their hearts out in a far-off land, if it had not pleased God to give Inch Orran the hand and the heart to help them—och ay, he's the one that will never drive the poor man off his land, as long as the water rins, and the heather grows—och, he's a blessed man, and blessed he will be, and the poor lad's death was a great blessing—och ay, 'deed was't."

Ronald's heart was brimming high; he abruptly wished old Nanny good day, and quitted the house.

CHAPTER XXXIV.

THE young wanderer proceeded on his way, but his mind was a chaos of contending emotions, for there are hearts of so generous a nature as to be more keenly alive to the sufferings of others than to their own.

"This, then, is my welcome!" said he to himself, in bitterness of spirit; "already forgotten, or rather remembered only as a riddance; and my return, it seems, instead of bringing joy, will only be felt as a misfortune; my very death to be the cause of rejoicing to hundreds! and *they—they* to be all so happy, while I——" Tears burst from his eyes as he thought how his heart had pined for the dear ones he had left. "And my mother! my mother! can she too have forgotten me?"

And on the bare supposition, he threw himself on the ground in an agony of grief, mortification, and disappointment, while a thousand wild thoughts rushed through his mind.

"And am I so selfish, then, as to wish to cause sorrow to those I love? and can I not bear to see them happy at my expense? But I will see them, I will satisfy myself that they *are* happy, and then—

they shall remain so, were it at the price of my heart's blood!"

Starting up, he pursued his course towards Inch Orran. As he came within the extensive bounds which he knew pertained to it, he everywhere read a confirmation of old Nanny's words, in the improvements he beheld. The glens were more thickly peopled, and with more comfortable-looking dwellings; mountains, which had once frowned in heather, were now smiling in verdure; dreary moors were now covered with young plantations; a neat church and schoolhouse stood where a wilderness had formerly spread; all denoted that the stream of wealth was indeed flowing in the channel of beneficence, and everywhere spreading its riches over the land. He entered several of the cottages, and all told the same tale— a happy and thriving peasantry had been redeemed from poverty and exile, and even while his own home was fondly remembered, and his sad fate lamented, still his death was regarded as a blessing.

"And all this I am come only to blast," thought Ronald, as he surveyed the goodly scene that stretched around him. "I come only to bring poverty and sorrow and exile to all these poor people, and to my own home! Oh! that is worst of all, even there I can bring no joy! But happen what will, they shall not have cause to mourn that I still live—if they are happy, if they are indeed happy, to them I will still be dead——" And, dashing the tears from his eyes, he hastened on his way.

Years had passed away, and with them the bitterness, though not the remembrance, of sorrow ; for
Ronald's name was still pronounced with emotion in
his family circle, and the blank he had left still remained a dreary chasm to the eye and the ear, accustomed to the animation of his presence, to his generous
affections, to his kindly accents, to his bright smiles,
to his "sweet laughter, and wild song, and footstep
free," and to all the charms and the treasures of his
opening mind. But there is no anguish, however
severe, that time and religion and reflection will not
gradually soften into a resignation so entire, as to the
casual observer to appear almost like forgetfulness.
And times there are—else who could bear the constant
woe and live?—when even the mother forgets the child
over whose grave she has shed so many a bitter tear,
and whose image, though shrouded from the common
eye, still lies buried in the depths of her own heart.

It was evening when Ronald reached Inch Orran,
and the setting sun was shedding its last glories on
the scene. His heart was keenly alive to outward
impressions, and dull must the soul have been that
could have gazed unmoved on such a spectacle. But
how doubly sweet to him, who had been the ship-
wrecked sea-boy, the captive in a far-distant land, the
slave beneath a burning sky, the wayworn houseless
wanderer, to stand upon his native land, and look on
such an earth, and such a heaven ! The sun seemed
as if melting away beneath its own bright effulgence.
The mountains gleamed with ever-changing hues of

gold and crimson and purple; each tufted isle and rock and tree shone in the "rich sadness" of eve's last splendour. Not a breath ruffled the surface of the water; not a sound broke the stillness of the air, save the distant bleating of the sheep, and the soft rippling of the waves as they crept gently along the shore, or broke with faint effort upon the bare fantastic roots of some stately beech, whose stem rose like a mast of gold from the bosom of the waters. But not all the pomp and glory of the scene could arrest the gaze of him whose eyes were fixed on the walls that contained the treasures of his heart, the first, the only objects of his young affections! He hastily drew near, then stopped, as if to restrain himself from rushing at once into their sight, and casting himself into their arms. And then the one cruel thought came like ice upon his heart to chill the warm gush of nature.

"I come to bring them all to poverty! Oh, if they have ceased to think of me—if I am forgotten—if my place is filled—would that I had died rather than that I should live to see them rue the day of my return! But they shall not. I will dig, toil, starve, but they shall be happy!"

He now stood amidst the ruins of Inch Orran, but the hand of taste had been there since he had visited them. A still greater portion of the old walls had fallen; but the rubbish had been removed, and the large openings gave light and air and cheerfulness to the dwelling-house, which was half hid by the jessamines and honeysuckles and roses that clustered around its windows. Ronald, with throbbing heart, leant against a part of the ancient tower, where once had been a window, but which was now merely an opening curtained with ivy. His heart beat as though it would have burst from his bosom. At one moment he had yielded to the passionate impulse to make himself known; but, long inured to habits of self-command, by a mighty effort he subdued the yearnings of nature, and repressed the feelings which strove for mastery. "I will wait—I will wait," he said to himself, while every fibre quivered to agony, and he gnawed his lip as if to enforce its silence. Opposite to where he stood was the family sitting-room, and from the spot he could plainly discern all that was passing within. But it was some time ere he could dispel the gathering mists from his eyes, so as to enable him to single out each dear one numbered in his heart. Ah !

> " There are no looks like those which dwell
> On long remember'd things !"

His eye was first attracted to his father, who sat nearest to him reading, but his back was towards him, and he could only perceive that his figure was thinner, and his hair grayer, than when he had parted from him. At one end of the room Lucy was seated at a piano, but it seemed as if merely an excuse for the lovers to be a little apart, for young Dunross leant on the back of her chair, and her sweet face was turned to him in conversation, while now and then she carelessly touched a few notes of the instrument. A tea-table was in the middle of the room, at which a lovely girl, whom Ronald recognised as his sister Flora, was presiding with the younger part of the family, who were gaily chatting and laughing together.

Over all these Ronald's eyes wandered in search of his mother, till they riveted themselves upon that cherished image. She sat apart at a window which looked out upon the lake and the setting sun; her pale brow and still lovely profile pencilled against the deep flush of the evening sky. Her air betokened "the careless stillness of a thinking mind." One hand hung listlessly on the shoulder of a little boy, her youngest born, the image of her long-lost Ronald, who, with head of curling gold, stood by her side, feeding with bits of bread Ronald's fondly-cherished dog.

Oh, how pensive was the look with which she gazed on the still water, and the silent beauty of the skies! It might be that her thoughts were then of sad but holy import; that they were of him who had found a grave in the deep sea, a home in the mansions of those glorious heavens; of him whose place at hearth and board still to the mother's eye stood vacant. Scarcely could Ronald restrain himself as his heart heaved almost to agony, and the large tear-drops gushed from his eyes, and he thought what rapture it would be to fall on his mother's neck and weep!

"No—oh no! she has not forgotten me; I am

sure she has not. Even now perhaps she is thinking of me!" and in a second he would have been in her arms. But at that moment his mother turned towards her little boy: a bright sweet smile lighted up her face at something he had said, and she looked and spoke fondly to him, as she parted the fair curls from his sunny brow.

Presently the young party of tea-drinkers started up and flew towards her as if with some petition. They spoke with eager childish gesticulation. They hung upon her with looks of loving entreaty, and one little fair girl, climbing upon the back of her chair, laughingly threw her arms round her neck, and kissed her. Lucy, recalled from her aberrations, struck up a lively air; the tea-table was pushed aside, and all were in motion for a dance.

"Yes, yes, they *are* happy, and I am forgotten!" exclaimed Ronald in a burst of passionate emotion, as he rushed from his hiding-place, and fled far from Inch Orran, and all he loved.

CHAPTER XXXV.

THUS Ronald came, saw, and was gone—unseen, unknown. Who can tell what a day may bring forth —what a moment may annihilate! Ere the sun complete its diurnal course, what clouds of events pass and repass o'er the surface of Time's dial! Surely man differs little from the atoms which sport in the sunbeam, and well may his life be compared to the vapour that passeth away—to the shadow which mocketh the eye—to the dream that scareth by night. He is born, and grows up like the grass, and like the grass he withers before it is noon, or falls before the scythe in all its pride and freshness. How vain are all our schemes for futurity! Human wisdom exhausts itself in devising what a higher power shows to be vanity. We decide for to-day, and a passing moment scatters our decisions as chaff before the wind. We resolve for to-morrow; to-morrow comes but to root up our resolutions. We scheme for our works to remain monuments of our power and wisdom, and the most minute, the most trivial event is sufficient to overturn all our purposes, and cast down to the dust the thoughts and the labours of a life. Truly, "it is not in man that walketh to direct his steps."

Though none may have been so foolish or so daring as to hope they might escape the final doom of mortality, yet there are many to whom the King of Terrors appears as an obscure, indistinct vision, seen at the termination of a long vista of years, whose dart is indeed uplifted, but out of the power of which their youth, their health, their strength, and other adventitious aids, have far removed them.

Such and so remotely was the pale monarch viewed by Glenroy, when Norman, the pride of his heart, the prop of his house, the desire of his eyes, was suddenly seized with a violent and dangerous malady. Expresses were sent in all directions, and doctors came full speed from all quarters—but in vain; the fever continued to increase, and poor Glenroy was at his wits' end. Yet, that his son, the heir of his house, the chief of a mighty clan, should actually die, was an apprehension too horrible to be admitted; it was a mere vague, nameless fear that took possession of him, and made him walk about the house, and talk to everybody as loud as he could, and bustle unceasingly, as though he were striving by his restless activity to get the better of some unseen evil. But, alas! Death was the evil, and vain the attempt to repulse *him* from whom all hearts recoil! After three weeks of racking suspense, the son of many hopes, the heir of many honours, was a lifeless lump of clay! "The eye that hath seen him shall see him no more."

It was some time ere Glenroy could fully comprehend the fact that Norman—the gay, the blooming,
the healthful, the active, the brave, should have been
cut off in such a manner; the thing was inconceivable,
impossible! Had he fallen in battle, or been killed
in a duel, he could have better understood it. But
death thus to have invaded his mansion, even as he
visits the cottar's hut, the peasant's clay-built shed;
to have been thus bereft by the hand of disease, under
his own roof, beneath his own bright skies, amid his
own mountain solitudes, where sickness seldom came
—with all that wealth and skill could do to save—
poor Glenroy was confounded!

In vain his benighted soul strove to picture to itself
another state of existence for the perished idol of
his affections; his eye had never sought to pierce the
dim opaque of mortal life, for that had hitherto been
the boundary of his hopes, his wishes, his joys; and
now all was gone—but where? He gazed upon
nature as though he sought his son amidst its bright
manifestations; but he was not on the hills raising
the wild bird, for the heather stood untrodden in its
lonely brightness, and his dogs roamed around as if
seeking their master; he was not on the plain chasing
the deer, for they lay in their silent wildness beneath
the shade of the green boughs; he was not on the
waters guiding his boat, for it was rocking idly on
the blue waves that curled gaily to the summer breeze;
and the sun poured forth his meridian splendour, and
all creatures seemed exulting in the joyfulness of

existence. Could all these things be, if he, who in his father's eyes had given life to all, was dead? he, the heir of all this goodly scene, laid in his cold grave, his eyes closed for ever—his the narrow house and the deep sleep of death? "There is hope of a tree, if it be cut down, that it shall sprout again, and the tender branch thereof shall not cease; through the scent of water it will bud and bring forth boughs like a plant. But man dieth and wasteth away! yea, man giveth up the ghost, and where is he?"

Glenroy's mind reeled beneath the stroke—all was dark within; his head became confused, his memory imperfect; his was the grief of warm affections and proud hopes blasted and overthrown. His gourd had withered, and he knew not where to look for shelter for his gray head; his cistern was broken, and he sought not the fountain from whence he might draw living waters to revive his soul. He was laden with grief, and "the darkness of age came like the mist of the desert." In vain did Edith struggle against her own sorrow, in attempts to mitigate the grief of her wretched father. In vain his two faithful adherents sought in their own way to turn his mind from the gloomy object on which it dwelt in a sort of panic-struck stupor—"One is not, and all seem to have departed."

CHAPTER XXXVI.

AND where was Reginald, that he was not with the mourners to mingle his tears with theirs, and by his presence to cheer and support them in the hour of sorrow? Alas! Edith could not answer; for although he had been written to, on the first alarm of Norman's illness, no answer had been received, and many weeks had passed since she had heard from him. Thus the fever of anxiety was now added to the endurance of anguish, and the tears that fell for her brother were rendered doubly bitter by the neglect of her lover. Yet still, not even to herself would she acknowledge that she distrusted him; it was *impossible* that Reginald could be false, and that single word was the sheet-anchor of her soul : to that she clung with fearful tenacity, and worlds could not have wrested it from her. True, it was equally impossible to account for Reginald's conduct; but *that*, she felt assured, would one day be fully explained. She would not, she said, she *could* not, an instant doubt it; but unconsciously the poison of distrust was creeping slowly and silently into her heart, and corroding her very life-spring. To add to her suffering, Glenroy, having surmounted the first shock of his son's death, now became impatient for Reginald's return; and, as if eager to turn his thoughts to another channel, he talked unceasingly of him, and all that was to be done *for* and by him; for Reginald was now the heir, not only of his honours, but of his whole estates, as all were entailed. The natural impatience of his temper was also aggravated by his personal infirmities; gout and indolence and high living, and mental affliction, combined, had all done the work, and more than the work, of time; for time alone would not have made him the old and broken-down man he now was. To add to his disquiet, he had no proper object for his irritation to work upon at that particular time, for Benbowie was at all times too passive to serve his purpose, and Mrs. Macauley had gone for a few days to pay a marriage visit to a niece of Mr. Macauley's, who had lately married, and settled in the neighbourhood. At least a dozen times a day he would ask Edith if there was no news of Reginald yet, and then he would ring the bell, and order the servants to go to the ferry, or to the clachan, and see if there were any signs of him; and he would call the housekeeper to know if Sir Reginald's rooms were ready yet, for that he expected him home that day; then, as he dozed and nodded in his arm-chair, he would suddenly start up with, " Was not Reginald to have been home before now, and what's keeping him then? And where's Molly Macauley, that she's not in the way?" (From the first hour of her departure.

that had been the constant demand.) Or, worst of
all, he would turn to Edith with a dreamy bewildered
look, and say, "Ay, ay, it's well you're to be married
to Reginald—very well; it will be all his own. But
where is he? When are you to make out the marriage? You'll surely be married soon now, my dear,
will you not?"

At length—O agitation unspeakable!—Edith received a letter in the well-known handwriting of her
lover. It bore a foreign post-mark, and the black
seal denoted that the intelligence of Norman's death
had reached him. Edith's hand trembled, and the
tear-drops swelled in her eyes. "He knows all," she
thought, "and yet he comes not to us! He can calmly
write. Perhaps it is to tell us that he is not coming.
Ah, how cold seems written condolence at such a
time!" and she remained for some moments passive,
under the mute agony of apprehension.

At length she opened the letter, and her doubts
were dispelled. It was brief and agitated, and evidently written under the greatest anguish of spirit.
He had only just learnt the sad tidings of Norman's
death, and the expressions of his grief were frantic
and full of self-upbraiding that he had not set off on
the first accounts of his cousin's illness. He said he
never could forgive himself for having been absent at
such a time; but he was just setting off for Britain,
and would be at Glenroy almost as soon as his letter.
A sentence had been begun, "And if you still love me
as I——" But his pen had been drawn through it, and

he abruptly added, "Would to Heaven I had never left you!" Altogether, it was evidently written under all the incoherence of the most passionate and unsubdued emotion.

Such as it was, it was welcome—oh, how welcome!—to Edith; and its tone of excitation seemed to her the surest pledge that the warmth of his affection continued unabated. "And if I still love him," she repeated, as she deciphered the half-obliterated letters —"Ah, how could he then doubt me? And what can he mean by what follows, 'Would that he had never left me'?"

In vain Edith read over and over again this strange expression. She could make no more of it at the last than at the first; so she concluded that Reginald himself knew not what he was writing in the anguish of his heart, for the loss of one who had been to him as his very brother, heightened too, it seemed, by the bitterest self-reproach at his own absence.

The intelligence of Sir Reginald's expected arrival gave a fresh stimulus to Glenroy's impatience, and he strove, poor man, in the bustle which he himself created, to drown the still small voice of secret woe, which yet spoke daggers to his soul.

So passed several succeeding days in the feverish excitement of hope deferred. It was the evening of the fourth day of watching and disappointment, when Edith, having left Glenroy and Benbowie dozing over their bottle in the dining-room, sat alone in the drawing-room, with her eyes fixed on the waters which she expected to bear the truant to her heart. Assuredly he would cross at the ferry. It would shorten the time and distance so much, instead of travelling the tedious and hilly road with tired horses, at the end of a long and dreary stage. It was the way he used to take even in boisterous weather, when absent only for a day, and many a time she had softly chid the impatience which urged him to trust the slender boat and stormy sea. Now the evening was fair and sweet, and her father's pinnace had been stationed at the ferry to receive him; but Edith sighed as she saw its white sails, gilded by the setting sun, still flapping idly in the evening breeze. All at once she heard the sound of a carriage advancing. Her heart beat as it drew nearer and nearer; and as it swept round the entrance, her eye caught a glimpse of an open travelling carriage, containing one gentleman, something—yet so unlike to Reginald! A single glance had sufficed to show that he was pale, that he leant back in the carriage with an air of languor, and eyes half closed. Could this be the gay, blooming, impetuous Reginald? But in a few seconds all doubts were removed, as the door was thrown open, and Sir Reginald Malcolm was announced. What a tide of mingled emotions rushed o'er Edith's heart as she rose to receive him to whom she had plighted her faith and love, but who now came thus late to claim them; —him from whom, on that very spot where she now stood, she had parted!—and oh, how differently did they now meet!

And one was gone, the playfellow of their childhood, the companion of their youth, the brother—the friend! Pale and motionless, Edith stood in silent emotion; in the tumult of her own feelings unconscious of the still more apparent agitation of Reginald, as he advanced, then took her hand, and pressed it to his lips. It was the hand on which he himself had placed the ring of betrothment. He started, and suddenly dropping it, walked with hurried steps to the end of the room; then as quickly returning, he clasped Edith in his arms, and tenderly kissed her cheek, but while he did so tears burst from his eyes. The hearts of both were too full for utterance; a spell seemed upon their lips, and they remained in deep and silent emotion. Yet an unconcerned spectator would have remarked that Sir Reginald's embarrassment was equal to his emotion, and that something more than sorrow struggled in his bosom and choked his utterance. But Edith was too much under the influence of powerful feeling herself to be a nice observer of what was passing in the mind of another. Her tears continued to flow, from the mingled tide of grief and joy which swelled her heart.

A long pause ensued. At length Sir Reginald, as if by a violent effort, spoke.

"I have been delayed by illness," said he. The tone and accent, though beautifully modulated, were languid and mournful, and they sounded so strange, that Edith could scarcely have recognised in them the gay familiar tones which still dwelt in fond memory's

ear. Still it was Reginald that spoke, and these few
simple words at once dispelled all the vague doubts
which had arisen from his unaccountable delay.

"You have been ill!" she exclaimed; "and I did
not know it—and you have hastened to us even before
you are recovered!"

"But it is too late," said he bitterly.

"No—no, dear Reginald, do not say so—we still
need your sympathy." Her voice faltered, and again
her tears fell. A sigh, almost a groan, broke from Sir
Reginald's heart. He rose and traversed the apartment, then resumed his seat, and leaning his head on
a table, tears forced their way through the fingers
which shaded his brow. But again he roused himself,
and strove to speak calmly and firmly, while he inquired—"How is Glenroy?"

"You will find him changed, much changed,"
replied Edith, striving to subdue her emotion also;
"but the sight of you will, I am sure, do him good.
Ah, Reginald, you are now his only hope." She
stopped, for her firmness was forsaking her.

"And you, Edith—and you," gasped he, as he
again buried his face in his hands, and his whole
frame shook with emotion—"what am I to you?"

Edith was silent. Reginald heavily raised his
head, but his inquiring gaze met only the deep blush
and the downcast eye of love revealed, though not
avowed. Then, in a tone of forced composure, he
said—

"Edith, should you have known me again? Am

not I changed?" he added, attempting to smile, while he grew very pale.

"We are all changed," said she sadly, "for we have all known affliction since we parted; but you have been ill in health, and you concealed it from me! while I—ah, Reginald, had you but guessed what——"

"I *have* been ill," interrupted he hurriedly; "but that is past,—at least the worst. But you say Glenroy is much altered? Had I not better go to him? The sooner the meeting is over the better."

"Perhaps so," said Edith, "if you feel able for it. But you are fatigued; had you not better rest and——"

"No—nothing—I wish it over," said he impatiently. "I will do anything—everything for you both," he added, with emotion

"I am sure you will," said Edith, with simple earnestness, "and if you wish to comfort us, you will yourself be comforted. Now go, dear Reginald!" She extended her hand; he took it, pressed it in his with a sigh, then slowly quitted the apartment.

CHAPTER XXXVII

EDITH remained motionless and bewildered—her heart sank, she knew not why—her tears flowed, she could not tell for what. Reginald was returned, ought she not to be happy? But was it her own—her long-loved, her loving Reginald she had beheld? Oh, surely he was changed. Others might think him improved, but no change could improve that image so deeply impressed upon her heart. Edith loved too profoundly to *admire*.

A long time elapsed ere she heard her father's slow and shuffling step crossing the hall to the drawing-room, which he entered leaning on, or rather clinging to, Reginald, as if afraid he would again desert him. The traces of agitation were still visible in his face, for his grief for the loss of his son had been all awakened at sight of his nephew, that son's once inseparable playfellow and companion, now come to fill his place, and succeed to all that should have been his. But the first burst of sorrow was over, and he again talked in his usual rambling, desultory way, of the worldly objects to which his soul still cleaved—his estates, his rents, his woods, his cattle, his improvements—everything, in short, which could still minister to his pride.

"Glenroy has lost none of his hospitality since I left him," said Reginald, addressing Edith, as he passed, supporting her father to his seat; "and I daresay you can guess how unavailing remonstrance is at those times."

"He has only been making up for my omission, then," replied she, "as I forgot to ask whether you had dined—perhaps," she added, with a slight blush, "that is because I had never before had occasion to treat you as a stranger."

"Treat him as a stranger!" exclaimed Glenroy angrily; "I'll have no strangers here. I never desire to see the face of a stranger within my door—remember that, Edith; and to treat Reginald as a stranger! my own nephew—the man that you're to——"

"Oh, papa," interrupted Edith hastily, "I beg your pardon, but you have quite misunderstood me. I did not mean—I——"

"No matter whether I've misunderstood you or not," cried Glenroy; "I say, once for all, that Reginald's not to be treated as a stranger in this house—he's to do as he pleases. Remember that, Reginald—you're to do exactly as you please. I'm getting old now, Reginald, and I've lost him that——"

Here grief for a moment got the better of his anger, and he groaned in the bitterness of his heart.

"My cousin does herself injustice," said Reginald, trying to soothe the weak and irritated feelings of the old man—"she received me with more kindness than I deserved," and he sighed as he said it.

"How could that be?" cried Glenroy impatiently; "and to treat you as a stranger, too! And what would become of me, if it was not for you, Reginald, and of her too? Remember, Reginald, you're just as much master here as if—as ever my own poor boy was." Here another momentary gush of sorrow checked him, but quickly mastering it, he called— "Ring the bell, Benbowie—he's grown as deaf's a post. Ring it again—give it another tug! What the plague are these lazy dogs about?"

Then when the summons was answered by the butler and deputy, bearing tea and coffee, "It wasn't that I rang for, but you all make one errand answer for two, if there should be a dozen of you. There, Boyd, remember I desire you, and all of you, to treat Sir Reginald with the greatest respect, and to obey him the same as myself. You hear me? And desire Mrs. Pattison to give us a supper like a dinner, and that quickly. Now don't you interfere, Reginald," as his nephew was about to remonstrate; "I'm master here, and I'll do as I please; and it is my pleasure that you should be well treated, and do as you please —remember that, Edith. And, Boyd, let all the servants have as much drink as they choose to-night, to drink Sir Reginald's health and welcome home. Where's that idiot Molly Macauley, that she's not in the way?"

"I have missed my kind-hearted, good-natured

old friend," said Sir Reginald. "I hope she is not far off?"

But before Edith had time to answer, Glenroy, with the rambling garrulity of an infirm mind, had started another subject. "You would see, Reginald, that my tenants had got the principal premiums from the Highland Society this year. M'Laren, that's he that has the farm of Kildrunnach, you know, up Glendochart, the same land M'Taggart had a lease of before your time; he got no fewer than three premiums; one was for the draining of the Dhu Moss —you remember the Dhu Moss, Reginald, up beyond the Roebuck Park? Many a time you've shot a roebuck there, and the very last time Norman was out, he shot three with his own hand. He had become the very best shot in the country—yes he had; but there was not his match for anything—nothing— nothing." Here another tide of fond recollection for a moment stopped the current of poor Glenroy's words; but he quickly rallied, and resumed—"You would observe the plantation on the Skirridale Hill, as you came along, Reginald? That's all new, and I'll venture to say, you never saw a finer plantation; and, by-the-bye, Reginald, there's been some thinning of the wood since you were here, and I must cut some more; they're too thick—too thick a great deal. I'll give you a good portion with Edith, out of the thinnings of the Glenhaussen Wood, and you shall mark the trees yourself, Reginald; we'll ride up to-morrow and look at them, if you'll put me in mind. Benbowie,

ring the bell. Do you hear, Boyd? you'll send one of
the men directly to the stables, to desire M'Nab to
have my horse ready for me to ride to-morrow. I'll
let him know at what hour—and he's to go directly.
And stay, do you hear, Boyd? he's to bring the black
mare for Sir Reginald—the black mare," repeated he,
as the servant left the room; "that was Norman's,
and the handsomest creature I ever saw. M'Nab tells
me Lord Allonby would give any money for her, but
I'll not part with her; for what's money to me, now
that he's gone? But it's yours now, Reginald; you
shall have anything that belonged to him—you shall
—you shall, Reginald. Ay, Lord Allonby wanted
to have her, so M'Nab told me; that's he, you know,
that courted Edith, when——"

"Oh, papa!" exclaimed Edith in a deprecating
tone, and blushing deeply, as Reginald turned upon
her a look of surprise, which fixed into a piercing gaze
of most earnest scrutiny.

"It's no secret, I'm sure," cried Glenroy angrily;
"and if it was, I'll have no secrets here, for the conceited puppy thought he might have her for the
asking, I believe. But, upon my honour, Reginald,
I would rather you had her, than any man living. I
would, upon my soul! What's Lord Allonby, or any
lord amongst them, to me? The king can make a
lord any day, but I defy him to make the Chief of
Glenroy; and that's what you'll be, Reginald, when
I'm gone; and you're more to me than all the lords
in the creation, now that I've no son of my own,"

grasping his nephew's hand in strong emotion. "And Edith shall be yours as soon as we can get everything settled; and, in the meantime, we'll take a ride to-morrow and see the trees marked; and, Edith, is there no word of that Molly Macauley yet?"

In this sort of bald, disjointed chat the evening wore heavily away, without the lovers having an opportunity of conversing for an instant apart; for Glenroy would not suffer Reginald to stir from his side, and seemed even loath to lose sight of him when they separated for the night.

CHAPTER XXXVIII

HITHERTO Edith had felt chilled and disappointed. Reginald, it was true, had been so engrossed by her father, that it had not been in his power to devote himself to her, but he had not even looked as if he wished it. His air had been sad and abstracted, and only once had she seen his eye kindle with its wonted fire, and that was at the mention of Lord Allonby as her lover. The report had gone abroad (though without foundation) that he was an accepted one, and it might have reached Reginald, and hence all the mystery: he had been piqued, angry, jealous; and her father's words had merely conveyed the impression that she had rejected him as a suitor. But could Reginald then have believed her capable, even in thought, of breaking her plighted faith, and renouncing her first, her only love? And would he have yielded her up to a rival without a word? Yes, generous and high-minded as he was, he would have disdained to remonstrate, but, oh, how he must have despised her! And Edith's cheek burned even at the thought. Then the strange expressions in his letter, his unaccountable delay in returning, his agitation at

meeting, his abstracted and gloomy air—were all
these to be referred to the same source? Yes, partly to
that, and partly to the mournful circumstances under
which they had met; the loss of Norman, the infirmities of her father, both in mind and body, must have
shocked one who had so much cause to love him as
Reginald had. And thus Edith strove to soothe her
wounded feelings, and bar her breast against the
admission of doubts worse than death. But all these
reflections did not enable her to meet her lover with
that easy, artless confidence of manner which had
formerly rendered their intercourse so delightful.
When they met at the breakfast-table, there was
mutual embarrassment. Reginald seemed less sad,
indeed, than on the preceding evening; but still there
was none of that gaiety and playfulness of manner
which had been so often wont to call up the smiles
on her cheek. His manners were all elegance and
suavity, but they lacked the affectionate warmth of
former days, and though his countenance was more
than ever expressive of the fire and sensibility of his
mind, still no bright or tender glance repeated the
oft-told tale of fond, happy, youthful affection—"the
kind sweet smile of old."

The conversation, or rather talk, was carried on
by Glenroy in the same strain of mingled pride,
vanity, lamentation, and tautology. There was all
the detail of the premiums and the Dhu Moss, and
the account of the new plantations greatly enlarged,
and the anticipation of the thinnings, with the purpose

for which they were to be applied; and then came
the black mare, and Lord Allonby; and, at the mention of his name, Reginald, who had been sunk in a
reverie, suddenly started, and again cast on Edith a
look which seemed as if it would have pierced into
her soul, and again the blood mounted to her temples
at the suspicion it implied.

"I hope, Edith, you will be of our party to Glenhaussen?" said he gaily. "What a charming morning this is!"

"I have been little in the practice of riding for
some time," replied she; "and am become such a
timid horsewoman that I fear I should only be an
encumbrance."

"Where is it we're going, Reginald?" cried Glenroy. "Oh, ay! to look at the Glenhaussen woods.
But what would take her there? Riding's not the
thing for a lady. Lord Allonby, that's he that wants
the black mare that I was talking about (he courted
Edith, too!), that belonged to my Norman—as if I
would part with it to any man breathing, but yourself, Reginald; and that's not parting with it neither,
for I hope you and I will never part, Reginald. You
shall be as much master here as I am; and when
you're married to Edith—— What have you dropped,
Reginald? Edith, will you mind what you're about,
and not set the table in a swim? And—and—why
is that idiot, Molly Macauley, not here to make the
tea wiselike? And we were speaking about riding,
or what was it? For I don't know what I am about;

not that it's your fault, Reginald; but, Edith, you really have not been yourself since that puppy, Lord Allonby, put nonsense in your head."

Poor Edith was aghast at this accusation, accustomed as she was to the capricious garrulity of her father's temper. But the fact was, Glenroy, by one of the inexplicable . contradictions of nature, even while indulging his spleen in chiding and censuring his daughter, sought at the same time to give her consequence in the eyes of his nephew, by perpetually adverting to the noble and wealthy suitor who had courted her alliance. Reginald seemed to feel for her confusion, for, taking her hand, he said, with a look of almost fond entreaty, "Come now, Edith, don't refuse my first request; do go with us?"

"I will," said Edith softly; "if you really wish it."

"Can you doubt it?" replied Reginald in the same tone.

But Glenroy seemed so bent on monopolising his nephew's company and conversation, as to grudge even a portion of it to his daughter, for he said peevishly, "It's not a woman's business we're going about; we're going to look at the Glenhaussen woods—are we not, Reginald? Then what can she know about the thinning of woods? she knows enough when she knows she's to have them for her tocher, and not a bad one either, Reginald; M'Intosh tells me seven thousand pounds worth will never be missed—and as many more as you like. But I'll be hanged if I

would have given a single stick to that lord of yours,
Edith. What cared I for him, and what was he to
me? a bit lowland lord, that has hardly a hill in all
the Highlands now. But, Edith, dear, do as you like,
and you shall have the first thousand of the cuttings
to buy your wedding trumpery, and you'll get that
fool, Molly Macauley, to help you. What the plague's
come over the creature?"

Reginald said nothing, but his countenance was
overcast, and when Edith rose from the breakfast-
table, he neither repeated his request, nor reminded
her of her promise; but as she was leaving the room,
she heard him say with quickness, "There can be no
hurry as to marking the trees, Glenroy; and if——"
But here Glenroy, with his usual impatience of con-
tradiction, broke in—"No hurry! but I tell you there
is a hurry, Reginald; and if it had not been for Norman's death, which I shall never get the better of
——" Here a passionate burst of grief concluded
the sentence, and Edith only learnt how the discussion had ended when an hour afterwards she saw her
father and lover ride off without her.

That Reginald was piqued and jealous she thought
was now certain, for how could she otherwise
account for such capricious inequalities? From the
moment of his arrival, her mind had been in too
great a tremor to admit of her marking accurately the
sudden changes of his manner; if she had, she would
have drawn a very different inference. Edith's feelings were all too pure and devoted to allow her

enjoying any womanish triumph at this supposed discovery; on the contrary, her gentle, guileless heart was pained at the thought that she was the cause of uneasiness to Reginald. A few words from her lips, she was sure, would instantly remove it, and she therefore resolved to take the first opportunity of coming to an explanation with him, and of undeceiving him as to her fancied predilection for another

CHAPTER XXXIX.

But it seemed as if Reginald avoided all opportunities of being alone with her. When he returned from his ride, he withdrew to his own apartment on the plea of having letters to write; and when he appeared at dinner, his air was still more melancholy and abstracted than it had yet been. Two or three chance visitors who had arrived rendered the conversation rather more general, and by their county news diverted Glenroy's attention from being quite so exclusively directed to his nephew, though every subject that was started still bore some reference to him—to the Dhu Moss, the planting of Skirridale Hill, the thinning of the Glenhaussen woods, the Highland Society, the black mare, Norman, and Lord Allonby.

Edith flattered herself when she left the dining-room that Reginald would soon follow her; she knew he disliked sitting long at table, and the party was not one to be upon any ceremony with: her father had a habit of remaining long after dinner, and as he became drowsy and confused, it would be an easy matter for Reginald to make his escape from him. But she waited in vain—Reginald came not; but

soon she caught a glimpse of him from the window,
as he slowly crossed the lawn, and disappeared in the
woods that skirted it on one side. Edith could not
restrain her tears at this new proof of Reginald's
estrangement from her. "Oh, cruel that he is!"
thought she, "thus to torture himself and me—could
he act thus if he loved me as I love him? No, no;
surely he would seek an explanation, and end this
mystery; and yet it is I who may be unjust. This
fancied mystery may be nothing more than grief and
self-reproach, and he is unwilling to give me pain by
communicating his feelings. Ah, did he but know
how sweet it would be to me to share in his every
sorrow, he would not thus withhold them from me!"

Thus did Edith mournfully commune with herself
till the evening was far advanced, when she was
roused by the sound of an arrival, and in a few
minutes Mrs. Macauley's jocund tones saluted her ear,
and presently she entered, all bustle, calling, "So he's
come—where is he?—let me see him;" then suddenly
stopping—"But bless my heart, my dear!" she exclaimed, as she surveyed Edith with a look of surprise, "what is the matter with you? Is not your
papa well, and your true love come home; and what
makes you look as if you had been crying, then?"

"Oh, Macky, how can you ask?" said Edith
mournfully, "considering——"

"Well, my dear, I know what you mean, and it's
very true, and I consider everything, and you know
very well yourself what a sore heart it gave me when

it happened. But you have sense to know, my dear, there's a time for everything, and this is not the time for you to be crying for them that's gone, when you ought rather to be rejoicing at them that's come back. 'Deed I think so!"

"I am sure your return will rejoice us all, Macky," said Edith affectionately; "papa has missed you very much."

"'Deed, and I thought he would do that, for he has always been so kind to me—and I thought sometimes when I was away, 'Oh,' thinks I to myself, 'I wonder what Glenroy will do for somebody to be angry with; for Benbowie's grown so deaf, poor creature, it's not worth his while to be angry at him; and you're so gentle, that it would not do for him to be angry with you; but I'm sure he has a good right to be angry at me, considering how kind he has always been to me.'" Then uttering an exclamation of joy as Sir Reginald entered the room, she flew towards him, and precipitated herself round his neck, uttering expressions of joy and delight, which were returned on his part with all the hearty warmth and ardour of his more refined welcome.

"And now," said she, releasing him from her embrace, and holding him at arm's length, "let me look at you—well, I declare you are ten times handsomer than ever you were, and you hold yourself up so well, you might pass for a prince; and I would know that smile of yours among a thousand. Oh, I hope my eyes will serve me to take your picture some day—'deed I cannot help looking at you, for you are like, and yet you are not like, what you was; you have not just the bonny bloom on your cheek that you had when you went away. What do you think, Miss Edith, dear?"

"I think Reginald *is* changed," said Edith, with a low sigh.

"All things change, you know," said Reginald, assuming an air of gaiety; "it was not to be expected that I alone, of all created things, should remain unchangeable, and return precisely the same individual I was a year ago; even you yourself, dear Macky, are somewhat changed; you are become still more *embonpoint*—still more youthful and merry and kind-hearted."

"Now, are you not flattering me, Sir Reginald? for though I like to be praised, I do not want to be flattered."

"You did not use to think me a flatterer, Macky?" said Sir Reginald, with a smile.

"'Deed, then, I don't think you are one now, my dear, for you always spoke the truth when you was a boy, and it is not likely you would change now, when you have got more sense and good principles. Now you need not colour up, Sir Reginald, for I'm not flattering you—I'm only just saying what I think; but oh, my dears, what a happy meeting you would have! except, to be sure, that there was a reason for its not being so happy as it should have been; and indeed it would be a shame to us if we were to be as happy and merry all at once,"—and tears twinkled in

her sunny eyes as she spoke. "But then, as 1 was
telling Miss Edith, when I found her with the tears
on her cheek, the time is gone by now, and we should
not accustom ourselves to be melancholy, for it is a
very bad habit; but once the distress is over, we
should just wipe our eyes, and thank God for His
mercies; and I'm sure I do it with all my heart,"
wiping her own eyes as she said it.

"I wish I had your philosophy, Macky," said Sir
Reginald, with a sigh.

"Now, what for should you wish for anything
belonging to me?" said Mrs. Macauley, with a strong
mark of interrogation, from which there was no escape.

"Don't be afraid," said Reginald, evading the
question; "I would not rob you of it, even if I could;
it sits so well upon you—you make such a good use
of it."

"Now, as sure as anything, you are flattering me,
Sir Reginald! But I want to know what use you
could have for what you please to call my philosophy
—though, 'deed, to tell the truth, I do not know very
well what philosophy is; but if you mean my contentment, I'm sure you cannot want that, when you
have everything to make you so contented and happy;
you yourself so handsome, and with such a grand fortune, and a beautiful place, and an old family, and a
title, and your own true love there, that——"

. "True," exclaimed Reginald abruptly—"what a
charming evening this is! Have you not been out,
Edith?"

"No," replied she in a tone of forced composure; "but I should like to take a stroll now."

"Then I hope you will allow me to attend you," said Reginald, colouring, and evidently embarrassed.

"Certainly," said Edith, in the same tone, and rising to prepare for her walk.

"But, my dears, have you had tea and coffee?" cried Mrs. Macauley.

"I beg your pardon," said Edith, "I had forgot;" and she rang the bell.

"I own myself too much of a Frenchman to dispense with my coffee," said Sir Reginald, seemingly relieved by the delay, while Edith left the room for her shawl.

"I really think that sweet creature's looking very ill," said Mrs. Macauley in a low voice to Sir Reginald, after dismissing Boyd and his satellite. "I thought the sight of you would have brought back the roses to her cheeks, and the smiles to her pretty mouth; but I think she looks almost as pale and mournful as she did before you came, and that's very extraordinary, is it not!"

"She certainly is much changed," said Sir Reginald, with a sigh.

"Ay, well, but for all that, I'll wager you have not seen the like of her among all the fine French and foreign ladies you have seen—tell me truly, have you?"

"Edith certainly *was* very pretty," replied Sir Reginald, in a tone that betrayed emotion.

"Well, my dear, but don't you be frightened for all that, and she'll soon be as pretty as ever she was; for she has a very good constitution, although maybe she does not look so stout as some of your great big fat people; and you know it is natural for her to be looking not so well, considering what distress she has suffered; and then, you know, she was so anxious about you, and so wearying for you to come home——"

"In spite of Lord Allonby?" said Sir Reginald, with a forced laugh.

"Oh, so you have heard about that already! But it would not be from Miss Edith herself, for she does not like the way Glenroy speaks about that at all."

Sir Reginald remained silent for a few moments, as if struggling with his emotion; then, sipping his coffee, he said, with affected carelessness—"Ladies seldom dislike having their conquests known, and my cousin has no cause to be ashamed of hers."

"'Deed, I think not, for Lord Allonby is a very fine, handsome man, though he has no clan; he has a very good fortune too, they tell me, though it is but in the Low Country, which makes Glenroy look down upon him so much; many a one would not be so particular in these things as he is. Not that it was for that he refused him for Miss Malcolm, but you know she was as good as married to you."

"Edith liked him, did she not?" said Reginald hurriedly.

"'Deed, I don't know whether she did or not," replied the innocent, unsuspecting Mrs. Macauley;

"but you may ask her yourself," as the door opened and Edith entered.

"Pshaw—nonsense," cried Reginald, crimsoning, while he tried to prevent Mrs. Macauley from proceeding.

But if it is dangerous playing with edged tools, it is no less so to tamper with simplicity, so Mrs. Macauley went on. "Well, if it is nonsense, where's the harm of it, for I declare I can't see it?" Then addressing Edith—"We were just speaking about you, my dear, and Sir Reginald was asking me if I knew how you liked Lord Allonby; 'deed, I said I did not know, but he might ask yourself."

Sir Reginald and Edith were standing almost opposite to each other; a slight blush and an expression of wounded feeling were upon her countenance, while strong agitation was depicted upon his, and if any one so graceful could possibly have looked awkward, he must have done so at that moment.

"If Sir Reginald wishes to know, he has only to ask myself," said Edith calmly; and turning away, she seated herself at one of the farthest off windows, while he remained standing, as if still dawdling over his coffee, but with a flushed cheek and downcast eye.

"Well," cried Mrs. Macauley, "I know very well you are both wishing me, as Glenroy, honest man, sometimes says, sticking on the point of one of my own needles, just now when you have so much to say to one another; so now that I've had my dish of tea, I'll just go and make myself a little wiselike before

Glenroy comes in, or he'll be noticing my cap, as sure as death, for you see how it is crushed with my bonnet."

" I—I—thought—were you not proposing a walk ?" said Sir Reginald, trying to detain her.

" 'Deed, then, Sir Reginald, I have a great deal too much sense to think of troubling two tender young lovers with my company, but I'm sure it is very discreet in you to ask me. Now, go your ways, my dears —and let me see you walking arm-in-arm, so lovingly as you used to do—well, I daresay I'm almost as happy as you are yourselves !"

And away trotted Mrs. Macauley singing, with the tears still upon her cheek.

A pause of some minutes ensued ; at length Reginald approached Edith, and in a voice which vainly strove to appear calm, said, "I thought you had been going to walk, Edith ?"

Edith made no answer, her heart seemed too full ; but she turned upon him a look so soft and tearful, that Reginald involuntarily caught her hand, but as suddenly dropped it as he again encountered the ring his own had placed there, while the flush on his cheek turned to an almost ashy paleness.

At sight of his agitation, Edith mastered hers, and though her voice was almost inarticulate from her emotion, she said, " Reginald, what is it you seek to know ?"

Reginald made no answer, and his agitation increased. Then again taking her hand, he almost

crushed it in his, while, in a low suffocated voice, he
murmured—"How I can best make you happy!" A
thrill of joy ran through Edith's heart at the words;
for, blinded by her tears, she did not perceive the
mute anguish of her lover's features, and for a few
minutes both remained silent. But she was already
happy, for her hand was locked in Reginald's, and she
felt assured that the time was now come when all would
be cleared up. But at that moment Glenroy and his
party came thronging into the room, and as he shuffled
along, supported by a friend on one hand, and a stick
in the other, he called—"Sir Reginald, you're here,
and I did not know it! What made you leave me?
But that's always the way, now! Have not you plenty
of time to be courting, without leaving me alone this
way? But, now that *he's* gone, nobody comes near
me," as his friends placed him carefully in a sofa.
"And where's Molly Macauley?"

"She will be here presently, papa," said Edith, trying to soothe him. "She is returned, and is merely
making herself a little smart for you."

"What do I care for her?" cried Glenroy peevishly; "or what do I care for any woman? Reginald, come here and sit down beside me. Reginald,
you're more to me than all the rest of the world put
together; and you must never leave me. She shall
be married to you as soon as you——"

"Your coffee waits, papa," said Edith, laying her
hand softly on his, as if to stop the current of his
discourse.

"Well, let it wait. Set it down, Boyd; and—
and—Reginald, I'll tell you what I'll do. You know
the Skirridale woods, the—the Glenhaussen woods?
M'Nab tells me I may cut ten thousand pounds worth
to-morrow, if I choose; and—and——"

"Well, my dear uncle, we shall talk about that to-
morrow," said Reginald impatiently; "but some of
us were projecting a walk—the evening is so fine."
And he looked to some of the company as though he
expected to be seconded.

"A walk!" cried Glenroy contemptuously. "Who
but silly women would think of walking at this time
of night? Edith may go, if she likes, but I cannot
part with you, Reginald, and, Auchnagruel, you may
go with her"—to a bashful, shining, red-faced laird,
with large white ears, and a smooth powdered head,
who awkwardly mumbled out his acquiescence, which
Edith waived, while Reginald made another effort, but
in vain, to disengage himself from his uncle's grasp.

"Stay you still, Reginald," cried he, holding him fast;
"and—and you shall have the black mare to-morrow.
She's the greatest beauty—there's not her match in
the country. I could lay a thousand guineas her
match is not to be found in Scotland. That Lord—
what do you call him, Edith? he that had the impudence to propose to me for her, and he would have
taken you, too!"

"There comes Mrs. Macauley, papa," said Edith,
as that worthy entered, and with all her speed made
up to her beloved Chief.

"Oh, Glenroy, how happy I am to see you!" exclaimed she, seizing both his hands. "And I hope you are happy to see me, too?" regarding him with an expression of unmingled delight.

"What should make me happy to see you?" demanded Glenroy, with a stare of astonishment—"the woman that I see every day of my life—that I've seen every day these forty years?"

"Well, but, Glenroy, for all that, you have not seen me for well on to a week."

"A week! Where have you been? I never missed you!"

"Oh, Glenroy, I was told, then, you had missed me very much," said poor Molly in a tone of disappointment.

"Miss *you!*" repeated Glenroy. "I—I've somebody else that I miss. Reginald, you know who it is I miss; and you are to me now what *he* was when I had him. Old Molly Macauley, where have you been? Can you not settle yourself at home, but you must be going about sorning on people that you've no business with? You should stay away altogether, since you're so fond of it." Then, pushing away his cup—"That coffee's not drinkable; ring the bell for the tea-things; and, Mrs. Macauley, you'll make tea for me, for that woman Pattison can no more make tea than she can shoe a horse. And sit down here at my hand, for I know you like to scuttle with the tea-things, Molly; and, Reginald, you'll stay where you are on the other side—there's room for us all."

And thus, with a debilitated mind and despotic temper, Glenroy maintained an ascendency over all around him, and rendered them subservient to his will. Thus another insupportable evening was consumed; but Reginald's words had taken a load from Edith's heart, and she felt assured that another sun would not set without seeing them restored to their former happy state of mutual confidence.

CHAPTER XL.

WITH this hope she repaired to the breakfast-table the following morning; but Reginald was the last to join the party, and when he did, he had the appearance of one who had passed a sleepless night. He looked pale and thoughtful, and did no justice to the good cheer Glenroy and Mrs. Macauley heaped upon him with unsparing hand.

"What's the reason there's nothing at the table Reginald can eat, Edith?" demanded Glenroy sternly.

"There is only too great a variety of good things," said Reginald, trying to deprecate the Chief's unjust displeasure. "I have been little accustomed to see such substantial breakfasts for some time."

"Substantial!" repeated Glenroy, still more indignantly; "it's no breakfast at all. Why is there no herring, Edith? Ring the bell, Benbowie—that woman Pattison's good for nothing. We never have a proper meal, now that your brother's gone. He looked better after these things. He would not have set you down to such a breakfast. Boyd, what's the reason there's no herring at table? I never saw a breakfast without herring. Not in season yet?

Don't tell me any such nonsense; I desire they may
be in season to-morrow, and that there may be plenty
of herring on the table after this. And no game—is
that not in season too? A pretty-like breakfast for
hungry men! Not in season! not in fiddlesticks;
everything must have its season now! in my day
there were no seasons."

Reginald said nothing, but looked as if annoyed
and oppressed by his uncle's overbearing hospitality.

"Well, Glenroy," said Mrs. Macauley, "for my
part, I think this might satisfy a dozen of hungry
men, and a score that are not hungry. But maybe
Sir Reginald does not think so much of our Heiland
breakfasts, now that he has seen so much of the
world. I have heard that in some strange countries
they eat pine-apples and grapes and peaches to their
breakfasts."

"And why have we not pine-apples and peaches
and grapes here, Edith?" cried Glenroy. "What is
the use of my having all these things, if they are not
produced at proper occasions? But you give yourself
no sort of trouble to please your cousin now. But
ring the bell, and I'll send to the hothouses for some
of those things. Now, Reginald, you need not say a
word. Boyd, you'll desire M'Nicol to have every
kind of fruit for breakfast after this. And bring
some grapes directly; and I desire there may be fresh
herring every morning. Is it because that puppy—
that Lord Allonby—turned up his nose at herring that
we never see them now? And he had the impudence

to want Norman's black mare! as if I would have parted with that to any man breathing but yourself, Reginald. She is yours now, and we shall take a ride to-day. What time will you be ready to go?"

Reginald looked embarrassed, and as if wishing to decline, without having an apology ready.

"Perhaps you would prefer a walk," said Edith softly; then blushed, as if she thought she said too much.

"A walk!" repeated Glenroy scornfully; "women are never happy but when they are walking. *I* can hardly walk a step now for that confounded gout; but I'll take a ride with you, Reginald, and we'll go to see the Dhu Moss—that's what M'Kinnon has drained forty acres of, and got a premium from the Highland Society. You—you remember the Dhu Moss, Reginald?"

Reginald coloured as he said, "I am afraid I shall be a dull companion for either a walk or ride—I have got so much of a headache this morning."

"A headache!" repeated Glenroy, in alarm; "how is that? But I very often have a headache myself, Reginald. But I'll tell you what, we'll not go out to-day—we'll just sit quietly here, and talk over some things that I want to speak to you about, and——"

"Excuse me, Glenroy," interrupted Sir Reginald impatiently; "but I am still more indisposed for business this morning. I suppose," he added, trying to force a smile, "I had taken too much of your champagne yesterday."

As he spoke, Edith passed into the drawing-room, and Mrs. Macauley rose to follow; but first going round to Sir Reginald, she laid her hand upon his arm, and whispered, "My dear Sir Reginald, take my word for it, the best cure for both your head and your heart will be to take a little walk with your own true love. I doubt there's something not right between you, for she's away with the tear in her ee— 'deed is she, and it makes me wae to see her."

"What is it you are whispering about, Molly Macauley?" cried Glenroy angrily; "can you not speak out?"

"'Deed, Glenroy, I was just saying that you ought not to hinder two tender young sweethearts from taking a walk together. Think how much they must have to say to one another after such a long separation."

"You are really a most officious goose, Mrs. Macauley," cried the Chief. "What can they have to say to one another, that they may not say before my face as well as behind my back, all the times of the day, if they like? Who hinders them from saying what they please?—I'm sure, Reginald, I've told you, you are as much master here as I am myself. You may say and do exactly what you please, for you're now the man that's to come after me——" Here his voice sank at the thought of his lost son.

"I am very sensible of your kindness, Glenroy," said Sir Reginald, shaking his uncle's hand, as he rose from table; "and I wish I could make a better return for it," he added with emotion. "In the meantime,

I shall try to get rid of my headache, and be ready to attend you on a short ride before dinner." And he hastily left the room, as if to avoid all further discussion.

He entered the drawing-room, where Edith and Mrs. Macauley were, but the latter immediately vanished, singing—

> " The luve that I ha'e chosen
> Therewith I'll be content,
> The saut seas shall be frozen
> Before that I repent.
>
> " Repent it sall I never
> Until the day I dee,
> Though the lawlands o' Holland
> Ha'e twined my luve and me."

Edith was arranging her drawing-materials, preparatory to copying a drawing which lay before her, and which she had already begun.

"I ought perhaps to feel ashamed of your seeing my poor attempts," said she, as Reginald looked at the outline she had begun ; "but," she added, looking on him with the clear and innocent expression of her soft eyes, "I do not wish to hide anything from you, Reginald, however painful it might be."

" You have no cause," replied he, bending over the drawing, and seeming to examine it very attentively.

"To you, who have lately been seeing so many fine pictures in Italy, it must be a penance to be obliged to look at my poor scratches; but I don't even wish you to praise them. I should think you were either laughing at me, or deceiving me, if you did so."

Sir Reginald stood with his eyes still fixed on the drawing, but his thoughts were evidently more profound; at last he said, in a voice of deep emotion— "It would be difficult to laugh at you, Edith; and, Heaven knows! I have no wish to deceive you!"

"I am sure you have not!" said Edith, with tenderness of tone and manner. "But, dear Reginald, are you not deceiving yourself?" And she blushed to crimson, as though she thought she had said too much.

Reginald made no reply, but shaded his face with the drawing he still held in his hand. After a pause, raising his head, he said in a voice that vainly struggled at composure—"I will not attempt to misunderstand you, Edith. You would tell me—that you ——" He stopped, as if suffocating with emotion.

"Yes, Reginald," said Edith tenderly; "I would tell you how much you have wronged yourself and me, if you ever supposed I, for an instant, could forget—Ah, Reginald, do you think I should have continued to wear this ring, if I had ceased to——" love you, she would have added, but the words died on her lips, and she bent her head to hide the blush which glowed even to her brow.

Reginald took the hand she had half extended to him, and pressed it in silence to his lips, but some minutes elapsed ere he spoke; then, in a deep and faltering voice, he said—"I believe you, Edith; my doubts are now ended. Say, when will you become mine ?"

Edith started ; for the accents in which this fond interrogatory was put were anything but those of hope and joy. She looked on her lover, and his face, even his lips were pale, and his features were contracted as if in agony.

"What is this?" exclaimed she wildly. "You are ill, Reginald! Oh, tell me why do I see you thus?"

"I *am* ill, Edith," said he, faintly attempting to smile ; "but do not be alarmed—it is a mere spasm, to which I am occasionally liable ; but it is past for the present, let us think no more of it." And, assuming an air of gaiety, he sought to quiet Edith's fears, and remove her suspicions, if she had any, as to the nature of his emotion. Edith was, of course, strenuous for medical advice : but Reginald assured her it was merely the effects of the *malaria* he had had when at Rome, and consequently a disorder not understood by the physicians of this country. "But time, and your good management, will perhaps enable me to get the better of it," he added, with difficulty suppressing a sigh, "if you are not afraid to undertake the cure."

"You had the *malaria*, then, and concealed it from me?" said Edith reproachfully. "Ah, Reginald, if you had known what your silence cost me ! but it was your tenderness for me made you conceal it from me ; and you were ill while I was unjustly blaming you, perhaps——"

"No, no," cried Reginald, in agitation ; "I ought

—But—oh, Edith, had I flown to you at the first, it might not then have been too late; I should not have been the wretch I am!"

"Dear Reginald, do not reproach yourself so bitterly; you could not foresee how fatally our dear Norman's illness was to terminate."

"Fatally indeed!" re-echoed Reginald, as he leant his head on the table, and buried his face in his hands.

"Had you been here, you could have done nothing for my poor brother," said Edith; "he would not even have known you; and you see you are not too late to be a comfort to us."

Reginald looked up, and spoke more calmly, as he said, "You were always gentle and forgiving, Edith; but you know not the depth of my self-reproach," he added, with renewed agitation. "Edith, you see me broken in spirits, oppressed with remorse—the victim of a hopeless—malady," gasped he, striking his bosom; "yet, if I can but make you happy—I can bear it all —Edith, a brighter, happier destiny might be yours— but if you will unite yourself with me—let it be quickly—let there be no idle delay—there has been too much already."

A painful surmise now darted into Edith's mind; she had heard of the baleful effects of the pestilential fever at Rome, in even affecting the mind of the sufferer long after the cause had apparently ceased; and trembling at the dread suspicion, she knew not how to reply.

" Speak, Edith," he cried impatiently, "do you repent ?"

Edith cast her streaming eyes upon him with a look of tenderness and affection, while she slowly and distinctly uttered, " Never !"

"Enough!" cried Reginald, as he pressed his quivering lip to her hand ; then, after a short pause, he said with calmness, " And now, Edith, I again entreat that there may be no trifling delays on your part ; on mine everything shall be done to accelerate matters ; for that purpose I must now leave you for a time. I must go to Dunshiern ; there must be much for me to do there, and the more that I have now to prepare it for its future mistress." His voice now faltered a little, and he stopped, but soon went on. "I have too long neglected it, but I must now live there for a part of the year if I can. I am aware of the opposition this will meet with from Glenroy ; but, much as I owe him, and desirous as I am by every means in my power to discharge my debt of gratitude, still I cannot devote myself wholly to him."

"It would be too much to expect," said Edith, with a sigh ; "and yet, my poor father ! how shall I leave him in his present state of mind ? and still worse, how will he bear your absence—you who are now everything to him ?"

"Yes," cried Reginald, again relapsing into agitation ; "my father's mistaken tenderness for me has placed me in a cruel situation. I have incurred a load of gratitude to Glenroy, which crushes me to the earth; his house hitherto has been my home—but, Edith—I cannot—I will not continue to drag out a useless existence here."

Glenroy's voice was at that moment heard loudly calling "Reginald," and presently he came slowly shuffling into the room, talking to himself, as he was wont to do. At sight of Reginald and Edith, he exclaimed, "What's the meaning of this, Edith—you taking up your cousin's time this way? I have been wanting you, Reginald, about something of more importance than anything she can have to say to you. Here's a letter from M'Gillivray, that's he that has the farm of Invercardnish—the sheep-farm, you know, that M'Intosh had, and made such a hand of, and——"

"I beg your pardon, Glenroy," interrupted Reginald hurriedly; "but I can scarcely attend to that business at present—I—I—find I must go to Dunshiera."

"Go to Dunshiera!" repeated Glenroy, in astonishment; "what would take you to Dunshiera in such a hurry?"

"I ought to have been there long ere now, Glenroy," said Reginald; "I know I am much wanted, and more especially now," he added, with a forced gaiety, "that Edith has just consented to be mine as soon as the arrangements can be made for her reception there."

"Consented to be a fiddlestick!" cried Glenroy angrily. "Is that you, Edith, that's putting such

nonsense in your cousin's head?" But Edith had
made her escape as her father entered, to be spared
the scene she feared would ensue. "Arrangements
for her reception! What reception, and what arrangements can she want? Haven't you this house to live
in, and as much room as would hold a dozen of you?
and are not you just as much master here as I am,
Reginald? and what would take you to a house of
your own, then? Consent!—reception!—arrangement!—What the plague! there's no hurry in your
marrying, Reginald; you must wait till we get the
woods thinned at all events; and—and whatever you
want from your own house you can send for it here;
and bring your servants, and your horses, and all here;
and—and—but you must not leave me, Reginald,"
grasping his nephew's hand in his.

"Only for a few days," said Reginald.

"Only for a few days!" repeated Glenroy; "and
what am I to do without you for a single day? I'll
tell you what, Reginald, if you'll wait till this confounded gout's out of my toe, I'll go with you myself
(if you must go), and we can take Edith and Molly
Macauley with us, if you like, and I'll stay with you
as long as you please; I will, upon my honour."

Reginald certainly showed no symptoms of delight
at this proposal, though he strove to utter some
general expressions about happiness, gratitude, pleasure, and so forth.

"But my house and establishment cannot be in
order to receive guests; only consider, my dear uncle,

that I have scarcely been there for more than a day
at a time, since I left it a mere child."

"And what's to have put it out of order, then, when
there's been nobody living in it? Come now, Reginald, don't be obstinate, stay where you are, and do
exactly as you like—you are completely your own
master here, Reginald, as much as if you were in your
own house; but I can't part with you, now that my
own poor lad's gone. So stay where you are, and you
shall have everything you can desire—you shall have
his black mare, Reginald, that—that—Lord—what do
you call him, had the impudence to think I would sell
to him."

Reginald saw it was in vain to attempt to use
argument with Glenroy; he therefore conceded so far
as to give up his intention of setting off the following morning, and even allowed him to remain in the
belief that he never should leave him for a single day.
Of course, the poor Chief became ten times more tiresome and exacting than ever, under this accession of
gratified affection; and though Reginald submitted
with the best grace he could, it was obvious he was
writhing under the weariness and torment of being
the engrossing object of a blind, despotic, doting
attachment. Although politely attentive to Edith in
as far as he was permitted to attend to anything but
Glenroy and his never-failing themes, nothing particular occurred to call forth any marked demonstrations
of the nature of his feelings towards her. Edith sometimes thought he looked sadder than anything she

had ever seen ; but that she imputed to the poignancy
of his feelings regarding Norman. Though she loved
him the more for this proof of his sensibility, she
trusted that time, and her tenderness together, would
gradually diminish his sorrow and self-reproach.

CHAPTER XLI

"Do you remember your courting days, Benbowie?" said Mrs. Macauley one day to the worthy Laird, as he sat, with a face of solemn stupidity, chewing his quid.

"Surely, surely," cried Benbowie, starting at the question, as some faint reminiscences of a rejected suit wandered through his brain.

"Because I don't know how it is, Benbowie—maybe the fashion's changed in that too, like everything else, and that it's not genteel for people to look as happy as they used to do; but, as sure as death, if I was Miss Edith, I would not be pleased to see my sweetheart look so dull as he does sometimes; he has not the canty face my good Mr. Macauley had when we were going to be married—the laugh and the joke were never out of his mouth; and, I daresay, you yourself, Benbowie, was merrier when you were thinking of matrimony than you are now?"

"True, true; it's a serious matter—it is, upon my conscience."

"Oh, now, Benbowie, that's not what I mean at all."

Benbowie's eyes grew rounder, but he made no attempt to come to an understanding.

"What is there serious," continued Mrs. Macauley, "in two handsome, rich, accomplished, sensible, well-born, well-principled young creatures going to be married? I declare I think they ought both to be ready to jump out of their skins for joy."

"On my conscience it's very true, so they ought," responded Benbowie; "and it will cost nothing—her money will not go out of the family."

"Oh, who cares for the money, Benbowie? that's not the thing at all—it's true love I was thinking of, and that's a far better thing. I'm sure my Mr. Macauley and I were as poor as two church mice when we were married, and for all that, we were as merry as two fireside crickets. Oh! how I wish I saw Sir Reginald look upon his own true love with that heartsome smile that he had before he left her!"

"He's a fine young man," said Benbowie; "he is—he is—he is a very fine young man, Mrs. Macauley, and he has a very fine property—on my conscience he has."

"Well, well, Benbowie; but I don't think you understand me,—I would rather see his smiles than his gold just now," raising her voice, as though the obtuseness lay in the physical, not the intellectual part of her auditor. But Benbowie only looked still more bewildered.

"Oh, Benbowie, I wish I could make you understand what it is I mean! and then I could know

whether it is my own fancy, or whether it is the real
truth, that—(for you know it would not do for me to
give a whish of that, either to Glenroy or Miss Edith,
for fear of distressing them, and there is nobody else
I would like to say it to); but I would give all I
have to be quite sure that Sir Reginald is as happy
as he ought to be!"

"His own estate is now quite free," said Benbowie,
trying to look wise, "and he is next heir of entail to
Glenroy."

"Oh, the stupid body!" thought Mrs. Macauley,
"how shall I ever get him to understand the difference
between love and land? But maybe, after all, I am
just putting nonsense in his head, and that it is just
as Miss Edith thinks—sorrow for him that's gone,
that makes her own true love look so mournful sometimes. How do I know what is in his heart? and
then, when he catches Miss Edith looking at him,
how he brightens up, and smiles and jokes in his
own way, as he used to do. But then, again, I do
not like to hear young people sigh—it is not naatural,
whatever they may say of lovers' sighing, for I know
my good Mr. Macauley sighed none, for as happy as
we were!"

Such were the *pros* and *cons* with which Mrs.
Macauley strove to solve the mystery of Sir Reginald's dejection; but the result of all her speculations
only amounted to this, that Sir Reginald and Mr.
Macauley had been quite different lovers. But it
was not Mrs. Macauley's nature to stop there.

Having made nothing of Benbowie, she next began to wonder whether Glenroy had observed anything. One day that she found herself alone with him she began to sound her way. Seating herself beside her Chief, as he sat in his easy-chair, she wiped her spectacles, put them carefully on her nose, and began to ply her needle, while she said, "Well, Glenroy, are not we all very happy at having got Sir Reginald back again?"

"What earthly difference can his coming or going make to you, Molly Macaulcy?—*You're* not going to be married to him?" was the peevish reply.

"'Deed I am not; but surely, Glenroy, I may be very happy, though I am not going to be married?"

"I know no business you have to think anything about happiness. If you had my gout in you, you would not be so happy, I can tell you."

"'Deed, and I believe that's true, Glenroy; but though I am very sorry that you have it, yet ought I not to be thankful too that I have it not?"

"Well, don't torment me with your thanks, and your this, and your that. Where's Reginald?"

"I'm sure I cannot tell, Glenroy. I hope he may be taking a little walk with his own true love, and that it will do him good; for as I was now saying, I do not think him quite—just—that's to say, I think—but maybe I'm wrong—that he's a little dowff just now."

"Dowff! what do you mean by dowff? I wish, if you will chatter, you would learn to speak intelligibly. What do you mean by dowff?"

"Just dull, Glenroy; as if he was not——"

"Was not what?" demanded the Chief, still more angrily.

"Was not—'deed, I don't know how to express myself to please you, Glenroy; but I think he is not just so—just in such good spirits as I have seen him."

"Good spirits!" repeated Glenroy, bursting forth in all his majesty—"Good spirits! 'pon my soul, you're the most unfeeling—hegh—good spirits, too! and you, Mrs. Macauley, that pretend to——but I never know one of you women that were better than another. There's not one of you knows what feeling is; you think of nothing but your own idle amusements. Where's that girl gadding to now, and keeping Reginald from me?—Good spirits! good spirits in this house, after what I've lost! if you must have good spirits, Mrs. Macauley, you must go somewhere else for them, for there's to be no good spirits here.—Good spirits! I really believe you, Molly Macauley, have just as much feeling as one of your own needles," stamping his stick upon the floor.

"Well, well, Glenroy, do not be so angry, for you know very well how bad my own spirits were at the proper time;—and—but you know there is a time for everything, Glenroy. Now that it is past, I want everybody to be happy, looking to Miss Edith's marriage."

"And what's Miss Edith's marriage to me, in comparison of the loss of my boy? And if she's to take away Reginald from me in this manner, what good will her marriage do to me? Can't you go and see where he is? I want to speak to him about that tack of M'Kinnon's.—*Will* you go?" he exclaimed, with redoubled impatience, as Mrs. Macauley carefully folded up her work, and then trotted off, not daring to dispute the commands of her despotic Chief.

"Well, there's no making anything of Glenroy," thought she. "I wish I could find out from Sir Reginald himself what ails him, that I might try to do him some good."

Entering the library, she found the object of her anxiety seated with a book in his hand, on which his eyes were fixed, but with the air of one whose thoughts are afar off. He either did not observe, or took no notice of her entrance; but stepping up to him, she accosted him, "So, Sir Reginald, you are here all by yourself, when I figured you gallanting your own true love."

"If you are in search of Edith, you will find her, I believe, in the drawing-room, with some visitors," said Sir Reginald coldly, and without looking up.

Mrs. Macauley stood irresolute for a few seconds, then looking him full in the face, she said, in a strong tone of interrogation, "Oh, my dear, I hope you are not angry?"

"Not angry," replied Sir Reginald, forcing a smile, "only a little bored."

"Oh, well, if that be all, that's nothing to signify; maybe you'll be so good as tell me what it is that bores you, for I hope it is not me?" with the same interrogatory accent.

Sir Reginald made no reply but by a slight gesture of impatience. "Well, I cannot think what I could say that did not please you, my dear; I only said I thought you would have been taken up with your own true love, and I'm sure that could not anger you."

"Surely, Mrs Macauley," said Reginald, speaking very quickly and impatiently, "you have lived long enough to know, what every child knows, that the best things become stale and tiresome by constant repetition."

"My dear!" exclaimed Mrs. Macauley, in an accent which testified she did not in the least comprehend the drift of this observation.

"You and everybody else, I believe," said Sir Reginald in the same impatient manner, "are aware of the engagement between Edith and me; the delay in fulfilling it is now on her part," added he, with increased agitation. "In the meantime, it is unpleasant to me, and must be painful to her, to have it made the perpetual theme of conversation, and for ever alluded to in the broadest manner, not only before strangers, but before the very grooms and footmen."

"And so that's the story, is it!" exclaimed Mrs. Macauley, in astonishment. "Well, how could I ever have guessed that, when my good Mr. Macauley liked so well to be joked about his marriage, and to have everybody coming and rubbing shoulders with him! But I'm glad to think that, when you was looking so

dull, it was only because you was not pleased; and
now that I know what it is that angers you, I will
never let on anything about Miss Edith and you, and
maybe it's genteeler not——" Here a furious peal
from Glenroy's bell recalled Mrs. Macauley to a sense
of her duty. "Oh, and I forgot! there's Glenroy sitting in his dressing-room waiting for you all this time,
and here's that worthy man Mr. M'Dow coming," as
the door opened, and the head of Mr. M'Dow pro-
truded itself, quickly followed by his whole person.
Sir Reginald, scarcely able to conceal how much he
was annoyed, was hastily passing him with a slight
bow, and a sort of murmured apology, but he might
as easily have attempted to escape from the arms of a
man-trap after having touched the fatal spring.

"How do you do, Sir Reginald?" with a violent
shake of the hand. "I rejoice to see you back again
—better late than never, hoch, ho;—but I can't say
you've brought any Italian beef upon you. I doubt
you've been rather ailing; but I've no doubt the air
of the Highlands, and the sight of a certain fair lady,
will set you all to rights again." Sir Reginald bit
his lip, and made no reply. Mr. M'Dow went on—
"I'm afraid you must think I've been rather deficient
in my duty, in not having waited upon you before
now; but the fact is, I've suffered a great deal from
the toothache this summer, and at last I was obliged
to get my tooth taken out. A most dreadful thing it
is the pulling of a tooth, and mine was an uncommon
strong one! 'Pon my word, I thought at first my

head was off. However, I was much amused with an anecdote the dentist told me—for I went all the way to Glasgow to get it taken out in the best manner—though bad's the best, hoch, hoch, ho! But, as I was going to tell you, the dentist, Mr. Bain, really made me almost laugh; though, to tell the truth, I was very much down in the mouth at the time—hoch, hoch, ho!—A gentleman (he would not tell me his name, but he's a justice of the peace) had come to him to get a tooth taken out, but after Mr. Bain had him fairly in the chair, there he sat with his lips screwed together like a vice. 'Be so good, sir, as open your mouth a little,' says Mr. Bain, 'and allow me just to put in my finger to feel your tooth.'

"'Na, na,' says the Justice, 'I'll no do that; you'll bite me!'—hach, hach, hach, ho!" Even Sir Reginald's features relaxed for a moment into a smile, at the overwhelming, vulgar jocularity of Mr. M'Dow, while he made another attempt to extricate himself from his grasp, but in vain.

"Excuse my detaining you for one moment, Sir Reginald," said he, grasping him still more firmly; "but I think it proper to let you know that I shall have occasion to be absent again very shortly for a few days—it's upon a most agreeable occasion, to be sure—no less than a marriage that's to take place in our family—my niece, Miss Alexa M'Fee—that's the eldest daughter of my sister, Mrs. Dr. M'Fee—is on the point of marriage with a very fine young man just set up in business in London, Mr. Andrew

Pollock; it's been a long attachment, like some others that I know, Sir Reginald—hach, hach, ho!—but the means were wanting; however now they think they'll be able to do; and so the marriage is fixed to take place this day se'ennight, and nothing will satisfy them but that I must perform the ceremony; but then, on the other hand, I consider my old engagement to you as paramount to everything else of the same nature, so I wish to ascertain that the one may not interfere with the other, for that would really place me in a most awkward dilemma."

Reginald's face had gradually been crimsoning during Mr. M'Dow's speech, and, with a haughty bend of the head, he merely said, "I beg, sir, I may not stand in the way of any of your engagements;" then quickly extricating himself from him, he left the room.

"Ay," exclaimed Mr. M'Dow, in a tone of amazement, "I don't know very well what to make of that; I suspect the Baronet's not over and above well pleased at my not having waited upon him sooner. I'm sure I'm at a loss how to act, for it will be a dreadful disappointment to 'Lexy, poor thing, if I should fail her; and yet I would be very loath to disoblige Sir Reginald and my excellent pawtron, Glenroy, to say nothing of the disappointment to myself."

"Oh, Mr. M'Dow," said Mrs. Macauley, "that's not the thing at all, things are not just come to that yet; but what's made Sir Reginald not just so well pleased is, that he does not like to be joked about his marriage; he says it's not genteel."

"Oh, that's it, is it?" cried Mr. M'Dow, in a tone of surprise. "Ay, ay! I had no notion of that giving any offence! and yet I don't think I said anything that could be taken amiss; for I'm sure the allusions that I made were of the most delicate nature. But there's a fashion in these things; it's one that I don't think I'll ever be tempted to follow—though there's no saying; for, as my worthy mother says, there's nothing so catching as fashion; and as I live much in fashionable society now, perhaps I may just grow neebor-like, and become a fashionable myself—hach, hach, ho!"

"Well, for my part," said Mrs. Macauley, "I hope I may never turn into a fashionable; for I think one had better be merry and happy, even though it should not be the fashion, than be mournful and genteel, as Sir Reginald is grown. Do you know, Mr. M'Dow," in a confidential whisper, "I did not just like his look sometimes; I was beginning to think—I don't know what!"

"Oh, you're quite wrong there, my good lady," said Mr. M'Dow, with a self-sufficient air, taking a pinch of snuff as he spoke—"quite wrong; it's mere fashionable awpathy, nothing else; I've always kept free from it myself, for I can't say I admire it, but it's creeping in. There are some young ladies in this country that I could mention, that I've known give themselves great airs of awpathy."

"By-the-bye, Mr. M'Dow, have you seen the young Lady Dunross, pretty Miss Lucy Malcolm, since her marriage?" said Mrs. Macauley, quite unaware of Mr. M'Dow's susceptibility on that score.

"Oh yes," returned he, with an air of contemptuous indifference; "she has got well married, which was more than I thought she would, for she was very high set, and rather gave herself airs above herself at one time; but as I've come to spend the day with my worthy friend Glenroy, and it's getting near dinnertime, I suspect I must be going to clean myself a little before dinner." And away he stalked to the chamber, which, from frequent occupation, had now become in a manner his own property.

Glenroy's gout confined him to his own apartment for the rest of the day, but Sir Reginald took his place and did the honours with so much grace and spirit, and exerted himself so effectually, that it must have been a more accurate observer that any that were present who could have discerned the force he was putting upon himself.

CHAPTER XLII.

ONE of the many acts of penance the Chief thought fit to impose upon his family was that of reading the newspapers to them every morning during a long protracted breakfast.

"And labour dire it was, and weary woe,"

for quick ears to keep pace with his tedious utterance and intermingled comments, although he rarely condescended to read the fashionable intelligence, so called. One morning he chanced to stumble on the following paragraph. "We have to congratulate the noble youth of Britain on the arrival of the beautiful and fascinating Baroness Waldegrave at her mansion, St. James's Square, after an absence of several years on the Continent. Her Ladyship is accompanied by her mother, the Lady Elizabeth Malcolm." Here Glenroy made a full stop, as if he had come suddenly upon some unlooked-for and unwelcome object; then muttered—"Ay, that's my pretty lady, and that other —that's the what-do-you-call her—the bit white-faced lassie that she had here with her—the creature you never could bear, Reginald?" Reginald's head was at that moment resting on his hand, which shaded his

face, but he had the air of being too deeply engaged
by a letter which lay open before him to hear himself
thus called upon; at least he made no answer.

"You mean Florinda, papa," said Edith. "Oh,
how I should like to see her again!"

"I never desire to see the face of her," cried Glenroy—"an upsetting, spoilt brat. What was it you
used to call her, Reginald? The skim-milk cheese,
wasn't it?"

But Reginald still looked upon his letter, and was
silent.

"Is that a cess letter that you've got, Reginald?
I've got one too, and so has Benbowie. It's from
M'Intosh, is it not?"

"I—I—beg your pardon," said Reginald, looking
up, and speaking very fast—"yes, I suppose—I believe
—I think—yes—I mean M'Intosh is the name."

"Ay, I thought so; it will just be the same as my
own, and I'm not at all satisfied as to the collecting
of the cess. I think there's great mismanagement—
and——"

"Oh, you have not read the whole paragraph,
papa," cried Edith, glancing at the paper which Glenroy had laid down. "It adds, 'The young Baroness
is said to be the Venus of Apelles realised, and com-
bines with the beauty and delicacy of the English fair,
the softness and grace of the Italian, with the gaiety
and brilliancy of the French. We may therefore
anticipate the *éclat* which will attend so rare and perfect a combination, when it bursts on an astonished

world!' Did you never happen to meet with Flor inda, when you were abroad, Reginald?" inquired Edith, as she still scanned the paper.

"Yes," answered Reginald hesitatingly; then turned to Glenroy, and resumed the subject of the cess.

"And I hope you made up your old quarrel, and were friends?" said Mrs. Macauley.

But Reginald was too much engrossed with his subject to hear the question. Edith took advantage of the first pause to say, "How came you never to mention her to us, Reginald?"

"Mention an old tobacco pipe!" cried Glenroy angrily. "What was there to mention? I daresay Reginald had more sense than to trouble his head about such an insignificant creature as that—a spoilt, troublesome monkey, that there was no living in a house with."

"Oh, but, Glenroy, you must not speak that way of her now, that you hear she has turned out so well," said Mrs. Macauley, always charitable in her judgments, and credulous in her belief; "and I daresay Sir Reginald will give her a very good character now; I'll wager anything they would make it all up—am I not right, Sir Reginald?"

"Lady Waldegrave was much admired," said Reginald, in a cold, constrained manner.

"What a cautious answer, and how unlike you, Reginald," said Edith, with a smile; "but don't expect to get off so easily; I must have a full and particular description of her—for, in spite of you, I always loved Florinda. I scarcely think she met with justice from you."

"Perhaps not," replied Sir Reginald, in the same abrupt, laconic manner.

"Well, then, you will make it up now by giving us a faithful representation of her, or, as dear Macky says, by giving a good character of her."

"What the plague does it signify whether her character's good or bad?" cried Glenroy, in one of his transports; "the character of the man that's to be collector of our cess is of more consequence, I think, than the character of an idle dancing *dorrity* like that —a creature that your brother——Here, Sir Reginald, come back; 'pon my soul, this is insufferable! you women, with your chatter, you've driven him away from the table! I really wish you would learn to hold your tongues when you see we're engaged in business. Reginald!—ay, there he's off, and he's away out without his hat! You women really are— hem——"

And Glenroy was obliged to break off, for want of words to express his indignation.

"Well, then, as sure as death, Glenroy," responded Mrs. Macauley, "I think we behave ourselves very well, and speak very little, considering. I'm sure I could speak a great deal more than I do, if it was not for fear of angering you; and I'm sure Miss Edith speaks less than anybody. But wasn't it naatural for her to be rather inquisitive about the little creature

she used to be so fond of? 'Deed, I think it was; for
how was she to think that Sir Reginald and she had
not made it up, the spiteful thing that she must be?
for I know it would not be his fault—he is so good-
natured and generous, and forgiving to his enemies."

But Benbowie, having found some knotty point in
his cess letter, was now applying to his Chief to solve
it for him; and thus Glenroy's wrath was for the
moment appeased, and his attention excited, and the
abuses of the cess seemed to afford them what is called
subject-matter for some hours to come. When Reginald joined Edith in the drawing-room, he looked ill
and dejected; and, in answer to her timid and gentle
inquiries, he admitted that he had had a slight spas-
modic attack during breakfast, but that it was nearly
over for the present.

"I flattered myself," said he, "they had left me,
as I have been less subject to them of late; but one
is commonly the prelude to others. Now don't be
alarmed," he added, with a faint smile, "although you
see me what you ladies would call somewhat nervous,
occasionally—in time, I trust, I shall get the better
of it," and he sighed as he said it.

"I fear your feelings are too acute for your peace,
Reginald," said Edith mournfully, as she gently laid
her hand on his arm. Reginald looked on that hand
for a moment, with a strange contraction of brow,
and something like a recoil; then, suddenly changing,
he took it in his, and said, in a voice that faltered
with emotion—

"When once this hand is fairly mine, I shall bo better, much calmer—I am sure I shall."

"You know it will ere long be yours," said Edith, and her colour deepened while she added, with simple earnestness, "and in the meantime, you cannot doubt that my best affections—that my heart itself, is wholly —solely yours."

"Oh that I were worthy of it, Edith," said he, in a melancholy accent; "and yet," he added, with emotion, "if you could but read mine, you would there see that its first desire is for your happiness."

"Yes, I am sure—I feel—it is!" said Edith; "but the way to make me happy is to be happy yourself."

"Well, then, let us now settle something, Edith," said he rapidly; "I shall go to Dunshiera soon; but since it is your desire, I shall make no alteration upon it. The credit of the improvements shall bo yours. Glenroy expects his lawyers in a few days, who will arrange all matters of business, and then—and then, Edith," added he, with a strong gasp, "you will surely put it out of the power of fate to divide us?"

Edith sighed, even as she smiled an assent; for the time she had fixed for her marriage was the expiry of her mourning for her brother.

CHAPTER XLIII

ALTHOUGH Glenroy's gout was much on the decline, it still confined him to his couch for the greater part of the day, during which either his bell or his voice was to be heard resounding, indicative of the restlessness and impatience of its master. The following morning, as the family sat at breakfast, a peal was heard from the bell, which surpassed all the peals that had yet been rung, followed by another, and another, in such quick succession, that only a flash of lightning could possibly have had time to answer the summons.

"I think I hear Glenroy's bell," said Benbowie, holding up his ear, and looking wise.

"'Deed, Benbowie, we may all hear that at the deafest side of our heads," said Mrs. Macauley; "as sure as death, he'll ring down the house."

"Something more than common has surely disturbed him," said Edith, rising, when, at that moment, the Chief's valet entered to say that Glenroy wished to see Sir Reginald *immediately*.

"Something about a new lease, or an old bridge, or some such parish matter," said Reginald carelessly, and he rose, and was sauntering out of the room, humming an air to himself; then looking back, as he saw Benbowie groping in the direction of his plate, he called, "May I beg, Edith, that you will not allow Benbowie to mistake my cup for his own?"

Edith sat patiently waiting Reginald's return for a considerable time; but still he came not, and all was silent.

"Oh, this is really not fair in Glenroy to keep Sir Reginald from his breakfast," said Mrs. Macauley.

"Is Sir Reginald not coming back to his tea?" inquired Benbowie, with a face of solicitude, for it was one of his peculiarities to cast a sheep's eye at other people's viands, even when surrounded by a profusion of untouched dainties. So, balked in his design, he betook himself and his newspapers to his own corner.

Mrs. Macauley was too busy and active to indulge long over the pleasures of the table, and she likewise trotted away, weary of wondering what was keeping Sir Reginald.

At length Reginald returned, but his features still bore the marks of recent agitation; and although he had a perfect composure of manner, either real or affected, yet his hand trembled as he raised the cup to his lips.

"I have had another of those foolish spasms," said he, "occasioned, I think, by the heat of Glenroy's room, though he would fain persuade me it is flying gout, and we have consequently had a long and interesting discussion on gout and malaria. He tells me my father had it in his constitution, which I never knew. But I beg pardon, Edith, you are waiting for me. Oh, by-the-bye, Glenroy has had a letter from—from Lady Elizabeth; a letter offering to pay him a visit here, which has of course agitated and annoyed him."

"An offer of a visit from Lady Elizabeth!" exclaimed Edith; "that is indeed very strange, after so long a separation. Don't you think so?"

"Rather," replied Reginald.

"How does papa take it?"

"I can scarcely tell. He seems both for and against it. He is, you may believe, very unwilling to receive the visit, and yet still more unwilling to decline it. He begged me to mention it to you, and talk it over."

"What can have prompted such an offer at this time?" said Edith, still rapt in amazement. Reginald was silent.

"Does she assign no reason for so strange a proceeding?" inquired Edith. Reginald hesitated for a moment; then, with a deepening colour, replied—"Sympathy is the motive assigned. She wishes to condole personally with your father and you in your affliction;" and he sighed deeply.

"Ah, how very kind!" said Edith; "much more so than I should have expected from Lady Elizabeth, either from my own recollection of her, or from anything I have ever heard of her. Perhaps she is much changed, and, if it is so, papa and she may yet live happily together—and then, you know," she added, with a rising colour, "he could better spare you when——"

"Oh, impossible; they are so totally different, and Lady Elizabeth is such an invalid, so constantly complaining; their habits are so dissimilar—so—in short, their ever living together is out of the question; she only proposes remaining for a week or two."

"At least there can be no harm in trying the experiment for a week or two; that will soon pass away, whether pleasantly or not. But does she say nothing of Florinda? Won't she come too?"

"I suppose—I believe—of course—here, Fido," to his dog, as he placed a saucer on the floor, with some milk and water, and bent down, as if deeply interested in the common action of Fido's lapping his breakfast.

"Oh, how delighted I am!" exclaimed Edith, her eyes sparkling with animation. "I cannot tell you, Reginald, how much I have longed to see her again, my recollection of her is so vivid! I am sure I shall love her, she was such an engaging creature; and you remember how often I used to make up your little quarrels together? I am resolved to make you both good friends for evermore."

Reginald made no immediate reply, for he was still occupied with his dog. At length he said in a cold, constrained manner, but without raising his head—"Excuse me, Edith; but we view this matter quite differently. I have already advised Glenroy to decline the visit."

"Ah, Reginald! how could you be so unkind?" exclaimed Edith, in a tone of reproach.

"Because I thought it my duty," he replied, almost sternly.

"But you may have mistaken it, dear Reginald," said Edith gently. Reginald was silent. "And will papa, then, not receive them?" inquired she, with a sigh.

"I cannot tell. He was much perplexed, and asked my advice, which I gave him, although it was not pleasant for me to be the umpire in such a matter."

"Tell me, Reginald, is it your dislike to Florinda that makes you so averse to receiving the visit?"

Sir Reginald did not immediately reply; when he did, he said very coldly—"I never said I disliked her."

"No; but I suspect you do," said Edith, looking at him with a soft smile; "and I long to reconcile you."

"You had better not try," said Reginald sternly; then added, in a voice of repressed emotion—"This visit can be productive of no pleasure; they are so different—they are both so unsuited to this place."

"But, for a short time, it matters little," said Edith.

"Even for a short time I am sure the visit will annoy your father, they will bring such a *suite* along with them. Lady Elizabeth has her travelling physician—and—and—there is a French lady—a friend——"

"But there is plenty of room, and we are accustomed to receive everybody. How unkind, then, it would be to refuse such near connections! Now, come, dear Reginald, do persuade papa to accept the visit."

"That might be the test of my obedience, but not of my love," said he bitterly. While he spoke, Glenroy's bell had been sounding a larum, and now a servant entered in all haste, to say Glenroy wished to know what was detaining Miss Malcolm, and to desire she would bring the letter immediately.

"Oh, by-the-bye!" exclaimed Sir Reginald, in some confusion, "I had almost forgot Glenroy charged me to show you the letter, and to request of you to answer it." And he drew forth a letter, and laid it before Edith. She took it from its envelope, and at the first glance exclaimed—"Florinda Waldegrave! I thought the letter had been from Lady Elizabeth."

"'Tis much the same thing, is it not," said Reginald, "whether I write a letter, or you do it for me? The letter is virtually Lady Elizabeth's."

"What a pretty, elegant little hand she writes!" exclaimed Edith, as, without further comment, she began to read as follows :—

"My DEAR SIR—At mamma's request, and in accordance with my own feelings, I beg leave to express to you the deep sympathy we feel on the mournful event which has taken place in your family. The early recollections of your kindness to me, and the tender affection I always cherished for you, and my dear brother and sister (for such I ever considered them), remain indelibly impressed upon my heart; and I wish nothing more earnestly than to be allowed an opportunity of proving to you how sincerely I participate in your affliction. Mamma is equally desirous of convincing you that, however circumstances may have unfortunately separated her for so long a period from you, she has ever retained a lively interest in your welfare, and that of all dearest to you. Should it not, therefore, be deemed an intrusion on your grief, we shall have much pleasure in being allowed to join your domestic circle, and pass a week or two with you quietly at Glenroy; when it will be our most earnest study to endeavour to mitigate your sorrow, by every means in our power. Mamma unites with me in every heartfelt wish for your health and returning happiness. And, with kindest love to my dear sister Edith, I have the honour to be, my dear Sir,

"Your very sincere and obliged servant
and daughter,
"FLORINDA WALDEGRAVE.

"*P.S.*—Mamma entreats you will not put yourself to the slightest inconvenience on her account; for, although somewhat delicate, she is not at all particular as to her accommodation; and as for me, you may put me in the turret, with which you used to threaten me when I was a naughty, troublesome little girl."

"It is a very kind letter," said Edith, with a sigh, as she finished it. "And yet——" She stopped.

Here another message from Glenroy admitted of
no further delay, and Edith was hastening to satisfy
his impatience, when Reginald stopped her.

"Do not allow anything I have said to prejudice
you against Lady Waldegrave," said he, in agitation.
"I ought not to have given an opinion—I—do not let
me think I have injured her in your estimation, Edith."

"No, no," cried Edith hastily, as a perfect volley
of bell-ringing caused her to fly.

"Are you to be all day writing that letter, Edith?
is it not done yet?" were the queries that greeted her
on her entrance.

"I beg your pardon, papa; but I have not had
time."

"Not had time! you've had time to write at least
a dozen of letters—it's really intolerable; what's the
use of you women learning to write at all? you should
all keep to your needles and thread, like that idiot,
Molly Macauley, and not torment people with your
trash of letters this way. Have you not written the
one I desired you yet?"

"It is not five minutes, papa, since Reginald
showed me the one you had received from Lady
Waldegrave."

"That's not the letter I am speaking about; it's
the one I desired you to write in answer to that."

"I understand you, papa; but I really have not
had time since."

"I tell you, the letter might have been half-way
to London by this time."

" My dear papa, you know the post does not leave this till the evening."

"That's nothing to the purpose; your business was to write the letter when I desired you."

" I will write it directly, papa, if you will be so good as tell me what I am to say."

" How often am I to tell you what to say ? I told you already, or at least I told Reginald, which is the same thing."

" Reginald said you did not seem inclined to receive the visit."

" How can I be inclined to receive a visit, lying in my bed here ? It's a most senseless and unfeeling proposal."

" It must be kindly meant," said Edith gently; "and, dear papa, sympathy ought always to be kindly taken."

"Sympathy ! what good will all the sympathy in the world do to me ? it will not bring back him that I've lost."

A pause of some minutes ensued.

"You may be quite well before Lady Elizabeth comes, papa," said Edith ; "and if not, you will at least have shown your hospitality and good-will; but yet, if the thought of it is so unpleasant to you, to be sure the visit had better be refused than that you should suffer."

" You don't know what you're speaking about! If I'm well, and if I'm not well ! How can I tell whether I'm to be well or ill ? I wish both these ladies of quality had my gout in their fingers and toes, to settle them, and keep them from disturbing me in this manner. And there's Reginald, he has got the gout too, or I'm mistaken; his father had it when he was not much older than he is now; but if he could get it to fix in his foot, there would be no fear of him. But what's the reason you have not written that letter, Edith?"

"I will write it now, papa, if you will only tell me what you wish."

"How can I tell you what I wish? Can't you ask Reginald, and he'll tell you what I wish."

"Reginald and I don't quite agree about it, papa."

"Reginald and you don't agree! And do you really pretend to disagree with the man you're to be married to? and before you're married to him! I never heard of such a thing in my life as people not agreeing before they were married—not agree with the man that's to come after me!"

"Reginald and I are very good friends, papa, and we shall be quite agreed when we know your wishes on this subject; but he is of opinion that it would be better to decline the visit; and I——"

"He's quite right—much better—what the plague brings them here now? After staying away so long, they'd better have stayed altogether. The mother not particular!—there's not a more troublesome, particular woman in the kingdom than she is!"

"Then I shall write and say the state of your health prevents you receiving their kindly meant visit at this time, or something to that purpose, papa?" said Edith, and she was leaving the room.

"The state of the fiddlestick!" cried Glenroy peevishly; "I wish you would not be in such a hurry —what's the matter with my health? You women are always so impatient and so ready with your pens! What is there in the state of my health to keep people from coming to the house?—you speak as if I had the plague! I've had a touch of the gout in my toe, which is now almost gone, and I'm better than I've been for months, and how can I tell people they're not to come to my house? It's a thing I never did in my life, and I'm not going to begin now; I wonder how you could propose such a thing, Edith, to refuse to admit a woman of rank, and my own wife too, within my door, and for two or three days; and her taking such a journey, poor thing, on purpose, and all for my poor boy! It's a piece of respect to him, and it says a great deal for her, and she shall be welcome to the best in my house for his sake."

Here poor Glenroy began to weep, and Edith, distressed and perplexed, after soothing him as well as she could by turning his thoughts to another channel, left him to have again recourse to Reginald for advice and assistance. But Reginald had set off to join a shooting party, and had left word he should not return till late in the evening. Edith had therefore to write the letter without further communing. Upon showing it to her father, he of course scolded and protested against it, and swore he would not receive any such visitors; but, at the same time, desired the letter might be sent off, accepting the visit.

CHAPTER XLIV.

Mrs. Macauley's astonishment on being made acquainted with this revolution (or rather restoration) was excessive.

"Well, Glenroy," cried she, as she repaired to his sitting-room, brimful of the subject, "I'm sure we may well say, wonders will never cease! As sure as death, I could hardly believe Miss Edith when she told me! To think of your lady coming back to you of her own accord, after staying so long away from you. Of all the wonderful things I've met with, and I have met with a good many in my day, this is the most extraordinary."

"I see nothing in the least extraordinary in the matter," said Glenroy, with dignified composure.

"Oh, that must be because you are so wise, Glenroy; for I have heard that very wise people are never surprised at anything, which I think very extraordinary, considering what curious creatures we are, and what wonderful things we meet with both by day and by night. It was but just the night before last I had such a curious dream;—but I'm not going to tell it to you, Glenroy,"—as she saw a volley ready to burst forth—"though I must always think it very uncommon that I should have dreamed such a dream at the very time your lady was coming back to you. I'm sure I hope she will behave herself now."

"Behave herself!" repeated Glenroy wrathfully; "I wish, Mrs. Macauley, you would learn to behave *yourself*, and not give your tongue such a license."

"Well, what did I say was wrong there, Glenroy? for 'deed I do not think she behaved so discreetly as she might have done to you; but now that she has seen her fault, to be sure we should not speak about what's past; and I daresay she will make you a good and an obedient and a well-behaved wife in all times to come; for once she comes here, I doubt if she'll be for going away again. 'Deed, I wondered at her leaving you when she did."

"And what right had you to wonder anything about it, Mrs. Macauley? And where was the wonder of her going to look after her daughter's fortune at the time she did? She acted like a sensible, prudent woman: and now that she has secured that, and got the girl properly educated, the first thing she does is to show her respect for me by bringing her back to me: but, I daresay, one reason of her leaving this was, that the child might not be corrupted by you. You would have been a fit person to have educated a peeress, to be sure! You've made a fine hand of Edith, to be sure."

"Oh fie, Glenroy," cried Mrs. Macauley, kindling a little at these aspersions, "I wonder to hear you!

'Deed, I don't think it sets you to speak in that disparaging way of your own daughter, and her so sweet and pretty and genteel, and so much admired; and I wonder you should set up the other one, considering what a little spoilt, impudent monkey she was, and, 'deed, I don't believe she's much better yet; for you see Sir Reginald has never said a good word of her, and I really think he cannot bear the name of her."

"You're an old goose, Molly Macauley, and don't know what you are speaking about. I asked Reginald if he had any fault to find with her, and he said none in the world; and he said as much as that they had been upon a good enough footing when they met; and I know it was only his fear of their disturbing me that made him unwilling to admit them here, for he thinks more of me than any of you, I know that; and he's everything to me now; so take you care, Mrs. Macauley, that you behave yourself properly."

"Oh, Glenroy, as if ever I could behave myself improperly to anybody, especially to your lady and your stepdaughter. I'm sure I shall put my best foot foremost to please them. And I'm just thinking what little marks of my respect I can contrive for them, that will be something out of the common." After much deliberation, she at last decided upon what she deemed a meet and appropriate offering for Glenroy's lady, in the form of a visiting card-case with a view of "The Castle" on one side, and on the other, a full-length representation of the Chief in the Highland dress; while Lady Waldegrave was to be made

happy with a gown, tamboured in coloured silks, with
what the artist called a running pattern, of heather
and thistles, of her own contriving. Benbowie, who
had only one mode of testifying emotions either of
grief or joy, ordered a new waistcoat for half mourning, which even Mrs. Macauley declared was ugly
enough "to spean a bairn."

Edith waited impatiently for Reginald's return,
but instead of himself, she received a note by the
gamekeeper who had attended him, to say that he
had been prevailed upon to take a night's quarters,
and spend a day or two with his old friend Dunross,
at Lochdhu, and that as he was now so far on his way
to Dunshiera, he would probably visit it before his
return; he therefore desired his servant and horses
might join him the following morning, and begged
Edith would write him a line to say how Glenroy was,
etc. All this was quite natural, and yet Edith felt a
little mortified that Reginald should voluntarily absent
himself from her even for a few days; it might be
chiefly on her account, indeed, as it was probably a
mere excuse to get to Dunshiera with a view to prepare it for her reception, and she was angry with herself for the momentary chagrin she had given way to.
She wrote him a few lines in reply, and told him what
answer had been returned to Lady Waldegrave's letter,
by her father's desire; then added a hope that he
would not be long absent, and a request that he would
do nothing to Dunshiera on her account.

There was of course a violent storm from Glenroy,

when he heard of his nephew's departure ; but upon
the whole he bore it better than could have been expected. The fact was, there was always some one
subject that reigned paramount in his mind, and for
the present that was the approaching visit of his lady.
It was something to excite him, to confuse him, to
keep him in talk, and make him fancy himself in a
bustle, as the letter was scarcely gone before he began
to watch for the arrival of his expected guests. But
he soon began to weary of expectation and preparation
—not even steam itself could have kept pace with his
impatience—how much less the tardy movements of
even the fleetest of post-horses, and the best paid of
post-boys, when they depend upon the movements of
fine ladies! He did not indeed pretend to say that he
anticipated any pleasure from the arrival of his guests
—on the contrary, he loudly declared that there
ought to be an Act of Parliament to prevent women
from travelling, and that he only wished his visitors
would come that they might go away again.

"I really wish this visit was over," he would
exclaim twenty times a day. " Why can't they come
and have done with it ? Do they think I'm going to
sit up this way, day after day, waiting for them ?
Haven't had time ?"—to Edith. "What do you call
time ? I know I have had time to repent that ever I
listened to such a madlike proposal. What is it they
mean to do after they come here ? Are they to take
up with Benbowie and Molly Macauley ? for I can tell
them, they're much mistaken if they think I'm to

gallant them about. They're coming to your marriage, are they? But they'll surely have the discretion to write before they come."

Edith assured him they would, as she had required
of Lady Waldegrave to let her know when they
might expect them.

"And what's the reason Reginald's not come back?
What am I to do if he does not come in time to receive them? I really wish, Edith, you would write,
and ask what's keeping him, and tell him that he must
come directly. It's a pretty situation I'm landed in,
with two strange women coming that I know nothing
about. What do I know about your Lady Waldegrave? she's nothing to me; and—and my own boy
gone!"

At length a sudden and alarming attack of gout
in the stomach put a stop to Glenroy's garrulous de-
batings. All was confusion and dismay—expresses
were sent off for medical assistance; and Edith wrote
a hurried line to Sir Reginald, informing him of her
father's situation. She had heard from him from
Dunshiera, where he said he had found so much to
do, that the time of his return was uncertain; but the
intelligence of his uncle's danger, she was sure, would
bring him instantly to Glenroy; and so it proved, for
he lost not a moment in answering the summons; but
before either he or the doctor arrived, the disorder
had taken a favourable turn—the gout had resumed
its station in the feet. Thus the danger was past for
the time, and Glenroy was himself again, and every-

thing and everybody resumed their former station and occupation. Reginald alone seemed restless and un- uneasy—abrupt in his answers, and unequal in his spirits; but whenever he caught Edith's eye, he in- stantly rallied, recovered his self-possession, and began to talk to her of Dunshiera, of all he was doing and had to do for her comfort and accommodation, and would then urge the necessity there was for return- ing there, having numerous work-people waiting his orders. But as the mention of such a purpose always threw Glenroy into an absolute paroxysm, and made him gout all over, he at length agreed to remain where he was, until his uncle's health should be more firmly re-established.

"You surely do not think of receiving Lady Eliza- beth now?" said he to Edith, one day when she was expressing her expectation of a letter from Lady Waldegrave.

"No, I scarcely expect them now," said she, " as I wrote to Florinda when papa was taken ill; but if they had set out, of course she could not have received my letter. However, I must hear from her soon, as she will at all events write to apprise me of the day of their arrival, if they are really coming."

"If they should come," said Reginald, in a tone of affected composure, "I shall take advantage of your having such good company to return to Dunshiera for a few days. Glenroy will probably be quite well by that time, and I am anxious to forward the opera- tions."

"Surely, Reginald, you will not think of leaving us at such a time?" said Edith; "how very unkind —I may almost say rude—it would seem to Lady Elizabeth and Florinda."

"That is a very secondary consideration," replied he; "*seems* signifies little to me in comparison of *should.* I ought to return to Dunshiera at that time," he added, endeavouring to retain the same artificial tone. "Nay, more, Edith, why might not you accompany me? Why," he continued, with more visible agitation, "may we not make out our marriage quietly at least, if not privately, now, before these people come?"

"Surely you are not serious, Reginald," cried Edith, in amazement.

"Perfectly so," returned he quickly.

"I can scarcely believe you," said she; "what can your motive be for so strange a proposal?"

"In the first place," said he, "I feel that I have been long enough exhibited as your lover. In the next, we should avoid the intolerable *éclat* which always attends on these things. And, lastly," he added, with a sort of mocking air, "since your father is going to be reunited to his lady love, 'tis to be supposed he will be too happy to be dependent upon other society, and consequently he could more easily spare us. What have I said to offend you, Edith?" he continued quickly, as she remained silent, and the tears swelled in her eyes.

"Much," said she, with emotion; "and yet I am

sure you did not mean to hurt me, Reginald," she added tenderly.

" If you are hurt, the fault must be your own, not mine," said Reginald coldly.

Edith's tears fell, but she made no reply.

Reginald proceeded, in the manner of one who had worked himself up to be angry—"Since my return, two months ago, I have never ceased importuning you to fulfil your engagement. I have repeatedly besought you to become mine—publicly or privately, I cared not which; but there has always been some frivolous pretext or another for delay; yes, even the colour of your gown has been made the excuse," he cried, with rising vehemence, "as if such weak, super-stitious fancies could have swayed you, had you really, truly loved."

" Unkind, unjust that you are !" said Edith, choked with her tears.

" No, the unkindness, the injustice is yours," cried he, still more passionately. " Heaven is witness, that I would have fulfilled our contract long before now. You must do me the justice to own that the moment I was assured your affection for me was unchanged, I would have made you mine; you need not blame me, then, if your behaviour leads me at least to doubt the reality of that affection."

Edith was too much overcome to reply. She was accustomed to the querulous fault-finding of her father; and from that and other evils she had been wont to find a refuge in the tenderness of Reginald;

but this burst of displeasure was too much for her, and she wept in meek and silent anguish, while he paced the room with the air of one who would rather be still more exasperated than mollified.

At that moment Benbowie entered the room, and was making up to Sir Reginald with an open letter, and beginning something about commissioners of supply, when, hastily brushing past him with an air of reckless hauteur, he quitted the apartment. At the same time, the dressing-bell sounded, and Edith retired to her chamber, to compose herself as she best could for meeting her angry and unreasonable lover at dinner.

CHAPTER XLV.

SIR REGINALD did not make his appearance in the drawing-room, and it was not till the party were all seated that he entered the dining-room, and then his looks and manner still betokened a mind ill at ease. He was silent and absent, inattentive to the company, and almost rude to poor Mrs. Macauley, when she attempted to coax him into a better humour by her simple and somewhat ill-timed allusions.

Edith felt unequal to bear a part in the conversation. It was all she could do to retain the tears that rose in her eyes, as she now and then encountered Sir Reginald's glance, which, if it did not speak positive displeasure, at least evinced a sort of impatient dissatisfaction. The dessert had been just placed on the table when Boyd entered with a face of importance, and announced that two travelling carriages had just entered the avenue; and while he yet spoke, the sound of approaching horses and wheels confirmed the fact; in another second, they swept round and drew up.

"Can this be Lady Elizabeth?" exclaimed Edith, rising from the table in some agitation, while Sir

Reginald, shading his face with one hand, poured out several successive bumpers of champagne, and drank them off unnoticed in the general confusion that prevailed.

"'Deed and it can be nobody else," cried Mrs. Macauley, who had hastened to the window; "there's the two ladies in a barouche, and a well loaded one too, and a gentleman—no, he's only a servant—behind; and there's two very smart-looking ladies' maids, I'm thinking, in the other carriage; and oh what a sight of imperials and trunks and boxes! it's a mercy Glenroy does not see them. But I declare I don't think it's Lady Elizabeth, after all, or else she's grown younger and handsomer than ever she was."

"Sir Reginald, will you go and receive Lady Elizabeth?" cried Edith; then, struck with the change in his countenance, she exclaimed, "But you are ill!"

"No—no—nothing," he cried, starting up, his pale cheek and downcast eye suddenly flashing and sparkling with false fire, while the sweetest and most melodious of voices was now heard in the hall, as if speaking to her dog, and presently Lady Waldegrave was announced. Edith flew to the door to receive her, but she started in surprise at the beauty, the surpassing beauty and brilliancy of the figure that met her view, and gracefully opened her arms to receive her embrace.

For some moments, Edith's emotion rendered her unconscious of everything but that her once fondly-loved Florinda was restored to her. But, at the same

time, the remembrance of her lost brother mingled
with the tide of feeling, and rendered her unable to
articulate the common expressions of welcome.

"You are very kind, dear Edith," said Lady Waldegrave, as she raised her head and shook back the
beautiful ringlets which shaded her face. "I scarcely
deserve to be so well received, considering how I have
broken in upon your family party. I am afraid I have
disturbed you."

"Oh! do not think of apologies at such a time,"
said Edith, again tenderly embracing her, and gazing
with looks of fond admiration through her tears.
"Dearest Florinda! how welcome you are to Glenroy!"

"I assure you I cannot be more welcome than I am
delighted to return," replied Lady Waldegrave, with
an earnestness of manner which left no doubt of her
sincerity.

Edith did not immediately answer, for her attention was attracted to Sir Reginald, who was standing
with his back to them, talking and laughing strangely
loud with the other lady, when Lady Waldegrave
called to her—

"Madame Latour, allow me to present you to Miss
Malcolm." Then observing Edith's look of surprise,
she exclaimed—"Ah! did I forget to mention Madame
Latour to you? She was my governess, and is now
my friend—she is a very charming, accomplished person, and excels in speaking broken English."

Madame Latour, thus called upon, saluted Edith

with all the ease and grace of her country, while Sir
Reginald, for the first time recognising Lady Waldegrave, made a slight constrained bow, and then turned
abruptly away. Edith was shocked at the rudeness
of such a reception. Lady Waldegrave blushed, and
said in a low voice, but sufficiently loud for him to
overhear—

"I scarcely expected to find Sir Reginald Malcolm
at Glenroy."

Such avowed marks of hostility at the very outset,
and from persons of such high breeding and refinement, struck Edith with surprise and consternation.
She knew not what to reply, and in some confusion
said—"I—we—expected to see Lady Elizabeth; and
I hope nothing has occurred——"

"Oh! mamma will be here," said Lady Waldegrave; "but her carriage is heavier than mine, and
I flatter myself," added she, with sweetness, "my
impatience was also greater than even hers, to reach
Glenroy and its loved ones," gently pressing Edith's
hand as she spoke. "But I am really shocked at having
deranged your little party," as Mrs. Macauley and
Benbowie remained in all the awkwardness of suspense, not knowing whether to sit or stand.

"I daresay your Ladyship will not remember me,"
said Mrs. Macauley, on coming forward.

"My dear Mrs. Macauley," said Lady Waldegrave,
affectionately embracing her—"how can you suppose
I ever could forget you? Indeed, I never do forget
those I love," she said with much earnestness. "And

you used to be so kind to me when I was a little,
naughty, mischievous creature !"

"'Deed, then, my lady, and you was that," replied
the simple Macky : "but I'm sure one need only look
at you to see that you are not that now."

Lady Waldegrave laughed, and there was melody
even in her laugh. "And, Benbowie, I hope I see
you well?" extending the tip of her finger to him.
"But where is Glenroy?" looking round, as she missed
him for the first time. Edith explained that he was
confined to his own apartment with a fit of the gout.

"How sorry I am !" said Lady Waldegrave, in a
tone beautifully modulated to pity ; then in a moment
changing it to one of delight, she exclaimed, "Come,
dear Fido !" as Sir Reginald's dog entered the room,
and flew to her with demonstrations of joy.

"How kindly Fido welcomes me," said she, as
she fondled it. "He has not forgot me — dear
Fido !" she repeated, as she continued to load it with
caresses, unmindful of the jealousy testified by her
own favourite.

Sir Reginald made no reply, but with a heightened
colour, called the dog to himself, and, striking it,
sternly bade it be quiet. Edith was still more confounded by Reginald's behaviour ; that he, who was
so uniformly polite and well-bred, should behave with
rudeness to any woman, but more especially to one so
lovely and fascinating, was quite incomprehensible.
His dog, too, of which he had hitherto evinced a care
and tenderness that seemed almost ridiculous, to lift

his hand against it, for no other reason, as it seemed, than because it had caressed Lady Waldegrave! Surely this was carrying antipathy to its utmost bounds! Rousing herself from these reflections, however, she said, "I need scarcely ask if you have dined; I can only apologise for the uncomfortable meal I fear you will now have."

"Were I to answer you myself, I should say I had dined," replied Lady Waldegrave. "As I really don't mind dinner so much as many people do, and we had some not *very* bad mutton chops at the last stage— only they did taste a little of peats and whisky," she added, laughing. "But if you ask Madame Latour, she will tell you she has not dined since she left London."

"Get dinner immediately for Lady—for Madame Latour," cried Sir Reginald hastily, to a servant who happened to be in the room; then colouring at his own impetuosity, he turned to Edith and said, "I beg pardon, Miss Malcolm, for presuming to anticipate your orders,—it is time Glenroy should resume his place, since I am already usurping his authority."

"Oh no," said Edith gently; "papa would be pleased to see you performing the duties of his proxy, by showing hospitality (which, you know, is all we poor Highlanders have to show) to those kind friends who have come so far to see us."

"I think I might be prevailed upon to eat some of these Alpine strawberries," said Lady Waldegrave, as she seated herself at table. A slight bend of the head was the only reply Sir Reginald vouchsafed as he helped the strawberries, without once looking towards his beautiful guest.

Glenroy's bell had been sounding vehemently at intervals for some time, and a message now came, desiring to see Sir Reginald or Miss Malcolm directly.

Sir Reginald instantly started up, as if glad of the summons, and merely saying to Edith, "I will save you the trouble," hastily quitted the room.

"How extremement Saar Ragenall est changé," exclaimed Madame Latour, addressing her friend; "ce ne que l'ombre de lui-même! how he is pâle et morne, what you call painseeve. Miss Maulcomb, you most be *sensible* of an extraordinaire changement of Saar Ragenall?"

Edith's attention had been so engrossed by Florinda, that she had little to bestow upon Madame Latour; but, thus called upon, she considered her more attentively, and the impression made was not of a pleasing kind. Madame Latour, though rather past her prime, was still a showy, handsome brunette, with quick black eyes, good white teeth, a well-got-up complexion, and an air of the most thorough self-possession. "Sir Reginald has not been very well of late," said Edith, casting down her eyes to avoid the piercing stare which accompanied the interrogation.

"Ah! I am much inquiet for him," resumed Madame, with a shake of the head, "he was si joli, si charmant, vat you call pleesante—Ladi Waldegrave, n'êtes vous pas frappé—strock with de change?"

"I have scarcely yet had time to observe Sir Reginald's looks," replied Lady Waldegrave carelessly; "but I thought you and he seemed very merry together."

"Oh, we talk—nous rions—laaffe for one moment, mais donc il est si maigre—vat you call sin."

Meanwhile a repast from the *débris* of the dinner had been quickly got up at the other end of the room, and no sooner was it arranged than Madame Latour started up with great alacrity, and repaired to it. Lady Waldegrave declined partaking of it, saying she preferred dining on the dessert. Benbowie, whose appetite was of a most hospitable nature, instinctively stalked away, and took his place by her, as if intending to do the honours of the banquet, which indeed he did, if devouring everything within his reach was deemed an exemplary mark of hospitality.

"Cette grosse est excellente, excellente," said Madame Latour, after she had helped herself to the back and breast of a moorfowl, leaving the legs and pinions for Benbowie, who, like panting Time, toiled after her in vain. She flew like a butterfly or bee, from dish to dish, extracting the very heart and soul from each as she skimmed along, while at the same time she kept calling for every species of sauce and condiment that ever had been heard of, which she contrived to mix with the most admirable dexterity.

"Madame Latour est une peu gourmande," said Lady Waldegrave, addressing Edith, "but otherwise she is the best creature in the world; so perfectly

good-hearted, and so devoted to me. I am sure you
will like her."

Edith could not violate sincerity so far as to say
she thought she should, for she already felt what she
rarely did, a strong prepossession against this "best
creature in the world;" so she changed the subject
by making a sort of apology for Reginald's protracted
absence—"But papa is so fond of him," she said,
"that he finds it very difficult to get away from him."
Then, with an air of hesitation, she added, "Sir Reginald and you met abroad, I believe?"

"Yes, we met occasionally," replied her Ladyship,
slightly colouring.—"What very pretty china this is
—Dresden, I am sure," examining her plate with
great attention; "after all, there is nothing so pretty
as flowers upon china."

Edith assented, and then timidly added, "Madame
Latour seems much struck with the change in Reginald's appearance?"

"He does look rather *triste*," said Lady Waldegrave,
as she drew another plate towards her; "what a
charming group—these carnations are perfect!"

"The loss of my dear brother," said Edith, with
emotion, "has affected Reginald very deeply."

"Ah, true," replied Lady Waldegrave, putting on
a very soft, melancholy look.

"That, and the remains of malaria which he had
at Rome, will account to you for the present de-
pressed state of his spirits."

"Oh, perfectly," said Lady Waldegrave, biting her

lip as if to repress a smile which lurked round her
beautiful mouth, and shone in her large blue eyes.

Madame Latour's devotion meanwhile had been
dedicated exclusively to her dinner, and having done
due honour to it, she was now on her way to the
dessert, when Lady Waldegrave rose, saying, "Pray,
dear Edith, let us go to the drawing-room; the smell
of two dinners is rather too much for those who have
not partaken of either." Putting her arm within
Edith's, she then gracefully sauntered out of the
room, stopping occasionally to remark upon some of
the pictures, which she did in the style of one who
was perfect mistress of the theory of painting. They
were soon followed by the rest of the party, with the
exception of Sir Reginald.

An air of languid discontent was now insensibly
stealing over Lady Waldegrave, in spite of Madame
Latour's efforts to amuse by her broken English, when
again the sound of wheels was heard. Presently a
heavy-laden travelling coach drew up, from the
windows of which dogs' heads were seen protruding
in all directions.

"There comes mamma and her tiresome dogs!"
exclaimed Lady Waldegrave in a tone of chagrin.

At that moment the hall resounded with the sharp
shrill treble of three lap-dogs, which was quickly
accompanied by a deep running bass from the various
dogs of the household, and then caught up by the
imprisoned yells of the more remote inmates of the
kennel, "in notes by distance made more sweet."

"Ah, I am happy to see Reginald has gone to receive Lady Elizabeth," said Edith, as his voice was heard in the hall giving orders to the servants; and then flying down the steps, he presented his arm to Lady Elizabeth, as she alighted, and appeared to welcome her with the semblance of the greatest cordiality.

"How differently he met Lady Waldegrave!" thought Edith, then hastened forward to receive her stepmother.

CHAPTER XLVI

LADY ELIZABETH was now a thin, weak, cross, old-looking woman, dressed in the extreme of youthfulness, with an unnatural profusion of flaxen ringlets dangling round withered, hollow, rouged cheeks. She but just touched Edith's hand, and laid her face to hers, then passed on to her daughter, and putting her arms round her, kissed her with a sort of hysterical emphasis; then, in a peevish, querulous tone, exclaimed—

"You may thank heaven, child, you see me safe and tolerably well! What a frightful road for me to travel! How could you leave me, my love? I have been excessively alarmed—those dreadful precipices, and that shocking water!"

"Quite charming, mamma," said Lady Waldegrave. "It seemed as if Scott's beautiful description of the Trossachs had started into life;" and in a low tone, but with perfect modulation of voice and manner, she repeated some of those glowing lines.

"Nonsense, my dear," exclaimed Lady Elizabeth; "it is a frightful, a *dangerous* road, and it was very improper of you, my love, to leave my carriage so far behind."

"I beg pardon, mamma; but it did not appear to me there was the slightest danger," said her daughter.

"My dear love, don't say so," cried her Ladyship impatiently; "I never in my life travelled so dangerous a road. If I had had the slightest recollection of it, I never should have attempted it, even to gratify you, my sweetest—those tremendous rocks on one hand, and the lake on the other—shocking! I had forgot it entirely, else I certainly never should have dreamt of such a thing as coming here."

"Don't you feel fatigued, mamma?" inquired Lady Waldegrave.

"Certainly, my love, excessively fatigued, and my nerves shaken beyond expression; and those dear dogs! Bijou was really quite ill. I'm surprised Glenroy can suffer such a road—it ought not to be permitted. If I had been travelling in the dark, or if my horses had taken fright—or a thousand things might have happened."

"Don't you think mamma *must* be much fatigued, Dr. Price?" said Lady Waldegrave, turning to a sickly-looking, elderly man, in a black wig, green surtout, white trousers, pale hands, and a ring.

"Unquestionably," replied the doctor, in a slow, hesitating manner; "her Ladyship has been much agitated, and consequently must be considerably exhausted. If her Ladyship is to dine now, I would recommend half-an-hour's repose after dinner, either upon a couch or easy-chair, whichever she gives the preference to; or if there is to be any delay in the preparing of her Ladyship's repast, then I would advise the rest to be taken previous to partaking of it."

Edith took the hint, and ringing the bell, ordered a third dinner to be prepared as soon as possible for her very considerate guests. Then, having procured some refreshments in the meantime, she offered to conduct Lady Elizabeth to her apartment. With a languid air she accepted Edith's arm, but as she was leaving the room, turned round and called—

"Florinda, my darling, you must come too. And, Dr. Price, you will give Rosalie her directions about the drops, and do see that the dogs get their dinners, for they are almost famished, poor loves. Do, Florinda, love, come with me. I assure you I have been excessively alarmed; it is all your doing, my dear—that road was really quite frightful—I shall never forget my alarm."

Here Lady Waldegrave swept her fingers over a harp which stood near, and thus contrived to evade the proposal.

Lady Elizabeth, after another ineffectual attempt to attract her daughter's attention, suffered Edith to lead her from the room; but it was with difficulty she managed to shuffle along, in shoes evidently much too small for her feet.

"Lady Waldegrave is a charming creature, is she not?" said she, stopping in the middle of the hall, and leaning her whole weight on Edith.

"Oh, beautiful!" exclaimed Edith; "I could not have imagined anything so faultless, and at the same time so captivating."

"Ah! very true—her manners are very good. I have bestowed great pains upon her; she is, perhaps, if anything—but it is scarcely perceptible—a single degree too much *embonpoint;* at least she *may* be, unless she is upon her guard. I was a perfect whipping-post at her age; and even now I don't think I am larger than she is. It is a great matter to preserve the figure; nothing makes people look so soon old as allowing themselves to grow fat, and get out of shape. Florinda's figure, to be sure, is perfection, —rather, if anything, too tall perhaps; she is taller than I am; otherwise, as Monsieur Perpignan said, we might very well pass for twins—a pretty thought, was it not?"

Edith could scarcely restrain a smile as she looked at the old wrinkled scarecrow, who sought to assimilate herself with her young and blooming daughter.

Her Ladyship went on—"She has been prodigiously admired and *recherché* wherever we went; but I don't intend that she should marry yet, for, in fact, Lady Waldegrave has nothing to gain by marriage; like myself, she may lose, but she can scarcely better herself; it is very well for *des filles sans dots* to be eager about a settlement; but with my daughter's rank, beauty, fashion, and fortune, what is she to look for? And if she were to marry now, she would have a daughter at her heels, while she herself was quite a young woman. I married a great deal too soon, and you see the consequence! I may be a grandmother in the very prime of life! Shocking and foolish!"

They had now reached the door of her Ladyship's apartment, and upon entering the dressing-room, the floor was covered with imperials, wells, trunks, boxes, *sacs de nuit*, and packages of every description, which her maid and footman were busily employed in putting to rights.

"Do, Rosalie, contrive to get my things unpacked and arranged as quickly as possible," cried Lady Elizabeth impatiently, and looking round the room. "Pray ask the housekeeper to let me have a *chaise longue*, I rather prefer it to a sofa; and bring up my dog-baskets and cushions; let me have a larger table, and have that commode carried away. I shall not have room to turn about here." Then addressing her footman, "And, Rousseau, look to my guitar, and have it brought here with my music books and *portefeuille*: I brought my guitar and Rossini's last opera, as I thought it would amuse Glenroy to have a little good music; but I am sorry to hear from Sir Reginald that he is so unwell. I shall make a point of Dr. Price seeing him; he is the best creature in the world; dresses so well; he is so skilful and gentlemanly, and is never out of the way. I have the most perfect confidence in him. It is very unfortunate for him, poor man, that he has such wretched health himself. Had it been otherwise, indeed, he must have been devoted to the public, and I should not have had the good fortune to attach him to my establishment; and I am in hopes change of scene and travelling may do him good.—How very tedious you are,

Rosalie—do get my things ready, that I may begin to dress."

"I beg pardon," said Edith; "but I think Dr. Price recommended your taking a little rest before dinner; and as we are quite a family party, I hope you won't add to your fatigue by dressing."

"Oh, Dr. Price does not at all understand that sort of thing," replied her Ladyship; "he is excellent in his way, but—I shall put on a black gown to-day, Rosalie—Florinda and I agreed to wear black at first, as a sort of proper compliment, you know "— glancing at Edith's deep mourning—"otherwise I never do wear black, it is so unpleasant, and puts such shocking thoughts in one's head; but we won't talk of it— it makes me quite ill to think of such things!" Then, as Rosalie announced that her Ladyship's toilet was ready, she gently pressed the tip of Edith's fingers, and said, "Now, my dear, I shall join you in half an hour." And Edith gladly availed herself of the hint to withdraw. Wearied and sickened at the frivolity, heartlessness, and egotism already so fully developed in her stepmother's conversation, Edith bitterly repented having been accessory to bringing her to the house.

"Reginald was right," thought she; "papa will never be able to bear this." And she trembled to think of the shock that would ensue when two such antipodes came in contact.

It was therefore with fear she returned into her father's presence, whom she found already apprised of the extent of the party, Benbowie having twice counted them over to him on his fingers, and thus demonstrated to him that there was an individual to each, thumbs included. Edith had, of course, to bear a storm of reproach and invective for having brought such a crew to the house, interspersed with threats of turning the Doctor and Frenchwoman, with their attendants, out of it; and of not seeing the face of one of them as long as they stayed.

CHAPTER XLVII.

In the drawing-room Edith found only Lady Walde-grave and her friend. The former was reclining languidly on a sofa, and Madame Latour was seated on a low stool by her, discoursing with much energy in her native language.

"Soyez sure qu'il est passionnément amoureux," exclaimed she vehemently, as Edith entered; then, on perceiving her, she called, "Venez ici, Mlle. Malcomb—dites moi, croyez vous qu'il soit possible d'aimer cette dame? n'est elle pas affreuse—wat you call oglie?" And making a grimace, she put her hands before her eyes.

Lady Waldegrave slightly blushed, and smiled as, half rising from her reclining attitude, she extended her hand to Edith, and said, "You have been sadly bored, I fear, dear Edith; but we must not allow mamma to monopolise you thus."

There was something so sweet and fascinating in Lady Waldegrave's every tone and look and movement, that Edith, won by the charm, seated herself by her, and soon forgot her momentary dissatisfaction with Lady Elizabeth and Madame Latour.

"How vivid my remembrance is of you," said she coaxingly to Edith; "and how like a dream it seems to find myself again here, where everything awakens some childish recollection; most of them to my own shame, indeed, when I think what a little saucy chit I was. And, by-the-bye, how very unkind and ungrateful you must have thought me, in never having written to you. But, indeed, you cannot conceive how much I have been under the control of guardians and governesses for the last twelve years. Thank Heaven, I am now pretty much emancipated from bondage; but, I do assure you, it is a very tiresome thing to be trained up to be a person of consequence; and I often thought with envy of the delightful liberty you enjoyed of rambling amongst your Highland hills and forests with the boys, while I was condemned to lessons from morning till night. My only relaxation was a walk in the Park with my governesses, or a still more tiresome drive with mamma. But you have forgiven me, dearest Edith, have you not?" and she put her arm round Edith's neck, and laid her head on her shoulder, and looked in her face with the most winning expression.

"I have nothing to forgive—I am sure I never shall have anything to forgive you," said Edith, with fond affection.

"Non, non, c'est un ange, un parfait ange!" exclaimed Madame Latour, putting her handkerchief to her eyes. "Mais, Ladi Waldegrave, ne faites vous pas toilette ce soir?" inquired she, as she rose from the lowly seat, and glanced at herself in an opposite mirror.

"No, I am too lazy; will you excuse me, Edith, if I remain *en déshabillé ?*"

"Ah, c'est le privilege de la jeunesse et de la beauté, de se passer d'ornemens; mais lorsqu'on est un peu passée, ma belle,"—Madame sighed affectedly. "Ainsi je vais sonner pour ma femme de chambre." And to Edith's great relief, Madame Latour retired to her toilet.

"*Apropos* of *dress*," said Lady Waldegrave, "I hope you admire cameos, Edith, because I have brought you some, and I shall be sorry if you don't happen to like them; I am very impatient to show them to you, so I shall send for them now;" and, in spite of Edith's remonstrances, she rang the bell for her maid, and in a few minutes the box was brought, and an exquisite set of cameos, of the most perfect design and execution, was presented to Edith, whose native good taste enabled her at once to appreciate the beauty and value of the gift.

"How my heart overflows with affection and kind wishes!" said Lady Waldegrave. "I now feel so forcibly the truth of that beautiful sentiment of Madame de Staël's, 'Il y a en nous un superflu d'ame, qu'il est doux de consacrer à ce qui est beau, quand ce qui est bien, est accompli.' Not that I can flatter myself with having accomplished the good," added she, with a smile, "*le beau* is so much more to my taste than *le bien.*"

"If to give pleasure is to do good, you have suc-ceeded in one instance," said Edith, as she continued admiring the various beauties of the classic gems; "but I am afraid there is too much of *le beau* here, to admit of much of *le bien.*"

Lady Waldegrave was silent for a few minutes, then, with a sigh, said, "Whether I shall ever do good is doubtful, but it is certain that I have already been the cause of much mischief. I cannot tell you how much I lament the unfortunate misunderstanding that took place between Lady Elizabeth and Glenroy. It grieves me more than I can express, to think that I should have been the cause, the unintentional one indeed, of their separation!"

"Do not distress yourself on that account, dear Florinda," said Edith tenderly, "for indeed Lady Elizabeth and papa seem so different, I do not think they ever could have lived happily together."

" You are very kind and considerate to say so," replied Lady Waldegrave, pressing her hand; "but we cannot tell what habit might have done. I must therefore always look upon myself as the cause of this, I fear, irreparable mischief."

"You blame yourself unjustly," said Edith ear-nestly. "Young as I was at the time, from what I remember, I should suppose you had only been one of many causes of disagreement."

"Perhaps so; but still I feel as a guilty thing. Oh, how glad I should be if I could see them fairly reconciled!"

"To tell you the truth, I have often, especially of late, felt the same wish," said Edith, with a slight degree of confusion; "but now I see—I fear—I do not think it will be practicable—they are so different."

"Of that you must be a better judge than I," replied Lady Waldegrave, "as my impression of Glenroy is probably very imperfect. I only remember him a very tall, fine-looking man, with a loud voice, and an authoritative manner, of which I was a little afraid; but perhaps circumstances may have softened these."

Edith shook her head. "Papa is very kind-hearted and affectionate," said she, "but he likes to have his own way, and Lady Elizabeth has, of course, been so long independent of control——"

"Ah, true," interrupted Lady Waldegrave; "mamma is not easily managed, and she is excessively fond of what is called a gay life, and therefore, I fear, we must be satisfied with a mere temporary reconciliation, without attempting a more solid union. It is unfortunate, for when I marry, mamma would be more respectable living with her husband than she will be by herself; and when *you* marry, which, of course, you will also do—now don't blush, Edith, love—I am not going to talk of lovers; I shall find out in good time whether you have any *affaires du cœur*, so pray don't make me your confidante—'tis the office in the world I have the greatest dread of."

Edith laughed and promised, and the conversation was ended by the entrance of Sir Reginald and Dr.

Price, looking like two people whom chance, not choice, had thrown together.

Sir Reginald drew near, as if about to address Lady Waldegrave, then stopped, and turned to the table where the cameos were, and taking up one of the bracelets, commended the beauty of it.

"They are indeed perfect," said Edith; "each cameo is a picture in itself, and I should have thought myself rich with any one of them; but Lady Waldegrave insists upon my accepting the whole set."

Sir Reginald said nothing, but hastily put down the bracelet, and, joining Dr. Price at one of the windows, immediately began to talk politics with him. Edith coloured with shame at this proof of her lover's rudeness and dislike to Lady Waldegrave. "And yet," she thought, "how is it possible to hate anything so beautiful and captivating? What can be the cause of this coldness which he seems to feel for everything connected with a creature so lovely and engaging?"

"How did you like my picture, Edith?" inquired Lady Waldegrave. "Should you have known me by it?"

Edith looked at her with the air of one who is at a loss to comprehend the meaning of a question.

"Your picture?" replied she; "I never saw any picture of you, except the little daub done by Mrs. Macauley, which, bad as it is, has always hung in my dressing-room. You don't mean that?"

"No—the picture I sent you from Florence. Whom did I send it by?" as if trying to recollect. "I certainly did send it—how provoking that I should not be able to tell by whom! There were a number of English there; but perhaps Sir Reginald Malcolm might, if he chose, assist my memory."

Sir Reginald took no notice, but continued talking with much energy with Dr. Price on the affairs of Europe. Edith called to him—"Sir Reginald!—Sir Reginald! I wish you would come and assist Lady Waldegrave and me in our attempts to recover a picture she gave in charge to some one at Florence for me, but which I have never received."

"Even if I guessed at the offender," said Sir Reginald, in a low voice, "Lady Waldegrave surely would not have the cruelty to have his name exposed to the indignation which his conduct merits."

Reginald was behind Edith, who did not see his face as he spoke; but he was opposite to Lady Waldegrave, who blushed deeply, while something like a smile was upon her lip.

"Is it Florinda or I whose indignation you think would be so excessive?" asked Edith.

"Both," he replied, as he turned quickly and rejoined Dr. Price.

"It must be from mere carelessness that it has not been delivered," said Lady Waldegrave; "but if it does not appear soon, you or I must draw up an advertisement for it, Edith. Seriously, it must be recovered, as a lock of my hair accompanied it, and it is not every one I should choose to be in possession of such things, valueless as they may be to the retainer."

Sir Reginald and Dr. Price were busily engaged looking at an atlas; and the two friends continued to converse together, till Lady Elizabeth made her appearance, dressed like fifteen for a first ball.

"My dear Florinda!" she exclaimed, "what do I see? not yet dressed? How very uncomfortable it makes me to see anybody in a morning gown in the evening—it is so very trying, an angel could not stand such a test. I do assure you, my dear, you look very ill."

"Thank you, mamma," said Lady Waldegrave coolly; and taking up a footstool cover, with Mrs. Macauley's needle still sticking in it, she began to work with an air of unconcern.

"Too ridiculous!" cried Lady Elizabeth, with a shrug of her little bare shoulders; "you only want a brass thimble to make you quite complete, Lady Waldegrave. Why should you wish to look like a dowdy, my love?" Then, in a whisper to Edith, "She is a beautiful creature, to be sure! what a profile! what a throat! what hands! Madame d'Aumont used to say she should have known her to be my daughter anywhere from the hands alone—hands and feet, you know, are the great criterions of birth. Heavens, how she was admired at Paris! She is a *little* spoilt, perhaps, by the sensation she caused."

Here her Ladyship's dinner was announced, and, as Edith rose to attend her, Lady Waldegrave exclaimed, "Poor dear Edith! this is really too much, to do the honours of three dinners in one day. How you must hate us all! Cannot good Mrs. Macauley relieve you from this duty? I am sure mamma will excuse you."

"Mrs. Macauley and Benbowie are always with papa in the evening," said Edith; "but, at any rate, Sir Reginald and I would wish to welcome Lady Elizabeth to Glenroy ourselves, and as you did not partake of the first dinner, perhaps you will join our party."

"No dinner! My dear child," cried Lady Elizabeth, "what do I hear? How very foolish. How could Madame Latour suffer such a thing? No wonder you look pale—quite *abattue.* Come, my love, you shall dine with me : my dinner, you know, is a mere make-believe. Sir Reginald, you will take charge of Lady Waldegrave"—putting her own arm within Edith's. Sir Reginald hastily recoiled at the proposal; then quickly recovering himself, was advancing, when Lady Waldegrave said, with an air of coldness, "Excuse me, mamma; I have already dined, and I prefer remaining here."

"But, my dear love, you will be alone—some one must stay with you. Not you," pressing Edith's arm; "I have much to say to you. Perhaps Dr. Price." But the doctor looked very glum at the proposal; and luckily at that moment Madame Latour appeared, which settled the point, and the party proceeded to the dining-room, leaving the two friends together. "I wish particularly to talk to you, my dear," said her Ladyship in a low voice to Edith, as she walked mincingly along. "There are many

things very interesting to both of us I have on my
mind at present. By-the-bye, my dear, your hair is
not dressed quite *à-la-mode*. It becomes you very
well, but still it is too simple for the present style—
the simple is now quite exploded; and, indeed, I'm
not sure that I like simplicity, though it does well
enough now and then, by way of a little variety.
Florinda, for instance, may simple now and then for
a whim, but *she* may do anything she chooses. You
have heard these pretty lines somebody made upon
her?

> ' Tender or free, in smiles or sadness drest,
> The reigning humour ever suits her best.'"

Then, as she seated herself at table, she repeated,
"Tender and free," etc. "Sir Reginald, do you remember who it was made these lines upon my
daughter?"

"I beg pardon," said Sir Reginald; "but I believe
the lines are to be found in Partenopex de Blois."

"Excuse me, Sir Reginald," replied the lady, with
an air of displeasure; "but the lines were made upon
Lady Waldegrave, as any one may perceive at once;
and, as Mr. Ellenton very well remarked to me, they
were a perfect picture of her. Mr. Ellenton repeats
verses better than anybody I know.—This soup is
very good—it is very good,"—sending away her plate
after taking two spoonfuls. "I know you don't recommend salmon to me, Dr. Price, but that looks so
particularly well, I will just taste it." Then, having
taken a little of it, it was also sent off. "Pray, send

me a *pâté*, Dr. Price—ah, chicken *pâté*, very well
seasoned, though?"—putting down the knife and
fork, after the first mouthful. "Yes, I will try the
fricandeau," and so on with game, tarts, jellies, and
dessert, in a manner enough to have raised the ghost
of Lycurgus, or Dr. Gregory. No sooner had she
finished, than, quickly rising, she again linked herself
to Edith. "Now, let us go to the library, or the saloon,
or anywhere to be quiet, as I wish to have a little
tête-à-tête with you, my dear. I have so much to say
to you; and, *àpropos*, do you know, I think Sir Reginald Malcolm excessively disagreeable? How very
rude to contradict me about these lines! I know he
is your cousin—but nobody minds cousins. To tell
you the truth, I never did like him—as a boy, you
know, he was shocking; he had very nearly killed
my daughter, as you may remember; he had beat
her in the most frightful manner; in fact, had almost
actually strangled her. I certainly never would have
forgiven it; and I did not approve of Florinda's having admitted him to her acquaintance. It began
when she was absent from me, with her aunt, Lady
Escott, at Naples, else I never would have permitted
it."

"Lady Waldegrave and Sir Reginald do not appear
to be very good friends yet," said Edith, in some
embarrassment.

"Why, no—I am not sure; he certainly was
admired; and he *is* rather handsome; don't you
think so? But Florinda, though the sweetest creature

in the world, is a little capricious—that between ourselves,'though—and I blame Madame Latour entirely
for whatever faults my daughter may have.   I don't
quite like Madame Latour; she affects a style of dress
which is absurd, and wears her petticoats so *very*
short, to show her foot—which, by-the-bye—is *not*
well shaped.   Such display is very bad taste, and
quite defeats the object," glancing at herself in a
mirror with great complacency.   "To tell you a
secret, my dear—but this is quite in confidence—I
half suspect her of a design upon Sir Reginald.   It is
rather ridiculous, to be sure, for Madame Latour is
by no means a young-*looking* woman—in fact, that
is one great advantage we blondes have over brunettes
in general, we retain a youthful appearance ·much
longer.   However, it is certain he paid her great
attention at Florence, and was much more in my
house than I thought either proper or agreeable."

Reginald an admirer of Madame Latour!   Edith
could not believe her ears; and yet with what vivacity he had met her!   How she sickened at the thought
—how degrading to Sir Reginald, to herself, to harbour it for a single moment!   While these thoughts
passed through her mind, Lady Elizabeth went on.

"Madame Latour is of a good family, and so was
her husband—to be sure she is older than Sir Reginald; but that is nothing—a few years one way or
other makes little difference, and he certainly *did* admire her, and paid her great attention; but, however,
it may have been merely *pour passer le temps.*"

Could Reginald, her own betrothed, have condescended to flirt, *pour passer le temps,* with a Madame
Latour? Oh, how Edith's pure and devoted heart
rose at the suggestion!

"I should not be sorry to see Madame Latour well
disposed of," continued her Ladyship; "she is rather
de trop now; indeed I had no intention of keeping her
so long, for in fact I merely engaged her for a year,
as a sort of something between a governess and a companion for Florinda; you understand the sort of person. My own health was wretched at that time; but
upon the whole she is objectionable—she talks so much,
and is so extremely gross in her eating, quite shocking,
and dresses with so much pretension—and, in short,
she is become so unpleasant, that I do assure you I
shall not be sorry to lose her; but of course this is
all a secret, and I don't wish to take any notice of
it either to Florinda or Sir Reginald just at present;
but we shall see how they go on. Did you ever see
anything so excessively *recherché* as her style of dress?"

In this manner she continued to babble on for about
an hour, resisting all Edith's attempts to return to the
drawing-room, from whence issued the most delightful
sounds of music.

"Yes, Florinda does play and sing very well," said
she, in answer to Edith's remark; "in fact, she would
not have been my daughter had she not been possessed
of all the requisites for a good musician; but I think
she has done enough now; I don't approve of her
singing too long at a time. Come, my dear, we shall

return to the drawing-room. I have much to say to you, but we shall take another time, when we can have a little quiet talk together."

On entering the drawing-room, they found Lady Waldegrave seated at the harp, pouring forth the full tide of song in strains of perfect melody. Her voice was rich, clear, and flexible, and she both played and sang with much taste and execution.

"Florinda possesses every personal requisite for the harp," whispered Edith's tormentor, as she still leant upon her, "quite a classic bust, the most perfect hands and arms, and the prettiest foot in the world. How shocking to see women pawing the harp with great ill-shaped hands, or awkwardly showing their long waists and clumsy feet! Such things ought not to be permitted; I have been obliged to leave off playing the harp since my health became delicate, it requires more muscular exertion than Dr. Price thinks good for me; but you shall hear me on the guitar."

Edith's attention was directed to Reginald, who sat apart at a table, with an open book spread before him, his head resting on his hand, which shaded his eyes. Madame Latour sat by him working a purse, which was every now and then suspended, while she held up her hands, threw up her eyes, and sighed in ecstasy at particular passages in the song. Dr. Price was reading the newspapers. Mrs. Macauley was sitting with her hands on her lap, listening to what she did not understand.

Scarcely was the song ended, when Lady Elizabeth

exclaimed impatiently, "Now, my dearest, you have done quite enough for to-night—I must not suffer you to over-exert yourself; I will relieve you now. Dr. Price, pray ring the bell for my guitar."

"You forget how late it is, mamma," said her daughter, with an air of chagrin, "and that we are all beginning to get tired, even of music."

"Nonsense, my love, 'tis not at all late—my fatigue is quite gone off. I feel as if I could even take a turn in a waltz," looking towards Sir Reginald, who now fixed his eyes attentively on his book. "Of course you waltz, Miss Malcolm? come, let us take a round together."

"Your Ladyship must excuse me; my spirits are not equal to dancing," said Edith; and her eyes filled with tears as she thought, "This is the boasted sympathy I was led to expect in our sorrow!"

"'Deed, and I think it would not be decent to be dancing," said Mrs. Macauley in a low voice to Madame Latour, "considering the misfortunes of the family, and Glenroy himself laid up in his bed, honest man!"

Sir Reginald saw that Edith was hurt. Quitting Madame Latour, he hastily advanced towards her, and taking her hand, drew it within his arm, while he led her to an open window. "You are ill—fatigued, I fear, dear Edith," said he in a tone of compassion. At that moment Lady Waldegrave rose, and called to her, "Excuse me, Miss Malcolm, but I must wish you good-night;" she was then retiring, attended by her friend, when Lady Elizabeth, folding her in her arms, kissed her forehead, "Good-night, my sweetest, you do look *abattue;* but a morning-gown in the evening is too trying for an angel—good-night, my charmer; and here comes my guitar. Miss Malcolm, you will return when you have seen Florinda to her apartment, and we shall have a little soft music before supper."

Sir Reginald opened the door for the ladies to withdraw, and as Lady Waldegrave passed, he made her a profound bow, which she noticed with a slight and constrained bend of the head. Madame Latour whispered a few words to him in Italian, then laughed gaily, and the door was closed. "Quelle grâce dans son salut! vat you call bow," said she, addressing Lady Waldegrave; then turning to Edith, "Ah, Meess Malcomb, votre frère est charmant! il a fait tourner la tête à toutes les femmes d'Italie."

"Sir Reginald is not my brother," said Edith, with a blush.

"Saar Reginaal n'est pas votre frère, your broder?" exclaimed Madame, in well-feigned astonishment; "Vraiment je n'en ai pas douté, ven I do see ses aimables petites attentions pour vous;—mais que je suis étourdie! I do remember dat he talk of sometime his bonne petite cousine Ecossaise."

Edith's cheeks glowed, and her heart rose at this insolence.

"Que je suis bête to meestak," continued Madame, as if in despair; "vous me pardonnerez, ma chère Meess Malcomb?"

"Edith, I am sure, looks too good to resent anything," said Lady Waldegrave, suddenly restored to good spirits, "much less so harmless a meestak," laughing, as she mimicked Madame's pronunciation; "but your patience is heavily taxed, dear Edith—mamma has such an inveterate habit of sitting up half the night, that it is quite distressing to think of your having to keep her company."

"How extraamement Ladi Elizabeth injure her estomac by so frequent eating," said Madame Latour in a tone of virtuous indignation; "et il est si malsain de souper! vat you call disealthy; den she will expose ses pauvres soldiers, ses épaules, and they die of de rheumatisme."

Edith embraced Lady Waldegrave, and, coldly saluting Madame Latour, returned to the drawing-room, where she had to sit for an hour listening to insipid madrigals and rondos, after which her Lady-ship, having pecked like a sparrow at everything that was at table, at length retired, and the house of Glenroy was once more at rest.

CHAPTER XLVIII

WHEN Lady Waldegrave appeared at breakfast the following morning, she looked still more beautiful than she had done the preceding evening. Madame Latour was as usual by her side, but Lady Elizabeth never was visible in the morning. Dr. Price was also there, as silent and sickly-looking as usual. Edith had planned a little excursion by land and water, to show some of the beauties of Glenroy to her guests, and she intended that Reginald should take the management; but her surprise and disappointment were great when she learnt that he had set off early in the morning to shoot. Here was a fresh act of incivility and unkindness, and Edith vainly tried to falter out some excuse for him to Lady Waldegrave, who heard her in silence, while an air of languid dissatisfaction gradually stole over her lovely features.

"Ah, le pauvre Saar Reginaal!" exclaimed Madame Latour, in a tone of deep commiseration, and heaving a sigh.

"If you please, Madame, what do you mean by that?" inquired Mrs. Macauley, with her usual blunt simplicity.

"Ah, que je le plains!" continued Madame Latour, as if not hearing Mrs. Macauley.

The cough and the trot of Amailye were now heard resounding in the stillness of the warm sunny morning, and presently she was descried passing the. window with her load on her back. In another second, the loud broad tones of Mr. M'Dow were heard interrogating the servant, and next entered the gentleman himself, his face "round as my father's shield," every line and lineament big with triumph and exultation, standing out in bold *alto relievo*. The customary salutations were scarcely over, before it was obvious that Mr. M'Dow's exclamation would not be that of Hamlet—"Let me not burst in ignorance," but rather that of his father's ghost, "I could a tale unfold." It was also evident that the secret with which he was burdened was of an agreeable nature, as not all the respect with which he strove to address Lady Waldegrave could master the inveterate hoch, hoch, ho, which burst forth even on his introduction. Seating himself at table, he fixed his eyes on her with a stare of astonishment; and while he stuffed one side of his mouth to its utmost extent, he discoursed at large with the other, and accordingly began, "It's most amazing to see how young people shoot up! It seems no time since your Ladyship was a little fair-haired missy in a frock, with a doll in your arms, and now you are quite a full-grown lady! It's really wonderful to see the changes a few years bring to pass!"

"I cannot apply that observation to you, Mr.

M'Dow," said Lady Waldegrave, with a smile; "for, as far as my imperfect recollection serves me, you have undergone very little change during those years."

Mr. M'Dow bowed after his manner, then, with a hoch, hoch, ho, replied, "That's precisely what some of my good friends find fault with me for, my lady; they say that I ought to have changed (my state) before now—hoch, hoch, ho!"

"'Deed, then, and I think so too," said Mrs. Macauley, with her usual simplicity; if you had a wife you would maybe like to stay more at home. But better late than never. I don't think but what you'll get a wife yet, Mr. M'Dow."

"Had you ever any doubts of that, Mrs. Macauley?" cried Mr. M'Dow, in a tone of pique. "I was not aware that ever I had professed celibacy."

"Well, then, I declare from your face I think you're going to get a wife now, Mr. M'Dow; you look so croose and canty," said Mrs. Macauley.

"Oh, you're a witch, Mrs. Macauley! just a witch," repeated Mr. M'Dow, with one of his exuberant roars. "If you had lived a hundred years ago, you would have stood a fair chance of being burnt!"

"Oh, as sure as death, then, that's just owning that you are going to be married, Mr. M'Dow," exclaimed Mrs. Macauley, in that accent of joyful surprise which always attends the discovery of a marriage. "And was it not clever in me to find it out? 'deed, I think it was. I declare I'm glad of it, for I think it

will be a great improvement to you, if she is a
sensible, well-principled woman, which I hope she is."

"Well, there's no keeping anything from you ladies
—you really are most amazingly acute! at the same
time I'm not sensible of having committed myself in
any shape—hoch, hoch, ho!"

"Ah, comme il fait chaud!" exclaimed Madame
Latour; "le pauvre Saar Reginaal!"

"By-the-bye, I was missing a certain gentleman,"
said Mr. M'Dow, with a significant glance directed
towards Edith; "but I hope he's not to be long
absent, as I'm anxious to come to an understanding
with him regarding certain arrangements that shall
be nameless,—as we're both bound for the same port,
we must take care not to run foul of each other. He's
had the advantage of me at the starting; but I suspect I'll make the harbour before him—hoch, hoch,
ho!"

This metaphorical flourish was, of course, Greek
and Hebrew to the whole party except Edith and Mrs.
Macauley. The former coloured and was silent; but
the latter exclaimed, "Well, that's right of you, Mr.
M'Dow, just to tell the truth, and not to think shame
about it. What for should not people tell when they
are going to be married?—and marriage such an
honourable state! As sure as anything, I'm very glad
you're going to be settled at last. . Benbowie, are not
you happy that Mr. M'Dow's going to be married?"

"Surely, surely," said Benbowie; "has she any
money?"

"Why, as to that," said Mr. M'Dow, with an air of great dignity, and conscious elevation of soul, "I have never made fortune my principal object; I consider it beneath a man of honour and integrity to lay himself out for money; at the same time, I would not quarrel with it if it came in my way—and upon this occasion, the lady's fortune is *shootable;* indeed, I may say, pretty handsome."

Edith tried to utter some complimentary words on the occasion, but found it very difficult to combine compliments with sincerity. Luckily Mrs. Macauley covered all deficiencies: "And what may be the name of the lady, Mr. M'Dow, if it is not a secret?"

"Why, if it is, it will not be long one," returned Mr. M'Dow, still very consequential; "indeed I strongly suspect the report had reached the country before myself, or I doubt if even my good friend Mrs. Macauley, with all her wit and shrewdness, would have taken me up so cleverly. It's amazing how a report of that kind spreads! It was for that reason I wished to lose no time in communicating the event myself to my excellent friend and pawtron, for I only returned home last night; but before this time to-morrow, I have no doubt it will be over the whole country. The lady's name is Miss Collina Muckle of Glasgow."

"Well, I think it's a very honest-like name," said Mrs. Macauley. "I had once a sister they called Colin, but she died, poor thing, of St. Anthony's fire; and Mr. Macauley had a cousin that was married a second

marriage to a Mr. Mucklehose, a very decent man.
I wonder if she can be any relation of his? He was
Bailie Mucklehose, of Portneuk; he was a——"

"The very same!" interrupted Mr. M'Dow.
"Bailie Mucklehose, of Portneuk, was the fawther
(by his first wife) of the lady in question; but, at the
time of their fawther's death, they dropped the *hose*,
thinking the other a more fashionable name, which
perhaps it is. The Bailie was a most highly respectable man, and left his daughters in good circumstances."

"Well, is it not curious to think that you and I,
Mr. M'Dow, who have been so long acquaint, are now
going to be connected together by marriage? I declare,
I think it is very extraordinary to see how things are
brought about! And I saw Bailie Mucklehose once,
when I was in Glasgow, about five-and-thirty years
ago. He was an honest-like, weel-fa'ured man, with
a fine rosy colour. He was a——"

"Perhaps you may be able to trace a family-like-
ness here," interrupted Mr. M'Dow, plunging his hand
into one of his huge pockets, and drawing forth—not
a decreet, or reclaiming petition, as in days of yore—
but a small, oval, red morocco case, which upon being
opened, disclosed the full-blown charms of Miss
Collina Muckle.

"I am no great judge of painting, myself," said
the exulting lover, as he handed it round; "but it
strikes me as being most beautifully painted—extremely high finished. I can't say I think the likeness

altogether so favourable as it might have been. It is painted by a very young man, who has just set up."

It is unnecessary to be so minute as the artist was, in depicting the charms of the original. Suffice it therefore to say there was the usual bad drawing and distortion; there was a large ivory and vermilion cheek, and a smaller burnt umber one, a nose all on one side, round pale eyes of different sizes, a simpering mouth, a range of hair-dresser curls sitting on end, a wooden arm, a white gown, a yellow scarf, a blue cloud, and a coral necklace.

Few and faint were the remarks passed upon Miss Muckle, as she made the round of the table; but luckily Mr. M'Dow's perceptions were too obtuse to enable him to feel any omissions. "I had, of course, to return the compliment in kind; but I doubt the painter did not succeed quite as well with me. In fact, the clerical dress is not the most becoming, in my opinion, for a man to sit in; the gown and bands are rather stiff and heavy, and not so fashionable-looking as one could wish. However, the lady was pleased, and that was enough."

"*Apropos* of pictures," said Edith to Lady Waldegrave, wishing to turn the conversation from the loves of Mr. M'Dow, "have you not yet been able to recollect by whom you sent your picture to me?"

Lady Waldegrave coloured, and in slight confusion answered, "Yes—no—not to a certainty. But I think I shall recover it yet; and if not," she added, with mock gravity, "the loss will not be irreparable.

It is one which I daresay Mrs. Macauley will be kind enough to replace. Won't you paint my picture again, dear Mrs. Macauley?"

"'Deed and I will that," cried Mrs. Macauley, in a transport of delight. "I have painted Miss Edith's already, which I will show to you after breakfast; and I've been wanting Sir Reginald to sit too for his picture; and then when I've done your Ladyship, I'm sure I may be well proud, for I'll have painted tho three greatest beauties that ever were seen!"

"Sir Reginald should make a well-looked picture," said Mr. M'Dow; "that's still a good likeness of him," pointing to a picture of him as a boy, that hung opposite, "though there's not just so much of the pickle in him now as there was then; he was really a wild little dog in these days, as your Ladyship may remember. You know what a work he had with you at the first, there was nothing like you; poor Miss Edith was thought nothing of; you were his sweetheart and his wife, and I don't know all what, and I was to promise to marry him to you in my kirk, whenever his papa came home; then you and he cast out about something or another, and I remember him coming to me one day that I chanced to be dining here, in a perfect passion.

"'Mr. M'Dow,' says he, 'you're never to marry me to Florinda; I shall never speak to her as long as I live.'

"'Oh, but,' says I, 'Mr. Reginald, how can that be, when you have promised to marry Miss Florinda?"

"'No matter for that,' says he, 'I'm determined I'll never marry her as long as I live, but I'm to marry Edith, and nobody else.'

"'But if you're to change your mind this way,' says I, 'I don't think I can venture to marry you to anybody.'

"'Oh, you may depend upon it, Mr. M'Dow, I'll never change any more, for Edith's very pretty, and she does whatever I bid her.'

"'Most capital and unanswerable reasons for choosing a wife,' says I, 'and I've nothing more to say, only you must take care that you're aff wi' the auld love before ye tak' on wi' the new.' However, there's been no more changing, and it's all well that end's well—hoch, hoch, ho!'"

With an exclamation at the heat of the room, Lady Waldegrave abruptly rose, and taking Madame Latour's arm, passed into the adjoining apartment.

"I hope I have not said anything that her Ladyship or you could take amiss," whispered Mr. M'Dow, fixing his great goggling eyes on Edith, as she was also rising. "It was all a joke together, and amongst friends, of course, there's no secrets in these things. But, Miss Malcolm," in a still lower and more mysterious key, "I'm really disappointed at not finding Sir Reginald, especially as it seems my worthy friend Glenroy is not able to see me at present; for this change that's going to take place in my own situation, I'm afraid may inconvenience Sir Reginald and you. I beg your pardon, Miss Malcolm, but I'll not detain you a moment," following her, and laying a great paw upon her arm; "but I find I must be at the manse the greater part of this week, and I also wish, if possible, to preach on Sunday, though there's a certain awkwardness in appearing in the pulpit too, at such a time. And on Monday I had fixed to return to Glasgow, to be at the disposal of my lady fair, who has not positively fixed the day; but I'm in great hopes it will be between and the 27th, after which we must of course take a marriage jaunt, and when I return I shall be ready to do to others as has been done to myself—hoch, hoch, hoch, ho! At the same time, rather than disappoint Sir Reginald, I would, if possible, endeavour to arrange my own affairs so as to be at his service when required. I'm really disappointed at not seeing him, for I've so much to do preparing matters at the manse that it's not in my power to spend the day here, and I doubt if it will be possible for me to ride over again before I go. I've a mason, a wright, two painters, a sklater, and a sempstress all hard at work at present, besides having all my own papers and books to shift out of the way of my wife's caps and bonnets; however, I take you bound, Miss Malcolm, that you're not to steal a march upon me in my absence—hoch, hoch, ho!"

Edith would have promised much more to get rid of Mr. M'Dow, and giving a hurried affirmative, she disengaged herself from him. And after going a little further into the depths of the Muckle family with Mrs. Macauley, he once more betook himself to

Amailye, and trotted away to superintend the adorning of the manse.

Edith found Lady Waldegrave seated at an open
window, while the zealous Madame Latour was gently
bedewing her with eau-de-Cologne.

"Ah, ce vilain Monsieur Makedu!" exclaimed she,
turning to Edith on her entrance, "he talk so mosch,
et sa voix est assommante! Cette chère Miladi a
les nerfs si délicats, he has made her vat you call
seek!"

Florinda gave a languid smile, while she said, "The
truth is, I have a headache this morning—the break-
fast-room felt oppressively hot, and Mr. M'Dow is
certainly very shocking. All these causes combined
have made me very useless, so not to bore you with
my megrims, I shall confine myself to my dressing-
room for the rest of the morning," rising as she spoke.

Edith in vain assured her the sight of her never
could be otherwise than pleasing, and begged at least
that she might be allowed to attend upon her. It
was evident that when Lady Waldegrave spoke of
studying others, she meant only to please herself, and
her pleasure was to shut herself up in her own apartment, where Edith left her reclining on a couch, with
a table before her, covered with flowers, poetry, and
French novels, her lap-dog in her arms, and Madame
Latour ever and anon touching her temples with eau-
de-Cologne, while a soft breeze from the lake stirred
now and then the beautiful ringlets which she had
allowed to fall in graceful disorder about her face.

It was impossible that Edith should not deeply feel the strange, capricious conduct of her guests, and be also aware that a scene was carrying on around her, the meaning of which she could not fathom. There was, on the one hand, Reginald's coldness and even dislike to Lady Waldegrave; his unwillingness to receive them at Glenroy; his anxiety to hurry on his marriage before their arrival; his rudely absenting himself from them. On the other, there was a visit offered under circumstances certainly very peculiar, and a long journey undertaken for a purpose which seemed to hold no place in the minds of either mother or daughter. The latter had indeed declared her aim to be that of effecting a reconciliation between Lady Elizabeth and Glenroy; but why, while she thus laid open her own mind to Edith, had she avoided all confidence in return? Was it—could it be possible, that Reginald had formed an attachment to Madame Latour, or she to him, and that Florinda's real object was to accomplish a marriage between Sir Reginald and her favourite? Edith's pride and delicacy alike revolted at such a supposition—no, she could not think so meanly of either herself or him. The alienation between Sir Reginald and Florinda seemed mutual, and how, then, could she be desirous of bringing about a union between two people—the one the object of her dislike, the other the friend, it appeared, of her warmest affections? In vain Edith strove to unravel the strange heap of contradictions in which she felt her thoughts entangled. Never was one less fitted by nature and by education to thread the dark intricacies of the human heart. The path of love and duty had ever been plain before her; she had trod it herself in singleness of heart, and she dreamt not (even when she marked her lover's dubious steps) of the treacherous quicksands that lay beneath.

CHAPTER XLIX.

BUT it was not in the present state of the family that Edith could long indulge in vague reflections. She was soon summoned to attend her father in his study (so called), a room adjoining his dressing-room, into which he had caused himself to be wheeled in his gouty chair. To her surprise, she found he had discarded his dressing-gown and night-cap, and all the insignia of the gout, excepting the fleecy stockings and cloth shoes. His countenance and manner were more than usually calm and benign, and altogether the change was no less agreeable than unexpected.

"I am in hopes I've got the better of the enemy at last," said he, pointing to his feet; "the pain's almost entirely gone to-day; and I've been thinking, that since that poor thing has taken the trouble to come so far to see me, it would be just as well to let her come here at once, and have it over, and then she can go when she likes, you know; but if I'm laid up again, she may think herself obliged to wait, and there's no knowing when we may get rid of them; and so, I think, Edith, the best thing will be for you just to bring them in here—you can tell them that

I've still a touch of the gout. And, Edith, give me that cloak to lay on my legs, these confounded stockings make them look like posts. Stay a little, don't be in such a hurry. I wish from my soul it was over, —what the plague brought them here, and a doctor too? Remember, I'm for none of their doctors—I'm neither for doctors nor ministers. And so M'Dow's going to get a wife? she must have a fine taste! They ought both to be sent to the treadmill. And how's that old goose Molly Macauley behaving herself?"—and so on, till he had landed in the Dhu Moss, and the Skirridale woods, Reginald, Norman, and the black pony.

Aware that Lady Elizabeth could not understand, much less "minister to a mind diseased," her own being nearly in the same state, Edith was desirous, if possible, to prevent a meeting which she was sure could produce nothing but irritation on both sides. She therefore sought to turn his mind from the subject altogether, or, at least, to prevail upon him to postpone the interview till near the time of their departure; but, with all the obstinacy and perverseness of imbecility, Glenroy's wishes strengthened, and his impatience increased, under opposition even in the mildest form, and Edith was obliged to yield the point, and depart on her embassy.

On craving an audience, she was admitted to Lady Elizabeth's dressing-room, where she found her Ladyship in her *robe de chambre*, holding a *levée* of Dr. Price, Rousseau, and Rosalie, and, like another Julius Cæsar, dictating to all at once.

"Dr. Price finds me pretty well this morning," said she, squeezing the tip of Edith's fingers on her entrance; "and I have just been giving him directions as to the sort of draught I should like to have to-day; 'tis of great consequence to have these sort of things suited to one's taste and constitution. By-the-bye, perhaps Glenroy would like to have one of Dr. Price's draughts, they are really very pleasant, something like lemonade, but not quite that neither.—Dr. Price, you will be so good as mix up a draught exactly the same as mine, and take it to Glenroy with my love. I am sure he will be pleased with this little mark of attention from me."

Edith trembled at the very thoughts of such an embassy, and almost fancied she beheld the Chief's crutch uplifted to smite Dr. Price and his potion to the ground; in great trepidation, she therefore entreated that the kind intention might be at least postponed, and then delivered the message with which she had been charged, though in rather softer terms than she had received it.

Having come expressly, as was supposed, for the purpose of seeing her husband, it was naturally to be concluded that her Ladyship's mind would be quite prepared for the interview; instead of which she fell into a childish flutter at the first mention of it.

"You have taken me quite by surprise, my dear; I really feel quite overcome; any sort of agitation is so dangerous for me in the present state of my nerves. Rosalie, fetch Dr. Price back immediately; you shall hear what he says; I am entirely guided by him. Rousseau, leave the guitar for the present, take my music, and look out—how my heart beats! I do assure you, my dear, it will be a prodigious exertion for me to meet Glenroy, poor man, at present!"

Edith was so utterly void of affectation herself that she could not comprehend its effects upon others, and she therefore gave her Ladyship credit for the reality of her tremors; she begged she would take her own time, was sure her papa would wish to do what was most agreeable to her, and so on, till the return of Dr. Price.

The Doctor was a stupid, inoffensive man, who, for two hundred a year, a luxurious home, and his travelling expenses, was contented to trot between his own room and Lady Elizabeth's about twenty times a day, to compound little harmless draughts and powders for her, and to have his advice constantly asked, and never taken.

The result of the consultation however was, that her Ladyship heroically resolved to go through (as she termed it) with the part she had to perform. Dr. Price was again dismissed, and Edith desired to wait until she should be dressed. Rosalie was then summoned, and Lady Elizabeth, in spite of her tremors, betaking herself to the labours of the toilet, was soon so completely engrossed by them, that the dreaded interview seemed almost forgotten.

"I always disliked black," said she, addressing Edith; "there's something so *sombre* about it, one

never looks dressed; otherwise I'm not sure that it is
actually unbecoming to me. It sets off a fair skin, but
then it obliges one to use a *soupçon* more rouge than
I like. *Apropos*, my dear, one comfort is, that black
satin shoes are the most becoming things possible for
the feet—all men think so. These are made by Mell-
notte, and I think are perfect," added she, while her
maid, with great exertion, was forcing them on, "and
fit me admirably. Florinda has got my foot. A
model of it was taken for the Gallery at Florence—in
fact, Princess Pauline was quite jealous of it. My
large gold ear-rings and bracelets, Rosalie—and—
what shall I put on my head? a cap looks so particularly dowdy in black. My purple hat and feathers—
purple, my dear, you know, is a sort of mourning.
There, I think, that looks very well—the feathers the
least in the world more to the left side, and a ringlet
or two pulled a little more down. Now," contemplating herself from head to foot in the mirror, and jerk-
ing her head and shoulders, "my gloves and shawl,
Rosalie. Now comes the true test of taste," turning
to Edith—"in fact, nobody that has not been abroad
can put on a shawl." And at length, equipped like
one of the *élégantes* in " *Les Modes de Paris*," her Ladyship set forth, leaning on Edith; then suddenly stopping, she exclaimed, "But I must have my dogs, and
I am sure Glenroy will be delighted with them—
Bijou is *such* a love!"

Here Edith was obliged to interpose, and, aware
of her father's abhorrence of lap-dogs, with much

difficulty succeeded in prevailing on her Ladyship to
dispense with their attendance for the present.

On arriving at the door of the study there was
another demur.

"I hope it is not necessary that I should say much
to Glenroy of the death of your poor brother, my
dear. Such a subject would quite overcome me at
present. I must try to rouse and amuse him a little,
poor man—don't you think so? Another time I shall
take my guitar, but perhaps it would be rather too
much at first—indeed I don't feel equal to the exertion."

Edith, with tears in her eyes, entreated she would
make no allusion to the death of her brother, but
merely converse on general subjects; and after a little
more delay they entered into the presence of the Chief.
He made an attempt, with the help of his stick, to
rise to receive his lady, who advanced, and with a
very good grace, saluted him after her fashion; then
seating herself by him, laid her hand on his arm.

"It's a long while since you and I met, Glenroy,
and I'm sorry to find you so great an invalid, though,
'pon my word, I think you look wonderfully well,
considering. You find the gout very painful, I'm
afraid. My poor brother, Heywood, is quite a martyr
to it. He really looks almost as old as you do. In
fact, he is completely broken down; and, do you
know, I am much afraid his son, Lord Lanville, shows
symptoms of it already, which is very alarming. He
is a charming young man, not actually handsome, but

extremely *distingué* in his appearance and manners.
He is a great favourite of mine, and quite *le cheri des
dames.* He is so very sensible and attentive—quite
amiable; but he certainly is delicate, and I know my
poor brother is at times wretched about him. An
only son! Conceive how dreadful if he were to lose
him!"

Here Glenroy burst out, "And why should he not
lose an only son as well as his neighbours? I know
what it is to have lost an only son. My Norman
was taken from me whether I would or not; and—
and——" He could not go on.

"Ah, true!" said his lady, in a tone of commiseration; "that was very sad. But we won't talk of
these things, Glenroy; they are too much for us. You
must not allow yourself to get hipped—you ought to
come to town for a little in the season. We are to
have Pasta next winter, and I have already secured
an excellent box. Her Medea is quite perfect. I am
sure you would be enchanted with it. Her despair
at the loss of her children was absolutely too much.
I assure you I was quite overcome."

Edith saw a storm ready to burst forth, and
hastily interposed.

"You have got a more pleasing sight to show
papa in Lady Waldegrave. I am sure London con-
tains nothing more beautiful."

"Very true, very true," said her Ladyship, with a
nod of approbation. "Florinda *is pétrie de grâces*, and
she will cause a prodigious sensation in the world.

In fact, wherever she has appeared, you can form no idea of the admiration she has excited. She has, of course, already had many splendid offers—at least what would have been splendid for any one else— but Florinda is too young to marry yet. Early marriages are foolish things, you know, Glenroy."

A sort of growl was here ejaculated by Glenroy. "And late ones worse," he muttered to himself.

"The weather is so fine, I hope you will soon be able to get out, papa," said Edith. Then turning to Lady Elizabeth, "Perhaps you will take a drive to-day in papa's low phaeton?"

"No, thank you, my dear; I seldom go out when I am in the country; and besides, while I am here, I wish to devote as much of my time as possible to Glenroy; that, together with my letters and music, will fill up my mornings entirely. *Àpropos*, I must bring my guitar next time. I have been practising that charming little *romance* to sing to you, Glenroy, '*Vous me quittez pour aller à la gloire;*' I think you will like it."

"I'm for no guitars, nor anything of the kind," interrupted Glenroy impatiently. "I take very little pleasure now even in my own piper, though he's the best in the country, and has carried off the Highland Society's prize three times at the competition. And he was *his* foster-brother too." Here Glenroy's voice faltered, and allowed his lady to strike in.

"Ah, well, we won't say any more about that—we shall talk a little about my daughter."

" *Your* daughter! what's your daughter to me?" cried Glenroy peevishly.

"There's no relationship, certainly," said her Lady-ship condescendingly, "but circumstances, you know, have formed a sort of connection, and I should have brought her with me just now to show her to you, but she has got a little of a *migraine* this morning; she has become rather subject to them of late, and I should be very uneasy if I hadn't the most perfect re-liance on Dr. Price. You must allow me to present Dr. Price to you, Glenroy; I am sure you will like him; he is quite a superior person. I assure you I consider my life perfectly safe in his hands."

"I'll have none of your doctors," cried Glenroy; "I desire never to see the face of a doctor—a set of ignorant, upsetting——What did the doctors do for —for—for my Norman?"

"Ah, we won't say anything about that, Glenroy! Let us talk of something else. You have never been abroad, I believe. Do you know, I really think you would find great pleasure in making a little excursion through France and Italy. You needn't stay long in one place, you know; and I think moving about might be of service to you; and, by-the-bye, I can re-commend the best creature in the world as a courier for you, quite a treasure,—a Greek, and speaks six different languages. My nephew, Lord Lanville, certainly benefited very much by change of climate. I assure you I was quite uneasy about him when he first joined us at Paris; for you know an only son one is always anxious about; and his poor father quite dotes upon him; indeed he is deserving of it, for he is a most superior young man, and I have a real regard for him. Besides, to let you into a little family secret, he is distractedly in love with my daughter, and I think she is attached to him. But I don't wish her to marry yet. She can at any time form a brilliant alliance. In fact, with Florinda's rank, beauty, fortune, talents, she may unquestionably be considered the first match in the kingdom."

"The first match in the kingdom!" exclaimed Glenroy, in a transport of rage; "what makes her the first match in the kingdom? A woman—a poor insignificant woman, to be the first match in the kingdom! The first match in the kingdom is the man who will come after me, and that man's Reginald Malcolm! And if my son had been alive, *he* would have been the first match in the kingdom! A woman to be the first match in the kingdom!" and Glenroy actually swelled out with passion.

To this burst his lady gave a little weak, angry, affected laugh, then said, "You certainly forget, Glenroy, who my daughter is! Lady Waldegrave is a peeress in her own right, and——"

"A snuff of tobacco in her own right! Pretty rights, to be sure; I wonder what right she has to be the first match in the kingdom! What are your peers and peeresses to me! creatures made by a word of a mouth or a scratch of a pen! The king could make a peeress of a turnip-shaw, if he chose—he could

make Molly Macauley a peeress, if he pleased, to-
morrow; but I defy all the kings on the face of the
earth to make the Chief of Glenroy!"

"Certainly the king cannot make a savage," retorted the lady, quivering with indignation, and rising
as she spoke; but Glenroy despised her too much even
to hear what she said, but kept muttering and murmuring to himself, "The first match in the kingdom!
A woman—*any* woman, to be the first match in the
kingdom! Who ever heard of a woman being a chief?
A woman's just as capable of being a chief as—as this
stick," stamping his own with an air of defiance on
the carpet. "Reginald Malcolm, my heir and successor, is the first match in the kingdom, either of
man or woman!"

Edith had made many ineffectual attempts to
interpose her still small voice between the incensed
parties, but in vain; neither of them would listen to
a word she had to say; and all she could do was to
follow Lady Elizabeth, as she tottered out of the
room, her flounces and feathers vibrating, and her
whole dress seeming as though it were a party in her
exasperated feelings. She declared her determination
of instantly leaving the house. She had been treated
with the greatest disrespect; her daughter most improperly spoken of. It was impossible to remain
another night under the same roof; go she would;
she must see Dr. Price and Rousseau immediately.

Edith strove to soothe her as she best could, but in
vain; till at length, with tears in her eyes, she alluded

to the shock her father's mind had received by the
loss of her brother, and feelingly deplored the little
aberrations of memory he had been subject to ever
since that sad event.

"Oh! now I understand," said her Ladyship,
brightening up all at once.—"I understand," tapping
her forehead significantly with her forefinger. "Poor
man! but I ought to have been made aware of that
circumstance before. It was quite wrong to conceal
it from me. Poor man! I am quite sorry for him;
at the same time, nothing can excuse the very improper manner in which he spoke of my daughter.
Sir Reginald Malcolm to be compared to her! too
ridiculous! A person of no consequence whatever,
and an uncommonly disagreeable man. He the first
match in the kingdom! Ha, ha, ha!—poor man. I
—but I must see Dr. Price directly. I have been
excessively agitated and alarmed." And Dr. Price
being summoned, Edith withdrew, and returned to
her father. She found him still boiling over, like a
huge caldron; and she was immediately assailed
with a torrent of invective against his lady. Upon
attempting to explain away the offence, it was immediately turned against herself.

"I always knew you were a weak creature," said
he, addressing her with an inflamed visage. "How
could you be anything else, brought up by that idiot
Molly Macauley; though, to give her her due, she's
a King Solomon compared to that other woman.
What could you mean by bringing a woman that's

not in her senses to molest me ?—A woman that's mad! And you're very little better, to bring her to me in the state of health that I'm in. She's enough to make any man mad! I shall quit my house if I'm to be tormented in this manner. *Her* daughter the first man in the kingdom!"

"*Match*, papa. She only meant as——"

"Now, hold your tongue, and don't contradict me. Man and match is all one. I know what she said, and what she meant. *Her* daughter, forsooth! What's her daughter? Reginald never could bear her. He showed his sense, and I should never have let them enter my door, considering how they behaved to him. And where's Reginald?—And—and send Molly Macauley and Benbowie. Are *they* away to the shooting too, that I'm left alone all day?"

Edith gladly consigned the Chief to the hands of his two faithful adherents, to whom he had the luxury of relating his injuries at full length; more fortunate in that respect than his lady, who found less willing and sympathising auditors in her daughter and Madame Latour.

CHAPTER L

SIR REGINALD returned from shooting, and on entering the dining-room before dinner, he found only
Madame Latour, Mrs. Macauley, Dr. Price, and two or
three chance guests of no note, who kept apart with
Benbowie. Lady Elizabeth was commonly the last to
appear, and Edith was sitting with Lady Waldegrave,
who chose to remain in her own apartment, on the
plea of continued indisposition.

"I wonder what all you young people are made of
now-a-days," said Mrs. Macauley, looking with eyes
of affectionate compassion on Sir Reginald, who certainly had nothing of the free and joyous air of the
sportsman, but looked languid and dispirited. "You
are all so tender now, so different from what young
people were in my day, when we were so stout and
hearty! There's Lady Waldegrave been shut up in
her room the whole of this fine sunny day, not well;
there's you——"

"I hope—there is nothing——" stammered Sir
Reginald to Madame Latour.

"Ah, oui," said Madame Latour, with a deep sigh,
and a shake of her head. "Ladi Waldegrâve est un

peu malade depuis ce matin ; c'est sa sensibilité extrême ! ah ! si elle avoit la tranquillité de Mademoiselle Malcomb, votre sœur !" and Madame Latour
heaved another sigh.

Reginald was silent for a few moments, as if
mastering his agitation, then said in a calm tone, "I
trust Lady Waldegrave's indisposition is not of a serious
nature. Probably it is occasioned by the uncommon
heat, which has been almost too much for me. Miss
Malcolm is not my sister," he added, in a less firm
voice.

"Ah, que je suis bête ! how I do meestak ! Assurément elle ne vous ressemble nullement, elle est si
calme ! si tranquille ! What you call enseepede—
n'est ce pas ?".

Reginald coloured, and was silent ; but Mrs. Macauley had caught at the word insipid as somehow
coupled with Edith, and she exclaimed, "Insipid !
You're not surely meaning to call Miss Edith insipid ?
or I'm thinking you don't know the meaning of the
word, Madame. Insipid, you know, means *wersh*, and
wersh means insipid ; and I can tell you she's anything
but *wersh*, though she's so sweet and gentle."

"Ah, pardon, Madame Macalic, si—if I do speak
of Mademoiselle Malcomb vat is not propaar—c'est
une personne très aimable, Miss Malcomb ; et quoique
sa beauté ne soit pas si éblouissante, si parfaite que
celle de Ladi Waldegrâve, elle est très bien—vat you
call prettie well."

"Pretty well !" repeated Mrs. Macauley, kindling

up at this fresh insult. "Pretty well! did I ever
hear the like of that?" Then softening down as
quickly as she blazed up, "But though I'm thinking
you're no just so ignorant of our language as you would
make us trow, yet I see you cannot express yourself
properly, or you never would speak in such a way of
Miss Edith, and so I should not be angry with you.
Pretty well! I cannot think enough of it! Pretty
well means just well enough; and to call Glenroy's
daughter just well enough!"

Madame Latour either did not or affected not to
understand Mrs. Macauley better than Mrs. Macauley
understood her; but seeing her displeased, pretended
to conciliate her.

"Pardonnez moi, chère Madame Macalie, assurément
vous not onderstand—if you tink me capable to say
de tings of Meess Malcomb pour vous offenser; c'est
une personne de beaucoup de merite dans son genre;
elle n'a pas les grâces ni l'éclat de Ladi Waldegrâve,
ni son air distingué, ni sa sensibilité extrême."

"I don't very well know what you're saying,
Madame," said Mrs. Macauley, rather impatiently,
"for I'm no great French scholar; but I can tell you,
though Miss Edith does not give herself any grand
airs, she's as ladylike in her quiet genteel way as any
lady in the land; and though she may not be so showy
and catching-like, for all that, hers is the face nobody
could ever weary of, it's so good, and so sweet, and so
sensible, and so loving too. I've often thought how
she answered to a verse of one of our Scotch songs.

I'll let you hear it, and see if it's not like Miss Edith."
And she repeated, slowly and distinctly, the most
beautiful, perhaps, of all Burns's beautiful verses :

> " As in the bosom o' the stream
> The moonbeam dwells at dewy e'en,
> So trembling, pure, was tender love
> Within the breast o' bonny Jean."

"Ah! quel amour transi !" said Madame Latour,
with a shudder, as she turned to Sir Reginald. At
that moment Lady Elizabeth and Edith entered, and
the conversation of course dropped.

All traces of the matrimonial *fracas* had entirely
disappeared from Lady Elizabeth's aspect, for the
variety of her frivolous pursuits seldom allowed her
mind to dwell long on one subject. Satisfied that
she had amply fulfilled her duty by the visit of condolence to her husband, she was now decked out in
pink and silver, and smiles, and short petticoats, and
white shoes.

"Florinda has not been quite well this morning,
Dr. Price, and I think she is rather out of spirits ;
'tis dull for her, you know, to be in the country ;
however, she has promised to join us in the evening,
otherwise I must make a point of her seeing you, Dr.
Price. I wish I could have had her picture as I found
her just now—in my life I never beheld anything so
perfect ! She was sitting at a table, her cheek resting
on her hand—you know her attitude—her hair falling
over her shoulders—

> ' Tender or free, in smiles or sadness drest,
> The reigning humour ever suits her best.' "

D.

"''Deed, then, I think, begging your Ladyship's pardon, the fewer humours people have, so much the better," observed Mrs. Macaulcy.

"Il n'y a rien de plus ennuyeux que les personnes qui n'ont qu'un seul ton—N'est il pas vrai?" said Madame Latour.

Sir Reginald looked as if he understood the innuendo, and he answered in French: "The human mind has often been compared to a musical instrument; perhaps most minds may be capable of giving a variety of tones, but it is not every one who has the power of calling them forth."

"Ah, oui, mais le jeu ne vaut pas la chandelle, to what you call draw out cette espèce de personne; les gens reservés ressemblent, à mon avis, à cet instrument de votre pays le bag-peep, which it take such a force to sound;" and her glance was directed to Edith, who sat near, reading.

"The analogy is not just," replied Sir Reginald gravely; "there are minds like the organ, of great power and melody when skilfully called forth; but it is not every hand that can touch the right chords, or every ear that can appreciate their excellence." And he sighed as he said it.

"Ah, oui, c'est vat I do say,—il faut de la sympathic dans le gout; sans sympathie l'âme ne peut être d'accord, et sans harmonie le cœur ne vaut rien."

Sir Reginald turned abruptly from Madame Latour to Edith, and, as if he felt that he owed her some reparation for the innuendoes that had so evidently been levelled against her, he devoted himself to her until they were summoned to dinner.

On leaving the dining-room, Edith was fastened upon by Lady Elizabeth, who again appropriated her to her own particular use, as an auditor.

"You will go to Florinda, Madame Latour, and, with my love, tell her I desire to see her in the drawing-room by-and-by.—You, my dear," to Edith, "will accompany me to my dressing-room, where we shall be quiet, as I must have a little talk with you. I have much to say, and I shall not have much time, as, of course, we cannot remain long here. And, by-the-bye, I have never properly introduced you to my darlings. I am obliged to keep them in my dressing-room for fear of your large dogs; and that was one of the things I wanted to say to you; you really must have those creatures shut up. You must know, I got Amor and Amoretta from Cardinal Caccia-Piatti, an uncommonly fascinating, fine-looking person. He paid me great attention when I was at Rome. I daresay you find this room rather warm, but I am obliged to have a large fire on account of my dogs; they feel the cold of this climate dreadfully. Dr. Price was of opinion that Amoretta's last attack was decidedly rheumatic. Unluckily her dog-basket has a window, and I think the cold air had streamed in upon her, so I was obliged to have it closed up, which makes it dull, and I don't think she has ever liked it since. If it were not for my eider-down quilt, I don't know how I should have kept them alive. That Cardinal really was a delightful person; he thought my pronunciation of the language quite perfect. When you go, you must make a point of getting introduced to him. I think Glenroy would like him." So flowed on the babbling stream of her Ladyship's eloquence; and even Edith's patience, great as it was, was nearly exhausted before it could be brought to a cessation, or she could prevail on her to return to the drawing-room. On entering the apartment, Edith beheld Lady Waldegrave and Madame Latour seated on a sofa, and Sir Reginald leaning over the back of it. A blush was on Florinda's cheek; but traces of deep emotion were visible on Reginald's features, as he bent his head towards her, and spoke in a low voice. Madame Latour was, or affected to be, engrossed by Fido, whom she was fondling with true French vivacity. A strange undefinable something, she could not tell what, struck Edith at the sight. "This odious Madame Latour," thought she. It was, however, a mere sudden sensation, unattended by any train of reflections, for as Lady Elizabeth advanced, Reginald hastily broke off from Lady Waldegrave, and, turning abruptly round, joined the rest of the gentlemen, who were standing at some distance.

"How charmingly you look, my love!" exclaimed Lady Elizabeth, quitting her hold of Edith for a moment, to embrace her daughter. "And what a very pretty dress! that is Madame Belcour, I am sure; how I wish I had seen it, and I should have ordered one the same—how extremely becoming!"

with an air of chagrin. Then in a peevish tone,
"But you ought to have more flowers in your hair,
my dear child; only look at the size of my head,
which you know is far from being *outré.*"

"You forget I have had a headache this morning,
mamma," said Lady Waldegrave, evidently annoyed;
"consequently my head is not able to bear much."

"Absurd, my dear!" in a peevish voice; "who
ever heard of a headache, or anything else, being an
excuse for being ill dressed? If you choose to say it
is your fancy to dress so and so, I can understand
that, and it may pass; but I do assure you it is very
bad taste to make anything of that sort a matter of
necessity. You must expect to be pitied if you do;
and when once a person comes to be pitied, there is
an end of her consequence for ever."

"Then pray, mamma, suffer me to hide my
diminished head quietly in this corner," said Lady
Waldegrave, trying to laugh away her mother's
absurdity.

"Ah, vous et moi, miladi," said Madame Latour,
with an air of mock humility, "devons nous contenter
de porter des fleurs sur la tête; mais quant à Ladi
Waldegrâve, les fleurs naissent sous ses pas. Et,
àpropos, Saar Reginaal, est ce que votre fleur favorite
croit dans cette triste contrée? vat you call Forget-me-
not?" But Sir Reginald was by this time deeply
absorbed in a book, and made no answer. "Voyons
donc ce qui vous occupe," cried Madame Latour, play-
fully drawing the book from before him; "de la

poësie !" and she ran over the lines, as if going to read them aloud ; then handing the book to Lady Waldegrave, "Lizez donc, chère miladi, votre voix charmante embellira même ces vers."

Lady Waldegrave took the book without answering, glanced her eye over the page, and as she closed it, exclaimed, "Ah, there *was* love !"

The play was Count Basil ; the lines which had drawn forth the remark were those touching and beautiful ones, uttered as he gazes on Victoria for the last time—

> " To be so near thee, and for ever parted !
> For ever lost ! what art thou now to me ?
> Shall the departed gaze on thee again ?
> Shall I glide past thee in the midnight hour,
> Whilst thou perceiv'st it not, and think'st, perhaps,
> 'Tis but the mournful breeze that passes by ?"

Sir Reginald's eyes had been fixed on Florinda intently as she read ; then suddenly starting, he said in a hurried manner, "Edith, won't you give us some music ?"

"Do you remember, Edith, you promised to sing me one of your Scotch songs ?" said Lady Waldegrave gaily. "Pray let me have one of your oldest of old ballads ; and don't lose time," she added in a whisper, "while mamma is busy talking to that very civil, attentive gentleman, who looks as if he would listen for half a century."

Edith arose, and, as she turned towards the piano, she saw and was struck with the expression of Reginald's countenance ; his eyes were fixed on the spot

where Lady Waldegrave and Madame Latour were
seated, while she passed him unnoticed, unheeded. A
strange pang shot through her heart; her eyes filled
with tears; she could not define the nature of her
feelings; she would have shrunk from the attempt,
even had it been in her power, as she would have
done from the point of a dagger. She began to busy
herself in turning over the music, as if seeking for
something, though she knew not what, till her agitation subsided; and having selected that most beautiful of all Scottish airs, Gilderoy, she began to sing a
verse of the old ballad. She possessed from nature a
melodious voice, a fine ear, and an intuitive refinement
of taste—gifts which, if they did not constitute her a
first-rate musician, rendered her at least a very touching and delightful one. But on the present occasion,
Edith's powers seemed all to have failed her—her
voice was weak and tremulous, her ear was unconscious of sound, and all her perceptions were of a
mixed and painful nature. Aware of her failure, she
rose from the instrument, and faltering out an excuse,
begged some one else would take her place. Lady
Waldegrave attempted some faint commendations,
then rose, and was led by Sir Reginald to the harp.

Poor Edith's failure was only rendered more con-
spicuous by Florinda's display. She was in brilliant
voice, and, with perfect self-possession, played and
sang several beautiful Italian and French airs, in the
manner of a perfectly well-taught and highly-finished
musician. Lady Waldegrave was much too well bred

to practise any of the little, commonplace, paltry airs of coquetry; at the same time, it might be discovered by a discerning eye that admiration was the aim and scope of all her actions, the stimulus to all her powers. Nothing could appear more natural and graceful than her movements and attitudes, nothing more simple and unstudied than her varied modes of charming. But as La Bruyère says—"Combien d'art pour rentrer dans la nature!"

Symptoms of impatience were now visible in the countenance of Lady Elizabeth, and Rousseau and the guitar were summoned, which seemed the signal for her daughter to retire from the field. With an exclamation at the heat of the room and the beauty of the night, she rose and passed into the small drawing-room. A few minutes elapsed without any one following.

"Ladi Waldegrâve a laissé ses gants," said Madame Latour, looking to Sir Reginald, as she held them up. Reginald extended his hand to take them, then turned hastily away, and addressed some remark to the person next him.

"I will take Florinda her gloves," said Edith, with an elasticity of spirit she did not stop to analyse, and could not easily have accounted for; and, without noticing Madame Latour's look of displeasure, she seized the gloves, and followed Lady Waldegrave. The glow of excitement which had so lately lighted up her beautiful face had fled, and the same expression of languid dissatisfaction was visible which Edith had formerly observed.

"I fear you have fatigued yourself by singing too much," said Edith. And she proceeded to praise her musical powers with all the ardour of a generous and sincere admiration. Lady Waldegrave appeared but little gratified with the commendations, for she received them slightly, and her thoughts seemed wandering while Edith spoke.

"I fear you are unwell, dear Florinda," said Edith, at a loss to account for the coldness and abstraction of one who, but a few minutes before, had been all animation and brilliancy.

"Oh no, not ill," replied Lady Waldegrave, in the accent of one who felt rather annoyed than soothed by the inquiry.

"Then surely you can have nothing to vex or disquiet you," said Edith softly. "Ah, Florinda, if you have, would that you thought me worthy to share your confidence!"

"You would be shocked were I to tell you the cause of my *vapeurs*," said Lady Waldegrave, with affected solemnity; "how shall I own to you that I am a *little* whimsical; and a little—the very least grain in the world—capricious?" Edith felt hurt at the taunting manner in which she was treated, and remained silent.

"I see you are shocked, Edith, love, at such an acknowledgment; most people would as soon confess that they lie and steal as that they are in the least degree capricious; but for my part, I have none of that virtuous abhorrence to a little caprice; it certainly renders the character, or at least the manners, more *piquant;* for example, I am tired of singing sentimental songs all the evening, and that you will call being capricious, and I now wish to amuse myself by talking nonsense; but I fear you are too wise to talk nonsense, Edith?"

"Not on proper subjects," answered Edith gravely, "but——"

"My dear Edith! for heaven's sake, don't use such an old governess phrase as 'proper subjects!' But, indeed, I am not aware we were upon any important subject in particular—were we, Edith?"

"You had not thought it so, else you would not have asked the question," replied Edith, coldly but gently.

"Ah, I am the most forgetful creature in the world, especially when there is such a moon—such a lovely moon, to gaze upon! Come, let us enjoy its beams, and escape the tinkle of mamma's guitar out of doors." There was an old-fashioned glass door which opened upon a sort of terrace walk, and she stepped out. Edith and she took two or three turns backwards and forwards, admiring the beauty of the night, while Florinda occasionally warbled a few notes or repeated a line or two of Petrarch, then half pettishly exclaimed, "Have you nothing to say on the charms of moonlight, Edith?"

Edith, roused from the reverie into which she had fallen, replied, "Nothing of my own, but I could be eloquent in the words of Ossian, only I suspect you could not enter into my enthusiasm for our mountain bard. Do you remember the exquisite opening of Thalaba?—

> ' How beautiful is night !
> A dewy freshness fills the silent air ;
> No mist obscures, nor cloud, nor speck, nor stain,
> Breaks the serene of heaven ;
> In full-orb'd glory yonder moon divino
> Rolls through the dark-blue depths ! ' "

"Such a description is quite illustrative of the night," said Florinda carelessly; "but it is too cold and abstracted for me—and so is the night itself, to speak the truth. It wants the charm of an Italian moonlight—the rich, warm, glowing, indescribable charm which there pervades the atmosphere and fills the heart; as some one, Madame de Staël, I believe, has well said, the very perfume of the flowers in Italy produces something of melody on the senses, and, to use her own words, 'Vous éprouvez un bien-être si parfait, un si grand amitié de la nature pour vous, que rien n'altère les sensations agréables qu'elle vous cause.' This is what she says of Naples—dear, dear, loved Naples !" exclaimed she fervently, as at that moment they were joined by Madame Latour and Sir Reginald.

"I cannot join in your eulogium on Italy," said Edith, "as it is still a sealed book to me. But here are those who will, I have no doubt. Were you, Reginald, as much enamoured of Naples as Florinda seems to be ?"

"Quite," he replied, in an emphatic tone.

"And, like her, do you too look with something of disdain on the loveliest of our Highland nights?"

"Not with disdain; but with more of admiration than love."

"I thought you had loved your own country, Reginald," said Edith pensively.

"I have a great respect for it," replied he; "love, perhaps, is peculiar to Italy," he added, with a sigh.

"Ah, oui," cried Madame Latour, "admirer, respecter, c'est *une* chose,—aimer, adorer, c'en est une autre! par exemple, j'ai un profond respect pour vos hautes montagnes, et pour vos sombres lacs—vat you call locks; pour vos forêts de pins—vat you call feers; et que quelques personnes appellent 'le deuil de l'été,' —et en verité il y a trop de deuil dans vos tableaux— ils sont tristes; j'aime comme Saar Reginaal le climat à la fois passionné et riant, tel que celui de la belle Italie."

"And I," said Edith, "however much I might admire, and even enjoy, the fair skies and the flowers and the melody and the odours of Italy, am sure I should ever *love* the clouds and the mountains, the firs and the heather, of my own native land; to me the very hooting of these owls has a charm, as associated in my mind with all that I love, or ever loved."

She stopped, and blushed at her own warmth.

"Ah, ma chère!" exclaimed Madame Latour, gently pressing her arm, and looking in her face with a smile, "croyez moi, c'est de l'amitié, non de l'amour, que vous avez éprouvé ; le hibou est l'emblème de la sagesse, jamais on ne l'associa avec l'amour."

Edith coloured deeply—she tried to laugh, but she could not succeed, for a sigh from Sir Reginald smote her heart. He walked slowly away, then returned with the air of one who is irresolute whether to go or stay. Madame Latour now complained of "a frisson," and, shivering, hurried into the house. Florinda, Reginald, and Edith remained some time longer, but the two former showed no inclination to converse; and after some fruitless attempts on Edith's part, they all followed Madame Latour's example, and soon after separated for the night.

END OF VOL. I.

Printed by R. & R. CLARK, *Edinburgh.*

www.ingramcontent.com/pod-product-compliance
Lightning Source LLC
Chambersburg PA
CBHW021342110726
47900CB00005B/1568